# NEXT IN LINE

## J. BENGTSSON

*A special thank you to my brother Mike Wheeler and his bandmates Matt Faulkner and Brandon Gambles for allowing me to use the name of their 80s metal band in my story. I hope I did the name proud.*

# WHEN YOU SPEND YOUR LIFE
# CHASING AN IMPOSSIBLE DREAM

# CONTENTS

# 1

## QUINN: FINE PRINT

"Quinn, you're on in two."

I nodded, stretching my arms back to loosen the shiny brown vinyl jacket vacuum-sealed to my body. I'd been assured the suit was the height of fashion. It wasn't. But what did it matter what I looked like, anyway? I wasn't here to walk the runway. I was here to make a name for myself, and truth be told, I'd prefer to do that in a pair of jeans and a t-shirt. The plastic suit was... well... not my idea. Rest assured, when the stylist sprang the getup on me during rehearsals, I'd protested loudly. I think my exact words were, "No way am I getting up on stage looking like a Slip 'N Slide." And that was when I learned my opinion was not required—nor appreciated. Apparently, there was a clause in the contract I'd hastily signed giving the show the right to dress me any way they saw fit.

In hindsight, yeah, I probably should've paid more attention to the fine print, but at the time, if they'd asked me to sign over my left nut—it would've been missed, but I still had another. I'd been advised to hire a lawyer to look over the contract, but patience had never been one of my virtues, and I was convinced that taking extra time to comb over the document would just slow down the process of fame and fortune. Besides, the show had been around for fifteen years. If there was anything nefarious going on, I would've heard about it, right? Well, not quite right. I later discovered there was a gag order hidden in the fine print I did not read.

But here was the deal: It wouldn't have made any difference. Even if I'd known in advance they were going to make me cut off my rocker locks—another unfortunate casualty of the fine print —and turn me into a vanilla pretty boy, I still would have signed. Nothing was going to stop me from competing. This was my chance to make a name for myself, and I wasn't going to let it pass me by on technicalities.

Ignorance really was bliss. In the beginning, everything was fine—great, even—and I felt nothing but positive vibes as I was encouraged to stay true to the artist I wanted to be. I'd auditioned as the token rocker, and had then gone through four grueling elimination rounds as the token rocker. But with the live shows looming, suddenly the token rocker wasn't good enough. The song I'd chosen—a stripped-down version of an Imagine Dragons song—was nixed by the show's producers in favor of a more upbeat number by an artist I didn't follow.

*Trust in the process*, they'd said when I'd fought for my song. *We know what we're doing*, they'd said. And who was I to question the producers of *Next In Line*, the most popular televised singing competition in America—a show that had spawned huge names in the music industry? They were the experts, I'd been told.

Oh, man. I should have fought harder for my song... and for my hair.

At this point, though, I didn't have a lot of options left. I'd toured the country playing in dive bars and fairgrounds in a couple of no-name rock bands. I'd gone solo. I'd gone duo. I'd even considered a boy band for a hot Hollywood minute, but nothing caught fire until I stepped up to the audition table a couple of months ago and sang for my ever-loving life. They'd sat up, taken notice, and it truly felt like they'd heard me—just in the nick of time. I mean, at twenty-three, I wasn't getting any younger, and in an industry that valued youth and looks over all else, I was pushing middle age.

And so, I bit my tongue and learned the new sugary sweet lyrics. In rehearsals, the judges raved about the performance, assuring me the song was the perfect fit for my vocal range. I'd even been awarded the pimp spot at the end of the show, given to the singer they thought would make the biggest impact on the audience. That was good, right? So then why did it feel all wrong?

The stage director pointed to me and whispered, "You're on."

It was too late for second thoughts now–too late to make my stand. Willing my legs to carry me across the stage, I squinted into what I hoped would be the blinding lights of the rest of my life. If all went as planned, I'd be exiting left in seven minutes' time, flushed with the thrill of accomplishment. The spirit of the crowd energized me, adding a spring to my step that bordered on boyish enthusiasm. Oh, shit. I had to get that under control right away. Skipping across the stage was not in line with the rock star vibe I was going for, although one glance at my boogie nights dance party outfit and I could be moonwalking across the stage and still *no one* would think I was cool.

Easing back into a more relaxed rhythm, I allowed myself to savor the moment. This was the first time in my professional life there was even the slightest possibility I might be judged on my own merit and not on the triumphs of others. I'd never been more ready. Every party I'd missed, every girl I'd stood up, every person I'd flaked out on in pursuit of my dream had all been in preparation for this performance. Tonight was my moment to shine–my chance to step out from behind my superstar brother and claim the coveted spot beside his throne.

Jake. My step faltered as I fought the frown threatening to crush my confidence. It wasn't that I didn't love or respect my brother. On the contrary, I worshipped the guy. To the outside world, Jake McKallister was a rock star, a survivor—a goddamn legend. But to me, he was the larger-than-life big brother I had the privilege, and pain, of sharing a bedroom wall with.

Yeah, I went there. Deal with it. I just found it easier to acknowledge my family's history rather than watch people awkwardly stumble around it. Only a little kid when Jake was snatched off the street, I'd grown up in the aftermath of the tragedy. While other kids were happily playing in the sandbox, I was hiding under press conference podiums listening to my parents beg for my brother's safe return.

Look, I wasn't going to go into the whole sordid tale. Everyone knew—or thought they knew—Jake's story. How he'd barely survived after fighting his way out of the clutches of evil. And everyone agreed that was some next level shit right there. But surviving had never been enough for my brother. Somehow, he'd found the strength inside to rebuild his tattered life, make a name for himself in the music industry, and find a woman to help him heal. He was what true kings were made of.

And therein lay the problem.

Like Jake, music was in my blood. From the time I could talk I was singing and from the time I could walk I was banging, strumming, or clanging on anything that made the ears ring. And, although my brother and I shared a love of music, that was where our similarities ended. As a professional, everything Jake touched turned to gold. But me? I was like that wide-eyed prospector migrating west only to discover he'd arrived at the river a decade too late. And because my brother had already staked his claim, no one wanted me anywhere near his homestead. I was universally dismissed in the music industry with little chance to prove my worth. Still, I kept trying, chipping away at the earth and hoping beyond hope that there might be one tiny nugget left for me.

It was that nagging faith in myself that brought me here today, ready to roll the dice again. Look, I got it, this wasn't the most prestigious way to stride into the limelight as a contestant on a reality talent competition. But there were some distinct advantages to a show like this—namely, no Jake. Add to that no naysaying music executives or loudmouth haters accusing me of piggybacking off my brother's fame and you handed me an honest chance.

Stopping on my mark at center stage, I looked out over the studio audience. My fate was in their hands. Up until today, it was the judges who decided which contestants moved on and I'd survived those elimination rounds with glowing praise. So much so that I actually thought I might have a real shot at winning this whole competition. But now that I'd made it into the top ten, the power had shifted to a voting audience of millions. If I could deliver the performance I knew I was capable of maybe, just maybe, they'd look past my lineage and find the true musician in me.

Fuck Jake's golden river!

This right here... this was my pot of gold.

~

"Please welcome our final contestant, Quinn McKallister. Let's take a look at his journey to the top ten."

The overhead lights dimmed as the big screens came to life. For the next two minutes, the prerecorded story of my life would play out over the monitors, broadcasting onto television screens across the country. I dragged in a deep breath, nervous despite knowing I had nothing to fear. The producers had promised my participation on the show would focus solely on me, not Jake, and not the long-ago event that had shaken my famous family to the core. Any mention of my tumultuous past, I'd been assured, would be cleared by me first.

Still, I had an uneasy feeling that refused to fade. This show was as much about the sobfest life stories as it was about the music. Spun right, even a stubbed toe could be worked into a message of empowerment and perseverance. So why show restraint with me? I shook that nagging thought from my head. Was it so hard for me to believe that I, for once, would be the focus?

The clip began with lighthearted footage of me in the earlier rounds, bringing laughter from the live audience and a smile to my face. Right on. This was what I was talking about.

But then, without warning, the video took an abrupt turn into doom and gloom, complete with a Humane Society musical soundtrack. Suddenly, the carefree tale of my rather boring suburban life became entangled in someone else's tragedy, plunging me headfirst into a hard-luck life story that trumped all the others. Even the poor girl who'd survived a mountain lion attack while playing hopscotch on her front porch was sidelined by my backstory.

The one they'd promised not to exploit.

They'd lied.

I steeled myself, knowing the deceit had just begun. As each second of 'my life' ticked by, I could feel my identity slipping away—my talent being cast aside by the famous brother who commanded attention just by being himself. My entire experience on the show was unraveling. Instead of the Jake, jerk, and hater-free experience I'd been hoping for, this was lining up to be like all of my other disappointing finishes.

I should never have come on this show. Why couldn't I just accept that there wasn't enough room on stage for the two of us?

Jake would always be king.

The music shifted, delving into the deepest, darkest 'beaten puppy' chorus I'd ever heard, and even though I should have looked away, my eyes stayed glued to the screen. The camera zoomed in on a little boy's face... my face. What the hell? Where did they get that video? In it, my arms were wrapped around my sister Emma's leg, and I was staring into the lens with the most confused and frightened expression on my face.

My hand began to shake at my side and my breathing faltered as I processed the shock of seeing myself so pathetic and broken. That footage was taken out of context! The producers were making it seem like it was *me* who'd suffered irreparable harm. This was all wrong. It wasn't me who'd been imprisoned by a monster. It wasn't me who'd come home beaten and broken. It wasn't me who'd screamed into the wee hours of the night. It wasn't me.

I was not the damaged one.

I was not my brother.

But even as I reassured myself, bursts of memory came flooding back, clicking in my head like flares from a flashbulb— Grace and me left to fend for ourselves during Mom's medicated sleep marathons, Emma and the bed tent, Jake's emaciated shadow walking through the halls. All the things I'd actively worked to push out of my consciousness so that I could live in peace were now collectively banging on the windows of my brain. By coming on here and watching that video, I'd inadvertently uncorked the plug that had kept my past at bay. I wasn't okay. I'd never been okay.

Looking out over the mesmerized audience, it suddenly all made sense. All these years I'd thought Jake and I were the same, that we shared a similar talent, that people weren't giving me a fair shake because they couldn't see past my brother's splendor, but maybe they'd just been humoring me because I was Jake's traumatized little brother—the first grader who'd grown up in the eye of the storm and who'd conveniently misplaced all the gory little pieces of the puzzle so he wouldn't have to face them all in one place.

Anger bubbled up inside as I realized that these people felt sorry for me. I was the participation trophy in someone else's victory lap—being cheered on like an out-of-shape runner at the end of a marathon. *Good job, buddy! Keep on trying!* No matter how I performed tonight, I would still move on to the next round... and the next... and the next. Not because I was the best singer in the competition, but because I had the sympathy of the masses.

The video clicked off as spotlights illuminated the stage. The band began to play. I counted the beats, knowing the exact moment I was expected to jump in and join them on my guitar. But my heart was no longer in it. I didn't want to stand up here and play a song I didn't feel, for people who didn't care.

Trust in the process? That's what they'd said. These people who'd promised not to exploit my family, while changing me into something I wasn't.

I missed my cue.

As the music continued to play, I could already see panic setting in on the sidelines. I'd just shoved a wrench into their well-oiled machine. The band circled back around, trying to rescue me. But it was too late. I no longer wanted to be saved.

I held up my hand to stop the music. The band members glanced around, whispering amongst themselves as the crowd fell silent. They might as well get comfortable back there because I wouldn't be needing them anymore. With some effort, I peeled my reflective jacket off and tossed it across the stage before stepping up to the microphone. A sea of confused faces stared back at me as I began strumming my guitar. If they wanted a show, I'd give them a show, and it wouldn't be the shitty paint-by-numbers version being forced on me.

From the corner of my eye I could see the show's producer, Andrew Hollis, jumping up and down on the side of the stage. Was he trying to get my attention or just throwing a tantrum? I imagined that Botoxed face of his turning bright red. *Too damn bad, asshole.* The liar had brought this on himself, pushing me past my boiling point until there was no stopping the fury ignited inside.

With defiant determination, I launched into an original called "Undercover," a song that spoke to the tragedy the room had just witnessed on the screen—a song that was raw and angry and dipped in pain. The audience sat transfixed as I dumped years of frustration into their unsuspecting laps. After hitting its highest plateau, the song tumbled back down, spilling out over the edge of the stage. When I crooned my last intro-spective note, the audience rose to their feet, trampling me in a stampede of cheers.

This wasn't my stage.

This wasn't my crowd.

But for one magical moment, I'd made them mine.

And before the lights went back up on the house, I turned and walked off.

I was no one's pity vote.

**2**

## JESS: ANGEL LINE TOURS

"Hey! Keep it moving."

The warning was issued by a security guard cruising up on his Segway. I sighed. Not another newbie. I swear they swapped these guys out quicker than I could fast-forward through a Progressive commercial. And the new guys were always so gung ho, believing their pseudo cop uniform and safety-first scooter helmet made them real-life law enforcement agents when in reality, their minimum wage salaries didn't leave much room for heroics.

Some of these guys were cool with me, even looking the other way when I crept ever so slowly past the homes they were hired to guard. We all had jobs, after all, and I'd been doing mine for a long time. Surely they could cut me some slack. I mean, come on, they had to know I was coming into this neighborhood no matter what their objections. This was Goldfinch Road, after all, home to more celebrities per capita than any other residential area in the world. Don't fact-check me on that, but it sounded true enough that I regularly spouted the narrative to my customers. And really, it was a logical conclusion to make given the number of heavy hitters who lived on the block.

Every day, sometimes multiple times a day, I guided a new group of sightseers through the streets and hills of the Los Angeles jungle. Born and raised in these parts, I liked to think of myself as a seasoned Angeleno. I knew where the hidden gems were in the Southland as well as where those famous gems were hidden... inside their luxury mansions well away from us normals.

Some might accuse me of being no better than the paparazzi, stalking the rich and famous for my own economic gain, and maybe to an extent that was true. Technically, it was my bus that blocked the entrances to their stately mansions as they tried to back their Bentleys out of the driveway. It was also my early-bird-catches-the-worm customers who got that makeup-free shot of a certain starlet walking her dog in the wee hours of the morning. And it was, no doubt, my faint voice projected forth by the bus's speaker system that wafted out over their open-air verandas while they were bathing in the sun.

Sure, there were times I felt bad about reducing the 'haves' to circus animals, but if they didn't want the inconvenience of celebrity, then maybe they needed to be... well... less awesome. The way I saw it, the Hollywood elite needed me as much as I needed them. After all, it was us ordinary folk—the ones who watched their movies, listened to their music, and bought tickets to see their stately homes—who kept the pretty people in the lap of luxury.

Paul Blart Rent-A-Cop raced toward me at breakneck Segway speeds of up to eight miles per hour. Oh boy, he was an eager beaver, that one. Did he really think I was going to comply with him—a guy fresh out of his one-hour online training course? Besides, what was he going to do? Arrest me for driving my miniaturized sightseeing bus into this tony neighborhood? Last time I checked, the rich and famous didn't yet own the streets.

Pretending not to hear his warning, I continued on with the lively story I'd been telling before his interruption. "... and then Katelyn's husband arrived home unexpectedly, forcing her boyfriend to jump out of that second-story window right over there."

I pointed out the one with the yellow curtains even though I had no conceivable way of knowing the exact window the man had actually jumped from. Not that it mattered. These were the stories my customers wanted to hear, so if I had to embellish a bit, so be it. As long as I kept the retelling exciting, and relatively kid-friendly for the young ones on my bus, no one questioned my facts.

"As I'm sure any of you who watch TMZ remember, Katelyn's boyfriend landed flat on his back, breaking several bones, which completely immobilized him. The ambulance and police were called, and there, splayed out in the spotlight of the news station's helicopter—bare as the day he was born—was none other than Hollywood bad boy Reggie Bowman."

I paused for the reaction I knew was coming and was not disappointed. Chatter instantly erupted among the crowd as they discussed the incident amongst themselves. A few heads bobbed. A couple of smiles. After four hours, I knew who in this group were my reliable tour-goers, the ones who laughed at my jokes and made eye contact when I hit them with an interesting fact. I also knew who to avoid—the grumps who came on the tour looking to be miserable and left feeling no happier than when they'd arrived. There were the wiggly kids, the bored teens, and the tourists who didn't speak a lick of English but who nodded enthusiastically all the same.

"I said, move your bus."

This time the security guard didn't just repeat his previous warning but also pounded on the side of my open-air trolley-style bus with a baton he used to... what... knock hummingbirds out of trees? It's not like there was a lot of high crime in an area where housing prices started in the tens of millions.

"This is public property," I replied, never letting the fake smile break from my lips. "According to the ordinance code 7845, all buses under thirty-five feet are allowed to pass on city streets without incident."

There was no ordinance code 7845. I'd made that up too. But hey, it sounded good, and I was banking on this wannabe cherry cop accepting my lie through ignorance alone. The truth was these high-end residential areas had all sorts of bogus laws they'd enacted to keep my kind out. But us entertainment whores—the city's tour guides and paparazzi—regularly shirked their rules and regulations. What the high and mighty never factored in when trying to intimidate was the near impossible task of taking on an industry that had no shame.

"You know what I think?" the security guard asked, posturing himself hips out, chest puffed. "I think you're full of shit."

I raised a brow. How dare he question my lies! I hated when dicks thought. "Sir, there are children on the bus."

He turned his head, assessing my passengers before focusing his attention back on me. "Then don't bring them along when you're breaking the law, miss."

Flipping open the windshield on his helmet, the security guard who fancied himself a cop spat out a stream of tobacco before fixing his stare on me. Our eyes both widened as instant recognition passed between us.

"Jesse?" he asked, genuine shock in his tone.

My brain took a second to compute. He was seven years older, rounder around the middle, and squinting at me through eyes that hate, but I'd know that face anywhere: Cody Weller.

Hastily, I looked to my left then my right, trying to find some way—any way—to disappear. Even diving headfirst into a manhole would've been preferable to the stare of the man who'd once conspired with other like-minded high school douchebags to destroy my life. I'd actively worked to avoid the whole lot of them since my varsity blues days, but I supposed there were two universal truths in life. One was that you could never outrun your past, and the other was that you'd never find an unsightly manhole on a street like Goldfinch... unless it were coated in gold.

"Still leading sightseeing tours, I see. Would've thought you'd have moved on by now," he sneered.

I would have said the same about his job... if I could speak. But for some reason, seeing Cody Weller caused my throat to dehydrate on the spot. Unable to form the words needed to get the bus moving, I turned to my driver, Vernon, and silently motioned for him to go.

"You're not even going to talk to me?" Cody asked, seemingly offended that the girl he'd had a hand in unraveling didn't have the good graces to reply to his smug insults. "That's not very nice, Jesse."

Nice? Back in the day, I'd been lukewarm nice to him, and what had that gotten me? Humiliation and a juvenile rap sheet. Yeah, I wasn't being nice anymore. Not with Cody or any of the other elite group of oppressors I'd once called friends. Seeing him reminded me of how gullible I'd been, trusting in people who turned on me the first chance they got. I'd thought I belonged. I'd thought I was special. I'd thought wrong.

Speeding up my 'move it' arm gesture, I had to discreetly kick Vern in the calf to get him going. Putting the bus in gear, he popped forward, sending me lurching into the passengers in the front row.

Had he been a split-second faster, my driver would've spared me, and my passengers, Cody's final parting words.

"Well, okay then. It was good seeing you too, Jesse. Oh, and I'll be sure to tell Nicky you said hello—you stupid bitch."

∼

Whoa. Damn, dude. Cody just demonstrated why I never allowed my personal life to encroach on my professional one. His less-than-complimentary parting shot penetrated the ears of just about every customer on my bus. Even the hard-of-hearing folks were filled in by their able-eared peeps.

"That's it," I said, forcing a smile. "He's off my Christmas card list."

That got me a spattering of nervous giggles, which was what I'd been aiming for. I had to warm my customers back up before I could make them forget any of that nastiness had ever occurred. This called for a scandalously delicious story, and I just so happened to have an arsenal of those at my disposal. Launching into a Hollywood tale of woe, I didn't hold back, delivering one tantalizing 'fact' after another until I had my passengers, once again, happily eating out of the palm my hand. Who needed Cody's drama when you had me spinning a much juicer tale?

And, really, what did I care what Cody thought of me? He was a nonfactor in my life. If he insisted on living in the past, well, that spoke more to his emotional health than it did mine. Although I will admit, his mention of Nick rattled me a bit. Cody sure did seem to imply he and Nick were unusually chummy. That was interesting, given the fact that last I'd heard, Nick had conveniently left the country and was now hiding out on some Caribbean island. Wouldn't he be oh-so-surprised when Cody shared the wonderful news with him that his former girlfriend had been spotted in LA—right where she'd always been? Asshole. I hoped Nick choked on his Bahama Mama.

"Angels, get your cameras ready," I said, shaking off the negativity. There would be plenty of time for that when I was alone and digging the peanut butter out of the bottom of the jar with a Hershey bar. "As soon as the bus in front of us pulls away, Vern's going to slide us into a sweet little vista spot where you'll be able to get the picture of the Hollywood sign that I've been promising you all day. The sign is, of course, an iconic Los Angeles mainstay and has been on the mountainside since 1923. It originally read 'Hollywoodland' to advertise a new housing development and was lit up with over four thousand lights that flashed in sequence. Changing the burnt-out lights was such a huge chore back in the day that the sign even had its own dedicated maintenance man who lived in a little cabin off the big D."

Well, would you look at that! My low-key dick reference must've woken the harshest critic of the day: seventeen-year-old Chase, who was now observing me through half-opened, marginally interested eyes.

In the beginning of the tour—when he'd still been conscious —I'd done my best to wipe that 'everything sucks' frown off his face, but once those eyelids started drooping, I'd left the surly teen for dead.

And I had half a mind to continue ignoring him, but that didn't make good fiscal sense. All guides knew that the last few minutes of a sightseeing tour were the most important. It was our last chance to remind our passengers of what awesome human beings we were. In my case, in particular, customer gratitude made the difference between a couple of bucks being shoved into the tip jar and a down payment on my electricity bill. I hated to be so focused on money, but that was the way of the world... or at least the way of my world.

Yep, if I didn't get a healthy amount of monetary appreciation today, I'd be turning my ride-share app on after work, and what do you know... working again. Wouldn't that be fun? Ugh.

So mingling it was.

Crouching down to address the sleepy teen personally, I said. "Three more minutes, Chase, then you're home free."

Chase afforded me his first smile of the day, proving that somewhere deep inside, he had a beating heart ... until I realized he was actually just looking down my shirt. The perv.

I narrowed my eyes on his complacent face and let him know in no uncertain terms that I had his pimply-faced number. Years of dealing with guys like him making lewd comments or gestures on my bus—even grabbing my body parts on occasion as I walked by their seats—had taught me a thing or two about perseverance. My go-to weapon of choice? Emasculation.

"In your dreams, little dude," I whispered in his ear before standing up, patting his head like the childish man-boy he was, and walking away. That oughta do it. I smiled before moving on to a more agreeable man. This one was in his eighties and possessed an infectious giggle—but no other real meaningful communication skills to speak of.

"How're you doing, Lloyd?" I raised my voice to accommodate his old age. "You hanging in there?"

"What's that, hon?" He cupped his hand behind his ear.

His wife backhanded him in the chest and screamed, "*She said, how are you doing!*"

My ears shrieked from the sheer volume of her helpfulness.

He smiled up at me with glazed-over eyes. "Yes, it is."

Fighting off a giggle, I nodded in agreement. Whatever he'd heard was fine by me. In fact, sometimes I wished I could go through life like Lloyd, with a wax log jammed into my ears preventing me from hearing the likes of the Codys of the world.

As I moved past the old man, he gently touched my wrist, his bushy brows furrowed in concentration. "If you want something you've never had," he said, his voice crackling with wisdom. "You have to do something you've never done."

I blinked back my surprise, looking around to see if anyone else had seen Zoltare turn on unexpectedly to foretell my future. But when no one else appeared alarmed, I had to question what I'd heard.

"What did you say, Lloyd?" I asked.

A contented smile settled back over his face. Lloyd was through prophesizing. That was okay because I didn't need him to repeat it. His words were now circulating through my head on repeat. As if it were that easy! There were a lot of things I'd never had. But things I'd done? Well, now, that was a different story. Some of those things were good—real good—but too many of them were bad. Had Lloyd wasted his words on me, or did he give the same advice to everyone he met? I wanted to believe this was divine intervention, but the likelihood was old Lloyd had swiped that quote from a *Reader's Digest* magazine forty years earlier.

So, why were his words still churning in my head, inspiring me? Lloyd was right. I had to try something new. This whole spinning my wheels thing was getting me nowhere, and I was too young to give up on my dreams—whatever they might be. *Yes, Lloyd,* I thought to myself. *Yes to all of it.* It was time to shake things up and go a little crazy... but not too much, because crazy and me had always been a recipe for disaster.

Committing his guidance to memory, I finished our bizarre conversation. "Thank you, Lloyd."

He nodded. "Yes, it is, dear."

Encounters like this were why I loved my work. Sure, it would've been nice to have a job that brought in more than minimum wage plus tips, but I doubted said fictional job would have sprinkled my life with the quirky people I met every single day. There really was nothing like connecting with people of all walks of life in an environment that unified us all. I mean, come on, if there was one thing humankind could agree on, it was that we loved celebrities. For a short snapshot in time, my passengers and I were all on the same team, all wanting the same thing—to feel special in *the* place where dreams come true.

And since it was my job to transport these everyday folks into that world of beauty, glamour, and wealth, I had to look the part myself. There was no rolling out of bed, winding my long dark hair into a bun, and going makeup-free to this job. I took care to rock the canvas I'd been given, and every morning, I emerged from my modest apartment looking and feeling like I belonged. I was selling a dream, after all, and the more presentable and personable I was to my customers, the more generous they'd be when our shared adventure came to a close.

Vern brought the bus to a complete stop at the vista point. My passengers sprang to their feet as the cameras began to click. I took those few spare moments to discreetly check my phone. Oh goody. I had a message waiting for me from the president of Angel Line Tours—my sister Andrea. Try as I might, there was no holding back the roll of my irritated eyes. Not exactly the sisterly thing to do, but then, we weren't really the sisterly types. Ever since *my* mother stole *her* father from *her* mother—and then had me—there had been a strain in our relationship; never mind that the entire affair had taken place over twenty-six years ago. Andrea proved slow to forgive.

I read the text. *"You're late!"*

That was Andrea for you—never a 'hey sis, how are you?' or 'love you, Jesse.' No, my sister started every conversation with an exclamation point, putting me on the defense before the first stone was cast. After years of trying to make amends for my very existence, I'd stopped trying. She was never going to like me or even respect me, so what was the point? Now I just lowered myself to her level and let the negativity fly.

I quickly tapped out a reasonable reply. *"No shit?"*

*"This is the part where you explain why you are rolling in twenty minutes late."*

*"Right, so here's the deal. The chocolate glazed donuts are back at Krispy Kreme—but only for two days. What was I supposed to do?"*

She shot back a response in record time. *"Not funny."*

I was going for sarcastic, but whatever. Andrea had a way of turning everything around and making it my fault. And while she might be justified in the story of our lives, traffic was one monster I wasn't taking the fall for.

*"I was stuck in traffic,"* I replied, as if it were even necessary to spell out the obvious. In LA, *not* being stuck in traffic was what made the news around here. *"Chill out."*

Now I was irritated. Andrea knew as well as I did the quickest way to lose our daily stream of tourists was to cheat them out of the experiences they'd paid for, like snapping that perfect picture of the Hollywood sign or getting up-close-and-personal with celebrity homes.

*"I can see your bus now,"* she typed back. *"Just hurry."*

Huh. A truce? Not like her. Why the sudden niceness? Was she sick? Possessed by Ed Sheeran? Whatever it was, I knew Andrea well enough to know she wasn't giving me a pass out of the goodness of her heart. I wanted to press her for answers, but my sister played dirty, and although I was no shrinking violet, I knew better than to strike a match next to her fuse.

After instructing everyone to return to their seats, Vern rolled the bus forward another block before sliding into our designated spot along the Hollywood Walk of Fame. Our hole-in-the-wall headquarters was located just above our substandard gift shop. In the '70's, Angel Line Gifts & More had been *the* place to go for cheap Hollywood souvenirs like gold Oscar trophies with 'Best Dad' printed on the base and matted photos of celebrities. But as the years passed, competition cropped up on every street corner, and our little shop fell into disrepair. Now we were just an afterthought as tourists skipped over us for the big, flashy shops with giant blinking signs and life-size cardboard replicas of their favorite stars.

"Well, folks, I hope you enjoyed your tour of the stars' homes. I can't tell you how much Vernon and I appreciate you spending this morning with us. We at Angel Line Tours know that you have a choice when it comes to celebrity stalking, and we sincerely appreciate you choosing us to guide you down that slippery slope of harassment and misdemeanors. And listen up, Angels—this is very important. Please don't forget to fill out the online survey. *If* you liked our services, I'm Jess and this handsome fella is Vern—yes, the same man who nearly took out the retaining wall in front of Britney Spears' house with his daring three-point turn. If you didn't like our services, well, the survey really isn't all that important.

"And here comes the part you've all been waiting for. If you feel inclined to donate to the *Vern and Jess Didn't-Go-To-College Fund*, there's a tip jar on your way out of the bus that will happily gobble up any and all contributions. Now, gather up all your things, watch your step, and remember, folks, you're in California. If you go into a Starbucks at nine a.m. tomorrow morning and spot a guy in a baseball cap and sunglasses that looks like Ashton Kutcher—it probably *is* Ashton Kutcher."

~

Today's crowd lingered, wanting to have conversations with me after climbing off the bus, and although the tour had officially ended, I gave them all the time they needed. I know I said it was all about the money, but that wasn't entirely true. I liked being around these people. At the risk of sounding super creepy, I sometimes imagined what it would be like to belong to them, to have a normal, loving family to call my own. It had been too long.

Once all the stragglers had departed, I climbed back on the bus and shut the door. "Whew... they were a chatty bunch today, weren't they, Vern?"

The world's most unchatty person grumbled something incoherent before dragging his skinny rump out of his seat and reaching for the tip jar. I could almost hear the bones creaking in his skeletal frame. He was up there in age, but this sedentary job combined with a lifetime of hard living had left him with a multitude of health issues that had, inevitably, caught up to him.

"Maybe you could try harder to be less accommodating," he said, offering up a condescending tip.

Most of the other guides feared Vern, groaning when they saw his name on the schedule beside theirs, but I wasn't so sensitive to his rumblings. Vern was all growl and no bite. One of the lifers—what we called the drivers who'd been working for the company since the disco era—I'd known the old grump since I was a child, so he tended to have more 'compassion' with me when delivering his insults.

"And maybe you could try harder not to hit road signs," I countered. "But that's not going to happen either, now, is it, Vern?"

He showcased a rare grin.

Emboldened, I pointed to the money Vern had just separated into two haphazard piles on the dashboard.

"See all that?" I said. "You can thank my winning personality and shapely behind for that bottle of vodka you'll be buying tonight—and you're welcome."

Vern didn't bother thanking me, instead handing me my portion of the loot before opening the lid to his cooler and rummaging through his stash until he found an acceptable food item. So eager was he to shove the sandwich into his mouth, I swear he got pieces of the plastic wrap in that enthusiastic bite.

"What was that back there, anyway?" Vern asked through a mouthful of processed meat. "With that security guard on Goldfinch?"

"Nothing worth mentioning." I shrugged, not wanting to get into it with Vern and his sandwich. "Some jerk I knew in high school."

"Ah. High school," he responded, conveniently looking away.

I resisted the urge to smack him upside the head. How long were these people going to hold that against me? My god, it had been nine long years. Give it a break already.

An awkward silence settled between us as Vern chewed on an oversized bite longer than seemed necessary.

"Okay, well, good talk," I said, arranging my money by denomination before counting my share.

"One hundred and twenty-five dollars!" I exclaimed, resisting the urge to high-five myself. "Damn, I'm good."

"I've seen better," Vern mumbled, but I knew he was just as pleased.

"And you know what that means? I don't have to drive neurotic strangers around in my car this afternoon," I said.

"Congratulations."

"Thank you. After last week's baby abandonment fiasco, I've been especially weary."

"Do I even want to know?" Vern asked, which I took as code for *Tell me, tell me, pretty please, tell me.*

"This lady I picked up actually left her baby in the car with me while she ran into the pharmacy. She was like, 'I'm just gonna leave him a second. You don't mind, do you?' And then she was gone."

"Like I said. Too accommodating."

"How is this my fault?"

"You have a nice face. You think anyone in their right mind would leave their kid with me?"

No, I supposed even the most neglectful of mothers would think twice about Vern.

"Anyway," he said. "I wouldn't give up your second job just yet because you never know what's going to happen."

Something in the tone of his voice told me he wasn't speaking rhetorically.

"What does that mean?"

Vernon's eyes shifted away, purposefully avoiding my question.

"Vern?"

He refused to look up. "I don't want no trouble, and technically you are related to management."

I winced. Technically he was right. Angel Line Tours had once been my birthright... and the promise with which I'd laid my head on the pillow each night as a young girl.

"*Someday, Jesse,*" my father would whisper into the dimness of the night. "*It'll all be yours.*"

"*Mine?*" I'd replied, wide-eyed with wonder.

"*Yes. You and your sister, side by side.*"

And I'd believed him, every fantastical word. Hey, I was just a kid. How was I supposed to know his promises were nothing but wishful thinking? See, Angel Line Tours was never his to give. My father ran the operation, but he didn't own it. That title went to Andrea, who had inherited the company from her grandfather on her maternal side. Our father had been a place-holder until Andrea was old enough to run the company herself.

What no one had factored into the equation was Andrea's lingering resentment toward our father for the affair that had produced me. Before the smoke had even cleared from the candles on her twenty-first birthday cake, Andrea had kicked him to the curb, leaving him—and me—penniless. We lost everything. The house, the car, the dog... my mother. But what was worse was that my unsuspecting father never saw it coming, nor did he ever manage to recover from Andrea's heavy-handed betrayal.

"Related in the very broadest of terms," I said, fighting the emotion that came with remembering my beloved father's destruction. "Now spill."

My driver scanned the empty bus for spies before lowering his voice and replying, "There's been talk that Andrea's fixin' to sell."

I blinked. Then blinked again, trying to make sense of his words. That couldn't be. Could it? Tension coiled in my muscles as I grabbed a pole for support. Was Andrea planning Operation Jesse's Destruction 2.0? If she sold the business, I'd have... nothing. No security. No job. Just like before. And if I had nothing, how would I provide for him? No, Andrea wouldn't do that to us again, would she? Maybe the better question to ask was, why wouldn't she? My half sister had no loyalty to us. She'd only given me the job with the company after I'd arrived at her doorstep as a desperate teen and literally begged on my hands and knees for mercy.

Perhaps reading my distress, Vern asked, "Is it true?"

Forcing a smile of reassurance, I resorted to the little white lies that got me through my daily tours. "Everything's fine, Vern. Eat your salami sandwich."

But as I turned to leave, I pulled up the drive-share app on my phone and signed in for my shift. It was going to be another long day.

## 3

# QUINN: ENEMIES IN HIGH PLACES

My march off stage was not well received. In fact, not one person appeared to be in favor of my hasty retreat. Some tried to grab hold of me as I passed, while others called my name, but the vast majority of onlookers just stood off to the side, their wide, disbelieving eyes glued to my exit. Maybe I was still too worked up from the performance to fully appreciate the shitstorm I'd just unleashed on myself, but at that moment I was feeling pretty damn good. Free, actually. Free from expectation. Free from judgment. Free from the forces that sought to control me.

Although exactly how I was going to be free and still be relevant in the music business, I had no idea. This might very well be the end of the road for me—professional suicide. So why then wasn't I more freaked out? Why wasn't I panicking? Maybe this was what I'd wanted all along—a clean break. No more music. No more comparisons to Jake. No more struggling to be relevant in a world that didn't want me in it.

I glanced over at Morris, one of the fellow contestants I'd been friendly with during the competition, hoping he might be able to shine some light on my unraveling epiphany, but he couldn't even meet my eye. Really? What kind of a friend was he? Then it occurred to me; he wasn't my friend. He was my competition. When it came to push and shove, these situational acquaintances would have no problem pushing and shoving me right off the fucking stage.

Not that I really cared what Morris thought of me, or anyone else I'd been up on that stage with. There was only one person I was in competition with... and it wasn't myself. No, I'd spent my life competing against the one person I had no chance of ever catching. Jake. And the older I got, the more I realized I couldn't compete with a superstar. I didn't have the talent, the bravery, or the tragic backstory. More and more it was looking like my choice was to spend the rest of my life getting kicked around like an unwanted dog or to change courses completely and find something else to do... something that wouldn't put me in direct competition with any one of my noteworthy brothers.

Sounded awesome. Sign me up. Community college, here I come.

I sighed. What was I even saying? Give up music? For better or worse, I loved it too much to ever walk away. Eventually I'd crawl back, tail between my legs... like I always did. See, the thing about being a McKallister was we never knew what was best for us. It was almost like we were genetically predisposed to screw up our lives—as if rash decisions were hardwired into our DNA. I suppose you could say it was a family curse, really. If only my brother Keith had said no to drugs or if my mother could have kept it together when we'd needed her most. Or hell, I might as well get to the root of the issue: if only Jake and Kyle had gone to the skate park like they were supposed to that day, their lives—all of our lives—would've been so different. But they hadn't. We hadn't. And now here I was, adding to the family's compost pile.

Speaking of family... what the hell was I going to say to

mine? I couldn't exactly admit that I'd opened the portal to hell up there on stage. Evading capture seemed the best way to stay one step ahead of the genetic firestorm coming my way. Although to be fair, bolting off the stage in front of a live audience really wasn't that far out of character for me. I had a reputation in my family for being unpredictable—the squirrel in the road. You never knew in which direction it would run until it was either under your tires or safely across the street. It was too early to tell whether I'd be roadkill or burying my nuts by morning.

What I needed now was guidance, and there were three members of my family that might see my point of view. First was my baby sister Grace. She'd always been able to talk me through a crisis. But Gracie was currently overseas on a semester abroad, and until I figured out how to tell time in other countries, she was not a viable option.

My brother's wife Sam was like a sister to me too, but involving her in my drama in her current state wasn't a good idea, seeing she was so pregnant at this point that any undue stress might set her off like a shaken can of carbonated soda.

And then there was Emma. She was available, yes, but my older sister had a tendency to be a tad opinionated. And by 'tad,' I didn't mean like a pinch of salt in the cookie dough. No, more like an entire tablespoon of judgment. Emma was always good to have around in someone else's crisis, but in my own? Uh... no thank you. I'd rather get my life advice from my brother Kyle, the guy who routinely referred to broccoli as tiny trees.

Sprinting past all the stage-side naysayers, I booked it down the long narrow hallway until I arrived at the dressing room door. Sidestepping one of the PR ladies, we did an awkward dance before I grabbed her shoulders and physically moved her aside.

"Sorry," I apologized as I slipped past her and then through the door. There was no time for further niceties because, by my estimate, I only had about two minutes to vacate the premises before the powers that be pounced all over me. I aggressively shoved Lucia, my most prized possession, into her guitar case before grabbing my belongings out of my locker and hastily ramming them into my backpack. Hold up. How the hell was I going to blend in with the tourists on Hollywood Boulevard in shiny performance pants and a frilly pirate shirt? Dammit. I was going to have to change.

Snagging my jeans out of the bag, I'd just begun the laborious process of peeling the skintight vinyl down past my waist, much like I might extract a fruit rollup from its plastic wrap, when the door blasted open on its hinges.

"Don't you dare take those pants off, McKallister!"

I froze as a group of well-dressed, middle-aged men filed into the room, each one more red-faced and fuming than the next. And as if they'd choreographed the entire intimidating performance just for my benefit, the men stepped aside to make way for the head producer of the show and Satan himself—Andrew Hollis.

Hollis beelined it straight for me, waggling his pointer finger in the general direction of my shaft. "I swear to god, Quinn, if I see dick, I will destroy you."

Phillip, the mild-mannered lawyer without the clout or backbone to stand up to anyone, jumped into the fray. "Oh, um, Mr. Hollis, that's dangerously close to sexual harass—"

"Zip it!" Hollis shut him down with the rise of a steely fist before lowering his voice to a menacing growl. "Here's what's going to happen, shithead. You're going to pull those pants back up and get your ass out on that stage. And once you're there, you're going to extend your sincerest apology to the audience and the judges for having the mental capacity of a dishrag. Now, let's go!"

Before I could get a word in, Marvin, the stage producer, chimed in with his own useless chatter. "Quinn will need to give some excuse, Mr. Hollis."

Hollis flung his arms in the air in a show of frustration, and I watched in fascination as the broken, dilated capillaries beneath the surface of his skin turned his nose bright red.

"Assclown here can tell the crowd he had an urgent call with the Pope for all I care," Hollis blasted before turning his vitriol back on me. "But hear me now, McKallister, you *will* fix this! And then, once everything is under control, I'm going to take you around back and beat some sense back into you."

"Oh, now *that* really is inappropriate, sir," the lawyer tried to arbitrate once more. Not that anyone but me was listening. I had the distinct feeling that Phillip was the type of person who got picked last for every activity. But today, somehow, this slightly built man had become the captain of my team. "We really can't be threatening the contestants with bodily harm."

"Says who?" Hollis scoffed.

"The Penal Code, sir."

"If you have an issue with how I run my show, Phillip, you can go back to your five-figure salary chasing ambulances."

And *that* was the end of Phillip. He shrank back into the corner he'd briefly ventured out of, offering me a demur shrug of his narrow shoulders as an apology for his cowardliness. So much for my savior. But I didn't need him to speak for me. I didn't need anyone to speak for me. Never had.

Shoving my dick back into the vinyl pants, I hastily buttoned them back up and took a step closer to the prince of darkness before delivering a daring reply. "No."

His eyes rounded. "No?"

I stood taller, towering over Hollis and letting him feel the full weight of my conviction. "You heard me. I'm leaving, and you can clean up my mess. How's that sound?"

The room fell silent, nervous eyes darting from person to person as if they were about to witness an execution. My execution.

Through clenched teeth, Hollis responded in the hushed, homicidal tone reserved just for me. "It sounds like a man digging his own grave."

"Maybe," I said, all full of a bravado I had no business displaying.

"No, McKallister, not maybe. I *will* annihilate you, and when I'm done, not even your brother will be able to save you. Mark my words—you'll never work in this business again."

Well, shit. How thoroughly had I thought this all through? My conviction wavered as reality set in.

Had I just canceled... *myself*?

It was then that Alan Forrester, the show's long-running host, stepped up to the plate. "People, there's no need for threats. Quinn, I think what Mr. Hollis is saying is that no one's trying to pressure you. Perhaps you thought we were too active in your song choice this week, and I would have to agree. You were right to choose the song you did. It suited you perfectly. Would we have preferred to have been warned? Sure. But what's done is done. And the crowd loved it, so no harm no foul. Isn't that right, Mr. Hollis? All we're asking is that you uphold your end of the deal and go out there and make your fans happy."

"Actually, Alan," Hollis said, his words dripping with contempt as he pushed the lesser man aside. "What I was trying to say is, if the kid walks away now, he should know that any song he releases in the next decade belongs to me!"

That detail hit me straight between the eyes.

"That can't be right," I challenged.

"Oh, but it can. Why you Gen-x-y-z-er's don't read the fine print, I'll never understand. But let me make it perfectly clear: I. Own. You. Quinn. Now, turn around and march back on that stage like you signed on to do, or I'll be that sniper on the roof making sure every dream you've ever dreamed dies a horrible, bloody death."

I scanned the group of the powerful Hollywood elite, the very last men any self-respecting, aspiring singer would want to mess with. Fucking fine print! Why hadn't I read it? What was I, five? Honestly, I shouldn't be trusted to touch knives. And now, I'd wedged myself so far into a corner that unfurling the white flag seemed the easiest way out. But did I really want fame on his terms?

"Okay."

I'd taken so long to utter that one word that when it finally arrived, a collective sigh united the room.

"Well, halle-effen'-lujah, McKallister. You aren't as dumb as you look." Hollis pointed me toward the door. "Now off you go!"

Irked by his dismissiveness, I actually looked forward to the second part of the sentence he hadn't let me finish. Hollis thought he had me by the balls, but the minute he'd issued his smug threat was the minute he'd lost me. The thing about intimidation and me was that I never shrank from it. Being the youngest of five boys, I'd learned to adapt and survive in harsh environments. Under beds. Inside headlocks. Hell, if I'd waited patiently for release every time one of my brothers shoved me in a hamper and sat on the lid, I never would've gotten anywhere in life.

By drawing up the battle lines with his fine-print fist, Hollis had given himself the upper hand—but the war was far from over. My nemesis was about to discover that the youngest boy in the McKallister family was never scrappier than when his back was up against the wall.

With my eye on the firing squad, I opened my arms wide and slowly backed out of the room.

"No, Hollis," I said, a wicked smile forming. "I didn't mean, 'Okay, I'll be your little bitch.' I meant, 'Okay, let the bullets fly.'"

Right so, my fuck-you moment didn't go down exactly as planned. Just as I turned to make my escape, I discovered a split second too late that the PR lady was still inexplicably standing right outside the door, but instead of doing our obligatory dance, this time I plowed right into her, knocking both of us to the ground in the process.

"Oh, man, I'm so sorry," I said, helping her up and smoothing down her collision-worthy hair. What the hell was she still doing hanging out by the door, anyway? Was that part of her job description? Because hell, I was currently unemployed. I wondered if they had any openings in the PR department.

Hollis's henchmen saw weakness and descended, manhandling as they tried to push me in the direction of the stage. Oh, no, they didn't. I broke free, and with no other weapon to speak of but my Gibson guitar, I started swinging my girl around like a bat.

"Back off," I warned. Granted, I had no earthly intention of slamming my Lucia into one of their noses. That would just be cruel to the guitar. But just the threat of a broken nose repelled the manicured men. When it came right down to it, none of them seemed willing to risk rhinoplasty for their boss.

I took their cowardliness as my cue to bolt for the nearest exit.

"Go after him!" I heard Hollis shout from behind me.

"Me?" Alan Forrester whined, his voice high and disbelieving. "Why me?"

"Because I pay for your gym membership. Make it worth my while."

I didn't hear the rest of the conversation, as I'd already flung open an emergency exit and escaped into an alleyway. A quick dash brought me to Hollywood Boulevard, where the hordes of tourists would work as my protection.

"Excuse me. Right behind you. Coming through," I said, issuing warning after warning as I zigzagged through the crowd —not an easy feat, mind you, with the whole lot of them walking with their heads trained to the ground reading the names of the stars on the Walk of Fame.

"Quinn! Wait!" I heard Alan call from somewhere behind me. Well, shit, that gym membership was really paying off. He was faster than his leather loafers might make you think. Ducking behind a t-shirt display in front of a gift shop, I waited until Alan passed before scanning the boulevard for a more permanent solution. My eyes zeroed in on a tan sedan with a bright-yellow ride-share sticker on the back window featuring the single letter 'R'.

And there it was.

My getaway car.

# 4

## JESS: RUNAWAY ROCK STAR

"RYde, wait!"

The urgent call touched my ears just as I'd let my foot off the pedal and begun rolling forward. I pressed back down on the brake and adjusted my rearview mirror, watching as a man raced toward me, coming to a complete and screeching halt right at my passenger side window.

Too caught off guard to be startled, I lowered my window a crack and peeked up at him over the rim of my reflective orange-tinged sunglasses. Holy mother of yoga goats! My eyes amplified at the sheer awesomeness of what they were seeing. The man was beautiful. So attractive, in fact, that if I'd seen him walking down the street while leading one of my city tours, I'd have pointed him out to my giddy tourists and made up some story about him being a rising Hollywood star... and I'd probably have been right.

Everything about him was spot on, like his DNA had been meticulously pieced together by a master artist. He was young, yes, but still within that sweet spot where PTA moms could eye-hump him without feeling icky. This was the kind of guy who landed acting gigs even if he couldn't act, the kind of guy who got upgraded to first class even if he'd purchased the basic fare, the kind of guy who could post something totally lame on Instagram and still get a thousand likes.

I soaked in his classically angled face, side-swept hair, and long, muscled physique like a flower might benefit from the first drops of morning dew. It was true, I preferred a man to have lived a few more years, but there was a generous amount of wiggle room when the subject in question had a guitar case slung lazily over his shoulder.

Did he have talent? Did I care? *No.* As far as I was concerned, any guy who had the ability to carry even the corner end of a tune was instantly five shades hotter. *Slow it down, Jess,* I lectured myself. No way could I entangle myself with this musical Thor. Not only was he too young to be anything more than a one-night stand, but musicians in general were a notoriously prickly bunch, and letting my guard down around them could only lead to an early morning walk of shame. If I were smart, I'd roll up my rent-a-ride windows and get the hell out of here.

If I were smart.

My finger hit the button and I slid the passenger side window down to get a better look. Wow, the outfit. What was this guy wearing? He looked like one of those shiny Christmas balls you hang on a tree. Yet, strangely, the odd getup did nothing to cancel out his hotness.

"I need a ride," he said, with more command than a dude wearing disco pants should be allowed to possess. He said it like he just assumed I'd open my legs... I mean... *door* for him.

Retracting my wagging tongue, I replied with as much composure as possible, "Sorry, it doesn't work that way. You can't hail a RYde – gotta order on your app."

"I know that." His frustration sharpened each word. "I just need..."

The man's stunning greenish-gray eyes darted back and

forth between me and something of interest down the street. "Look, just let me in. I don't have a lot of time."

Um... hello, dictator. This guy obviously didn't hear the word 'no' very often. Granted, I hadn't yet decided if he'd hear it from me, but one thing was certain, I needed to establish some ground rules before my lust allowed him to walk all over me.

"Nor do I, bud. Not a chance I'm driving you around for free."

"And I'm not expecting you to. I'll pay you cash."

Cash? Now why hadn't he said that in the first place? Twenty-something guys rarely carried that dinosaur accessory around anymore unless they were on vacation—riding my tours with their wives or girlfriends. My eyes narrowed in on his ring finger... and found nothing. All right, another plus. Sexy, possibly single, and definitely safe because anyone dressed like Elton John was no threat to me.

Now all we needed to do was come to a mutually beneficial financial agreement.

Or not.

I watched in stunned disbelief as he jiggled the handle on my passenger side door without so much as a negotiation. Seriously? Did he think I was an amateur? I hadn't survived all this time in Los Angeles with an unlocked door.

"Ah, ah, ah." I shook my finger. "Cash first. Then getaway."

He dipped his head into the open window, a slight smile erasing the stress lines in his forehead. I gulped, taking in that marquee-worthy face of his and understanding that, going forward, this hot, young stud was going to star in a good deal of my nighttime fantasies.

"That's not how getaways work," he explained, adopting a more patient stance. "I say go. You drive."

Please. He acted like I hadn't inhaled all forty-five installments of the *Fast and Furious* franchise. I think I knew what a getaway entailed.

"Well, you see," I countered, summoning every bit of my reserve sass, "without cash up front, that sounds more like a carjacking to me."

His eyes widened, clearly surprised by my spunk, and that barely-there smile of his tipped up even higher. Good god, he had full-on leading man dazzle. Who let this guy out of his gilded cage?

"You don't mess around, do you?" he asked, the amusement in his tone almost enough for me to hand over my keys. Almost.

"Oh, I've messed around plenty in my life, which is why I'm now dusted in a fine layer of shame."

*Okay, Jess. Too much information. We talked about this.*

As you might imagine, that little tidbit about my past exploits perked the man right up. There was nothing like the promise of a woman with questionable virtue to get the juices flowing in a red-blooded male. His eyes slowly roved over me, letting it be known he was forming all kinds of preconceived notions. This was probably a good time to mention to him that the sprinkling of rebellion I'd once enjoyed had long since died. But the idea that I might actually star in one of *his* nighttime fantasies kept me from correcting his wandering mind.

"Quinn, wait!"

"Ah, shit," my guy swore. "I thought I lost him."

Suddenly another participant butted into our conversation, and this one was even more fancily dressed than the first. Pulling his head out of my window, my would-be carjacker turned to face the caller, tensing as the other guy grabbed his arm.

"Get your hand off me," the hot guy demanded, jerking free.

Oh dang, I liked his fire. This showman was not the pushover his outfit suggested.

"Let's talk this out," the accoster replied, still gasping for air.

"There's nothing to talk about. You sold me out. You sold my family out."

"I can see how you might feel that way. Is this about the video? Because I agree. It was... unfortunate."

"Unfortunate?" my guy barked, his fists curling. "It was more than *unfortunate*. It was exploitive. You promised this wouldn't happen, that I'd have a say, but then you, what... you just went behind my back? Was I just a ratings boost for you?"

I watched the exchange with unparalleled interest, wishing a tub of popcorn would miraculously appear in my hands. Whatever was going on here was better than any binge-watch on Netflix.

"Of course not, Quinn," the man said, still trying to get his exaggerated breathing under control. "Your talent speaks for itself. Look, I'll admit your last name was a big draw, but it wasn't why you made it to the top ten. That was all you."

Talent? Top ten? Last name? And the plot twists kept on coming. Pass the Milk Duds.

"Then why lie? Why try to change me?" Quinn pressed. "Why force me to cut my hair and wear these shitty clothes?"

Did someone say hair? Well, now, that was an interesting development. Had my boy toy, who I'd now determined was named Quinn, once been rough around the edges?

"Look, I'll be honest with you. Yes—the haircut—that part *was* for the ratings. We knew the girls would freak."

I nodded from my place of utter insignificance. Good call. I mean, I didn't know what he looked like *before*, but the *after* was pretty spectacular, so I had to agree with Wheezy on this one. Even a mole rat could see Quinn was ratings gold, and although I was still in the dark as to what the two were discussing, I'd been around show business long enough to understand their dispute was entertainment-related.

It wasn't until the other man turned my way and his face came into view for the first time, that all my questions were answered. Quinn was arguing with none other than Alan Forrester—the ultra-famous TV host of *Next in Line*. And, by way of logical thinking, that made Quinn a contestant on his show. A top ten contestant. A *talented* top ten contestant with a last name of some significance.

I needed a soda to wash this all down.

Quinn took a step back toward my car until his ass was flush with the window and his hand was again testing the doorknob. Still locked. Glancing my way, his nonverbal plea for help was just the push I needed to be his hero.

I unclicked the lock.

He spun around without a second's hesitation as if instinctively he'd known I'd be there for him when he needed me most. In one fluid motion Quinn opened the door, shoved his guitar into the back, and slipped onto the seat beside me like he'd rehearsed it a thousand times.

Slamming the door shut, he slapped his hand on the dashboard.

"Go!"

Our getaway was epic, complete with the satisfying squeal of my speed-limit-rated tires. Darting a gaze to my rearview mirror, a rush of adrenaline shot though me as I watched Alan Forrester slip away into the congregating mob of tourists. Quinn was also focused on the scene playing out behind us, fully rotated in his seat to take in the action. Once we were too far away to see, he righted himself, and we both sat in silence as I drove.

Exiting right and off the boulevard a few blocks down, my rapidly beating heart began to slow. God, how I loved the thrill!

Too much, some would say. I'd spent my life repenting for my wild ways, but if you dangled a string in front of me and wiggled it around, you could expect me to pounce. It was just in my nature, I supposed. I was meant for adventure and fun, and had my life not gone the way it did, I would have been out in the world really living it.

I glanced over at my accomplice, expecting to see the over-confident man from minutes earlier flushed with the same excitement. Instead, I found him decompressed like a wilted balloon, his body limp in the seat and the palms of his hands covering his eyes while he mumbled tidbits of doom and gloom.

"Shit. What have I done? What was I thinking? I'm fucked. Totally fucked."

I continued to glance between Quinn and the road, wanting to comfort him with words of hard-earned wisdom but not knowing enough about his situation to give a qualified response.

"You all right there?" I asked, after he'd let loose another string of self-directed insults.

Not bothering to uncover his eyes, he said, "Depends on what you mean by all right."

"Standard dictionary definition."

"Then no, I'm not all right."

More silence ensued, but the longer we went without speaking, the more questions I had. And really, if you thought about it, he owed me a little something. Sure, I was his driver for hire, but I was also his savior of sorts. Who knew what would've happened to him had I not unlocked my door? Maybe Alan Forrester would have dragged him back to the stage and forced him to perform like a puppet on a string. Or maybe the tourists on Hollywood Boulevard would have drowned him in a sea of drool. As far as I was concerned, he owed me an explanation before I left him in some undisclosed location and never saw him again.

"So, Quinn, I'm assuming you're a contestant on *Next in Line*?"

He let his hands fall from his eyes as he turned to squint my way. "How do you know my name?"

Jesus, so suspicious. He acted like I was a stalker when he was the one who'd tracked *me* down. "Alan Forrester screamed it from down the street."

"Oh, right." He winced as if recalling the scene as vividly as I did. "And, yes, I *was* a contestant on *Next in Line*. As in, past tense."

Remembering the exchange between him and Alan, I replied, "That's too bad. Sounds like you were a really good singer."

"Great," he moaned, as if already pegging me as a nuisance. "So you do know who I am, then?"

His douchey response irritated me. The guy was a contestant on a shitty television show. Did he really think the world was clamoring to know him?

"Relax, dude. Not everyone is up to date on their *Next in Line* trivia. I haven't watched that show since my acne cleared up in seventh grade."

"Oh, I... it's just... you said I was a good singer," Quinn stammered, realizing his mistake too late to save himself. To his credit, he actually looked embarrassed by his narcissistic comment. "I thought..."

I knew what he thought—that I was some groupie girl scrambling to get inside his shiny up-and-comer pants. That was far from reality. Well... okay... maybe not that far. But I wasn't one to hold grudges, especially with a guy as attractive as this one.

"I get how you were confused. No worries," I said. "But let's just assume, for the remainder of your car ride, that everything I know about you was obtained in that three-minute conversation you had with Alan Forrester."

"Got it." Quinn tipped his head back on the seat. A long pause ensued, and I wondered if our conversation was over. I wasn't ready... not yet.

"Hey," he said, sounding tired. "Sorry if I snapped at you. I'm on edge. I get that way when I ruin my career."

"I'm sure you didn't ruin your career," I replied in a lame attempt at solidarity.

"Oh yeah," he groaned. "I'm pretty sure I did."

Our eyes met, and in that moment, I knew he believed it. Whatever had happened was serious enough that a well-known television personality felt compelled to chase him down the street.

"What happened, if you don't mind me asking?" I probed, knowing I was overstepping my bounds as a complete and total stranger but hoping he wouldn't notice.

Quinn slid his fingers through his hair, looking pained. "I walked off the stage during my performance... in front of a live audience."

My eyes bugged from their sockets. Oh wow. Yeah, he was fucked.

"That's... not so bad." I forced the encouraging words out of my lying mouth. "Did you walk off because of the video?"

He lifted a brow. "You sure learned a lot about me in three minutes."

I nodded. "I come from a long line of eavesdroppers."

"I can see that. And no, not just because of the video, but that was the tipping point, for sure." Quinn paused, and I worried that he might cut me off after realizing he was having a heart-to-heart conversation with his ride-share driver. But no, he seemed not to discriminate, and the words kept coming. "I never should have auditioned in the first place. I'm a rocker, and the show's not really known for my type of music. But they made me feel like I belonged, you know?"

Oh yes, I knew. In fact, I'd experienced a very similar situation myself once, wanting to belong so badly I'd allowed myself to be dragged around like an old ratty blanket by people who were cloaked in cashmere. I'd been young and dumb, lured by the promise of fitting into a world that was not my own. And like Quinn, my reckoning had been just as big and flashy. I'd thought once I would never recover, but I did, and now I was thankful for the experience because without it, I probably would have continued down that same path of destruction...just like my father did before me.

"I don't know what I was thinking," he continued. "I should've known they'd change the rules. Everyone warned me, but I didn't listen."

"Who's everyone?"

"My family."

"So, then why audition in the first place... if you'd been warned?" I asked. It was not an accusation but a real and valid question. I wanted to know why a man as talented as Quinn had apparently set himself up to fail.

"Because I have the listening skills of a scurrying rodent."

I chuckled. He didn't.

Okay, then.

"I don't know." Quinn sighed in clear frustration. "I think I just let the promise of fame cloud my better judgment."

"You wouldn't be the first."

"No. But I might be the most pathetic. I almost sold my soul to the devil."

"But you didn't."

He paused a moment before admitting, "But I wanted to."

I caught his eye and corrected him. "But you didn't."

Quinn stared long and hard with an expression I couldn't

read before leaning his head back on the seat and closing his eyes. "No, thank god. I didn't."

A breath caught in my throat. His regret was real, and the vulnerability he displayed damn near blew me away. It was rare indeed for a man to open himself up for all to see. I felt nothing but empathy for this lost soul who'd chosen honesty over lies. Behind his perfect façade, Quinn was lost and searching, just like the rest of us.

"Why is fame so important to you, anyway?" I asked.

He turned his head, opening one eye. "Why does anyone want to be famous?"

"I don't know." I shrugged. "I don't want to be famous."

Everybody had starlit dreams of some sort, of course, but only the very lucky ever got to live them.

He narrowed in on me. "So, you're saying if someone came up and offered you fame and fortune, you'd say no?"

"I mean, maybe if I had your talent, I'd go for it. But I wouldn't want to be famous just for the sake of being famous."

"I don't want that either. I just want..."

I waited for the rest of his sentence, but in the end, I had to coax it out of him. "What do you want, Quinn?"

His reply was slow to come, but when it did, his sincerity nearly broke me. "To be seen."

Silence fell over the two of us. This guy... damn. Something in the way he said those three little words tore at my heart-strings. If a man with all his talent and beauty felt invisible in this world, what hope was there for the rest of us?

"By who?"

"By..." Quinn hesitated. "By everyone, but mostly by the hero of my story."

"Wait—you're not the hero of your own story?"

Quinn replied with nothing more than a tempered laugh. So the story of his life was being narrated by someone else. But who was this hero to Quinn? His father? A sibling? Whoever it was had cast a shadow so wide that my runaway rock star couldn't seem to find his way out from under the cover.

"Explain to me how you're not the star of your own show," I asked.

"How much time do you have?"

"Depends on how much cash you have in your pocket."

"Not nearly enough." He chuckled.

I eyed him, curious enough about my passenger to offer up freebies. "How about I throw in counseling for free?"

"You'd do that?" he asked, his sarcasm smothering us both. "For me?"

"For you," I confirmed. "But just so we're clear: the psychotherapy is free. The car ride is not."

"Ah." He leaned back. "Got it. And thanks, but no thanks."

"Okay. Your loss."

He didn't respond, and we drove in silence for a minute or so... until I could stand it no more. I had to know this guy's story, and I'd pay *him* if it meant satisfying my curiosity. "Hear me out on the whole psychotherapy thing. I happen to have valuable experience when it comes to dealing with biologically related scene stealers."

He grinned, glancing my way. "You don't say?"

"I do say."

Quinn shifted in his seat. "Okay, then. Who?"

"You first."

I didn't think he'd actually answer but he was surprisingly quick with his reply. "My brother."

I followed with my own admission. "My sister."

He nodded, and an understanding passed between us: two castaways floating aimlessly in a sea of greatness.

"So, what's your story?" he asked.

I shrugged. "I'm the result of a desktop dalliance."

"A what?"

"Exactly as it sounds, Quinn. My father did the secretary on top of his drafting table and nine months later..." I displayed jazz hands to showcase my unplanned arrival. "Hello."

His eyes rounded. "Oh, shit..."

"Yep. Lucky me. Think about it. Had my father kept his moneymaker in his pants and not cheated on his wife with the pretty young secretary, I'd have been erased from history like Marty McFly."

Quinn laughed, keeping his curious eyes on me. "Damn, I just have abandonment issues, but you—you're fucked up, girl."

I performed a little in-car curtsy as I laughed along with him. What did it say about me that I wasn't even the slightest bit offended?

"So, what happened to your parents?" he asked, still gripped by the cheating scandal that had created me. "Did your dad get caught?"

"He's a man," I replied, as if that was enough to guide Quinn along in his quest for answers. "What do you think?"

"I would think he paid dearly."

I turned away from his prying eyes and winced. "And you'd be right."

Obviously highly engaged in my tale of woe, Quinn asked, "Then what?"

"Then—nothing." I shrugged. "Everyone lived happily ever after. The end."

Quinn eyed me knowingly before leaning back in his seat and gripping the back headrest. With great appreciation for his manly form, I watched him stretch out his long body.

"Yeah, no way is your story so straightforward."

"Oh, really?" I asked. "Why not?"

"Because I date uncomplicated women, and you, Getaway Girl, do not strike me as one."

Well, he wasn't wrong. I was complicated, but then what woman wasn't?

"Huh. I didn't realize uncomplicated women even existed. Good for you, finding them under those rocks."

"They're not that hard to find if you know where to look."

"High school?"

Quinn puffed out a laugh. "Whoa, let me stop you right there, Buckaroo."

Buckaroo? I wasn't sure if I should be impressed with his 1940's vocabulary or irritated. Any guy who used that type of language around a woman clearly wasn't trying to woo.

"What I meant was, I don't date women with a past," he clarified. "I have what I like to refer to as a tragedy barometer. Any woman with a history more devastating than, say, flushing her pet fish down the toilet is a no go for me."

My eyes widened at the news of his utter shallowness. "Wait—so what you're saying is because I flushed Ms. Bubbles down the toilet eighteen years ago, I'm not a contender for your affections? Am I hearing you correctly, dickhead?"

"Damn, right to the insults," he noted playfully. "No, you're still a contender... I mean as long as Ms. Bubbles wasn't followed down the shitter by your aunt May."

I blinked, shocked. "Your policy is seriously flawed, Quinn."

"Oh, yeah? How?"

"Because the perfect woman doesn't exist," I said, raising my voice to punctuate my point.

"I didn't say perfect. I said uncomplicated." He slid back up in his seat, taking in my irritated face. "Wait, are you offended?"

I expelled some weird whooshing gust of air to show just how ridiculous his question was. "Of course not."

"Then why are your nostrils flaring?"

"I'm not offended for myself," I explained. "I'm offended for womankind."

"Ah." He smirked. "Good for you. Taking one for the team. So commendable."

Oh, my god. What a dick. I fought the urge to reach out and smack him for no other reason than his shitty policy excluded me from the running.

"Actually, you know what, Prince Gaston?" I raised a hand to stop him. "You're right. You deserve a fun, bubbly, uncomplicated woman. In fact, let me be the first to congratulate you and Hannah Montana on a super happy life together."

Quinn gave a hearty laugh at that one, eyeing me with interest before replying, "Thank you."

I grumbled something incoherent—à la Vern—and silently chastised myself for being so rankled by this guy.

Clearing my throat, I asked, "So, where do you want to go?"

Without skipping a beat, Quinn sent his finger soaring through the skies. "To the stars and back."

And just like that, he was back in charge.

"No," I said, fighting off a smile. "I meant in *this* universe."

"Oh, sorry. I misunderstood. You'll have to give me extra time to think."

"You've had plenty of time. How about I give you thirty seconds to decide before dumping your ass on the side of the road?"

"Okay, well, first—I don't do anything in thirty seconds," he said, raising a brow and leaving me with no question as to what he meant by that suggestive statement. "And second—I can't formulate a plan that fast, so I guess you'll just have to drop me off on the side of the road."

I cast him a sidelong glance. "Seriously?"

He shrugged.

"This isn't a safe area, Quinn."

"I hardly think it matters," he replied. "A nice mugging might do me good."

"Perhaps, but you seem attached to your face... and your guitar."

"My face? Not so much. But my guitar? Yeah, me and Lucia, man, we go way back. Maybe you can hold onto her until after I get out of the hospital."

"Oh, I'm sorry, but that's against the ride-share rules. According to the regulation handbook, everything must go home with the customer. Further down in the manual is how incredibly cliché it is to name your guitar."

"Don't hate." He chuckled. "I got Lucia from my brother when I was a kid."

"I understand it's sentimental and all, but naming your guitar is like naming your genitals."

A guilty smile spread slowly across his face.

My eyes popped open and a laugh burst from my gut. "Oh, my god, you didn't?"

He shrugged. "Every guy does, and if he says he doesn't, he's lying."

"Okay, give it to me," I said, beckoning with my fingers. "What did you name your tripod?"

"Like I'm going to tell you."

"Why not me?" I asked, all innocent-like.

"I can think of a whole lot of reasons not to tell my ride-share driver what I nicknamed my dick and balls," he said, laughing.

"Fine. It's probably something totally lame, anyway."

"Not only is it *not* lame but it's inspired," he bragged. "Totally original."

Now he was just taunting me. I expelled a long, drawn-out sigh, as if his refusal bored me beyond belief, when in reality, the suspense was killing me.

I snapped my fingers, returning to business as usual. "Location, Quinn, or I'm turning this car around and taking you back."

That got his attention. He shot up, looking my way. "You think I should go back?"

"That's not what I meant," I said, confused by the eagerness in his tone. Quinn really was lost. Where was his support system? Why was he relying on hired help to determine his path forward? "Do *you* want to go back?"

"No. The last thing I want to do is grovel to the warlords, but it's not that simple. If I don't go back, I've destroyed my future. If I do go back, I'll live someone else's life. No matter what, I'm screwed."

"Not screwed. The way I see it, if you can live with being someone you're not for fame and fortune, then awesome. I'll turn this car around right now and wish you a happily ever after. But if you think it's going to eat away at your soul and spit you out somewhere down the line, then give me an address, and I'll take you wherever you want to go."

"Gee." Quinn exhaled. "If only I could figure out which way you lean on the subject."

"Neither way, actually," I said, taking my eyes temporarily off the road to give him the sincerity he deserved. "There's no right or wrong answer here—only what you're willing to accept."

"Am I a bad person if I say I'm willing to accept living a lie?"

"People have all kinds of reasons for doing things, Quinn. That doesn't make you bad. It makes you human."

He slumped back into his seat, clearly pondering my words. I couldn't remember the last time a man had given my opinion such value.

"What does your gut say?" I asked.

My passenger turned his head toward me, really considering his options, before reaching into his bag and pulling out a wallet. He riffled through the contents and, chancing on a couple of bills, he shoved them in my direction. "My gut says drive me as far as thirty dollars will take me."

"Okay then." I smiled, taking the cash. "Right on."

"Right on," he repeated, his smile meeting mine in the middle. "You're all right, Getaway Girl."

"You're not too bad yourself, Hollywood."

He leaned back, appearing way more relaxed now that the decision was made. "Who needs fame anyway?"

"Exactly," I agreed, matching his mischievous tone. "It's totally overrated."

"And the paparazzi suck," he added.

"Sure as shit they do. And don't forget about the stalkers."

His eyes popped open wide. "Oh, my god, I forgot about the fucking stalkers."

His smartass comment brought a smile to my face. Attractive *and* sardonic. I soaked in his edgy disposition, fascinated by the way he engaged with me. It felt like I'd known him forever even though I still had everything about him to discover.

"Although"—he flashed me his killer grin—"can we agree the money is nice? And the adoration? And the first-class flights?"

"Yes, I will agree with you on those points. However"—I raised a finger—"not worth the loss of your dignity, right?"

"I thought you didn't have an opinion on that."

"Well, now that you made the right decision, I do."

Quinn groaned, but it was more playful than pained. "So now what, guru?"

"Now you blaze your own path."

"Maybe you haven't been listening to my ball-crushing story of woe," he countered.

"No, I have. But you seem like a scrappy guy. Why not have the best of both worlds? Walking off the stage in the middle of a performance is next-level drama. If it gets any traction on social media at all, it could blow up. Maybe by losing, you might actually win."

"Okay, sure. Let's go with your working theory," he said, leaning forward to bust out a drum solo with his fingers on my dashboard. "Do you happen to know a couple million people so we can make this happen?"

*We?* I liked the way that sounded. How long had it been since a man had included me in their planning process? "Um... I might be shy a couple million on my social media accounts. But stop shitting on my plan, dude. Think about what I'm saying. You might not come out of this the loser you think you will."

Stopping the impromptu concert, Quinn finally seemed to give my theory the serious consideration it deserved. "I hope you're right."

So was I. Of all the random people I'd picked up over the past couple of years, Quinn stood out as being the worthiest of a second chance.

He resumed the beat. "You're the kind of person I need on my team."

"I'm already on your team. I let you in my car, didn't I?"

"Yeah, about that," he said, glancing up at me through the fringe of his hair. "What the hell took you so long to open the door?"

"I don't open my door for just anyone, Quinn."

"You're a RYde driver! That's literally your job!"

"Right. But you weren't following the rules."

"Because I was being chased!" His voice rose an octave.

"By a guy in a silk suit and shiny loafers. I hardly think your situation was critical."

Quinn abandoned my dashboard altogether, shifting in his seat to give me his full attention. "So, you're saying if I were being pursued by someone like Liam Neeson or a nine-foot troll, you'd have opened the door and sped away when requested?"

"I would have sped away, yes. But you wouldn't have been in the car with me."

"Oh, okay." He lit up. "I see you. All for one. Good to know. Remind me not to bring you along in a tornado."

"As if that would ever happen. Don't forget, according to your tragedy meter, I'm not allowed to go to tornado alley with you because my dog died when I was in fifth grade."

I took in his self-assured grin, and as he leaned in, his heat ignited me. The close contact caused the hairs on my arms to stand at attention. I could smell the scent on his skin. My heart began to pound. This man was fire.

And then came his voice, soft and deliberate.

"I might be willing to relax my rules for a trip into the heartland with you."

Oh. My. Dear. God. Dead! I was dead. His was possibly the sexiest come-on in the history of come-ons, and it hit me squarely where it counted. Quinn was everything I could want... and more. What would it be like to be chosen by someone like him? I'd been told my whole life I was up there on the attractiveness curve, but I was nowhere close to tipping the scales like the man sitting beside me. Quinn was like one of those teenage crushes that made you feel all giggly inside—that unattainable dream guy who was just personable enough to make you think you had an actual shot with him. Like Nick.

*No, Jess. Shut up. Not like Nick at all.*

Fighting off his allure with everything I had, I replied with as much sarcasm as I could muster, "I'll be waiting on your decision with bated breath."

Quinn's eyes lit up, seemingly pleased with my response. I then watched as he dropped back into his seat and adjusted it to make room for his long legs. Through the skintight vinyl, I could see the movement of the muscles and could almost picture what was beneath. I was mesmerized by his freshness and strength.

Oh, yeah. I had to stop. I could not be fantasizing about this guy while he was still sitting in my car. There'd be plenty of time for imagining when I got home.

"I wouldn't get too comfortable there," I said, pressing my thighs together to hide the evidence.

"Why?"

"Because you're about to tell me where I'm driving you to."

He rolled his head to the side, gracing me with another wide grin. "Do I look like I have anywhere to go?"

Come to think of it, no, he didn't. Was Quinn planning on riding around with me all day? "Well, thirty dollars isn't going to get you far, big spender. So I suggest you start thinking."

Quinn groaned. "I don't want to think. I just want to chill."

"Maybe you can chill at home."

"Nah, I don't want to be alone in my time of need."

"Family, then?" I tried. "Friends?"

"Uh... definitely don't want to see my family right now, and as far as friends go, I don't have many to speak of."

"Really? Why not?"

"Eh, I don't know," he replied, distracted. "I probably should've tried harder to make 'em when I was still young and cute."

What guy who looked like Quinn didn't have friends to spare? They should be lined up around the corner, taking numbers. He didn't add up. There was something about him that didn't jibe with his perfect exterior, like there was some big reveal that might help explain why a professional singer would walk off the stage in the middle of a performance. But he didn't offer up any clues, so I forged on, trying to figure out where to take this wayward rocker.

"Come on, Quinn, focus. Where am I taking you?"

He sighed, long and loud. "Fine, just take me somewhere fun."

"Fun?" I asked. "Like an amusement park?"

"Not that much fun."

"A museum?"

He rolled his eyes. "Please."

"Quinn." I bit down a smile. "I'm about to push you out of my moving vehicle."

"Damn, Getaway Girl. Chill out. Maybe you need some fun too."

"Sure, just as soon as I drop you off."

"Or you can chill now...with me."

"Oh, right." I laughed, glancing his way only to find him... not laughing.

"I'm being serious. Come with me."

*YES!* I cut him off in my mind. *Yes, of course I'll come with you. We'll laugh and talk and go wild, and then after a fancy dinner at Red Robin, I'll let you absolutely rock my shit in the car. It'll be the perfect afternoon of entertainment and the hottest sex EVER.* My breath quickened at just the thought of all the carnal fun I could have with this young stallion in a few hours' time. But then reality kicked in. What was I thinking? I couldn't do that. Not now. Not ever. I wasn't that girl anymore. I *couldn't* be that girl anymore. Stability was what was required in my life now.

And although I wanted to beat the reasonable girl in my head to a bloody pulp, I deferred to her judgment. "It's a generous offer, but I'm gonna have to pass."

He sat up, clearly stunned by my refusal. "Why?"

"Why?" I replied, racking my brain for an acceptable lie.

"Because I know the guy on Hollywood Boulevard dressed up like Chewbacca better than I know you."

"Right, but I've got a better head of hair than that dude," he said, sliding his fingers through his highlighted strands.

"Debatable," I countered. "Besides, you don't even know my name."

"Does Chewbacca?"

"No. But he's asked...numerous times."

"I'm sure he has. And I was actually getting to that myself," Quinn said, tilting toward me and as his head dipped closer, I swallowed hard. Quinn was a pile of smoldering embers, and he was threatening to spread.

*Responsible Jess, where are you? I'm dying here.*

"What's your name, Getaway Girl?"

That self-assured smile. Oh god.

*Strong, Jess. Hold strong.*

"Again, not spending the afternoon with you, so there's really no need for my name."

"Ah, got it. You have a boyfriend."

I glanced his way. "Just because I said no to you doesn't mean I have a boyfriend."

"So you don't."

I met his eye, wanting to lie but knowing he already had me hopelessly cornered.

"No. I'm actually between boy toys at the moment. And you?"

A slow smile hitched up one corner of his mouth. That moment of vulnerability he'd displayed earlier was long gone, replaced with a magnetism that refused to be ignored. It was then that I could picture him up on a stage, girls crashing to the ground around him as they screamed his name. Holy shit. This was no down-and-out musician I had in my car. Quinn was a rising star, one that would someday see his name in lights and fill stadiums to capacity. And I, Jesse Olivia Bello, had a chance to grab a tiny piece of his shine, and I was... *declining?*

"No. I'm not currently attached," he replied. "And thanks for asking."

"You asked first," I reminded him.

His amused eyes flickered over me. "You don't like to lose, do you?"

"Does anyone?"

"Actually, to tell you the truth, I'm getting somewhat used to it."

Oh, he was so self-deprecating, so charming. How was I expected to fight this attraction? It was just cruel—torturous. Quinn took my obvious inner turmoil as his cue to push for the outcome he desired. "Come on... stop stalling. You know you want to spend the day with me."

Was there any debate? Of course I wanted him... uh, to spend the day with him. I mean, what girl didn't love a guy who challenged her, drew her into debate... Wait, exactly what were we debating—his sexiness? If that were the case, he'd win that argument hands down. There was something so endearing in his approach. He didn't need to play games to win me over. He simply conquered through directness and honesty. And by doing that, he made me want to hand him that victory. Jess of yore would've jumped at the chance. Hell, she'd already be in his lap by now. She was fearless and fun and sexy. She lived like there was no tomorrow... until tomorrow came calling and delivered her an ultimatum: repent or risk losing it all.

And that was when responsible Jess was born, the good girl who paid her rent and watered her plants and put others before herself. Old Jess grew to admire new Jess. The new, improved version of myself represented stability and a roof overhead. But sometimes... sometimes I missed that reckless girl. Wild Jess. God, she'd been so fun.

"That bullish charm is not going to work on me, Quinn," I said, feigning disinterest. "So, why don't you just go ahead and cross me off that list of women who fall all over you the minute you show them any interest."

"Okay, sure," Quinn agreed playfully. "I'll do that. Let me get my pad and pencil."

He reached into his bag and pulled out imaginary writing supplies. Mesmerized by his easy charm, I watched as he fake-scribbled on his make-believe paper, all the while swiping wayward strands of hair from his eyes. I was instantly reminded of an iconic movie and a young Leonardo with a sketch pad.

It had been a long while since I'd met a man so... alive.

"What's your name?" he asked again, fake pencil poised at the ready.

I narrowed my gaze.

"What?" His smile widened. "How can I cross it off my list if I don't know what it is?"

My name dangled on the edge of my tongue, begging to be spoken. What would be the harm? I actually had the week off from responsibility, so technically nothing was holding me back. One mindless afternoon of fun. Surely I could spare that for a future rock legend. Besides, no one had to know. I could bring old Jess back for just one day. And as my mouth watered in anticipation, the words unexpectedly slipped off my tongue.

"My name is Jess."

"Nice." He nodded, his tongue peeking out from between his lips as he wrote my name down on his pretend pad of paper. "Is that short for Jessica?"

I smiled. This was all so easy for him. This straightforward seduction. "Jesse, actually. I dropped the 'e.'"

"Jess-e," Quinn said, savoring the last vowel. He repeated my name a few times, trying it on for size.

"Jess, actually. Just Jess."

He smiled that disarming smile of his, the one that said he would call me what he'd like and I'd love it. "Last name, please. For alphabetical purposes only."

"Just write 'Jess, the getaway girl.' That should be enough to remember me by."

He raised a brow. "Ah, being mysterious, eh? I like it."

Oh, man. Where did I sign? This guy was female catnip. The minute he'd set his sights on me, I was done for. In fact, I'd never had a chance. If Quinn's looks weren't enough to complete the savory dish, he was served with a big ol' helping of charisma and a slippery side of sex. I knew what I was getting myself into. Quinn was all over the place, and he'd drag me along for the ride. It would be fun. It would be wild. And I would feel free. All the things I'd promised to never be again.

*Sorry, responsible Jess. I really tried.*

When a smile sprang to my face, Quinn knew he'd won.

# 5

## QUINN: THE END PIECES

I t was almost too easy.

Jess had fallen right in line, just as I knew she would. Who needed a famous last name or decent threads—or a job— when even aimless losers could score the girl?

The girl.

I glanced over at Jess. My smile faded. Oh, shit. I'd just picked up my RYde driver. Was that bad? It suddenly felt... wrong. Was I leading this girl on, when I had no intention of extending our playdate past midnight? No offense against Jess. She was a cool girl, but I'd recently come out of a short-lived relationship with human Saran Wrap and wasn't eager to get myself wound up in that sticky shit again. Not that there was any evidence that Jess was already planning on changing her personal pronoun from *I* to *we*, but then again, I'd just met her —in a car—so how could I know if she had a tendency to smother?

"You all right there, Hollywood?" Jess asked, seemingly reading my distress. "You're lookin' a bit nauseous."

"Not at all," I lied. "That's actually my thinking face."

"Oh, damn. I hope you don't do that very often."

"What, think?" I chuckled. "No, not very often."

"What a relief," she said, her teasing tone a welcome reprieve. I didn't want heavy right now. I didn't want to think. All I wanted was a few hours of peace, away from those who judged, and Jess offered that to me. She had no skin in the game, no reason to steer me wrong. And even though we were effectively strangers, she understood there was no turning back. The show was over. The audience had gone home. The damage—and it was colossal—had already been done.

I could almost hear the commentator in my head.

*Congratulations, Quinn. Now that you've successfully blown up your life, what will you do next?*

*Well, Chuck, I'm going to Disneyland!*

Oh god. My brothers were going to absolutely destroy me. Not that they needed a reason to lay me out, but this... Oh, yeah... They wouldn't be able to contain themselves. And how could I blame them? Had the roles been reversed, I would've absolutely annihilated them too. No, it wasn't my brothers I was worried about, but my parents. They'd look at me with the same disappointed acceptance in their eyes that they'd had when I'd quit my last band... and the one before that. And when I'd turned down Jake's offer to produce a solo album last year. I didn't want handouts, I'd explained at the time, but it was clear they thought I needed them. Look, I got it. Fiscal fatigue was setting in. My parents were probably tired of shelling out the supplemental income they paid monthly to me so I could go off in pursuit of my dreams... dreams that might never come to fruition.

Shit. They were going to cut me off, weren't they? Who could blame them? They'd given me ample time to get my act together, even suggesting other avenues of employment—for example, trade school. Not the worst idea. Maybe I could become a plumber. Really, I was already halfway through the education. I had a strong stomach, knew my way around a plunger, and could eventually learn to love Hanes classic brief underwear.

Of course, there was always college. I could be that hot older guy in the back, pulling in all the eighteen-year-old chicks. But what would I study? Besides music, I really wasn't good at anything other than psychoanalyzing myself, and I sure as hell didn't want to major in that. Music was my beating heart. Take that away and I wasn't so sure how long the rest of me could survive.

A quick glance at the notifications on my phone confirmed the inevitable—missed calls or texts from at least half of my family members. How did they even know? Had Hollis called and tattled on me? I contemplated answering them but thought better of it. The consequences would be the same whether I checked in with them now or whether we touched base tomorrow morning. They'd be 'disappointed' either way. They always were.

Silencing my phone, I shoved it into the depths of my backpack, and when I looked back up, I noticed Jess staring. She was a perceptive one. I offered up my 'you caught me' smile and left it at that. To my surprise, Jess didn't comment on my shifty behavior, and I was struck by her unobtrusive solidarity. Lately it seemed most females I encountered either giggled extensively upon first introduction or talked at a high rate of speed. Jess seemed content to just absorb.

Settling in for the drive, I sat mindlessly, taking in the concrete scenery until it occurred to me I had absolutely no idea where we were going. In the beginning of our journey, Jess had made a few freeway changes, but that was about the same time I got myself all wound up in alternate employment options and lost track of direction. And now, it seemed, Jess was taking us south on the freeway. I really didn't care where she took me as long as it wasn't into the nearby mountains for an invigorating nature hike. If there was one activity I'd never been a fan of, it was scaling up steep terrain for no apparent fucking reason.

"Um... I have a question," I said, raising my hand.

"Yes, Quinn. Go ahead."

"Does your fun involve hiking, biking, or ants crawling up my pants?"

"Dude, if an ant can get up those pants, it deserves to build a hill."

She made a good point. And getting out of these pants was of highest priority, but Jess was avoiding my question, and I was pretty sure I knew why. "We're hiking, aren't we?"

"I take it you don't like the great outdoors?"

Oh yeah, we were definitely scaling a mountain.

"No, I like the outdoors just fine—I just don't like dusty trails and tiny hunters and gatherers making pup tents out of my skin."

"Hmm." Jess tapped a finger to her tinted lips. "I wish you had clarified your hiking, biking, and ant nesting guidelines before telling me to, and I quote, 'Take me someplace fun.'"

"Okay but, in my defense, you didn't strike me as an outdoorsy type either, so I figured I'd be safe."

"What makes you think I don't like nature?"

"I mean..." My eyes traveled ever so slowly over Jess's fashion-friendly body until they landed on the wedge heels strapped to her feet. "You."

Jess. How to explain my getaway girl? She was exactly what I'd needed today—and the very last thing I'd expected. When Jess had first rolled down her window for me on the boulevard, only a few steps away from my brother's star on the Hollywood

Walk of Fame, I'd been surprised to find a female behind the wheel, considering ninety-five percent of the time my RYde drivers had facial hair and day-old body odor. Nabbing an honest-to-god five-percenter—and a smokin' one at that—was like winning the ride-share lottery.

My first instinct had been to miscast her. Maybe it was because I'd met her under the glittering lights of show business, but I'd just assumed her true passion was in the entertainment industry. Most of us wannabe stars, myself included, had side gigs as waiters or ride-share drivers or pizza delivery boys. And Jess looked the part of aspiring actress, with her long raven hair dipped in gloss. Pair that with her tanned skin, black t-shirt, and jeans ripped in all the right places and Jess was the poster girl for LA cool. Everything about her was put together, from her airbrushed face, her full, lush lips, and her fluttery lashes. Even the gathering of beach-chic knotted cloth and silver charm bracelets climbing halfway up her forearm screamed showbiz.

Really, Jess could have been any up-and-coming starlet desperately pursuing her dreams or any of the talented *Next in Line* singers who'd been holed up in the hotel with me over the past month. But to my surprise, she seemed to be actively shunning celebrity, and that made her a rare breed... in my world, at least.

"Nice. So now you're stereotyping me?" she asked, her perfectly arched eyebrows side characters in her angry bird act.

I met her disapproving query and raised her one. "You called me Prince Gaston, Jess."

She bit down on her lip, grinning. "Oh, right."

I rested my case.

"Okay, listen. I'm going to be completely honest with you. There might be a tiny bit of physical exertion involved in my fun," she said, measuring the amount between two narrowly spaced fingers. "But don't you worry, I have my tennis shoes in the trunk."

"Oh, well, I'm relieved that you're covered," I replied. "Now, if your finger measurements are to be believed, I won't even be breaking a sweat."

"That's correct," she replied, holding my gaze the entire time she lied right to my stinkin' face.

Damn, I liked this girl.

"You're a horrible liar," I replied, laughing.

"I beg to differ. I lie all day long and no one has ever had a problem with it before you."

I didn't even know where to begin with that. So many questions. "What do you lie about?"

"You know, a little of everything."

The way she said it, so matter of factly, made me laugh. Jess was definitely not the stereotypical Quinn girl. She wasn't a stereotypical *any* girl. I had to assume that if she took one of those DNA tests, the results would come back with a percentage of Bond in her.

"You lie to your ride-share passengers?"

"Sometimes, but this is just a side gig. I mostly lie on my real job."

I wasn't sure if I wanted to laugh or shake her. "What the hell do you do that has you lying all day long?"

"My duties consist mainly of being the head angel."

"The what?"

"Inside joke." She chuckled. "Never mind. I suppose you could say I'm in customer service."

Was Jess purposefully being vague or did she normally talk in tongues?

"Wait, so... are you lying to me right now?"

She held up her two fingers and again measured a small distance between them. "Only this much."

"Oh, my god." I laughed. "I got in the car with Milli Vanilli."

Jess shrugged. "I'm not holding you hostage, Quinn. You're free to go at any time."

Uh-huh, like that was going to happen. If her streak of evil wasn't enough to keep me strapped in beside her, the matter of having nowhere else to go sealed the deal. Besides, I was perfectly happy in her cramped car. It provided me both immeasurable entertainment *and* a place to lick my festering wounds.

"Nah. I like it here," I said, hooking my fingers behind my head. "I might never leave."

She smiled. "Is that right?"

I nodded, adding, "Luckily for you, I literally have nothing better to do."

"Ah." She sighed, stars twinkling in her liquid brown eyes. "I love being a backup plan."

"Most girls do," I agreed.

She laughed, alternating her focus between me and the road. "You're a quirky guy, Quinn. Definitely not what I would've suspected, looking at you."

I met her curious grin. "I get that a lot."

Actually, I didn't. If ever one had been typecast into the Sodapop Curtis role, it was me. Not only had I been strategically placed in a supporting cast part, but genetically, I'd been gifted with certain lady-pleasing attributes, which made it easy for people to dismiss me as someone who sailed through life on a perpetual high. But that had never been me. Don't get me wrong —I was always up for a good laugh, but when the day came to a close, I tended to retreat into my own head, where even good genes couldn't save me.

Thankfully, Jess would never see that side of me. No one would. As the old saying went, what happened in my head, stayed in my head. There was no big mystery how I'd become such a mind freak. By all accounts, I'd been a normal little human all the way up until the year Jake disappeared. That was the year my mother locked herself in her room with sleeping pills. The year my father wore the soles out of his shoes searching for a ghost.

And the year I realized I just didn't matter.

People sometimes asked if I was screwed up because of what had happened, and I never knew how to answer that. Life after the kidnapping was all I'd ever known. And although I'd deny it in public all day long, privately I might even admit to being jealous of my older siblings who got live a normal life before Disappearance Day—or D-Day, as I liked to call it in my head. They rode their bikes to the park alone, hung out with friends unsupervised, and lived their early years without fear and without Mom standing off to the side serving as their wingman.

Not to downplay what my older siblings went through after D-Day, because no one would deny they went through hell. But at least they knew what life was like before the grim reaper came-a-knockin'. Grace and me, we grew up thinking the Prince of Darkness was a long-lost relative—one who'd drastically overstayed his welcome.

My siblings and me all adapted to our new normal in our own unique ways. Jake screamed. Keith lost himself in drugs. Kyle got friendly with knives. Grace morphed into Pollyanna. And Emma folded in on herself. My method of coping had always been to silently seethe. There was nothing pinpoint specific about my anger; it was just an overall feeling of being slighted and overlooked my whole life. Then add to that a past that needed to stay in the past but didn't always oblige—like today. *Come on, people. I shoved those memories far down into my consciousness for a reason.* If they'd just stop digging shit up, maybe I'd be a more pleasant person.

The thing I'd learned about suppressing memories was they had a tendency to resurface at the most inopportune moments.

Like the time at band camp when one of the counselors growled like a monster outside our cabin before busting through the door laughing. Everyone else thought it was hysterical. I did not. And while the normal kids went on with their day, I crawled under the cabin and refused to come out until my parents arrived many hours later to bring me home.

And let's not forget about the time some kid in the McDonald's ball pit called my Obi Wan Kenobi socks dumb, triggering the dormant anger in me to break free of its constraints. Let's just say that eight-year-old fashionista would forever think twice before disrespecting the legendary Jedi Master again.

I wasn't normally a violent, unstable guy. In fact, I'd say I was your average everyday Joe ninety-eight percent of the time. It was that other two percent of trip-wire moments that made others take a step back. Maybe if I'd been more like Jake as a kid, storming around like a fucking lunatic one hundred percent of the time, I would've gotten it all out of my system before I grew up and that behavior wasn't as cute anymore.

"Are you carsick?" Jess asked, mistaking my trot through McKallister hell as a gastrointestinal issue. I wasn't sure what would make me less attractive to a female: reliving crippling childhood memories or having a stomach so delicate it couldn't withstand a ten-degree angle.

"Something like that," I mumbled.

"Sorry, we're almost there."

"Where is *there*?"

"You wanna guess?"

No, I really didn't want to guess, but by the peppy expression on her face, she was expecting me to.

"Uh... we're headed toward Anaheim, so..."

"No," she stopped me mid-sentence. "Not Disneyland. You already said amusement parks were entirely too much fun for you."

"So that knocks out my second guess, Knotts Berry Farm. All right," I said, squaring off. This girl came to play? "How about boating?"

"Is there a lake nearby?"

"We have a whole fucking ocean over there," I said pointing in the direction I thought might host the mighty Pacific.

"No, we're not boating, but you're getting warmer."

I was tired of the game now. Patience had never been one of my virtues. "I don't know, Jess. Hell?"

"Not that warm," she said with a smirk. Jess's sparkle caught me totally offguard. She was beautiful in that way people who truly knew themselves were. There was a depth to her that intrigued me. She was confident and guarded, but also relaxed and upbeat. It was an interesting mix of personality traits, yet somehow they all worked together to create Jess, the world's most perfect getaway girl.

"You win," I said, conceding defeat. "I've exhausted my knowledge of the area."

"Norwalk," she blurted out, naming some random-ass city I'd only ever heard of but would be hard-pressed to point out on a county map.

"Well, of course." I palmed my forehead. "Norwalk! Why didn't I think of Norwalk? What's in Norwalk?"

"Only the best miniature golf place ever. You get golf and go-carts and bumper boats. Dude, it's going to be so much fun..." Jess stopped and raised a finger. "But not *too* much fun. Just what you asked for."

I nodded, impressed. She'd actually listened to me. Not many people did.

"Well done," I acknowledged. "Just confused about how I was getting warmer when I said boating."

"Bumper boats."

"Ah, right. I had no idea Norwalk was such a thrilling place."

"Watch it." She chuckled. "I grew up there."

"Fun," I mumbled, looking out the window.

"I'm sure it's not as fun as whatever high-income enclave you come from, but it has its charms."

"How do you know where I come from?"

"I don't. You just scream trust fund."

I glanced over and caught her eye. "You don't know anything about me."

"Whoa, geez, relax. I was kidding. I assumed you came from a family of prominence because Alan Forrester said as much."

"So naturally I'm dripping in wealth?"

She held my eye, not backing down. "Aren't you?"

I hesitated. How to answer that? The wealth in our family was tied to one person—Jake—and he had a lot of it. Jake was our pot of gold. And, yes, I'd grown up in one of the richest areas of Los Angeles, but my parents were working class people and I'd been raised with that mentality. Jake's generosity had given us all an easier life, but I'd never considered his money mine... and it bothered me when other people made assumptions that I did.

"I'm not rich, if that's what you're asking. Up until I got the spot on *Next in Line*, I was waiting tables and playing a zombie for Horror Nights at Universal Studios."

"A zombie?"

"Yeah, you know—shuffling around, eating brains, terrorizing the most freaked-out person in every group?"

"How do you know which one is the most freaked out?"

"Easy. It's the person in the middle. They wedge themselves in, thinking they're safe. Their whole mentality is to let the end pieces die first. Selfish. So those are the ones I target."

She laughed. "You're a very interesting person, Quinn. I've never met a real-life zombie rock star before."

Still trying to shake off the trust fund comment, I grumbled, "Well, now you have."

"Are you mad?"

"Nope."

She eyed me.

"What?"

"You seem mad."

"Well, I'm not. I'm just anxious to get to Norwalk and all that fun."

"Oh, okay." She side-eyed me. "Well, you've got the right guide. I know every inch of the area. You know, back in the day, I was known as something of a rebel. Me and my friends, we roamed these parts like a pack of coyotes."

Jess's mention of her feral past was all it took to erase my sour mood.

"That's all you did?" I asked suggestively. "Roam?"

"Hmm..." Jess smiled; her fingers danced atop the steering wheel. "Well, we might have dabbled in a bit more than that."

"Uh-huh. Tell me."

"I would, but... well... there were some narcotics involved... and copious amounts of a hard liquor... so I can't really remember most of it."

I pivoted in my seat, studying her. Narcotics even? Interesting. She glanced over, and to my surprise, there wasn't an ounce of regret. No excuses. When Keith had been in the thick of addiction, he'd been a bundle of lies and justifications. But Jess, she owned every last bit of it... and with a side of sass to wash it all down.

"Although," she said, her eyes up as if searching her brain for clues, "I do remember the sketch monsters. Those were an unruly bunch of freaks."

"What are sketch monsters?"

"Sketch monsters?" she asked, as if I should already be

informed. "You know, the scary little hand-drawn hellions that terrorize the mind when inebriation sets in?"

I shook my head.

"Huh, I thought they were common knowledge. Do you think maybe I made them up myself?"

Given her wild upbringing, I wouldn't put it past her. Jess was funny... so self-assured.

"Maybe."

"Anyway." She waved off the confusion. "You know what I'm talking about."

"Can't say I do."

She raised a brow.

"What?" I shrugged. "I've never been much of a partier."

"I don't believe you," she said with a mischievous grin. "A musician without a drug past is like a nun without a Bible."

I held a finger up. "Not if you were a pretentious teenage musician like I was."

"Really?"

"Oh, yeah. Had the whole stick up my ass and everything. Fancied myself a prodigy back then. It was all about practicing and writing and perfecting. I was going to be somebody someday, you know? Anyway, as you can see, I didn't have time for fun... or for those freaky sketch monsters of yours. In hindsight, I probably should've lit it up."

Jess studied me more closely, and I mentally scanned back over our conversation for anything even remotely incriminating.

"I'm sorry," she finally said.

"For what?"

"For misjudging you. For insinuating you were a spoiled brat. You're a solid guy, Quinn. And can I just say your dedication to your passion is admirable? I suppose I just assumed all musicians were tortured little creatures—but look at you, Mr. Well-Adjusted."

I held onto the bitter laugh threatening to blow my cover. If ever there was an adjective that least described me, it would be *well adjusted*.

Maybe in another life, but not in this one.

Never in this one.

## 6

# JESS: SPECIAL KIND OF DESTRUCTION

F lashes of skin could be seen through the windows of my car as Quinn changed from his performance attire into something that would be more comfortable for the both of us. Those vinyl pants left nothing to the imagination. And trust me, I'd been imagining.

But his modesty wasn't the only reason I was happy he was making the change. Despite preferring a more contemporary wardrobe for myself, I was a purist when it came to men's clothing. Just the basics, please. I'd take a pair of nice-fitting jeans any day over fancy duds. Maybe I just hadn't had enough swanky in my life to appreciate it when it slapped me in the face.

Tilting my sunglasses up, I made more of an effort to see inside the fogged windows and was glad I did because I was definitely catching some of Quinn's strapping chest behind the condensation. He'd insisted on changing in the car, so I'd parked in the back of the lot to give him some privacy. Not that I was affording him any. I shouldn't have been staring—I knew that—but it was near impossible to look away.

Quinn was an enigma, even after we'd talked nonstop for nearly an hour. Just when I thought I had him pegged, he went and flipped the switch on me. Those tiny droplets of truth he sprinkled into our conversation made me want to know more. Clearly, this was not an info-dump kind of guy. Getting what I needed out of him would require work. Luckily, no one had ever accused me of backing down from a challenge. Still, I had to be careful with Quinn because he would be so easy for me to fall for... and then watch, devastated, as he walked away.

I should get out now while I still had a chance. But I wouldn't, because deep down, I craved his special kind of destruction. Quinn was fun. He was gorgeous. He was deep. And, my god, he was so far out of my league. Guys like Quinn were the confidence levelers—the ones that took girls like me down a notch... or two... or ten. Don't get me wrong—I considered myself a reasonably attractive, self-assured woman, and operated under the assumption that most men were attainable if I gave it my all. But Quinn was the man at the bar that didn't need to send a girl a drink. He didn't need to try. Female attention must be lavished upon him. He'd expect it. In fact, had Quinn and I not met in such an intense way, he probably wouldn't have given me a second glance.

But now that I had his attention— if only for one day—what was the point in wasting it? At the very least, I could spend the day with a future star. Yes, I knew he'd just imploded on stage, but I had a feeling about Quinn. There was something special about him that I couldn't exactly pinpoint, but I knew extraordinary when I saw it. Sometimes people came along in life you just knew would make a difference. They had an aura around them, something intangible that made them shine. In a weird way, it felt as if I was witnessing a star being born right before my eyes—that this career-ending mistake he'd made really wasn't a mistake at all but a speed bump on his road to fame.

The questions I had circulating through my head only grew

louder. Who was Quinn, and why had Alan Forrester woven his family's name into the fabric of his success? And why did he look so damn familiar? I'd seen him somewhere before; I just couldn't put my finger on where. Had he once been a child star? Maybe a one-hit wonder? Of course, I knew the information I was seeking was readily available. All it would take was a couple of keywords typed into my phone and I'd know everything there was to know about this afternoon delight. Fact-checking him on the internet wouldn't be as fun as drawing the information out of him one tantalizing bit at a time, but it would satisfy the curiosity building up inside.

I pulled out my phone and entered the keywords into the search engine.

*Quinn. Next in Line.*

My finger hovered over *send*. In a matter of seconds, every-thing ever written about my studly companion would arrive right there at my fingertips, yet I was hesitating. Did I want a behind-the-scenes glimpse of Quinn, seen through other people's eyes, or did I want to hear it straight from the living, breathing source? And could I even believe what I'd learn about him on the internet—the place where even truths could be wrapped in lies? Most of all, would I want Quinn to google me? My past wasn't exactly a shining beacon of success. But I wasn't the sum of my researchable facts... and neither was Quinn.

Hitting the back button, I deleted the keywords from my search engine and turned my attention to another man altogether.

Opening my messages, I tapped out, *Any word on my dad?*

There was no need to identify myself. The person on the other line already knew who was texting—who was always texting. I sent the same message out every day. Sometimes it took hours to get a reply, but not today. This time my answer arrived only seconds after delivery, making me wonder if Maria had set me on some automated response program.

*No, sorry, sweetheart. Maybe tomorrow.*

Yeah, sure, tomorrow. Pain flared up in my chest as it always did when I got this familiar response. At least she was nice about it. The last person I'd sent my daily texts to, Harry, had pawned me off on Maria after getting his fill. At least he'd handed me off to someone with more patience.

But nice person on the line or not, the answer was never the one I wanted to hear. No news was good news, or so the saying went, but in this particular situation, that assumption was all wrong. No news on my father was always and forever bad news.

A multitude of worst-case scenarios filled my head, threatening to take me to a place I didn't want to go. Not today. I couldn't keep doing this to myself. Dad had chosen this path he was on through his own reckless decisions. It wasn't fair for me to go backwards just because he refused to go forward.

I send off a thank you to Maria before returning my phone to my purse, my heart breaking a little bit more as I tucked my dad away for another day.

Checking my watch, I was surprised that only six minutes had passed. Six minutes without Quinn felt like an hour. But then, it probably had less to do with him and more to do with me being a notoriously punctual person. Getting people places on a strict timetable was what I did for a living, and I'd adopted into my personal life the strict protocols that went with it. Nothing slowed me down these days except traffic, teenagers crossing the road, and unbeknownst to me until today, hot guys changing out of their concert pants in the front seat of my car.

"Do you need help getting dressed?" I called out. "Pants? Shirt? Anything?"

Quinn stuck his head out the passenger side door. "My, aren't you helpful."

I burst to life inside his flirt-bubble. "That's me. Always willing to lend a hand to my fellow man."

"I'm inspired by your selflessness."

Right there. That sarcasm. I loved it. Where had this dude been all my life? He was perfectly wired to complement my energy flow. Usually I nitpicked any potential suitors to death. They were too loud or too dull or too arrogant or too timid. None had hit the bullseye until this unassuming superstar crash-landed in my lap. God, he was going to ruin me. From here on out, every man I met was going to have to live up to *that*! Quinn was like a long-awaited sequel, one you'd worried might suck but turned out to be a masterpiece of cinematic perfection.

Quinn was my *End Game*.

"Would you mind terribly speeding it up?" I teased. "The sun will be setting soon."

"It's two o'clock."

"I know but each minute waiting on you is like twelve in Jess years."

"Which makes you...?"

"Is that your way of asking how old I am?"

"Yes, but in Jess years."

He was too cute to deny an answer. Besides, I had nothing to hide. Quinn might have been younger but we were at least born in the same decade. I pulled out my phone and punched in the numbers.

"I'm currently three hundred and twelve," I announced, impressed with how well I was aging.

"So..." He paused for a moment. "That makes you twenty-six."

"Whoa, you do math in your head?"

"I do." He chuckled. "One of my many party tricks."

"I thought you didn't party."

"I don't; hence the reason my party tricks involve math."

He was just so perfectly witty. I could barely wait for more.

"Okay, well, let me know if I can do anything to speed this along because I have a very low patience threshold."

"I can see that. If you want, I can come out now—naked."

I perked right up. "Like completely?"

"Damn near."

"Hell, yeah. Bring it on. Naked guys don't scare me."

"Spoken like someone who's never showered in a guy's locker room."

Quinn took a quick surveillance of the area, no doubt to confirm we were alone, before the passenger side door swung open and he unexpectedly backed out of the vehicle shirtless and with his naked bum visible just above the waistband of the jeans. Obviously, he'd been trying to pull them up over his hips when I'd interrupted.

My eyes. I couldn't control them if I tried. This was sensory overload at its finest.

"Oh, shit," my muscled Adonis cursed as gravity took hold, slipping those jeans of his further down his muscular legs and revealing ever more of that noteworthy ass. Quinn grappled with the waistband before yanking them back up.

"That wasn't supposed to happen," he said.

"No worries, I enjoyed it."

Quinn again scanned the perimeter, confirming he wasn't about to be collared for indecent exposure. It occurred to me then that he wasn't a risk taker, which made what he'd done on stage today all the more significant. "Yeah, you weren't who I was worried about."

Once he was all tucked back in, Quinn turned to face me, shirtless and in a pair of faded jeans that looked to have been conceived on his body. I full-on dry gulped, that was how thirsty he made me. But the reverse strip tease wasn't over yet, and as Quinn pulled a jersey-knit t-shirt over his head, I watched in hushed anticipation as the material fell into place, expertly clinging to every muscle in his broad, sculpted chest as if it were just happy to be of service.

As was I.

"Better?" he asked.

Most would be hard-pressed to improve on perfection, but not Quinn. He'd done it effortlessly. Of course, he did have *a lot* to work with. See, Quinn was the type of handsome that carried over from childhood. There had been no awkward stage for him. No embarrassing middle school photos. This guy had come out of the womb a fully formed flower.

*Thank you. Thank you, Old Jess. You made the right decision.*

"The best."

~

Two things became abundantly clear the moment Quinn was released onto the public. First, he attracted a lot of attention. As soon as we arrived at the clubhouse to buy a round of mini-golf, people were staring... and whispering and giggling. I wasn't the only one to see star quality in this guy.

The second thing I realized was that despite knowing everything there was to know about established Hollywood celebrities on my route, I was woefully behind the times when it came to new talent and pop culture. Had I been more up to date, I would've recognized Quinn as a contestant on a popular reality show, like apparently everyone else did.

"Are you"—the clubhouse girl jumped in place—"on *Next in Line*?"

Quinn didn't hesitate to engage, answering the questions coming his way with endearing responses. He was enjoying this. For a guy still making his way up the ladder of success, he sure seemed comfortable dealing with fans. I had to say, it was fun to watch someone on the cusp of stardom actually appreciating the windfall rather than the jaded celebrities I typically covered on my tours.

"How come you're here and not on the show?"

Quinn looked my way, the two of us exchanging a knowing nod. It was clear by the reaction of the crowd that the news hadn't yet hit the social media wires, and probably wouldn't until it first aired on the East Coast a couple of hours from now.

"It was filmed earlier," Quinn answered before switching the focus. "Are you going to watch tonight?"

"Are you kidding?" the counter girl said. "I can't wait."

"Neither can I," Quinn replied, glancing over at me and winking. "We're all in for a treat."

That was an understatement. It was impressive the way Quinn had bounced back after the doubt he'd revealed in the car. In fact, after the meet and greet with his fans, I wondered if maybe my advice hadn't been as sound as I'd thought in the moment. Had I deprived Quinn, and his fans, of the next big star?

"Just so you know, we don't offer refunds for rain," the counter girl said as she laid out our clubs and golf balls.

Quinn and I looked up at the blue sky. This was Southern California, where the sky was only ever shades of blue or filled with choking smoke.

Perhaps seeing our confusion, the girl added, "There's a thirty percent chance of rain."

"Ah." Quinn nodded. "Well, thanks for the warning. I think we'll take our chances."

He snagged the clubs and the golf balls off the counter and handed me mine.

I held up my ball. "Wanna trade?"

"Uh..." He rolled his golf ball through his fingers, the slightest hint of a grin. "Nah, I like pink."

"No, you don't. You only took it because you know I like pink."

"How could I possibly know you like pink?"

I lifted up one foot and pointed to the pink swoosh on my tennis shoe.

"Right." He scoffed. "Because a guy is certainly going to focus on the tiny details."

"So, are you going to trade me or not?" It really wasn't a question but a demand. I wanted that pink ball, and as far as I was concerned, it was rightfully mine.

"You know." He stroked his chin, considering. Taunting. "I don't think I will."

I stared him down, but Quinn didn't budge. Now he was just being ornery.

"Okay, fine. I actually like the color"—I glanced down at the sickly-looking ball in my hand—"puke green."

"Oh good." He perked up with fake cheer. "Then we're all happy."

Such a dick. I wasn't sure if I wanted to smack him or lick him—that was how deliciously frustrating he was.

"Yes, so happy," I said, one-upping his fake cheer. "And I'll get my retribution once my vomit ball kicks your Barbie ball's butt."

Our banter did not go unnoticed by those around us. In fact, they all seemed to be swooning for me as if to say, *You're so lucky.* And yes, I was lucky, but for how long? Would I have been better off to never have met him rather than the alternative—which was pining over him for life?

As we turned to leave the counter, a girl behind us in line gushed, "Tell your brother I love him so much. He's my favorite singer of all time."

Quinn's step faltered before he composed himself and raised his club to acknowledge her request. "I'll be sure to pass it on."

Neither one of us spoke as we walked to the first hole. I even teed up my ball before addressing the elephant on the green. "I'm guessing that's the hero of your story."

He performed a curt bow. "That's right, Jess. He's my king."

The rain started on hole eleven, if you could even call it rain. More like a very light afternoon drizzle. But the polite sprinkle did nothing to dampen our mood... or our competitive spirit. We'd spent the past forty-five minutes in the most intense matchup of interactive miniature golf I'd ever been privy to. Until I whipped his ass, I wasn't conceding to cloud dribble.

"Yes!" I thrust my club in the air after the barf ball once again dropped in the hole after one stroke. "Another hole in one. Suck that, pink ball! How many is that again, Quinn?"

He purposely ignored my taunting in favor of a morality lecture. "Didn't anyone ever teach you humility, Jess?"

"Um... can't say they did. Now, how many, Quinn? I want to hear you say it."

"You have three hole in ones, Jess. Are you happy now?" Quinn chuckled. "I swear, you're the worst winner ever."

"I think it just gets easier when you win all the time," I continued, not feeling the least bit concerned that I might offend him. Some people you just knew could take it. Quinn was one of them. Dare I say he even enjoyed it? No way was I going to let up now, not when I had his full and undivided attention. "But don't take it too hard. I mean, Buzz Aldrin was the second man on the moon, and you hear his name, you know, *sometimes.*"

He laughed, hooking my waist with the club and pulling me toward him. "You're such a brat. I thought my brothers were bad, but you just might be the cockiest winner I've ever come in contact with."

The clouds rallied in that moment, turning the thirty percent chance of rain into a downpour. As was common with confused Californians caught in the rain, we stood there dumbfounded, not knowing what the proper protocol was. Did we run? Did we play? Did we make a post on social media bragging to the rest of the country about our monster storm?

I grabbed Quinn's hand and led him off the green and around the back of the giant castle. "Come on. I know where we can go."

Reaching behind the trellis nailed onto the castle, I came up with a key.

Quinn's eyes widened. "How'd you know that was there?"

"My boyfriend used to work here. This was our designated make-out spot during break time... and even when it wasn't break time. Actually, I gotta say, we pretty much macked twenty-four seven in here."

"Okay, Jess. I got it," Quinn joked. "You had a jolly good time in here. Stop bragging."

He pointed to the small sign on the castle door. "It says no trespassing."

"I know."

"And that doesn't bother you?"

"It's just a cheapy sign, Quinn," I whispered. "They probably bought it at Walmart."

"I don't know about that. It has a city ordinance on it. Let me read it for you. It says, 'Violators are subject to arrest.'"

I rolled my eyes, letting it be known what I thought of city ordinances. "Oh please, who's going to arrest you—Lord Farquaad?"

"You are strangely up to date on your animated princes."

Maybe because Quinn reminded me of royalty. "Anyway, don't worry so much. The sign is really more ceremonial than anything else."

"*Ceremonial*?" His eyebrows shot up. "That will be of little consolation to me when I'm Jim Bob's jailhouse bitch."

"Wait, hold up there. Are you telling me you've never trespassed before?"

"Well... I... uh..." He paused. "Is that so weird?"

"It's...," I began, searching for an appropriate response. "A little weird, yes. Wait—I knew you looked familiar. You were once a Musketeer, weren't you?"

"You got me, Robert Downey Jr."

Quinn's quick-witted nod to Ironman's breaking and entering days made me want to hug the man. It wasn't often I connected with people at my level, but Quinn was just a perfect fit.

"You know, Jess. You borderline terrify me," he said. "I can't tell if I like it or not."

I knew how most men worked. Exciting girls almost always trumped the boring ones... until it came time for marriage. That was when us rule-breakers fell to the back of the pack. But this was a day of fun, and I was going to stick to the plan. I might not end up with the guy in the end, but he sure as hell was never going to forget me.

I slid the key into the lock and opened the door.

"Oh, you like it."

"Obviously others know about the key," Quinn said, shaking out his wet hair as we stood inside the castle walls, every square inch of which was littered with colorful graffiti.

"Believe it or not, most of this came from the same group of trespassers a decade ago."

"Oh, I believe it. And I'm going to go out on a limb and guess that the group of trespassers was none other than your coyote pack."

I laughed. "Such a quick study."

Walking over to the far wall, I slid down onto my butt. Quinn claimed the spot beside me.

"See that opening?" I asked, pointing to the space opposite us. "It's the hole you hit the golf ball into that then drops to the lower level. When I was a teen, I'd hide out in here and quietly roll the ball back out. They didn't know I was in here, and they couldn't figure out how come the ball kept returning to them. You can imagine how pissed people would get."

Quinn eyed me, amused. "You're diabolical, Jess. I love your wicked mind."

"I was such a shit back then. Don't be me."

"You? Don't be *me*. I'm about to be humiliated on national television."

Quinn adjusted his leg, resting it against mine. The contact sizzled through me, and I envisioned my hand sliding down his muscled thigh. Oh god. "You know, I almost googled you. Back at the car when you were changing."

He didn't seem surprised. "What stopped you?"

"The thought that you might google me."

He sat up straighter at my admission. "Why? What would I find?"

"Nothing good. I was arrested once."

"For what?"

"Trespassing."

He busted out laughing. "How am I not surprised?"

"Right?" I laid my head back against the wall. "Actually, I'm being modest. I was charged with breaking and entering. Destruction of property. Burglary. Theft."

"Okay, well, that's worse," he said, appearing a little less amused but far from judgmental. This guy was a keeper. "What did you steal?"

"My mother's jewelry. My stepfather's money."

"Oh, shit! You burglarized your own house. Again, I say, diabolical."

"Not my house. I'd long been discarded."

Quinn didn't say anything; he just sat there staring at me with an unreadable expression. I'd lost him. Honestly, how long did I think I could hold on?

"I know a thing or two about being discarded."

Now it was my turn to gawk at him. This perfect, handsome, self-assured man had once been rejected like me? It seemed almost unfathomable, but just from his expression, I knew it to be true. "Then you know the anger?"

He looked away, nodding. "Oh, I know the anger."

We sat in silent understanding. He and I seemed so different, but we weren't. Not really.

"This place here," I said, knocking my knuckle against the wall. "It wasn't just a love shack. It was also a roof over my head on more than a few occasions."

"Were you a runaway?"

"Not technically. My parents divorced when I was eight. At first, I bounced between the two—my mother's during the week-days and my father's on the weekends. But then Mom met this rich Hollywood producer guy, and suddenly I was at my father's during the week and hers on the weekends. Eventually, she gave up custody altogether, and I went to live with my father full time."

There was no way to hide the pain that still lingered. I'd been thrown away. You didn't just get over that. Quinn's fingers gently touched the back of mine. "You were nicer than me. I probably would've torched her house."

No judgment. He understood. My fingers mingled with his. "The thought did occur to me."

"Were you at least close to your father?"

"I was as a child—preferred him over my mother—but my dad had an alcohol and drug problem, making him a very unstable force. And he just got progressively worse as I got older. He couldn't hold a job. There were times he'd leave our apartment and be gone for a week or more, and I'd be all alone. I never told anyone because I didn't want them to take me away."

"That had to be hard on you."

"It was. When I was seventeen, my dad went into rehab. Mom refused to take me in while he was away. She told the social worker that she was concerned I'd be a bad influence on her new daughter... the one she'd had with the rich guy. Anyway, I was hanging with the wrong crowd. Pissed at my mom. It was a perfect storm. My friends and I stole a bunch of stuff. Hawked it. Got arrested. I went to juvenile hall, which, on the bright side, solved my housing problem..."

I paused, realizing I was rambling, and instantly shut down. What had I been thinking, spilling my messy history to Quinn? That was *never* a first date revelation. And now I'd left myself open and exposed, his to judge as he pleased. "This is the part where you run," I whispered.

His eyes caught mine... and there was no horror in them, no indication he couldn't get away fast enough. "Now why would I do that?"

"Because you prefer uncomplicated women."

He considered my words a moment before responding. "At this moment... I prefer you."

His admission ranked up there with one of the most unexpected moments of my life. Unbidden, a spark of hope flared. I'd only dared dreamed of finding a man who not only accepted me for who

I was now but also sympathized with the messed-up girl I once was. Of course, Quinn was only getting the first half of my story. If I didn't lose him in part one, there was still part two to scare the boy away.

"And just so you know, I'm not that girl anymore."

He nudged his shoulder into mine. "I know."

"Do you?"

"I'm not fragile, Jess. Far from it. And my childhood wasn't picture-perfect either. In fact, *terrifying* is the adjective I most often use to describe it."

Quinn watched for a reaction, waiting. For what? How was I supposed to respond? People didn't use that word to describe a death in the family or a bankruptcy or a drug-addicted dad who got them kicked out of their home. No, people used the word *terrifying* in relation to their childhood when they'd been traumatized by some major event.

"What happened?"

The muscle in Quinn's jaw tightened. Whatever he was hiding still had him in its grips.

"You shoulda googled me," he said, pushing off the wall and rising to his feet.

As he turned his back on me, I took the opportunity to mouth my complete and utter shock at his admission. Was this guy's life story in the public domain? "Are you saying if I googled you, I would've discovered your secret?"

"See, that's the thing, Jess. It isn't a secret." He turned around to face me. "All you need to know is just one tiny piece of my puzzle, and then everything about me will fall right into place."

*WTF?* The intrigue was killing me. I had half a mind to pull out my phone on the spot, but one glance at Quinn's fiery expression stopped me. This wasn't a tabloid story to him. This was his life, and whatever had happened to terrify him during his childhood still had a hold of him today.

I rose to my feet, offered my hand, and whispered, "You want more?"

I wasn't sure if Quinn cared to know more about me, but he didn't hesitate to grab my hand. He trusted me. And something told me he didn't extend that privilege to just anyone.

We walked toward the back of the castle where it narrowed and offered a more compact and protected place to sleep. Nick and I had used it for other things too, but that was a discussion for another time. Or not. I crouched down in search of my contribution to the wall of graffiti. It was just one small declaration of love, but instinctively I knew it would have survived the test of time. And sure enough, it was right where I'd left it, almost as if the love gods had conspired to protect its sanctity. My memories of Nick—of us—had been warped with time, but this little piece of us, preserved in ink, proved we had once been good.

"Here," I said, directing his attention to my initials framed inside a heart.

Quinn stooped down to take a closer look. I waited as he examined my drawing, knowing exactly what he was going to ask.

"You're JB?"

"Yes."

"And NL is your boyfriend."

"Was. Now he's more like a ghost," I replied.

"Like a real ghost?" Quinn asked, raising a brow. "Or are we speaking metaphorically here?"

"That's a good question. He makes himself scarce nowadays, but I'm told he lives."

"Well, that's good."

I took another glance at my inked heart, and suddenly my own beating one hardened. "I suppose."

He stared, no doubt assigning meaning to my words. "I'm sensing it didn't end well?"

"Does high school love ever end well?"

"My brother's been in love with the girl he met in high school pretty much his whole life. They're married now. Expecting a baby. So, it happens. Sometimes."

I chewed on that fact for longer than seemed necessary before replying. "How nice for them."

"Yes, I can see how happy you are for their union." Quinn laughed before shifting gears. "I'm guessing you still love NL."

He guessed wrong. I didn't love Nick anymore—not at all. "No. Quite the opposite. NL made sure there was nothing left of us to love. He turned on me, Quinn. Actually, they all did. My friends—they handed me over to the police. Told them I had been the mastermind, when in reality, I hadn't even known about the plan until the morning of. At the time, I thought I was protecting NL, so I took the fall for all of them. When I returned to school a few weeks later, I was a pariah, a laughingstock. Everyone turned against me, including"—I pointed to his initials—"NL."

Anger flashed across Quinn's face—for me. "What a piece of shit."

"I didn't show you this because I wanted sympathy. I showed you this because, despite everything that happened in my past, I'm still standing. And despite everything that happened in your past, you're still standing. See? We're survivors. You and me."

Quinn watched intently as I rustled around my backpack for a pen. And when I found one, I used it to scribble out NL's name, effectively erasing away the memory of the only boy I'd ever loved—the same one who'd stolen what little trust I'd had left in the world. I didn't have patience for his games anymore.

"There," I said. "Much better."

Quinn wrapped his hand over my fingers and leaned in close

to my ear. "Any guy who has your initials in his heart and lets you go, never deserved you in the first place."

My breath quickened as he pulled the pen from my hand and turned toward the wall. I couldn't see what he was doing, as his back blocked my view, but he appeared to be using my pen to add his own tribute to the wall. Once he was done, he moved to the side and gave me my first look at what he'd written. Above NL's crossed out initials, Quinn had added his own.

QM

## 7

## QUINN: MORAL SUPPORT

The rain had picked up enough to make finishing our round of mini-golf impossible, so we returned our clubs and called it a day.

Expansive puddles formed in the parking lot, with Jess's car sitting in isolation in the middle of the biggest one.

"Carry me," she said, pulling on my arm.

"Carry you?" I smiled, already liking the sound of having her attached to my body. "Is there something wrong with your feet?"

"Yes, they're inside my shoes."

I gave her the crazy look her words deserved. "So are mine."

"I know, but it took me four months to save up for these shoes. I don't want to ruin them."

Her reasoning was so endearing that I would've bought her a new pair of shoes on the spot. I'd never dated a woman as independent as her, one who was completely on her own with no family to catch her if she fell. In the span of one afternoon, I was already contemplating what it would be like to be that safety net for her.

I turned around and knelt down. "Hop on."

"My hero," she said, strapping onto my back and wrapping

her legs around my waist. And then, in a move that brought the protective instincts out of me, Jess crossed her arms over my chest and buried her head into the crook of my neck. It was intimate and trusting. I liked being her hero.

"Do you have your key with you?" I asked as we approached her car.

"Crap. It's in my backpack."

"Where's your backpack?"

"On my back, where it belongs. Just put me on the trunk, and then I'll dig it out. Sorry. I'm like a helpless newborn in the rain."

I eased her onto the trunk and watched as she searched through her pack.

"Got it!" She held the keys up and unclicked the lock.

I leaned in, intending to scoop her up and carry her to the front seat, when I got a good look at the girl. Jess's dark hair was sopping, those perfectly brushed strands now long and stringy and clinging to her cheeks. Water poured down her face and pooled in her eyelashes, but there wasn't an ounce of frustration. She smiled up at me, finding the joy in the moment. Her face, those lips. In a move that was totally unexpected on my part, I dipped in, cupped her face, and kissed her. Jess didn't flinch away, instead meeting me halfway and crushing her lips to mine. It was frantic and wild, exactly like I expected it to be with a woman who lived free.

And as our mouths wrestled in the rain, I trapped her lip in my teeth, grinding us to a halt. Jess groaned, pushing out with her tongue and fighting me for control. I could've taken her right there on the trunk of her car, and I honestly thought she might let me, but that was when the hail began.

"Oh! Fuck you!" I yelled up to the skies.

Jess dissolved into a fit of giggles as she once again wrapped herself onto my body. Lifting her off the trunk, I kept my hands squarely on her ass while carrying her the short distance to her car door. I deposited my new prize onto the driver's seat—where she'd been all day—and was about to jog around to the other side when Jess grabbed hold of my neck and drew me back in. Her tongue took a swipe at my lips, forcing them open and once again locking our mouths in a primal kiss.

Still gripping my face, Jess drew back, her eyes smoldering as streaks of water cut lines across her face. In that moment, I wasn't sure I'd ever seen anyone as beautiful. I snuck in and took another kiss from her.

"You're crazy." Jess laughed, and it was a joyous sound. I wasn't sure how to even describe what I was feeling other than to say Jess was quenching a thirst that I hadn't even known I had.

"No," I replied. "You make me crazy, and I swear, I don't know if I like it or not."

Jess buried her head into my neck and whispered, "You like it."

~

"Cats or dogs?" Jess asked, using her nails to comb through her wet, tangled hair like a makeshift brush.

"Dogs," I answered.

"Me too," she said. "Okay, now you go. Remember: opposites. No explanations."

"Yes, Jess, I get the concept of the game." I grinned. She was a bit of a micromanager, that one, but maybe her organization was just what I needed to get my life back on track.

"Odd or even?" I asked.

"Odd, of course."

"Odd?" I balked, blinking in rapid succession. "What kind of monster are you?"

"The kind who likes the number thirteen."

Oh, god, she was one of those. "I can't even go to sleep unless everything around me can divide into itself."

She laughed, no doubt picturing me counting my surroundings before shut-eye.

She continued with our game. "Kids or no kids?"

"Meaning do I have kids, or do I want kids?"

"Either or."

"Hold on. When did this turn into a full-on discussion? You're contradicting your own rules."

Her eyes flashed, and she snapped at me like a yappy dog. "Just answer the question."

I flinched, thinking she was serious, but she threw her head back and howled with laughter. "Sorry. I couldn't help myself."

"What is wrong with you?" I laughed.

"You bring out my playful side; what can I say?"

I liked that answer. I'd always been the least playful of my siblings—well, that is, if you shoved Emma in a closet—so it felt good to be cast in the role of 'fun guy in a car.'

"I currently have no kids," I answered her question, then added, "But I suppose I want them someday."

"Suppose or want?"

"Want."

"Okay, so when is someday?"

"When I'm no longer a complete and total fuckup—that's when. You sure seem overly interested in my sperm. Is that because, at three hundred and twelve years old, your clock is ticking?"

"Something like that. See, when you get to my ripe old age, you're willing to accept less as more. So at this point, even a reasonably fucked-up suitor will do."

"Ah, well, in that case, let me properly introduce myself. My name is Quinn."

"Nice to meet you, Quinn." She laughed, taking one hand off the wheel to shake mine.

We continued the handshake for longer than I'd intended, but I felt at home with her touch and wanted to extend it.

"Have dinner with me," I blurted out.

Her eyes darted from the road back to me. "You want me to go to a restaurant looking like a wet dog?"

"Actually, I wasn't suggesting dinner out. I thought maybe we could go back to my place and order something in."

She glanced my way. "Ah..."

"Hear me out," I interrupted before she could turn me down, which was where this looked like it was headed. "Just dinner and..."

"And what?" she asked as I hesitated.

"The East Coast feed of my performance should be coming up in an hour."

Her mouth dropped. "You want to watch it with me?"

"Yes, with you... and a large quantity of alcohol."

"You sure that's a good idea?"

"What? Watching the performance or getting shit-faced?"

"Both."

I laid my head back on the seat. "Tomorrow I'm going to wake up to a clusterfuck of my own doing. I have to know how the show is spinning it so I can tackle the problem in the morning."

"...with a raging hangover," Jess added.

"Exactly."

"Uh-huh. Solid plan."

"So, you in?"

She looked me in the eye. "I'm in. I'll have dinner with you. Maybe even one drink. We'll watch the show together, and I'll hold you while you cry. But I can't stay over."

"Jess, I'll take whatever charity you're handing out."

"Oh, trust me, Quinn. You're no charity case. If I stay, I might never leave."

~

"You said I could pick anything, right?" Jess called from my room.

When we'd arrived at my place, I'd offered her dry clothes of her choosing, and she'd been more than happy to go shopping in my drawers.

"Anything," I confirmed, fine-tuning the satellite connection.

Jess emerged a minute later in the vintage Van Halen t-shirt I'd taken from my father's drawer and a pair of my boxers.

"Wow. When I said make yourself comfortable, you took it to heart."

"All your pants are too long for me." She shrugged. "Oh, and I hope you don't mind, but I put my clothes in your dryer."

Again, wow. Jess didn't wait for things to happen, she just forged ahead. That was a characteristic most of my uncomplicated girls did not possess.

"That's my favorite shirt, by the way."

"Mine too," she said, doing a model pose for me. "I gotta say, Quinn. This place surprises me."

"What surprises you about it?"

"Just that your apartment is crappier than mine, no offense."

"None taken." I chuckled.

"I mean, you have a full-on freeway in your backyard."

"I know. Cool, huh? You wouldn't believe the accidents I've seen."

"Oh, I can believe it. It's just... I thought..."

"That I lived like a king?"

"Well, yes. Alan said..."

"Don't listen to what Alan says. Listen to me. Yes, my family has money. I do not. As a musician, I travel around a lot. I got the cheapest place I could find so I'd have somewhere to lay my head down when I was back in town."

"Gotcha," she said, grabbing her white food bag and dropping down onto my sofa. "Yum."

Dinner, such as it was, consisted of a Chick-fil-A drive-thru meal. I was a big spender like that. Actually, the choice had been Jess's. Traffic had been fierce on the way back to my place, and we were pushing it if we were going to catch the last performance of the night... my performance.

The feed came up just in time. Suzette, the contestant who'd taken the stage just before, was singing. My heart raced. In a few minutes time, my life would change—in what direction I wasn't sure.

"I'm up next," I told Jess.

She sat up straighter, chicken nugget in hand. "Holy shit, I'm nervous."

"How do you think I feel?"

Jess grabbed my cheek in her pinched fingers and cooed. "Does someone need a drop of liquid courage?"

I'd almost forgotten. Jumping from the sofa, I headed to the kitchen with Jess right on my heels.

"Where are *you* going?" I teased, boxing her out as we fought for position in my tiny kitchen.

"I've gotta see what my choir boy has in his liquor cabinet."

"It's not going to be impressive, but I know that I at least have a nice big bottle of Grey Goose the show gave me when I made the top ten."

"That'll do the job."

I nodded, searching my cupboard for a shot glass.

"Is this your family?"

Jess was standing at the fridge, staring at the photo. The picture had been taken at Keith's wedding. I braced for impact.

She leaned in closer, then slowly turned to me, and the disbelief on her face told me she'd seen the main attraction—and me standing right beside him.

"Surprise." I forced a smile. "Fun, right?"

"I... uh... good god, Quinn. Is Jake McKallister your brother?"

"I told you, Jess. I said one piece of the puzzle was all you'd need to have me all figured out. Was I right?"

Jess wasn't really listening to me. She'd gone a shade lighter. "That's why you looked so familiar but I couldn't place you."

"Because I look like him. My whole life people have been trying to *place* me."

"So, Jake is the hero of your story," she said, still working through the pieces in her head.

"And what a freakin' stud hero he is, am I right? Imagine living up to"—I pointed to the picture—"that!"

"Quinn." She gripped my face, sensing my rising panic. "Hey, easy, boy. It's going to be okay. You're up next, so we don't have a lot of time. Hand me that bottle—stat."

I passed her the bottle.

She snapped her fingers. "Glass."

I handed her the shot glass. She poured the vodka, which I expected her to guzzle down herself, but instead, she handed it to me. "Throw it back. You'll thank me later."

I did as I was told, and I could feel its goodness flowing through me like a lava river. I slammed the glass down on the counter. "Hit me again."

She raised a brow. "You sure? I get a sense you're a bit of a lightweight."

"Jess!" I said, warning her of a full nuclear meltdown if she didn't oblige me.

"Fine, but one more and then you're done. Got it?"

I nodded. She poured. I tossed it back and roared, everything in me burning. *Now* I was ready to face my fate.

~

We sat transfixed as I walked out to center stage. It was like an out-of-body experience. I remembered every second, but still, it all felt like such a blur. This had been my big moment, the one I'd been waiting for all my life, and what had I done? No really... what the hell had I done?

Jess sat fidgeting by my side. Even she was nervous for me.

"This is the video," I narrated, wanting to look away but knowing I had to face this head-on if I wanted to give myself a fighting chance to salvage what I'd destroyed.

She gripped my arm, and together we watched the exploitation. It wasn't as bad the second time around, but that was only because I was prepared for the assault.

"Is that you?" Jess asked as the camera panned to me clinging to Emma's leg.

"Yes."

"Oh, Quinn. That's heartbreaking."

She squeezed my arm a little tighter. The video ended. My face. My fucking face! You could see my anger. My frustration. My confusion. I was an open book up there, my pages splayed out for all to see.

The music started. Then stopped. Then started again when I stepped up to the microphone and sang.

Jess scooted to the edge of the sofa, leaning toward the television. I couldn't see her face, but I assumed that was deliberate. She didn't want me to register her reaction. Now that she knew I was Jake McKallister's brother, she was comparing my voice to his. My song to his. My looks to his. I had no doubt who would come out the winner—the guy hanging on the fridge.

The song ended, and the crowd jumped to their feet. But what I hadn't seen after my hasty retreat was that they'd stayed there—on their feet—chanting for my return. How had I not heard that?

The scene was cut, and Alan was back on the stage with the other contestants. They'd obviously spliced things together to make up for the time lapse created while Alan was chasing me down the street. My absence was glossed over—an emergency that needed tending to, he'd said. Did anyone believe that? One by one, the show recapped each singer, flashing a number on the screen for the home audience to call in and vote. Unexpectedly, my picture popped up on the screen. My voting number to call. The show wasn't through with me yet.

I was lucky number ten.

Rustling with the remote, I hastily clicked off the TV. I couldn't see Jess's face, but I assumed she was getting it ready to let me down easy—to tell me 'It wasn't so bad.'

"Jess," I said, running my finger along her back.

She turned her head to me, and I could see the emotion in her eyes.

"Quinn," she croaked out my name. "That was…"

I shook my head, frustrated in myself. "I know."

"No. You don't know. I could feel it down to my toes. Your pain…"

God, she was so beautiful. Watching her try to articulate her feelings about something I'd created from my heart—it was all that I'd ever wanted. To be heard.

I ran my thumb along her parted lips, aching for this woman. Slowly, she lifted her eyes to me. The same hungry stare that had held me captive in the rain was back. Jess licked my thumb, and that was enough. I grazed her cheek with my lips, then moved along her delicate skin, laying tiny kisses along the way. Jess drew in a breath, and I felt her shudder. My hungry lips hovered over hers, demanding she be the one to take what she needed.

And she did. Kissing me, sucking my lips gently, her tongue circling around mine. I gave in to her completely. Jess's fingers slid up my neck and through my hair, our lips still locked, our tongues still turning. As she lowered her back to the sofa, she pulled me down on top of her. I drew back, everything throbbing. I took her in, lying on my couch, her bare knees tilted to the side, wearing my favorite Van Halen shirt. I noticed then that she'd thrown her bra into the dryer and her pinpoint nipples were poking through the thin fabric. If I hadn't already been pulsing, that right there would have sealed the deal.

I slid my fingers along her thigh, over my boxers—the ones that looked sinful on her now—and up to her nipples. I grasped one with my palm, both of us groaning as I bent down and flicked it with my tongue through the fabric. Jess arched her back, thrusting her breasts at me, demanding more. Oh, god. I almost didn't feel worthy. She was too much. More than I deserved. My complicated woman. Give me more.

Greedily, I kissed her hard and deep while sliding my hands on the underside of her shirt, that silken skin of hers setting my throbbing shaft into a fury and nearly sending me to an early grave of shame.

"Jess..." I pulled back, panting. There was so much I wanted to say, but my brain could no longer articulate the words.

Her breath was shallow, her body twisting below me. She squeezed her thighs together, emitting tiny whisper-thin gasps, and then they parted and she grabbed my hand and pressed my fingers into her. As she writhed below me, I unbuttoned my fly.

Jess didn't wait, her fingers reaching into the opening and drawing me out, her encircled fingers sliding the length of me. I arched my back, dragging in what breath I had left. My oxygen level dropped. I thought I was going to fucking die. Lowering my weight onto her, my fingers probed deeper. She couldn't stay still, her hips thrusting back at me with every press.

"Don't stop," she cried, grabbing my hand maybe to direct me, but I required no instruction. I knew just what she needed.

"No, baby," I panted into her neck. "I promise to take you all the way."

Our bodies set into a rhythm then, both of us writhing to the beat of each other's drum.

Jess arched, her body shuddering and her legs pressing together in a scissor-lock that trapped my hand between her trembling thighs. The feel of her body, the quaking of her desire. Jess could have released her grip on me and I still would have detonated.

We quaked on the sofa, both of us lost in ourselves. In each other. I slid my hand around the back of her, gripped her bum, and yanked her into me as we caught our breaths. Nibbling her neck, I took advantage of her heaving breasts by sliding back under the shirt and teasing them. Jess grabbed my face, her eyes still awash with passion, and she pressed the purest kiss to my lips. I'd been with my share of women, but never anyone like her. She was premium quality.

We lay there in each other's arms, no words spoken between us as our fingers lazily explored. It felt right. Perfect. It was in that moment of quiet contentment that we heard the phone buzzing.

"Is that me or you?" Jess asked, not seeming the least bit interested in leaving the nest that we'd built.

"Who cares?" I answered, tipping her chin up and kissing her.

But I could feel her uncertainty, and as the phone continued to buzz, she unfolded herself from my arms and walked to her backpack.

"Come back to me," I called to her.

Jess pulled her phone out, tucking strands of hair behind her ear. Her shapely tanned legs crossed at the ankles as she stood there looking like my every teenage dream in a rock tee that barely covered her mound. I stiffened, ready for more.

"I just got a call from this number," she spoke into the phone, her brows furrowing. "Yes, this is her."

I watched her expression change from one of triviality to horror. "Is he okay? What happened exactly? Oh, god. Where are they taking him? Okay. Okay. I'm coming."

She hung up in a panic. "I have to go."

"What happened?" I asked, springing to my feet. "Is everything all right?"

Fear flooded her eyes. "I don't know. I have to…"

"Here—let me come with you."

"No," she blurted out, her eyes widening. "You can't."

"I can't? Why?"

Jess sprinted into the hall and grabbed her clothes out of the dryer, but she didn't even take the time to put them on. Instead, she sprinted toward the door in my t-shirt and boxers.

"Wait, Jess!"

"I'm sorry, Quinn. It's an emergency. I have to go."

"Give me your number. I'll text you in the morning."

Jess called it out to me as she opened the door. And before she disappeared, my perfect, complicated woman swung around and said, "You're a star, Quinn. And now everybody knows it."

# 8

## JESS: WHAT IF...?

I t was the call no one wanted to get. The kind that turned the blood cold and sent shivers down the spine. It was an accident, I'd been told. Hit his head. I heard *blood*. I heard *broken bones*. I heard *concussion*. And then I heard nothing because the person who'd called to report the news was no longer answering his phone.

Scenes of revenge played out through my head. Someone was going to pay for this. I'd trusted them with his life, and they had failed—miserably. I tried the number again, and it rang and rang. Panic began to creep up on me inch by inch, wrapping itself around my neck and squeezing tightly.

What if...

I sped up, daring a cop to pull me over so I could explain my dire situation. Surely, instead of a ticket, they'd give this woman in need a police escort. Yes, I was in need. I *needed* him to be all right, because if he didn't make it...

*No! Stop with the negativity!* The man who'd called hadn't mentioned *what-if*s. He'd said everything would be okay. And I had to believe that. I had to get into a positive mindset. Quinn. Yes—I could focus on my rock star golden boy. If anyone could keep my mind from wandering too far down a dangerous path, it would be him and his magic hand.

So much for keeping things friendly. I didn't know what had come over me. I heard him sing and knew what was sitting next to me. A bright and shining star. Quinn wasn't just going to be something someday; he was going to be *the* thing. The man I'd spent the day with was on the cusp of greatness, and I couldn't, in good conscience, *not* get a taste of his splendor. But immediately following our encounter on the couch, I understood Quinn McKallister was not a sampler at Costco. No, he was that nummy tester you gobbled up then circled back around seconds later, making some excuse for why you were such a needy little piglet.

Wait, what was I even thinking? What if I was *his* sampler? Maybe Quinn was just dipping his toes into the shark-infested groupie waters and I was his very first horny nibble. No doubt after that song hit the airwaves—he'd be swimming in the deep end.

I couldn't get Quinn's lyrics out of my mind. Or his voice with its soft, forgiving lilts shifting into something so wrought with emotion and power you thought you might not survive his pain. He'd suffered. There was no mistaking that. And after that performance, he'd be hard-pressed to find anyone not moved by his perseverance.

I was sold. But then, I had been ever since I'd rolled my window down back there on Hollywood Boulevard. My exit had been so abrupt. I wished I'd had time to say goodbye, to make him see how special he was. Because somehow he didn't know. How was that even possible? How had someone with his talent matured into a man who didn't think he had any? It wasn't right and it wasn't fair. Quinn deserved every good thing that was coming his way. And I had no doubt it was coming—in crashing waves.

Quinn would be a star—like his brother. Oh god. I'd almost

forgotten about the brother. How did you wrap your brain around that one? I mean, Quinn wasn't just the gallant hero who'd carried me through the rain or the sweet man who'd written his initials into my spray-painted heart. Quinn was also the younger brother of a superstar.

I knew the story. Everyone did. Jake had lived a nightmare. But I'd never really given much thought to what the other family members had lived through until I saw the look on young Quinn's face in that video. He'd been visibly traumatized, making me wonder what impact an experience like that might have had on the development of one so young. Certainly if the song he'd sung up on that stage had been autobiographical, which I suspected it was, then Quinn had lived a heartbreaking tale of loss and fear—and had struggled mightily to put his fractured life back together.

It explained the conflicted man in my car. And it explained his empathy toward me when I'd laid my past out on the line for him. Okay, well, maybe I hadn't laid out everything. I had left out one glaring truth. Which if revealed, it would explain to Quinn who I was over all else.

Pulling into the hospital parking garage, my tires squealed for the second time that day as I banked into an open spot. I was almost out of the car when I realized that I was still wearing Quinn's clothes. The t-shirt would work, but the boxers would not get me through the emergency room doors. I struggled into my damp jeans before dashing from my vehicle and taking the stairs two at a time.

*This is what you get*, a nasty voice popped into my head. *He was injured because you put yourself first.* No, it was just an accident! That's what they'd said. An accident with blood and broken bones. I fought the tears threatening to fall because, deep down, I feared that voice was right. Anytime I focused on my own happiness, I put his at risk.

Oh, god. What if...

A quick sprint across the hospital roundabout led me straight to the emergency room, where I nearly spun a hospital doc around like a revolving door.

"Whoa, slow down, young lady," he called to my back. There would be no slowing down. Not until I got to him, until I could see with my own eyes that my flesh and blood had survived.

Coming to a sliding stop at the triage desk in the middle of the lobby, I slapped my hand down on the counter. Through bated breath, I gasped, "Noah Ledger. Where is he?"

The woman put her palm up to slow me down. "First, I'm going to need some information."

"He was brought in here about an hour ago. Eight years old. Brown hair. Blue eyes. He fell and might have broken something."

"Yes, I remember him," she said. "And who are you?"

I straightened, standing strong and proud. That little boy in there was my one all-encompassing truth.

"I'm his mother."

The soothing elevator music made me want to crawl out of my skin. My kid was in the hospital. My injured kid. The least they could do was have a little "Crazy Train" blaring out of the speakers. The other three people in the elevator must have sensed my instability because they moved to the side, away from the fidgety mess I'd become. But there would be no apologies or excuses from me. I had reason to be anxious. Noah was all I had. The love of my life. My pride and joy. If I didn't have him, I didn't have anyone.

The elevator door opened on floor four, and I came face-to-face with the camp counselor, the man who'd promised me safety but had delivered me back a broken kid.

"Tell me," I insisted, resisting the urge to slap him across the face.

"Miss Bello," he said, "Please come sit down."

Resisting stomping my foot in protest, I replied, "Tell me here."

He appeared slightly taken aback, but he'd created the situation we were in, so why should he be comfortable? "Of course. First, let me say, I've spoken to Noah's doctor and have been assured he's going to be all right. Your son fell and broke his arm. They're keeping him here overnight to monitor him."

"For a broken arm?"

"No, for a concussion. He hit his head on the ground. And because Noah was complaining of pain and soreness in the upper left part of his belly, the doctors are worried he might have bruised his spleen."

This kept getting worse and worse, like he was starting with the least horrifying injury and working his way up.

"His spleen? I don't…I don't even know what that is."

"No one does," the camp director said, and as if responding to a joke, the corner end of a smile threatened to break free. If it made landfall, I'd punch him.

No doubt catching my murderous expression, the man cleared his throat. "Anyway, they don't think it's ruptured because his blood pressure is normal and there is no sign of bleeding."

"Okay. That's good, right?"

"Yes. Very good."

I let out the painful breath I'd been holding. And now that I had some assurance my little boy would be okay, the focus shifted to placing blame.

"How could this have happened? Wasn't anyone watching him?"

"Oh, I assure you, your son was being watched," the man said with the slightest inflection of amusement in his tone. "But as you know, Noah has a mischievous streak and can be quite the showman. He broke away from the pack during rope-making class, climbed the equipment shed, and told the other boys he could fly..."

My eyes widened. "He didn't..."

The director nodded. "I'm afraid he did."

Noah had done this—to himself. Embarrassment spread all the way up through my cheeks.

"I'm...I don't know what to say." I slumped my shoulders in defeat. "He knows better."

But did he really? All sympathy for my poor, innocent son evaporated. He'd freakin' jumped off the shed—of his own free will! There was nothing I could do or say to defend his actions. I couldn't even claim this to be out of his character, because it wasn't. Not even close. The truth was, I'd been to the hospital before. Once when Noah dropped off a rope swing that wasn't even over water. Another when he'd attempted to jump over my car with his trick bike. And yet another when he'd decided the neighbor's guard dog needed to roam free, and he got bitten on the butt for his efforts. I wasn't sure if Noah lacked sound decision-making skills, if he was Evel Knievel reincarnated, or if my relaxed mothering style allowed for such moments of recklessness from my son. I suspected it was a combo of all three.

"Miss Bello," the director said, taking pity on me.

"Jess," I corrected.

"Jess. Noah's a good kid—a crack-up, actually. He loves attention like Putin loves poison. And he's been thriving with the staff. This isn't a reflection on him or you. Sometimes accidents just happen... on purpose."

I tossed that astounding piece of wisdom around in my head before repeating it back for clarity.

"Accidents that happen on purpose?" I smiled. "How diplomatic of you."

"That didn't come out right, did it?"

"No," I agreed.

"You know. I was once a lot like Noah."

"Oh, really? You jumped off storage sheds too?"

"Well, no." He grinned. "But I did once fall out a second-story window."

"Oh, god. Please don't tell my son that story."

"We can keep it our little secret. Anyway, I grew up and went on to bigger and better things, and with the right guidance, so will Noah."

There it was. The subtle dig—the universal belief that a child born to a high school senior and raised by a single mom could not possibly get all the guidance he needed from her— from me. I hadn't put him at this sleepaway spring break camp for low-income kids because I thought he needed guidance. I'd enrolled him there because he'd received a scholarship to attend and I needed a break.

"Look, I know how hard it is to raise a son as a single mother without a man around. My mother did it on her own too, and look how I turned out."

The director opened his arms to showcase his awesomeness.

Was he...? I glanced at the man who was staring back with a wide toothy grin. Nah. No way would he be hitting on me so soon after my son was accidentally injured on purpose under his watch, would he?

"Very impressive," I smiled politely. "And thank you for making me feel better."

He kept ahold of my eye, nodding more times than seemed necessary. Oh god. Please no.

I stood up, putting some distance between me and a guy who didn't understand social cues. So much for being raised by a single mother.

"I'm going to go see Noah now, Mr....?"

"Craig," he said.

"Mr. Craig."

"No—Mr. Connor."

Wait, what? Was he Craig or Connor? I took my best guess. "Connor?"

"Yes." He chuckled. "I mean, no."

I blinked, unsure where to go from here. The dude couldn't even get his name straight, and he'd been put in charge of my child?

"Connor's my last name. Craig is my first. So it's Craig Connor."

Whoa, yeah. So, I didn't trust anyone who actually had to *explain* their name. I reached my hand out and shook his. "Thank you for getting my son to the hospital, Craig Connor. I'll stay in touch with the camp and update you on his condition."

"Yes." He nodded, not letting go of my hand. "Jess, I know this is random, but if you aren't doing anything next week, I have a day off, and..."

"I'll be with my son," I cut him off. It wasn't like me to be so clipped, but I was in no mood. Not only had my son been injured on his watch, but I had no patience for any man who wasn't named Quinn McKallister. "Sorry, I'm just overwhelmed."

And without a backward glance, I turned and walked away.

～

I pushed the door open and spotted a sleeping Noah across the room. My heart clenched. It didn't matter that he was directly responsible for his own misery; he was still my son and had suffered injuries that needed his mom. There was only one thing I'd promised myself the first time I'd held Noah in my arms, and that was I'd never abandon him like my parents had me. And I always kept my word.

Approaching quietly so as to not wake him, I looked over my sleeping angel. His shaggy head of hair had been forced into compliance by an alarming number of cords and tubes attached to his body, and his slight frame was dwarfed by a bed intended for a person twice his size. Noah looked so small and helpless. It was moments like this I was overwhelmed by my love for him. Yes, my boy was a handful, but he was also wickedly funny and a sweet soul who loved his mamma above all else.

Noah's eyes flew open. "Boo!"

I jumped back, slamming into a tray and knocking everything to the ground with a colossal ruckus. And just like that, any goodwill my son had banked was grievously spent.

"Dammit, Noah," I swore, slapping a hand to my chest. "Don't scare me like that."

"Sorry," he replied. "But you should've seen your face."

"Did it look something like this?" I asked, contorting mine into something worthy of a slasher flick.

"Worse." He giggled.

"Worse?" I teased, palming his face with my hand. "Don't you be dissing my looks, stinker."

I couldn't describe the relief I felt to hear him laugh, even at my expense. I'd pay any cost to keep him safe and by my side. At least I still had the opportunity to teach him the difference between right and wrong, although in this particular situation, it should have been quite obvious.

Playtime over. I needed answers. "What were you thinking, Noah?"

"It was windy." He shrugged. "I thought the gusts would carry my weight."

"Why?"

"'Cuz I saw it in a cartoon."

"Hmm... and you understand that cartoon characters don't have spleens that splatter on impact, right?"

"Yeah. But the nurse said it didn't splatter."

"Not for lack of trying. Honestly, Noah. I worry about you. What would you say if someone asked you to jump off a bridge?"

"I'd ask how high."

I flashed him the evil eye.

"Fine. I'd say, 'No, it's a bridge and my mom says I can't.'"

I shook my head, pulling the sheet down to assess the damage. "Does it hurt?"

"Not anymore."

"Did they give you pain medication?"

Noah dropped his voice to a whisper, checking for spies. "No, they gave me drugs. I told the nurse I wasn't old enough to take them yet, but he said it was a good drug. So I said sure."

"You said 'sure'?" I chuckled. "How agreeable of you."

"Can I still go to baseball practice tomorrow?"

"No, Noah. You jumped off a shed. That rules out sliding to home plate for at least a few weeks."

"Uugghh." He threw his arm over his face and groaned. "I have to practice."

"You don't even like baseball."

"Yes, I do." His eyes flared.

"Okay. Fine. You like baseball," I conceded. We'd had this discussion before. Noah only liked baseball because his father liked baseball. "Sorry."

The nurse walked in to check Noah's vitals, effectively saving me from a conversation about Nick and his absentee parenting.

"How's my favorite patient?" he asked.

"I'm fine. Can I have some ice cream?"

"Let me check first to see if it's allowed on your diet, okay?"

"I'm not on a diet," Noah replied.

"I meant your hospital diet." He laughed and then turned to me. "I love this kid."

"Me too," I agreed, taking Noah's hand in mine as the nurse finished his duties and left.

"You hear that?" I beamed. "He loves you."

"Yep." Noah nodded with such confidence. "Lots of people love me. You. Dad. Grandma Ledger. Grandpa Ledger. Dylan."

I blinked. Had I just heard him correctly?

"Dylan? Babe, me and Dylan broke up seven months ago."

"So? He loves me. He told me so himself."

I almost fell back onto the tray for a second time. Dylan and I had dated a grand total of two months. "When?"

"That day we went to the lake to fish. He took me to the pier while you were waiting on the beach. I asked him if he loved you, and he said yes, and then I asked him if he loved me too, and he said yes."

I could only imagine the sheer horror in Dylan's eyes when he'd gotten that doozy of a question from his brand spankin' new girlfriend's kid. "Oh, honey... that's just... uh."

"Call him, Mom," Noah said with such confidence. "He'll want to come see me."

This conversation had only one way to go and it was down.

"No, Noah. Dylan won't come see you."

"Yes. He. Will."

I could hear his frustration. Noah had easily bonded with the few boyfriends I'd had over the years and had been devastated with each and every breakup. But he'd never verbalized his disillusion until today. "Just because he doesn't love *you* anymore doesn't mean he doesn't still love me."

I looked away, not wanting Noah to see the sadness in my eyes. I wasn't sad about Dylan. We weren't right for each other. No, I was sad that he'd given my son hope that a man might stay.

"Noah, listen. Dylan has a new girlfriend. He's moved on. I'm sure he was really fond of you—who wouldn't be—but he's not coming to see you."

"Because you won't call," he blurted out. "You told him to go like you tell everyone to go. Marc loved me too. And so did Elijah. But you made them leave. Not everything's about you, Mom."

Tears burst from his eyes. I grabbed hold and held him until he'd had his cry, but I couldn't stop thinking about Noah's accusation. What damage was I inflicting on my son by introducing him to men who would fill that empty hole in his heart only to rip them out of his life when it ended?

"I'm sorry," I said. "I didn't know he meant that much to you."

Noah didn't respond. His normal jovial self didn't laugh or even smile. "I want my dad."

Oh boy. I should have known that one was coming. The demand for his father typically followed a discussion about my shortcomings as a mother.

"Honey, you know your dad is hard to track down."

"Call Grandma, then," Noah insisted, jutting out his jaw in a move strangely reminiscent of the man he sought. "She'll know where he is. Once she tells him I'm hurt, my dad will want to come see me."

I died a little inside. This boy never gave up his faith that his father would one day put him first. Nick rarely, if ever, showed any interest in Noah. His apathy toward his son had begun a few months after conception, when I'd first told him I was pregnant. First came the denial, followed by the slut-shaming, followed by the demand to end the pregnancy. He'd vowed to me back then that if I went through with it, he'd never be a part of Noah's life. And he hadn't lied. Nick had only ever spent a handful of days with his son since his birth nearly nine years ago... not to mention that the child support checks were few and far between.

Most of our dealings went through his parents, who'd gotten involved only after the court-ordered test had proved their son's paternity. Still, they always set aside a portion of each conversation to accuse me of ruining their son's baseball prospects. As if. Nick had done a fine job of ruining them himself when a frat party went horribly wrong and Nick not only lost his baseball scholarship but was kicked out of college.

Still, in his parents' eyes, all that blame fell on me... and the little boy who had done nothing but idolize his deadbeat dad his entire life. I tried hard not to crush Noah's faith in his father, thinking of Nick as a bit like Santa Claus. I wanted my son to believe in him as long as feasibly possible.

"I can't promise anything, but I'll contact Grandma Ledger and ask her to let your dad know."

Noah lit up. "Okay. Maybe he can sign my cast."

*Maybe he could sign a few checks while he's at it, too,* I thought to myself.

"Just don't get too excited. You know your dad isn't always easy to find."

"He'll come this time," Noah said, but even I could hear the cracks in his faith. He knew as well as I did—his dad wasn't coming.

## 9

# QUINN: TRENDING

A strangled scream caught in my throat as I shot up in bed, confused and winded. I covered my ears to block out the wail of sirens whizzing by my window. Normally, I slept right through police chases, but a night of drinking had delivered a morning of nausea and a head-splitting migraine. Possibly the only positive to waking up with a massive hangover was that I couldn't focus on the end of my very short career.

The buzzing on my nightstand temporarily drew my mind away from the throbbing in my brain. Texts, one after another, were coming in quick succession. I grabbed my phone and silenced the vibrations. I didn't even bother to check the senders since the only person I wanted to talk to was the one person who didn't have my number.

Jess. My god. Yesterday. Last night. My fingers sliding over her body. The way she moved. I hardened. I needed her. Wanted her. Would give anything to have her again. She'd left in too much of a hurry for proper goodbyes, leaving me with a drunken urge to text her. But my prior experience with emergencies told me she needed her space. Besides, Jess and I had made a plan, however hastily it had been put together. I would text her in the morning, and that was that.

Easing my body back onto the mattress, I was surprised by my need for her. I'd felt something with Jess yesterday. She'd eased that lonely spot inside me. The place that no one got to go to or see. Why her? Why now? This time yesterday, I didn't even know she existed, and now I couldn't imagine being without her. Jess was someone I could see myself with, not just for a night but for life. And sure, people connected all the time. They fell in lust. They fell in love. But not me.

I didn't bond easily with others. Never had. Actually, that wasn't true. There had been a time—before—but I barely remembered *before*. But *after*? Oh yeah, I remembered that. Imagine aging a decade in a matter of months. That was me, which made the *after* especially difficult when it came to connecting with kids my own age. While they were laughing and cheerfully running around, I stayed a safe distance from the action, hyper-aware of the danger that lurked. I couldn't relax. I couldn't connect. Gone was the brave, inquisitive boy who'd led his peers. Gone was the sporty kid always carrying a ball tucked under his arm. And gone was the chatty talker who couldn't walk down the street without making a new friend.

That punishing self-isolation carried on through grade school, gradually easing through my middle and high school years, but the feeling of being different never fully went away. Maybe it was the glare of existing in Jake's wake—first after the kidnapping and then after the fame—that kept me isolated from my peers. As I got older, I thought maybe it might be different with women. My confidants—Grace, Emma, and Sam—were all women, so maybe I just expected it to be easier to connect with females. But it never was. In every relationship I'd ever had, there'd been a disconnect from the very start. I struggled to make the investment with them even though I knew I should. I was embarrassed to even admit that the point where I was now with Jess was further than I'd ever been with any woman I'd ever dated. Jess had flicked a switch inside me. With her I didn't feel like I was crawling around in the dark. I had to know why. I had to see this through.

It wasn't lost on me that I'd seen a very similar scenario to Jess and me play out before. It was a moment that was etched into my memory forever—the very first flickerings of love. I'd seen it through the eyes of my brother and the woman who would one day become his wife. Jake had fallen for Casey in the span of just one night. I still remembered the electricity in the room and that razor-sharp focus projecting off both of them. Neither one was able to pull their eyes away from the other. Somehow, they knew. I'd been sixteen at the time, and it had made an indelible mark on me. Even now, years later, I still considered that the gold standard of love... and why I knew I'd never found it.

But yesterday—last night—the electricity was there. The razor-sharp focus was there. My eyes seeing only the girl. It was there. I knew it made no sense, but was it supposed to? Jake and Casey hadn't made any sense at the time either, but they'd never wavered. I blinked up at the ceiling, shocked by the thought slowly crystalizing in my brain. Was this my 'Casey' moment?

Was Jess *my* one?

My phone lit up, now the only indication of incoming calls. I tilted the screen toward me and soured upon seeing the Facetime request from my brother Kyle. Somehow I'd successfully kept my family at bay, probably only because I'd managed to send off another group text last night minutes before getting shit-faced drunk. In it, I'd reassured them that I wasn't inching my way along a ledge somewhere. My family was funny like that. Even the most innocent of things could go from zero to worst-case scenario in a matter of seconds. And no one in the family seemed to have much faith in my solitary coping skills, despite the fact that I'd been weathering the storm alone my whole life.

Still, I was almost insulted that they'd sent Kyle to make sure I was all right. Who in their right mind would put him on the front lines? But then, maybe that was the strategy. Toss the most harmless member of the family in first to test the waters, and if he survived, send in the rest of the troops.

"Yeah?" I answered, hoping my gruff morning voice and appearance would be enough to scare him away.

"Damn, dude!" He jumped back. "You look rough. I can almost smell your breath from here."

I breathed into my hand to confirm his theory and then cringed.

"Exactly." He nodded. "Well, at least you're alive. The fam will be happy to hear."

"It was a nail-biter there for a while."

"Nah. You'd never leave without getting the last word."

Had he not seen my performance last night? If that wasn't getting the last word, then I didn't know what was.

"What do you want, Kyle? I'm severely hung over, and seeing your face makes me want to vomit."

"Well, all right. Check you out. In a relatively good mood...considering."

Years of being Jake's punching bag made it near impossible to insult Kyle.

"And I wanted to thank you. See, when Kenz and I first heard you were going on *Next in Line*, we were both worried that you'd take our place as the favorite McKallister on a reality TV show. We worked hard for that title, as you know. Anyway, I should have known you'd screw it all up. I mean, what were we even worried about, am I right?"

"You guys are always underestimating me."

"I know, and I'm sorry."

"Is there anything else, or can I go back to my misery?" I asked, rubbing my weary eyes. I was not in the mood for his grandstanding.

"Actually, there is just one other tiny little thing. Have you happened to look outside today?"

The way he said it implied I was missing something, so I rose from my bed and looked out the window. Squinting into the morning sun, all I could see was traffic for miles.

"Not that window," he said, overseeing my movements through Facetime.

"It's the only window I have, Kyle."

"Ah, well, that explains it."

"Explains what?"

He didn't answer my question, instead opting for another one of his own. "Have you, by chance, checked social media?"

Now I was getting irritated. If Kyle didn't spill soon, he wouldn't make it back to the bunker to tell the others I'd survived. "Just get to the damn point, Kyle."

"Okay, so. Don't shoot the messenger, but there's a crowd gathered outside your apartment building."

"My apartment building? Why?"

He blinked. Then shook his head. "Why do you think?"

"I don't know. That's why I'm asking you."

"Oh, my god. You really are the worst reality star ever, aren't you? Okay, let me spell it out for you—B. O. O. M."

"Wait, what?"

"Dude, you blew up. Twitter. Instagram. You're breaking the goddamn internet."

That unbelievable piece of information took a second to process, but once it sank in, I had to know which direction I was trending. "In a good way or bad?"

"Does it matter? No publicity is bad publicity, bro."

"Tell that to Jake," I said.

"I have."

"Kyle, come on. Good or bad?"

"Good. Real good."

"So... they liked my performance?"

"Why wouldn't they? It was bomb."

It was? What I saw last night was anything but. "So, what do they want, these people outside?"

Kyle shook his head, tsking me. "It's almost as if you didn't grow up with a rock star for a brother. How do you not know what they want?"

"Because I've never had this happen before, dick!"

"Okay, fine. Let me paint the picture. You know when, like, Jake goes to a grocery store and people are ducking behind the avocados to take pictures of him and then those same people post the pictures to social media just to brag that they saw him? Now, pluck Jake out of that scenario and insert yourself. That, my friend, is what those people outside want. You, Quinn. They want you."

I stared at him, blinking. That couldn't be right.

"Don't believe me? Check your followers on Instagram. Go ahead. I'll wait."

It took all of ten seconds to discover my brother was telling the truth. My followers hadn't just doubled, they'd quadrupled —maybe even more.

My jaw dropped. "What the hell?"

"Exactly," Kyle confirmed. "Now, don't start getting a big head. You're nowhere near Jake levels—or even my levels, for that matter—but it's a solid start for our little troublemaking Quinn. You're just so cute, I want to squeeze those cheeks of yours."

I cut him off. "I have more."

"More what?"

"More Instagram followers than you."

"No, you don't," he scoffed.

"Yes, I do."

"Shut the fuck up," he said, his screen going black while he checked his own Instagram profile.

Once he came back on, disgruntled, I was ready to pounce. "Ah, look at you. So cute. Totally schooled by your own baby brother. Sorry, Kyle. How does it feel to be third best?"

"Shut up," he grumbled.

I popped back over to my profile once more just to bask in the glory.

"Where did all these people come from?" I asked, more to myself than to anyone else.

"It's not rocket science, Quinn. You went rogue in front of twelve million people. And then those twelve million people told their friends..."

I stopped listening when I saw the magical check next to my Instagram handle. "I have a check mark!"

"Yeah. Yeah. And you know what else you have? A security problem. Your apartment building isn't equipped to handle a guy with a blue check mark next to his name; you know what I mean?"

"I'm starting to." I nodded numbly, clicking back over to Kyle. "Does Jake know?"

"Dude, everyone knows."

"And?"

"And what?"

"What does he think?"

Kyle stared at me. "Does it matter what he thinks?"

It always mattered. Jake's support was gold to me, especially since he so rarely had the opportunity to give me his stamp of approval.

"It doesn't," I mumbled, looking away. "I was just asking."

Kyle took pity on me and offered up some rare sincerity. "He's proud of you, Quinn. We all are. You killed it last night. Plus, we're all on pins and needles waiting to see how you're going to get out of this latest mess."

Of course. I was a screwup. Even when I won, I lost. But I couldn't let that get me down. I had a blue check mark, and what I did with that power was up to me. I sank into the chair beside my bed, unsure what to say or how to feel. This had been my dream for so long, but I'd never really allowed myself to believe it could actually happen for me.

"What should I do?" I asked. "About the security problem, I mean?"

"First, pack a bag. You're staying at the main house for a few days. Second, brush your fuckin' teeth and take a shower. I'm thinking you smell like Bigfoot's dick right now. And third, be ready in thirty minutes. I'm coming to get you."

"You don't have to make the trip over. I can drive myself."

"No worries. We all have to be at Mom and Dad's by noon anyway."

My stunned expression said it all.

"Seriously, Quinn? It's Mother's Day."

"Again?"

"Yes, again. It happens every year. Haven't you been reading the family group chat?"

The truth was the family group chat had been blowing up my feed as of late. Once it started interrupting practice sessions for the show, I'd silenced them.

"Unbelievable." Kyle shook his head. "You've been muting your own family? Do you realize how many people would kill to be in a McKallister family photo?"

"We're taking photos too?" I whined. Nothing brought frowns to our faces faster than trying to fake happiness for a family photo.

Kyle shrugged. "The man has so little joy, Quinn. Just give him what he wants."

Yes, you heard right. Somehow, over the years, Mother's Day had become about my father. He took credit for everything because, and I quote, 'You kids should thank me instead because chances are your mother wasn't in the mood.' So, now, in addition to his birthday week, we all had to celebrate him on Mother's Day.

"I'm tired of living in fear of Dad's special holidays. Someone needs to put an end to his tyranny."

"Great. I nominate you. But please let me be in another state when you rip the beating heart out of his chest."

I cringed at just the thought of being the Grinch who stole Mother's Day *from my father*.

"Never mind. I'll be there."

"Ah, good. Doesn't it feel nice to be agreeable for a change?" Kyle dissed. "Oh, and Quinn? Don't forget to wear white."

"White? Are we going to a Spanish rave?"

"Pictures, shithead. Dad's request. Just do it and stop complaining. Jesus."

I exhaled audibly. "My god. Fine. I'll come dressed like the Pillsbury Doughboy. Are you happy now?"

"Ecstatic. Love the enthusiasm. Now get in that shower, Sasquatch. I'll be there in thirty minutes."

We hung up, but I held the phone, staring at the screen. I'd just gotten the biggest news of my life, and there was only one person I wanted to share it with. Bringing up Jess's contact information, I started, stopped, and backspaced multiple times before finally settling on the message and sending off a text.

# 10

## JESS: NOAH'S ARC

Sleep finally came for Noah late into the night, allowing me a moment to reflect on everything that had happened. The on-purpose accident, Quinn, the passion on the couch, the revelation that my son was strong-arming my exes into professing their love for him. I wasn't sure how to feel about any of it, but the sick feeling building in the pit of my stomach told me that something was going to have to give, and it wouldn't be that little boy hooked up to monitors on the bed.

Noah. The force of his emotions shocked me. Did he want a father figure so badly that he was willing to create a dad where none existed? Not one of my exes had bothered to tell me about the conversation they'd had with him, which told me it had meant nothing to them. How could a little boy begging for affection not be worthy of a mention? And Dylan? I didn't know what I was thinking with him. If ever there was a less fatherly figure, I'd like to know. I could picture Dylan getting that question while fishing off the pier with Noah. He'd have been shocked. Blindsided. How else would he have answered? *No, Noah. I don't love you. I only love nailing your mom.*

But this wasn't Dylan's fault. He had no allegiance to my son. Noah's needs came down to Nick and me, and since Nick had already tagged out of the whole fatherhood game, the blame fell squarely on my shoulders. I was the one bringing these men into Noah's life, which meant I was the one who needed to carefully consider the effects they had on my son. If Noah thought every man I brought home was a potential father for him to love, then I was doing a great disservice to everyone involved—because when those 'potential fathers' left me, they also left him.

So, where did that leave me and Quinn? I felt stupid even bringing him into the equation seeing that we'd only just met a few explosive hours earlier. But I couldn't *not*, because the attraction I felt toward him was too powerful to ignore. It wasn't just the way he looked or the things he did to slay me. It was that I wanted him right down to my core. I'd never been so sure of anything in my life. Quinn and me, we had something. I felt it, and I was convinced he did too. If given a chance, we'd burn bright... but for how long? Quinn was too young and too talented to stay in one place for long. If what I believed was true —that Quinn was on the cusp of stardom—then it wouldn't be long before he was gone for good.

If it were just me, I'd go for it. Live in the moment. Love hard and fast and free. But it wasn't just me. Noah would always be part of the equation, and every decision I made would affect his life. He and I, we were drawn to the same type of people. The more fun and dynamic, the better. There was no doubt in my mind that he and Quinn would bond quickly. It would be puppy love at its finest, and Quinn would probably make a great temporary daddy to Noah. They'd laugh. They'd play. They'd pass flatulence jokes between one another. Hell, Quinn might even teach Noah how to lose gracefully at miniature golf. But when it ended between the two of us—and it would surely end —Quinn wouldn't just take my heart with him. He'd take

Noah's too.

There was another option, of course. I could keep my son a secret from Quinn and sneak around like some desperate house-wife carrying on an affair with her hot, young lover. Quinn wouldn't know. Noah wouldn't know. But I would know. And how could I show Quinn who I really was without sharing the most important part of me?

I lay my head back on the chair and fought off the tears. Why did things always have to be so complicated? It had been a balancing act since the day Noah was born—how much of myself to give to him and how much to keep for myself. On any given day, the scale tipped in Noah's favor, but today was differ-ent. *If you want something you've never had, you have to do some-thing you've never done.* My god, I'd almost forgotten Lloyd's words. Was his prophecy about Quinn and me? And if so, what did it all mean?

Why did Quinn have to be such a risky bet? If he'd been someone like 'new' me, someone who paid his bills and watered his plants—maybe. But he wasn't. Quinn was destined for bigger and better things—ones that didn't include a single mom and another man's son.

My phone buzzed, and my eyes narrowed in on the screen. *How much is this going to cost Nick?*

Why was I not surprised by Grandma Ledger's response? Nothing in my earlier text implied I was asking for money, yet of course she would take it that way. I was, and would forever be, a gold digger in her eyes. Never mind that there was no gold to be dug. The Ledgers had money, don't get me wrong; they'd just figured out how to keep Nick's portion of it care-fully hidden, inexplicably giving him a management-level posi-tion in his family's company with the salary of a part-time fry cook.

That would show me. That would show his son who needed

food and a roof over his head. That would show us gold diggers who lived in low-cost housing.

*Noah's in the hospital, Hilary. He's asking for his daddy to come see him not for money*

Her response. *Again, I ask how much?*

My lips pursed in irritation and I contemplated adding a string of multicolored middle finger emojis to my line of text, but nothing good ever came from antagonizing the maternal gatekeeper.

*We have Medicaid*

And then I waited. I imagined her relaying the information to Nick. That was how all our conversations went after Nick conveniently 'lost' his phone a couple of years ago, forcing me to go through his mother Hilary for all my gold-digging needs.

*Nick's not available.*

*It's been over a year. Please ask him to reconsider—for his son's sake.*

More waiting and then the reply. *That was his final answer.*

His final answer? What was this—a game show?

*Ah, okay. I see,* I typed. *Well then, could you please tell Nick to kindly fuck off. Thank you, Hilary. Have a good night.*

*So classy,* came her reply.

I turned off my phone before our exchange turned deadly. Hilary and I had gone many rounds with each other over the years, and I'd come to the conclusion it wasn't worth my time anymore. As much as it pained me, I couldn't force Nick to love his son.

~

"Mom. Mom. Mommy. Mom. Mommy. Mommy. Mom."

After hours of tossing and turning, I must have fallen asleep only to open my eyes to Noah hovering over me, his hands manipulating my face as he crowed grating sweet nothings into my ear. "Ma. Mom. Mommy."

"Stop it." I giggled, removing his hands. "That's so annoying."

"You're the one that lets me watch *Family Guy* with you."

"Giant parenting fail, that one," I mumbled to myself.

"Nah. I don't want a boring old mom. You're fun."

"Too fun, apparently," I said, adjusting myself in the plastic hospital chair so Noah could position himself between my knees for a hug. He leaned in until his nose touched mine. There was never any personal space with him. My existence belonged to him.

"Why are you still sleeping?" he asked.

"Because I was up all night watching you breathe."

"That was dumb."

"You mean about as dumb as jumping off a shed?"

"I was flying, not jumping."

"It's not flying if you belly flop to the ground."

"I'm still working on sticking the landing."

I laughed. God, how I loved this muddy handful of a kid. He was my best friend, my confidant, and my partner in crime. And when Noah wasn't supergluing his hands to the desk at school or jumping off sheds, he really was the perfect little companion.

Sometimes when I was putting him to bed at night, I marveled at the joy and purpose he'd brought to my life. Nick had no idea what he was missing. Noah was full of color—and not just the standard, tiresome ones like yellow or green but also the cool, obscure shades at the end of the color wheel like puce or gamboge. And he didn't reserve his fun and fearless misadventures just for home, either. Noah was a beacon of light and universally loved at his school. Even the teachers and blacktop staff who occasionally doled out his punishments had to do so through thinly suppressed giggles.

"What are you doing out of bed?" I scolded.

"I was bored. When is my dad coming?"

I froze. This was always the worst part of 'Nick' discussions —trying to explain to my son the unexplainable.

"Honey?"

One word coated in compassion was all he needed to hear. Tears sprang to his eyes. "He's not coming?"

"No. Grandma Ledger says he's unavailable. Maybe he's traveling, or he might have a lot of work. She didn't specify why."

Noah fell into my arms, his soft cries gut-wrenching. He'd had enough, and I didn't blame him. There was just so much rejection a person could take before it carved out a little piece of your soul. I knew the feeling. I rocked him in place, my heart breaking for his innocence.

"Come on. We'll get you back in bed before the nurse finds out," I said after his tears dried up. "*Let's Make a Deal* is about to start."

Listless and dejected, Noah complied without protest as I maneuvered him into the bed, mindful of the tubing attached to his body.

"How did you manage to do this by yourself without getting all caught up in the wires?" I asked, always amazed at Noah's resourcefulness.

He shrugged, so miserable. "It was like limbo."

"Ah," I said, offering him my bent pinkie. Noah reluctantly hooked his into mine, and we both kissed our interlocked fingers. It was our bond and my promise. Noah might not have his dad in his life, but he had me. And that would just have to be enough for now.

∼

We were watching the game show on the hospital television when the text came in.

Noah's eyes widened, full of hope. "Is it my dad?"

*Please be Nick*, I silently prayed. *Just once, Nick. Please care.*

But it wasn't Nick. It was Quinn... and the text he'd promised me last night.

"No, hon, it's just a friend."

Noah turned his attention to the TV, silent and stoic. I squeezed his fingers. He squeezed back.

I pulled up Quinn's text.

*Hey Jess. Hope the emergency you were called away on wasn't too serious. I've got some news but I'm sure you already know. If not check my Instagram. Blue check, baby! Text me when you get a chance*

Another text immediately followed.

*Miss you already, Getaway Girl*

I placed my hand against my wildly beating heart, trying to settle it but knowing that wouldn't be possible. Quinn McKallister missed me. Quinn frickin' McKallister. He'd reached out, expressed his concern, then wanted to fill me in on his day. I'd been right. Our connection was as real to him as it had been to me. My heart raced at just the thought of seeing him again. And that kiss. And that song. It had been haunting. Beautiful. From his heart.

But wait... hadn't I already made the decision to put Noah first? Which, in turn, meant cutting Quinn loose. I glanced over at my son, a look of concentration on his face as the lady dressed like a stapler tried to determine which prize to choose.

"Door number two," he instructed the woman on the other side of the TV screen. He was so sweet, so innocent. Bringing Quinn into his life would bring him joy; that much I wasn't disputing. Quinn's humor and humility were qualities I wanted to instill in Noah, and I had no doubt he'd be a good influence on my son. But given what I'd learned last night about Noah's fixation on my former boyfriends, I couldn't in good conscience bring a man into our lives that I knew would not stick around. Quinn's life was about to blast off, and as much as I wanted to be on that rocket ship with him, I knew I couldn't... because for me, the scale would always tip in Noah's favor.

With a heavy heart, I closed my screen.

# 11

## QUINN: I DID IT FOR YOU

"There he is! The man of the hour," Keith exclaimed, clapping as I entered the area where my family was congregated. "You're so cool, Quinn. I wish I could be your boyfriend."

I smirked, flipping my brother off. So this was how it was going to play out. Avoidance and mockery. *That'll work.* I'd take sarcastic ribbing any day over sentimental gushing or pinpointed accusations.

"You'd be so lucky," I bragged.

"*I'd* be so lucky," his wife Sam said, trudging into the room and giving me a hug. "Please take him, Quinn. I'm sure Keith would make a wonderful addition to your harem."

"Yes, Quinn. Please take me. Sam has entered the 'Cross me and you die' gestational month of pregnancy. I'm not sure I'm going to make it to the delivery."

"Entirely your fault, Keith. Everyone knows you don't make comments about a woman's hair... especially when she's nearly seven months pregnant."

"All I said was the only thing worse than bangs is short bangs. How is that inflammatory?"

Sam pointed to her newly shorn bangs, and the women in the room gasped.

And yet, still, Keith continued to dig his own grave. "But you didn't cut them *too* short, so you're good."

"Ugh. Do me a favor, Keith. Just keep that mouth zipped for eight more weeks. Do you think you can do that for me?"

"I... I honestly don't think I can."

"Then you die," Sam said matter of factly.

I busted out a laugh. Sam was a favorite of mine, and when she wasn't actively growing a human inside, she was my go-to surf buddy.

My oldest brother Mitch—he was a half brother, actually, but no one talked about that—stepped into the fray. "If Keith's life depends on him keeping his mouth shut, we might as well all say our goodbyes now."

While the debate heated up on Keith's chances of survival, my still-throbbing head searched for a place to land. Eyeing Emma sitting alone in her oversized chair, I crossed the room.

"Scoot," I said, waving her over.

"Ah... not so fast." She held up a hand. "What's the magic word?"

"I'm not going to tell you the magic word because you're only asking it to shame me," I said, pushing her to one side and trying to squeeze in. Emma flung her legs up, nailing me in the thigh.

"The magic word first," she insisted, batting her lashes.

This whole ritual went back to the time when Emma had been my primary caretaker. One day, long ago, I'd opened my hands in prayer, begging Emma to let me have a full-on cookie lunch, and to my surprise, she was all for it—if I gave her the magic word. I didn't realize the magic word was *please*, so I gave her the only magic word I knew—the one she was now expecting of me.

"Abracadabra."

"There you go," she said, removing her legs and allowing me to slide into place beside her. Emma placed her arm through mine and used the other to check my forehead temperature with the back of her hand. "Uh-oh, Quinn. You look like a crusty little animal."

"Thanks... I guess."

"Seriously," she said, eyeing me. "Are you all right?"

I nodded. "Nothing a round of vomiting won't fix."

"Well, I don't think I need to remind you to keep your chunks well away from me or you'll be joining Keith in the dead man's pile."

"I'm well aware of your rules, Emma. Some nights before I go to bed, I still unconsciously recite them in my head."

"As you should." She grinned before switching gears on me. "That was quite a show you put on last night."

"Did you like it?" I asked, adding fake excitement for her benefit. "What was your absolute favorite part?"

"My favorite, you ask?" Emma matched my enthusiasm. "Wow, Quinn, I'd be hard-pressed to choose just one thing."

"In that case, let's not talk about any of them. How about that?"

"I suppose. For now." She nodded. "But only because I don't want to risk pissing you off after not seeing you in what seems like forever. I've missed you."

"I've missed you too. Have you heard from Grace lately?"

"We text all the time. She's in love."

My head shot up. "No, she's not."

Emma cocked her head, blinking at me in surprise. "Yes, she is."

"I think I'd know if my baby sister was in love. She tells me everything."

"Oh, really? Ever heard of a guy named Elliott?"

I blinked. "No."

"Then she doesn't tell you everything."

My mouth dropped open. "That sneaky little... why wouldn't she tell me that?"

"Probably because you're a one-man wrecking crew when it comes to her boyfriends. She doesn't want you to ruin it for her."

I resented the accusation that I was out for boyfriend blood. "Like I would do that. I don't even know this guy."

"One word, Quinn—Rory."

Rory? No way was I going to apologize for that. Rory had dug his own grave. I'd just covered it over with dirt. As far as I was concerned, I'd done Grace a favor with that one.

"Just keep your grubby hands away from Elliott. She really likes him."

"Please. I'm an angel."

She laughed. "A fallen one, maybe."

The conversation with Emma halted the minute my father entered the room with a 'Happy Mother's Day' party hat on his head, a plate of food in one hand, and a brightly colored drink sporting an umbrella in the other. Heading straight for his favorite armchair, he lined himself up and prepared for touchdown. It was a disaster waiting to happen, and everyone knew it... except for, apparently, the man himself. With no hands to guide his entry, Dad was going in butt first and blind. Even if he stuck the landing, there was no guarantee he'd escape the backsplash that would surely launch from his drink when gravity deposited him deep into the old recliner's manmade sinkhole.

Dad claimed to love this chair; he even had a list somewhere that highlighted its selling points. Things like superior squish factor, foam that 'remembered' the shape of his ass, and the recliner's otherworldly ability to smother the smell of his farts all ranked high on the list. But we all knew it was a lie. My father was no martyr. Like any other middle-aged man in America, he'd prefer a brand-new state-of-the-art remote-controlled recliner with advanced massage settings, a built-in power station, and the ability to cure cancer. Yet the man stuck to his fourteen-year-old chair for one incredibly selfish reason—he didn't want to share.

See, as of now, no one wanted to sit in his chair for the exact reasons he'd outlined as bonuses on his list. But where his chair was situated in the room was also the most coveted spot: the perfect angle and length from the big screen TV. A new chair meant fierce competition, which my father's dad bod could not withstand.

Dad started the descent slowly, but inevitably, gravity took over, pulling him down at a rate of speed not approved for his advancing age. The whole thing was like a cringeworthy sitcom, and none of us could look away.

"Ah shit," he swore, as a splash of red splattered onto his white shirt and a pile of chips transferred onto his shorts. Undeterred, the man forged on, flicking the folding side table out with his elbow and setting his drink on it before surveying the damage. All in all, not a bad performance. I'd seen worse. Much worse.

"You all right there, Dad?" I asked.

He looked up, surprised to see me. "Oh, good. You're home. Your mom was worried."

"Like I was the only one," she replied.

"Well, you were the loudest."

It was only when my father had transferred everything onto his TV tray that he sat back and I saw what was written in large bold lettering on his shirt. "Ask me about my colonoscopy."

"You really can't get enough attention, can you?" I laughed.

"I don't know what you're talking about."

"Whatever you do, do *not* ask him about his colonoscopy," Jake warned.

"It's a trap," Kenzie seconded the warning.

"Anything he says cannot be unheard," Sam added.

"Relax, ingrates." Dad smiled, relishing the horror his existence invoked in his children. "This is a different story."

Keith scratched his temple. "How can one person have two colonoscopy stories?"

"I have benign polyps, Keith, that's how," Dad scoffed.

"All right, fine." I bit down on the line. "Tell me about your colonoscopy."

"Nooo," the others groaned in unison.

"Oh, stop. This new story has no excrement involved. Anyway, after my last colonoscopy, my doctor came to check in on me and I said, 'Wow, Doc, now I know what it feels like to be a Muppet.'"

Mom's eyes rounded in horror. "Oh god, Scott. Please tell me he laughed at that."

"What do you think, Michelle? The man's a gastroenterologist. He specializes in diarrhea. Of course, he laughed."

She shielded her eyes with her hand. "And that's precisely why I no longer go to his appointments with him."

"I just hope this funnyman gastroenterologist of yours doesn't know you're my father," Jake said. "But that's probably wishful thinking, isn't it?"

"Well, I did wear a shirt once that read, 'Ask me about my son, Jake McKallister,' so it's possible he deduced from there."

Jake covered his head with a pillow. "I'm never taking you anywhere, ever again."

"Speaking of being a shitty son..." Dad smirked. "Jake, do you care to explain why you're not wearing the white clothes I specifically requested for Mother's Day pictures?"

"Sure, Dad. Because one, you're my father. And two, I have a reputation to uphold. To be perfectly honest with you, I never even considered your request."

"Ah, I see." Dad smoothed his fingers over his jawline. "Interesting, since it's, you know, Mother's Day and all. But okay. Quinn? What about you? I also noticed your blatant disregard for the sanctity of the day I convinced your mother to have sex with me... in order to have you."

"Blech! That's wrong on so many levels. And I'm sorry but no way are the first paparazzi pictures circulating in the media of me going to show me dressed like Colonel Sanders."

Dad took mental note of my refusal before turning to Keith, also not in white. "And you?"

"What?" He shrugged. "I just forgot."

"That's not cool," Mitch fussed, gesturing toward his lily-white outfit. "Jake, Keith, and Quinn shouldn't get off scot-free. It should be all or none."

"Exactly," Kyle complained, all decked out in his finest snowy duds. "The hypocrisy sucks."

My brother-in-law Finn didn't seem to want to get involved, but relented when all eyes fell on him. "Obviously, I side with Mitch and Kyle. The others should be punished for their insubordination. These ten-year-old party pants are so tight they're cutting off my circulation. I can barely breathe."

"You make a good point, Finn. Listen up, boys. I want you all to take a really good look at Finn's junk. It's so crammed in there that at any minute his plums could blast through those seams like a busted can of biscuits. That, my friends, is loyalty. Did he have to load those pants like gunpowder into a musket? No, he didn't. Finn is the only one of you boys who didn't come out of my nutsack and look at him. He looks absolutely ridiculous... all because he loves me."

Finn accepted the backhanded compliment with his characteristic aplomb. "Scott, I'm not sure if I say this often enough, but you always make Mother's Day a special one."

"I say the team players should get some sort of reward," Kyle suggested.

"Your reward is knowing that you are loved more than your brothers."

"That's it?" He bristled.

Jake nodded. "I can live with that."

"Me too," I added.

"I just forgot." Keith shrugged. "I don't know why I need to be punished."

"Wait? So, there are no pictures?" Mitch asked. "This was just a test?"

"That's correct. You passed. Well done, Mitch."

"Asshole," my brother grumbled.

"Oh, and as an added benefit to my now-favorite sons, I will also be cutting Jake, Quinn, and Keith out of their inheritance."

Keith gasped. "But your 'postal worker' fashion collection is our legacy. I was counting on the proceeds from the auction to buy a candy bar."

"Welp, I really can't help you, Keith. You should've thought about that before being a dumbass."

Casey entered the room. "Thought about what?"

"Oh, I've just been cut out of Dad's will," Jake replied.

She shook her head. "My god, Jake, I leave you alone for five minutes and now I'm never going to get the money to buy the box of Hot Pockets from the grocery store."

"I'll save up... just for you."

"Thank you, babe," she said, giving him a kiss.

"Is he sleeping?" Jake asked once she'd settled in beside him.

"Yes. Finally."

I didn't have to ask who they were talking about—Jake and Casey's youngest son.

Jake saw me staring. "You arrived about three minutes after Slater melted down to the core."

"Ah, yeah," I said. "Slater."

"Ah, yeah," he mimicked, his lip drawing into a thin line. "Slater. Casey calls him high energy. I call him Chucky."

I'd seen the little dude in action. He was no joke.

"Stop." She elbowed him. "He didn't get his morning nap. We won't make that mistake again, will we, Jake?"

"No, *we* will not," Jake said.

"What'd you do, pinch the poor kid?" I asked.

"Let's just say I didn't know I could ruin a person's day by giving him the wrong color sippy cup."

"Purple, Jake. Always purple," Casey said, laughing as she laid her hand on his leg. No further words needed to be passed between them. They understood each other at a deeper level. Like me and Jess. Or at least where I thought the two of us could go if given the chance. I was confident we'd get to the point where she could lay a hand on my thigh and all would be well.

"Who cares about Slater's meltdown when we've got Quinn's totally epic tantrum on stage last night?" Keith said. "Or are we all just going to pretend like it never happened?"

"I vote we pretend," I answered.

"Dude, I gotta know what was going through your head," Keith said.

"Obviously not much." I shrugged. "I got mad."

"You got mad?" Mom repeated.

"You know," Keith continued, "I'm wondering if Quinn might have benefitted from more timeouts as a child."

"We had a full-on Quinn Corner," Dad countered. "I assure you, we tried."

Mom ignored the others in her quest for details. "What's your plan, Quinn? Are you considering going back?"

"To the show?" I asked, surprised she'd even thought that an option. "Obviously not."

"Well, do they know that? The show made it seem like you

were performing next week, so you might want to clarify that with them."

"I plan to."

"Good. And next time something like this happens, I'd really appreciate if you answered my texts. I was worried about you."

"Next time?" I scoffed. "You act like I do this all the time."

I was met with silence as if, yes, they all did think this was a recurring theme. I drew my head back, stunned. What fresh fuckery was this?

"It's not that you do it *all* the time, Quinn," Emma said, trying to ward off my coming storm. "But you know how we are. A little communication goes a long way. What were you doing that was so important you couldn't return a text?"

*Avoiding you all* was what I wanted to say, but I held my tongue. In light of the day I'd spent with Jess, I hoped to be a better, more introspective man, so instead of arguing—which was my first instinct—I mimed throwing back a shot.

"Quinn!" Mom shook her head in disappointment. "I hope you're joking."

"Uh-huh," I humored her. "Just joking."

"No joke," Kyle snitched. "I saw him this morning pre-shower. He looked like he'd been nibbled on by a gaggle of rats."

"And did drinking solve any of your problems?" Mom asked.

"No. But it tasted good going down."

"How about coming up?" Mitch inquired.

"I know how to hold my liquor, dickhead."

"Less so how to hold onto a job."

All heads turned to Jake and his coarse comment. Leave it to him to shut the room down. I could see my family nervously glancing around. Clearly, they'd had a discussion about my joblessness before I'd arrived.

"Dude," I said, glaring at him. "Low-fucking-blow."

But Jake showed no signs of backing down. In fact, after the sippy cup incident, he appeared to be itching for a fight. "All I'm saying is, good for you. You made your stand. But then what? You run away? Turn off your phone? Don't deal with the situation when your whole career now depends on you making quick, sound decisions? If you're going to take a risk like that, at least be a man and back it up."

I was not liking one thing that came out of my brother's mouth. It didn't matter that everything he said was probably true. I'd never been good at accepting criticism from Jake. When it came to me, he had a way of wrapping everything in condemnation.

"Good thing it's none of your business, then."

"I disagree. The minute you walked off that stage, Quinn, you made it my business—hell, you made it all of our business."

My leg began to thump, an early sign of combustion. "I'm so sorry to have inconvenienced you all. I didn't realize I was supposed to clear all my fuckups with the family first."

"Wait. Is that a thing?" Kyle asked. "I haven't cleared any of mine."

His joke dropped like an anchor.

Kenzie whispered something only he could hear.

Why had I even bothered coming here? The paparazzi would be preferable to this inquisition. "I didn't do it for attention, if that's what you all think."

"Then what did you do it for?"

"Jake, stop!" Casey warned, grabbing his arm. "Quinn is right —it's none of your business."

I unraveled from Emma and rose from the oversized chair, my fists clenched. "I did it for you!"

"For me?" Jake protested.

"Yes. I did it for you. And you and you," I said, pointing out various family members. "I did it because the show disrespected our family."

"By showing the truth?" Emma asked.

"No. By exploiting it."

"But you had to know they'd do that," she countered. "The show thrives on drama."

"No, I didn't know it. Because they promised me the focus would be on me and my career and not Jake and his goddamn kidnapping. I mean, does everything in our lives have to revolve around that?"

The room fell silent, my hastily spoken words ricocheting back at me. Shit. It slipped out. We never talked about the kidnapping. It just wasn't done. And now, thanks to me, it couldn't be undone.

Jake got up and left the room. Casey followed close behind.

I stomped off in the other direction.

How was I the asshole? Jake's comments were no less damning than mine. Okay, mine were way more damning. The kidnapping was a taboo topic. I knew better. But I also knew Jake would get over it. He always did. The unusual part of growing up McKallister was that despite the feelings of rejection and neglect I still harbored toward my family from the time when I was a small child and left to fend for myself, I was also fiercely devoted to them. Maybe it was because we'd been forced to come together as a cohesive unit to fight against an outside force trying to destroy us that we'd all bonded like glue. So, when blowups like this happened, I was barely fazed. I knew it was only temporary. That was how it was done in our family. We huffed. We puffed. We blew the place down. And then we came back together like we'd never been apart. That was our family. Dysfunction at its finest.

I found a spot outside by the fire pit, a place to be alone until the storm settled, and that was where I checked on Jess, hoping she'd responded to my text, but there was nothing. I'd thought for sure she would've texted back by now. Why the delay? Now I was getting genuinely worried. Was her emergency of the irreversible kind? God, I hoped not. Jess didn't deserve to deal with stuff like that. Her life had already been hard enough without added stress piled on.

"Hey, hon," Mom said, walking over the grass to take one of the many empty spots beside me. "You've had an eventful few hours, haven't you?"

"Skip the pleasantries. I'm in no mood."

"I can see that. You came in hot."

"No, I came in like campfire ash—cooled and contained. You're the ones who fanned the flames."

Her lips pursed as she nodded. Clearly, she did not agree with my version of events. What was new?

"Quinn, what your brother said wasn't nice."

Nice? What did I care about nice? He attacked my character and questioned my motives so I struck back. An eye for an eye.

"I know Jake's approval means everything to you."

My jaw constricted. "I don't care what he thinks of me."

"You do care. You've always cared."

She knew me too well, and yet, really, not at all. Because if she did, she'd know why it was so important for me to best Jake. She'd understand that the only way for me to truly stand out in this family, to be worthy of their love and attention, was to achieve a status equal to or greater than my brother's. But it wasn't an attainable goal, not when my talent was forever being compared. Jake was the hurdle I'd never been able to clear. His bar was too high, and no matter how close I got to making it over the pole unscathed, I always came up short.

"He's proud of you, Quinn. You should have seen him watching you perform. He was so impressed. Mentioned several times what a great singer you were. And that song—he went so far as to say he wished he'd written it. From Jake, that's the highest praise."

She'd always been quick to defend him. He was the golden boy, the tip of the deadly mountain I had to climb. He could say or do whatever he wanted, and the rest of the family was content to give him a free victim pass, no matter how poorly he acted. But not me. Never me.

"So why didn't he tell me that himself instead of ripping into me for standing my ground?"

She paused, shaking her head. "Probably for the same reason you throw the kidnapping in his face every time the two of you have a disagreement. Look, I understand that you're mad and that you're lashing out any way you think will hurt him most, but blaming him for the kidnapping... Quinn, you just can't. Maybe you don't fully understand what he went through —what he had to endure. You were young, and I kept that information from you at the time, but you need to know that your brother suffered terribly. There was torture and abuse. I have the police report if you want..."

"I don't want," I clipped her off. "What would I want to see that for?"

"Because then you would understand why we don't blame him for something he had no control over. Attack his behavior, Quinn. Attack his music. Attack anything else about him. But don't attack him for being forced into a truck at gunpoint. Don't attack him for being stabbed multiple times or nearly starving to death. Don't attack him for surviving a hell none of us fully understand. Just don't do it."

Never had things been presented to me so plainly. Usually conversations centered around Jake's kidnapping were done in hushed tones with carefully selected words. But this... Now I felt like shit for always tossing around the kidnapping like it was no big deal. And to me it really wasn't. I didn't know exactly what Jake had been through because I didn't want to know. My whole life all I'd cared about was how his tragedy affected me. I blamed him... for his own kidnapping.

What the hell was wrong with me? I dropped my head into my hands and groaned. I had to be better than this. There had to be another way to be seen without weaponizing someone else's suffering.

I stood up.

"Where are you going?"

"To apologize."

"He went home."

Of course he did. I wouldn't want to stick around to be victim-blamed either. I sat back down. "I don't know what's wrong with me sometimes. It's just... this family. The pressure. The expectations."

"Nothing's expected of you, Quinn."

My head shot back up and I searched her eyes. "Why?"

She looked startled by my question. "What?"

"Why does no one expect anything from me?"

"That wasn't what I meant."

"But you *don't* expect me to succeed at the same level as Jake, do you?"

"I never said that. I think you have every bit the potential your brother has."

"But?"

"But why compare yourself to him? Why not carve out your own space in this business and be happy with your own unique successes?"

Oh, if only it could be that easy!

I shrugged. "Wins aren't wins unless they're Jake-sized wins."

Mom's eyes widened. "That's your measure of success?"

"Yep. So now you see my dilemma."

"Quinn...I..."

"I know." I put a hand up to stop her. "There are factors in play that make it impossible for me to achieve his level of success. I get it. Look, Mom. I appreciate the pep talk, but I've had a rough day, and I already have to apologize to Jake. If we continue this conversation, I'll have to apologize to you too."

"Okay, but let me just say this, and then I'll be quiet. Your dad and I would love to see you succeed, whether it's by stepping over your brother or by forging your own path. We'll be proud of you either way."

Sure they would. I nodded, pretending to accept her naïve proclamation of parental equality, but I'd learned pretty early on that you had to go big in this family to warrant any attention at all. And in music? Forget it. In my parents' eyes, Jake would always be the clear winner.

She grabbed my hand and squeezed, pleased with how the conversation had ended.

*Right.*

"I love you, hon."

"I love you too."

She patted my hair. "I don't think I've seen you with short hair since we had to cut it off when Kyle accidentally got that toy racecar stuck in it."

"That was absolutely *not* an accident. He rolled those race-cars back to wind them up and then stuck four of them in my hair."

We laughed at the memory.

"Anyway, you look so handsome. I love being able to see your face. You're going to have to fight the girls off."

"I was fighting them off with long hair too."

"That you were." She smiled. "You've always been a charmer, haven't you? I can't believe someone hasn't snapped you up yet."

"That's pending."

Mom whipped her head up. "Pending? Who?"

"Her name is Jess."

"Look at you smiling. How long have you known her?"

I checked my watch. "About twenty hours."

"Twenty hours?" she whined, nudging me. "You got my hopes up. I thought she was the one."

"She just might be yet."

## 12

---

# QUINN: THE SHARK

It had been a full three days since my stage exodus, and I was in complete limbo. For the first time in my life, I was on the brink of stardom, but I had no idea how to seize the moment... or even if I was legally allowed to do so. Despite being majorly pissed at me for the fight I'd yet to apologize for, Jake nevertheless sent me his lawyer, who instructed me to hang tight until he could figure out just how much trouble I was in.

So far, I'd successfully managed to keep the *Next in Line* hitmen from getting to me, but it was only a matter of time before Andrew Hollis bulldozed through the front gates of my parents' house and dragged me back to the stage where he would proceed to beat the hell out of me. More importantly, I had to figure out what was next, how I was going to take my blue check mark and turn it into gold.

I needed a plan, and until I had one, I couldn't go forward and I couldn't go back. I needed direction. Help. But instead, I waited, growing more impatient by the hour. To calm my nerves, I took advantage of the unseasonably warm post-rain weather and opted to drift aimlessly in my parents' pool, earbuds tucked in my ears as I let other people's music transport me into a place of clarity.

Maybe even to a place where Jess, my dream girl, would text me back. Because, god knows, it hadn't happened yet. I'd sent off a handful of follow-up texts over the past couple of days, and while they were delivered to the number I'd entered into my phone, they had not been read or responded to. I'd decided that there were only three possible scenarios that made any sense. One: She was ghosting my ass. But there was nothing about our afternoon together to support that theory. Two: The emergency she was dealing with was more serious than I'd thought, and Jess had emotionally shut down somewhere between my place and the one she'd gone. Or three: I'd entered the wrong number into my phone and was now paying dearly for my mistake.

The more time that passed, the more plausible the third option became, given that Jess had fired the numbers off so fast that I'd struggled to keep up. And if just one number was off, Jess would be the one thinking I'd ditched her. How was I supposed to correct this when I didn't even have her last name? Jess was the only one who could fix this. She knew who I was. She knew where I lived. But for whatever reason, my getaway girl was nowhere to be found.

And so I floated.

In the full heat of the sun, a shadow fell over me. I could almost not be bothered to investigate, but something told me to open my eyes. A man was standing on the deck of the pool, watching me. It was a moment of panic, of uncertainty. For obvious reasons, I didn't like being snuck up on, and even more so when the sneaker-upper was an unfamiliar man. I took in his pressed slacks and crisp button-down shirt. If he was here to do me harm, he certainly was smartly dressed for the occasion.

The man pointed to his ears, and I popped my earbuds out.

"Who are you?"

No need for pleasantries until I knew what he wanted from me.

"Hey there. Quinn, right? Name's Tucker Beckett."

"Who?"

"Tucker Beckett," he repeated again, pausing a moment as if I was supposed to know him.

I blinked.

"The band *AnyDayNow*? I was their creator and manager. Made them international pop sensations. Tucker Beckett."

That got my attention. I lifted my head up off the pool floatie and squinted into the sunlight. Now I knew who he was. This dude was a legend—and had more enemies in Hollywood than Katherine Heigl. Total prick. Rumor had it even his son, Bodhi Beckett, the head heartthrob in the boy band *AnyDayNow*, hated him. What the hell did he want with me?

"How'd you get back here?"

"Your father invited me in."

Of course he did. You'd think with all the horror movies my dad consumed, he'd have learned to never invite bloodsuckers into his home.

"Look," I said, wanting to get rid of him as quickly as possible, "I'm not sure what he told you, but I'm an untouchable—Andrew Hollis owns me for the next ten years."

"Ah, but that's where you're wrong. I know all about your contract, Quinn. That's why I'm here. I can help you."

"I seriously doubt that."

Tucker pulled a handkerchief—a handkerchief—out of his pocket and used it to wipe the sweat off his forehead. "I'm a busy man, Quinn. No way would I waste my time here if I thought you couldn't be saved."

"From what I hear, you actually aren't that busy."

It was a low blow, I knew that, but he deserved it for coming in here acting like he owned the place. My comment was a nod to another rumor I'd heard about Tucker, namely that in addition to being the creator and manager of *AnyDayNow*, he was also responsible for the band's demise.

Tucker didn't flinch. In fact, he bared a tooth or two. "Don't believe everything you hear."

Ah, challenge accepted. Might as well fire away. "I also heard you almost got your son killed in a wildfire."

Those teeth flashed brighter. God, he was so confident. "I'm good, Quinn. But not good enough to control the weather. Now, come on over here. I can't take you seriously on a unicorn pool float."

Was he seriously already micromanaging me? What a douche.

When I didn't comply, Tucker swiped the sunglasses off his eyes and sighed. "Please."

I almost laughed. This little power struggle we had going on was the most fun I'd had since Jess on the couch with my hand up her shirt.

"Now was that so hard?" I asked, hand-paddling over to the edge. The pathetic splashing moved me one inch at a time through the water, even spinning me in a full three-sixty turn before my plastic blow-up bed hit the side of the pool. But that was only step one of the two-part extraction process. I still had to get off my floatie with as much swagger as possible. Wiggling around, I finally managed to finagle my way into a sitting position, but it was only a short-lived reprieve until the flotation device began to sink, plunging me sideways into the water.

Tucker didn't say a word, didn't even give a twitch. Who didn't find people disembarking a pool float funny? Jesus, this dude was ruthless. But maybe that was what I needed. A shark. Someone so hated in the business he'd make me look good.

I hoisted myself up and out of the water, shaking out my hair.

"Are you done?" he asked, a smile finally materializing as he handed me my towel. "That was quite an encore there, Quinn... really just inspired."

"Well, you know, it's all in the dismount," I said, swiping the towel over my wet skin. "So, Tucker. Explain how you plan to liberate me."

"That's privileged information for my clients only. Are you my client?"

"You're kidding, right? You come over here while I'm busy..."

"Doing nothing," he finished the sentence for me.

I glared. Maybe if I'd been properly informed he was coming, I wouldn't have met him poolside in a pair of rubber duckie swim trunks.

"No offense, Quinn, but this setup you got going on here, this is why you're going to sink with the ship. Where's the urgency? Do you even realize how tight a corner you've backed yourself into?"

"I get it. My lawyer is working on it as we speak. I don't need some Hollywood player to tell me what needs to be done."

"No? Tell me, Quinn, how many studio heads have you heard from? You've got a whole new legion of fans dying to buy whatever you send their way. The labels should be knocking down your door. Where are they? Oh wait, I forgot— you're poison. See, the minute you took on Andrew Hollis, you became the kryptonite of the music world."

Goddamn, this guy went straight for the danglers. "So, if all of that is true, why are you here?"

"Because I know how to get you in the back door. And I've got the know-how, the power, and the determination to launch you straight to the top."

"How? And don't give me that crap about privileged information. How do you plan to get my music back from Hollis's grip?"

"By making it *not* your music."

"Not my music. What are you talking about?"

"Hollis owns solo artist Quinn... and all future music written under that name for a certain timeframe. What he doesn't own is your band or the music you'll write for it."

"My band? I don't have a band."

"You will if you hire me."

My eyes narrowed in on Tucker Beckett. It seemed too good to be true. There had to be a catch... and then it hit me. My voice dipped in octave. "You want me to join a fucking boy band!"

"No," he said. "Not a boy band. I've moved away from that. I'm looking to manage the next big rock band, and I absolutely believe that it'll be the one you're fronting."

Jesus, it seemed so simple. Too simple. "And what makes you think Hollis would leave that loophole open?"

"It's not a loophole. He could only take what was available to him at the time of the signing, and that was you. Quinn McKallister, solo artist. Look, I have a friend on the show that owed me a favor. He 'loaned' me the standard contract they make all the contestants sign. I had my business attorney look it over. He's dealt with these deals in the past and has signed off on my plan."

"So, if you're saying all I have to do is start a band, what do I need you for?"

Tucker lowered his glasses, peering at me over the top of the rims. He then whipped out a business card from the same pocket the handkerchief lived and thrust it in my direction.

"Oh, you need me."

~

*Call me—sooner rather than later,* he'd said as he walked away. *We've got a lot of work to do and not much time to do it.*

Fuck Tucker Beckett!

I watched him stride off, convinced I'd rather shove bird seed up my ass and let a blue jay go to town than hire that guy. He thought he had all the answers. So smug. Tucker was so wrapped up in slick packaging you'd think he was the spokesperson for a condom commercial. No wonder his son had risked first-degree burns to get the hell away from him.

And just because he said I was doomed didn't make it true. Although, okay... yes... it probably *was* true, but that was beside the point. Look, there was no denying that I was wrapped in lead and Tucker Beckett might possibly be the only one in Hollywood strong enough, and ruthless enough, to lift the chains off me before I sank to the bottom of a very muddy pond. But the question remained: did I want it bad enough to trade one captor for another?

My father met me halfway to the main house. "So, how'd it go?"

"You couldn't have given me some warning?" I asked.

"You would've said no."

"You don't know that."

He eyed me. "I do know. What did you tell Tucker Beckett?"

"Nothing."

"Nothing?" my father questioned, irritation filtering over his normally jovial features. "Why do you always have to be so bullheaded? That was your chance. Maybe even your only chance."

"Tucker Beckett is not a chance. He's a curse. I'm gonna call him back tonight and tell him no."

Now I was just being a dick because I knew my father wanted it so badly, and I was still irritated that he'd arranged this marriage of convenience without my consent.

"I see," Dad said, his lips pressing tightly together. "And why would you do that?"

"Because he's Tucker Beckett. His reputation proceeds him."

"Yeah, well, so does yours."

Ouch.

"You have no faith in me, do you?"

It was meant to be a meaningless reply, but my father hesitated... He actually fucking hesitated.

"Seriously? Thanks a lot," I said, knocking into him as I passed.

He grabbed my arm. "Don't walk away from me. I'm talking to you."

"Do you really think I can't make this decision on my own?"

"No, Quinn. No, I don't think you can make this decision. Do you have any idea what it's like to watch you throw away every opportunity you've ever had? It kills me to watch you sabotage yourself over and over. I mean my god, Quinn, you are so talented. So damn talented. You say you want it. You work so hard to get it. And then when you're right there at the moment of release... you don't finish."

The slap to my face stung as much as if he'd used his hand. What the hell was he talking about? I finished... didn't I? What possible reason would I have to sabotage myself when fame, when besting Jake, was all I'd ever wanted? But now that he'd said it, I couldn't get the words out of my head. Shit, was I actually doing this to myself?

My voice low and contemptuous, I replied, "Maybe I don't want to finish because none of those earlier opportunities were right."

"But that's the thing, Quinn—they *were* right. You told your mother the other day that it's not success unless it's Jake-level success, yet there you were, steps away from a record deal with your last band... and you walked."

"Because it was a shit deal."

"Who cares?" Dad said, raising his voice. "It was a deal! And now *Next in Line*? My god, kid, all you had to do was sing that song the other night and *stay on that stage*. Literally, Quinn, all you had to do was stand there, and all your dreams would've come true. But instead you ran. Like you always do. Things don't have to be perfect. Sometimes we have to adapt to the situation even if it's not ideal."

"Jake never adapted."

"If you believe that, then you know nothing about your brother's early struggles in this business. It's not always about how good you are or about how good he is; it's about how much you want it. You, my friend, are every bit as good as Jake, and the only reason you aren't where he is now is because you're not living up to your full potential."

"Like you lived up to your full potential?" I said, narrowly containing my irritation. "Didn't you also have aspirations of becoming a rock star? What happened to that dream, huh, Dad?"

"That was different. I sucked. Like really sucked. I didn't even realize how badly I sucked until I saw you and Jake and realized...my god, Scott, you really sucked. Maybe if someone had believed in me growing up..." My father's voice unexpectedly broke. "You have no idea what it's like to make your own way in the world."

I scoffed. "Yeah, I think I know."

"No, you don't! There was a time that you were neglected, yes, and your mom and me, we'll never forgive ourselves for that. But after Jake came home and we were able to heal, I dedicated my life to you kids. I was a fucking awesome dad to you and you can't deny that."

His anger floored me. My father rarely lost his temper. That was my mom's job.

"I don't deny it," I said. Everything he said was true.

Dad shook his head. "You think you had it so rough, try being neglected your whole life."

Neglected? My father? By my grandparents, affectionately

known as JimSuey? They'd never been solid fixtures in our lives, but they did come around every so often... when it was convenient for them. But they didn't seem like bad people. I mean, they wore knee socks, for god's sake.

"JimSuey were shitty parents?" I asked, genuinely surprised.

Dad's posture stiffened, the muscle in his arm rigid. "I misspoke. They were fine. The point I was making was..."

"Wait. No. No. Go back. Did something happen with JimSuey? Do you not get along with them? Am I the only one who doesn't know this?"

"Quinn, leave it alone."

"No. I want to know."

Dad fidgeted from one foot to another. He was nervous. Why?

"Look, they never cared about me, all right? I was just living in their house until I was old enough to... not be there."

"Did they treat Uncle Paul that way too?"

"That was different."

"Why was it different?"

Dad looked away, like he wanted to be anywhere but here. Had I just stumbled onto something big?

My father—the most open book I'd ever read—had a secret.

It had to be the single strangest conversation I'd ever had with my father, but it did make me think. Where did I want to be in thirty years? Because I now understood it wouldn't be on Jake's throne. He had that gig solidly wrapped up. But did I really need his level of success to be relevant in the music world? Could I be happy as a minor player *and* have my parents deem me worthy?

I unlocked my apartment door and let myself in. My parents' house, with all its earthly comforts, was feeding my complacency. It was time to leave. Some hard decisions needed to be made, and I couldn't do that on a pool floatie. Hell, by the state of things, I might already be too late. The parking lot had been buzzing when Kyle picked me up here three days ago, but look at it now. The photographers were gone; the reporters had moved on to fresher news, and I was quickly sliding back into obscurity—with a blue check next to my name.

Jess. I needed her now. She'd know the correct path for me to take. I grabbed the near-empty Grey Goose bottle and prepared a glass. Might as well drink *to* my girl since I couldn't drink *with* her.

There was a knock at the door. Holy shit! Had she read my mind? I shot up from the chair and jogged over, so proud of her for realizing her error and coming to rescue me. I swung the door open, unprepared for what greeted me on the other side: my brothers Jake and Kyle.

"Oh, hey," I said, fighting off my frustration. I might possibly be the only human on earth disappointed to find Jake McKallister standing on the other side of my door. "What are you doing here?"

"I got paged. Something about a cleanup on aisle Quinn."

"Ha," I said. "Funny. But true."

We exchanged a knowing laugh and I could tell I'd been forgiven without even uttering an apology. That was often how it went down.

"I'm actually *also* in the hallway." Kyle declared himself with a wave.

"Yes, I see you," I replied. "You wanna come in?"

"Uh...yeah." Kyle held up a bag. "I come bearing gifts."

"Taco Bell, of course," Jake announced the obvious. Not only could I see the overflowing bag of munchies in his hand, but Kyle was rarely spotted without.

Kyle knocked into Jake on his way in. "Don't be hating on my bean burritos, dude."

"Then don't be rippin' ass in my car once they've made their way through your digestive tract."

Shutting the door behind my brothers, I waited as they bickered about the potency of Kyle's Taco Bell exhaust.

"So...," I interrupted. "What brings you here?"

"Mom and Dad would very much like for me to talk some sense into you."

"Oh, isn't that nice of them?" I said through faked enthusiasm. "And why are you here, Kyle?"

"I..." Kyle stood there with bag in hand, looking back and forth between us. "... actually don't know. I have nothing relevant to add. I just came because Jake offered me food."

"Didn't want to be alone with me, huh?" I asked.

Jake gave a slight nod. "He's here as a witness."

"For me or you?"

"I suppose that depends on how our conversation goes."

"Um, guys, am I needed here?" Kyle asked. "If not, I'm just going to scoot on over to the table and lay waste to this bag of heaven."

"Knock yourself out." I motioned him to the chair.

Jake looked around. "I don't think I've ever been here before."

"No. You haven't."

"Where's your freeway?" he asked, my backyard always a source of amusement for the family.

We walked over to the window, both watching the traffic creep by. "Is it weird that I find this strangely inspiring? I want to pull up a chair and sit here all day and write songs."

"Not weird at all. I do it all the time."

Jake continued staring out the window, stalling. Or maybe he was waiting for me to start the conversation.

"Dad invited Tucker Beckett to the house without telling me. You know who he is?"

Jake nodded. "I know who he is."

"Basically wanted to pawn me off to the worst manager in Hollywood. Oh, and on a side note... Have you ever heard Dad mention having a bad relationship with Grandma and Grandpa?"

Jake seemed surprised by the question. "JimSuey?"

"Yeah."

"He's never said anything. Why?"

"Nothing. He was just acting weird."

"He's been under a lot of stress lately."

"He has?"

"Yes, Quinn," Jake said. "Because of the phone calls."

"What phone calls?"

"The ones Dad's been fending off for you from *Next in Line's* higher-ups for the past three days. They've been threatening him and you."

I knew he'd been getting calls but didn't know to what extent. "I don't understand why they keep calling him."

"Because you won't answer, and apparently you gave the show his number as an emergency contact. And now he's the one stuck dealing with your business because you won't. He's not your manager, Quinn. He doesn't know this business, and it's not fair to put this on him."

"I know. That was shitty of me. I'll fire Dad in the morning. Kyle," I called out. "You're my new manager."

My brother looked up from his chalupa. "Sweet."

Jake drew his hand across his throat, nixing the plan.

"I can see you, Jake," Kyle said.

"You can't even effectively manage yourself, dude. Kenzie sent you to the store for one thing—baby formula—you came home four hours later with a sixty-four-inch smart TV... and a puppy."

Kyle wadded up the wrapper, only to pull another item from the bag. "One time, Jake. That was one time... and I got the formula."

"Kyle," I said. "I'm sorry, man. But due to recent evidence, I'm gonna have to let you go."

"Eh. It was fun while it lasted." He shrugged and laid into his taco supreme.

"About your other problem," Jake said. "The way I see it, you've got three options. One: Go back to the show. Two: Quit music and find something else to do with your life. Or three: Hire Tucker Beckett."

"Why him? Tucker told me his plan, Jake. He wants to start a band with me as frontman to escape Hollis's solo artist clause. I can hire a different manager and do it myself."

"You can hire anyone you want. But if you hire some meek-ass manager just so you can push him around and make him do your bidding, how far do you think he's going to take you? Yeah, Tucker has a reputation as an asshole. News flash, Quinn—so do you. But being an asshole isn't a bad thing as long as people are still opening the door when you knock."

"How do you know they'll open the door for him?"

"Because I'd open the door for him."

"Why?"

"You know his story, right? Tucker didn't just create *AnyDayNow*. He made them. Just because you put five good-looking guys together doesn't guarantee success. Tucker made a series of decisions for the band that sent them soaring straight to the top...and, more impressive, he kept them there for five years. A boy band, Quinn. Imagine what he can do with a band that has more staying power."

"Jake's right," Kyle said through a mouthful. "I watched a

documentary about the band. Tucker Beckett was their driving force. The dude's a genius."

"And face it. You need someone with a significant amount of clout in this business to get you out of the hole you've dug. Someone who can stand up to Hollis. Someone ruthless."

"Someone like Tucker Beckett."

Both Jake and Kyle nodded.

"Oh, man," I said, sinking down into the chair opposite Kyle and rifling through his Taco Bell bag. "Why do I feel like I'm trading one dictator for another?"

"That's what your contract is for. Limit his power. Make him work for you."

Kyle's phone rang. "I know how powerful my input is here, boys, but it's the ol' ball and chain. I gotta take this," he said, smiling at the image of his wife filling up his screen. Kyle licked his fingers as he ducked into the hallway to take the call.

I laid my forehead against the table.

"What's going on in that head of yours, Quinn?"

"It's just a lot of pressure. I don't know if I'm good enough for all this hype."

"You're good enough. I rewatched your performance last night, and please don't take this the wrong way, but I've only ever heard you sing like that twice in your life. Once at my wedding. And then again on the *Next in Line* stage. Both times you were angry. Lost. Vulnerable. Remember at my bachelor party, we'd gotten into a fight and you were mad at me. The next day you performed that song you wrote for me at the wedding and you blew us all away. The other night, same thing. You were visibly pissed. Emotional. Before you even opened your mouth, I knew you were going to slay it.

"That's the magic, Quinn. It's what separates good from great. Find that anger that lives inside you, and instead of holding it in until you burst, take it out on the music. That's how

I learned to survive. All the darkness. All the pain. I threw it into my songs, and then I unleashed it on the world. And that's what you need to focus on—the darkness inside you. Where does that come from? Why do you always seem like a simmering volcano? You've got this danger to you, but you're always fighting it. It's not a crutch, Quinn; it's power. It's what makes you great. Always sing from *there*. If you do that, I promise, there will be no one who can hold you back."

"Even if I pick the shittiest manager in Hollywood?" I asked, bringing some levity into the life-affirming moment.

"Even then." He smiled. "You're *that* good, Quinn. You always have been—now you just have to believe it."

Thirteen years of formal education and never had I learned more wisdom from a lecture than I had today. I finally understood what needed to be done. If I wanted to go all the way, that portal to hell I'd opened up on the *Next in Line* stage could never be closed again.

My apology long overdue, I said. "I'm sorry for what I said to you at Dad's Mother's Day party, Jake."

"You don't have to apologize. I was egging you on. You're too easy, always one insult away from pulling the pin and..." Jake simulated an explosion with his hands.

"I'm serious. I should never have said those things to you."

My brother looked away, his jaw twitching ever so slightly. "Yeah, well. You're not the first, and you'll definitely not be the last. If I let shit like that affect me, I'd never leave my house. Maybe you ought to be more like me and stop listening to all the noise."

*Yeah*, I thought. *I definitely should.*

## 13

### JESS: HISTORY REPEATS ITSELF

I'd just settled Noah onto his throne in front of the TV, a game controller in one hand and a chocolate milkshake in the other. If I were an eight-year-old boy freshly home from the hospital, I wouldn't want to spend it any other way.

"Thank you, Mom," he said, tipping his head up for a kiss, and I gladly obliged. There was nothing like nearly losing it all to make you feel like a winner.

I sank down in a chair opposite Noah and reread the last message from Quinn. It had come in yesterday, and I wondered if it would be the last.

*Hey Jess. Not sure if you're getting my messages but I just wanted to make sure you were okay. Answer me back. Jesus, am I a stalker? I feel like a stalker*

I smiled, almost hearing his voice speaking those words. God, I was so mean. What I was doing was cruel. I knew that, but I also knew how quickly things could change. I remembered being curled up in front of the TV, much like Noah was now, moments before my life caved in. My parents had already divorced a year before, but of the two, my mother was the stabilizing force. Days spent with my father were fraught with uncertainty. After Andrea took his livelihood away, he'd floundered, usually drinking his weekends spent with me away. I couldn't wait to get back to my mother. The day she'd brought *him* home was the day I ceased being the center of her universe. Weekends spent with my father extended into weeks until finally she dropped custody claims altogether. Maybe if my mother had given me the same consideration I was now giving my son, she wouldn't have chosen him over me.

And the worst part of it all was that it didn't have to be that way. Even after she'd callously thrown me away, I would've forgiven her. And I would've eventually accepted her new husband into my life, just as Noah had accepted the handful of men I'd brought home to him. But my mother never gave me the choice. She'd made the decision for me and cut me loose. So, yes, maybe keeping Quinn away was an overcorrection, but I could not risk history repeating itself.

The doorbell rang. Noah looked up from his game, a momentary flicker of hope passing over his face.

"Who is it?"

"I don't know."

"Maybe my dad?"

*Don't count on it, buddy*, I thought as I peeked through the peephole. "What the hell?" I whispered.

"Is it Dad?" Noah brightened.

"No, it's Andrea."

"Who?"

"My sister."

"You have a sister?"

I could understand his confusion. He'd only met Andrea a few times in his life, and she didn't come up often in discussion.

"I have two, dork. You know that. Now be good, I'm going to let her in."

Why was I so nervous? She was my sister. But at the same

time, housecalls were not our thing. In fact, I'd never been to her house, and she'd never been to mine. I was surprised she even knew my address.

Anxiously tucking my hair behind my ear, I swung open the door, my hand actually shaking in the process. "Hi."

"Hi."

We stood there awkwardly, staring at each other.

"Can I come in?" she asked.

"Um... do you have any weapons?"

A smile pushed forward. "No. Do you?"

"Just these babies," I said, flexing my less-than-impressive muscles.

"I'll take my chances."

Andrea stepped into my apartment. I couldn't even believe I was saying that. Andrea. In. My. Apartment. Her eyes immediately zeroed in on Noah.

"Oh, my god, Jesse, I can't believe how big he's gotten."

"Yeah, these things...they grow. Who knew?"

Andrea laughed... in my apartment. First Quinn. Now this. Was I living in a TV show?

"May I?" Andrea asked as she approached Noah.

I nodded, still too dumbfounded to process her request.

"Hi, Noah," she said, extending her hand formally. "I'm Andrea."

He shook it, a floppy eight-year-old boy handshake. "Mom's sister."

"That's right. I'm sorry I haven't been around much, but it sure looks like your mom is taking good care of you."

"Aside from the scraped-up face, the bruised spleen, and the broken arm, you mean?" I asked.

"Yes, that's what I meant." Andrea smiled. "I brought you a gift, Noah... if... oh, I'm sorry." She turned to me. "Maybe I should have asked you first. Is it okay?"

God, so awkward. How had we gotten this way? That we couldn't be in the same room without spewing politically correct verbiage?

"We're equal opportunity gift getters in this house, aren't we, Noah?"

"We are," he confirmed, accepting the present with a smile on his face. I watched from my place near the door as he ripped open the paper to reveal a game inside.

"Totally Gross!" he called out, his eyes sparkling. My sister had just gifted Noah with the only game that catered specifically to a little boy's love of grossness. "Can we play now, Mom?"

"Maybe later. Don't forget your manners."

Noah, in all his pureness and without any knowledge of the rift between my sister and me, rose to his feet and gave her a hug. "Thank you."

"Oh," she said, taken aback by his gesture, awkwardly patting his back. "Aren't you a sweet one."

Had she made even the slightest effort to be in his life, I would've gladly shared him with her. As would I have with my mother, stepfather, and younger half sibling, Mabel. But none of them had ever shown an interest, so I'd gone it alone, raising my son without a tribe. It had been a lonely path to travel.

Andrea released Noah and turned to me. "Can we talk for a minute?"

"Sure," I said, then addressed Noah. "We'll be in the kitchen. Call me if you need anything."

Once we were out of Noah's earshot, I offered up a glass of wine to Andrea.

"Yes, please," she replied, eyeing me as I poured a glass for both of us. "I didn't think you drank anymore."

"I do occasionally, but normally I don't have much of a reason. You, here, is a reason."

"Yes. It surely is," Andrea said, pausing as if she were struggling for words. "I hope you don't mind me buying Noah a gift."

"Why would I? You're his aunt," I said, handing Andrea a glass and sitting down at the table. "I am sort of pissed that I now have to play the game with him, but..."

We laughed, and it was an odd moment for both of us. I couldn't remember the last time we'd done that together.

"So, what brings you to my doorstep, Andrea? Is a meteor plummeting to earth?"

"Not that I'm aware of. When you called in and told me about Noah's accident, I just... I realized that I didn't even know him. All these years. How old is he now—nine?"

"He'll be nine in a few months."

"Unbelievable. It seems like only yesterday you showed up at my doorstep drenched, pregnant, and desperate."

I couldn't help but react to her nonchalant retelling of one the worst days of my life. Did she have any idea how hard it had been for me to throw myself at her mercy? Obviously not. Worse still, she didn't seem to notice my surprise.

"Well, he's a darling boy. And handsome. I can't get over how much he looks like Nick with his light hair and eyes."

"He got my headstrong temperament. Does that count?"

"I suppose it does," she said, her speech faltering. "Speaking of headstrong temperament, I have news on Dad."

My head shot up.

"I know you've been looking for him."

"You know where he is?" I cut her off, eager for more.

"He's in a hospital in Pasadena with a broken leg. I'm not sure of all the details, but he was hit by a car. They say he's shown some interest in getting clean, and they have him on a waiting list for a public rehab. A transitional housing facility close by you is willing to take him until a spot opens up."

"When is he coming back?"

"Whenever you go and get him."

I brightened at the news, even if her ultimatum sent a pang of irritation through me. Since when had this become a 'me' problem and not a 'we' problem? Since forever. "I'm so happy he's been found. A broken leg, you said? It could've been so much worse. And maybe now he can get clean and get a job and..."

"Don't get your hopes up." Andrea cut me off. "You know we've been here before."

"Yes, but he's alive, and that's all that matters."

"Is it?"

"What's that supposed to mean?"

"He's barely there, Jesse—a drunken, strung-out shell."

"And whose fault is that?"

It just slipped out. Usually I had more control with my boss —who also happened to be my sister—but Andrea deserved everything she got.

"You think this is *my* fault?" she protested.

"If you hadn't fired him, none of this would have happened."

Andrea sat back in her chair, a stunned expression on her face. "And why do you think I fired him?"

*Because you're a selfish bitch*, I wanted to say, but I held onto that thought, choosing instead to throw the question back to her. "You tell me."

"Jesse! He was stealing from the company. Coming in wasted every day...if he came in at all. I had no choice. He had to go, or the company that my grandfather built would have been totally destroyed. You think I wanted to take over a company I had no idea how to run? No! I thought I'd have years to learn it, but he didn't give me that option. I had to either sink or swim."

Andrea paused, perhaps getting her blood pressure back under control before continuing. "Look, I'm sorry about what happened to you. It wasn't fair, but that wasn't my fault. If you want someone to blame, then point that judgmental finger right where it belongs... at that father you idolize for no reason at all."

I sat rigid, my heart beating wildly as memories flooded back. I'd been young, but I still remembered my father's erratic behavior. The fights with my mother. The acetic, sweet smell of alcohol on his breath. I looked up at my sister, realization dawning on me for the first time. She'd been such an easy target, what with her smug, aristocratic attitude, that I'd readily accepted, even perpetuated, the belief that every wrong ever done to me was a direct result of her; when all this time, we were both casualties of the same broken man.

I had nothing to say. Andrea looked down into her glass. The conversation irreversibly stalled until... "I'm getting a divorce."

My god, she was full of admissions today, each one equally stunning. Andrea divorcing? She'd always seemed so stable in her marriage; at least that's how she always made it seem in those pictures on Facebook, bragging of lavish vacations and fancy dinners. In every image, they were either laughing or kissing. It never meshed with their actual personalities, which were decidedly bland and unfriendly, but I always just assumed he brought out the best in her. Now I wondered if those photos were all a lie, a way for my sister to showcase to the world a false reality.

"Is it a mutual decision?" I asked.

She expelled a bitter laugh. "Depends on which of the three of us you're asking. Len and his girlfriend are quite in agreement — me, not so much."

I cringed... for her.

"How ironic, right?" she said, anger wrapped tightly around each word. "History repeats itself."

She was, of course, referring to the affair that had produced me. I wondered if she even realized how her words reflected on me. Did she not hear the accusation? I fought off the desire to strike back. Andrea was clearly at her lowest. Easy prey. I could either take the high road or the low. Swallowing hard, I went high.

Reaching over the great divide, I laid my hand on her outstretched arm. "I'm sorry. That truly sucks. He's a giant wanker."

She laughed. "Yes, he is...among other things. But thank you. I know I don't deserve your sympathy, but I'm going to take it anyway. What about you, Jesse? How are you doing?"

She looked around my modest apartment. It was nothing special, but I kept it modern and clean, or at least as clean as possible with a young child. Compared to her two-story home with landscaping and a pool, I'm sure I appeared to be on the cusp of poverty.

"I can't complain."

She looked back in Noah's direction. "No, I suppose you can't. Do you have a man in your life?"

Now it was my turn to stare into my glass. "I...yeah... That's a tough one."

"Really? You're so confident. Pretty. I'm sure you have them banging on your door."

"You'd be surprised," I said. "Most guys can't see past my seventy-pound accessory."

Andrea again turned her head to look back at Noah. "Do you... uh... do you ever wish you hadn't, you know, taken on so much so young?"

"If you mean do I ever regret having him, no. It hasn't been easy, but he gives my life happiness and meaning."

She nodded, taking a healthy swallow of chardonnay. "I think if I could have given Len a child, I might have been able to make him happy."

I looked away. Andrea? A mother? Had she forgotten her words the night I'd come banging on her door?

*Yes,* she'd said. *I'll give you a job, but you can't stay here, Jesse.*

*Please,* I'd begged. *Just until the baby is born, and then I'll find more permanent housing.*

*Absolutely not. You know I don't like kids.*

Dragging in a breath, I shoved those memories down. I couldn't get into it with her here, not with Noah's ear just a room away.

I pretended I hadn't just heard her ludicrous comment and turned to another topic near and dear to my heart. "Are you selling Angel Line Tours, Andrea?"

She startled at my question. "Where did you hear that?"

"Rumors amongst the staff."

"What staff?"

Like I'd tell her. "Everyone's talking about it."

"Well, that's a shitty thing to spread around."

"So it's not true?"

She hesitated. "It's complicated. When I married, I gave Len a stake in the company. He owns fifty percent."

"Andrea! Why would you do that? It's your grandfather's company."

"I know! I was young and dumb and in love. I wasn't the same person back then."

I begged to differ.

"He's forcing you to sell?"

"Either that or buy him out. And I don't have the revenue to buy him out, so..."

I took a healthy swallow myself before bopping the glass back onto the table. Through a barely controlled growl, I said, "I can't believe you're just going to roll over."

"What else can I do, Jesse?"

"Fight it. Fight him. I don't care. Save the company!"

"For who? Me or you?"

"I know you don't care what happens to me or Noah, but this

job is the only thing paying for a roof over our heads. If the company sells, what am I going to do?"

"What are *you* going to do?" she scoffed. "What am *I* going to do?"

Of course, she *would* say that.

## 14

### QUINN: WALK AND TALK

Carrying a cold-brew espresso in one hand and a laundry list of to-dos in the other, Tucker rattled off information faster than I could process. Since calling him minutes after ushering my brothers out the door last night, he hadn't stopped working. I don't think he'd even slept. If I'd had any doubts about my new manager's competence, they were squashed after spending two hours with him.

I'd had an agent in the past, and although I knew agents and managers had different duties, I was shocked by the hands-on approach Tucker took. He was singularly focused on me, acting as if I were his only client. My success, he'd said, was his success. Then it occurred to me... maybe I *was* Tucker Beckett's only client. A quick Google search confirmed my suspicions. The asshole had made it seem like I was lucky to get him, when in reality, the guy was hella lucky to get me—and I was no treat.

Turned out Tucker was every bit as much a pariah as I was. After having taken the fall for the highly publicized breakup of *AnyDayNow,* no artist would be caught dead associating with Tucker. Except me. Because... well... what did I have to lose? I was already dead in this business anyway. In fact, knowing he was untouchable actually made me trust him more, because under all those layers of confidence, Tucker Beckett needed me as much as I needed him.

As we walked, Tucker talked. "Would your parents be okay having the press conference in front of your house tomorrow?"

"A press conference?"

"Yes, the one you're going to give as a public statement of apology. We talked about this earlier, didn't we?"

We'd talked about a lot earlier, but given recent history, I definitely would've remembered if I'd been asked to apologize for something. Nowadays apologies were on a first-come, first-served basis.

"Remind me who I'm apologizing to?" I asked.

"*Next in Line.*"

"*Next in Line*? Shouldn't they be apologizing to me?"

"Think of it like damage control. If you apologize first, it makes them look like shits if they don't accept it. It's all a game, Quinn, and we want to come out on top."

"So, basically it's a non-apology?" I asked, growing ever more impressed with his devious mind.

"Exactly."

"Well, damn. I like it."

He smiled. "I'm glad you like it."

"So, why in front of my parents' house?"

"Sympathy, of course."

Oh, yeah, he was losing me now. "I don't want their sympathy."

"In this particularly delicate situation, yes, you do. We need all the goodwill we can get, because, see, *Next in Line* wants to destroy you, and they'll do it however they can, and that usually means attacking your character. Trust me, as someone on the receiving end of this, I know what I'm talking about. Right now, *Next in Line* is still in negotiation mode, trying to woo you back.

But once they discover that you're reneging on the contract, they aren't going to play nice. I know Hollis well. There's a very good chance he'll smear your name and make things very difficult for you. The press conference is necessary to stay a step ahead. Get the public on your side, so Hollis's team are the ones who look like the bad guys if, or when, they go after you."

Good lord, Tucker was good. Me, the guy who hated sympathy above all else, was actually nodding in agreement. Like Jake said, I had to be committed to change in order to grow, not only as a musician but as a man. Tucker was ushering in a new dawn, and with his leadership—and my newfound focus on greatness—we really couldn't fail.

*Hell, yeah, bring on the pity party, fuckers!*

"Okay. Press conference it is," I agreed. "What do you want me to say?"

"Is telling the truth an option?"

"Depends on what truth you're asking me to tell."

"What made you leave the stage? The rumor going around is that the video triggered a type of PTSD episode. That theory makes you very sympathetic, and given your past, people are eager to forgive. If that's what happened, then that should be our angle. And, honestly, Quinn, even if that wasn't what happened, it should still probably be our angle."

I sucked in a breath, wishing it hadn't come to this but understanding why Tucker thought it necessary. Besides, what did I have to lose? If people already assumed I'd suffered a flash-back, all I was doing was confirming what we all knew to be true.

"It's close enough," I admitted.

"All right then. We're in agreement."

"Yeah, sure."

Tucker smiled, clearly pleased by the ease with which I fell in line.

"Excellent. That's settled. I'll schedule it for tomorrow. And hopefully at the same time, we can announce the other big news."

I cast him a questioning stare.

"Your band."

My eyes expanded. "We'll have it picked by tomorrow?"

"We'll have it picked by three in the afternoon today," Tucker corrected, glancing down at his watch. "Speaking of that, Neil just texted me. We've got fifteen plus guys already gathered at the studio for the auditions. You ready to select your band?"

See, this was the speed at which things happened in Tucker's world. You either had to keep up or fall behind. It honestly surprised me that I wasn't falling behind.

"I feel like everything is happening..."

"Too fast?" He finished the sentence for me. Tucker did that often, like his mind was working so fast it didn't have time for periods.

"Yes."

"It is fast. I've never done anything like this at this speed, but we're working against time, Quinn. We have to jump on this while you're hot. The plan is to release that song we talked about by the end of next week. Do you think Jake and Kyle would publicize it? Maybe even post links in their bios?"

"I can ask. I'm sure they would. I can ask Finn too."

"Jesus, I forgot about Finn Perry. Your family is a gold mine of free publicity. And I'll talk to Bodhi and RJ and the other guys in *AnyDayNow*. See if they can help us out too. Contrary to popular belief, they don't actually hate me with every fiber of their being."

"Well, that's good to know."

"And," he continued, "your newfound following alone should be enough to get it trending. Then, with the added push of some big-name celebs, no one in the business is going to be able to ignore you."

"Is it just me, or does this seem too..."

"Easy? Yes, Quinn. Sometimes it is. You're uniquely positioned right now—and only right now—to make it big. Every minute we wait is another minute wasted." He paused, and I could practically hear his mind churning. "I can feel this in my bones, kid. You gotta trust me."

There was nothing about Tucker and his slick appearance that projected dependability—hell, no one in this business even trusted him—but I did. Implicitly.

"I do trust you."

He stopped walking. An expression I'd never seen on Tucker's face emerged. Was it... gratitude? "I'm going to tell you something I've never told anyone. I made promises to my own kid that I didn't keep. Biggest regret of my life. I swore to myself that never again would I lose myself to fame. You've given me a second chance to prove who I really am and what I really stand for. I won't let you down, Quinn."

His sincerity proved to me I'd made the right choice.

"Don't you mean you won't let the band down?"

"I didn't misspeak. Don't mistake what this is. The band is your smoke screen. You're the star. Think of it like Bruce Springsteen and the E Street Band. They exist to prop him up. Your band will do the same."

"Do those guys waiting to audition know that?"

"Every single one of them knows the deal. They saw you on stage and know who you are. They also know where you're going. And they want a piece of the action. I mean, think about it. Would you rather play side gigs at bars the rest of your life, or be on stage touring the world? These guys have waited their whole lives for an opportunity like this. Trust me when I say, they are well aware of the stakes."

Tucker had a way of making everything sound achievable. Whether it was or not remained to be seen, but I was inclined to believe the man. He had no reason to steer me wrong since both our livelihoods were tied to the success of this one shared mission.

"Final piece of business before we go in," Tucker said as we resumed speed walking. "Have you given any more thought to that matter we discussed last night?"

I knew exactly what he was referring to: a shady backdoor deal to keep Hollis's dirty little paws off my earlier music. Tucker wanted me to share the songwriting credits with a phantom cowriter. It was, he'd said, the only way to hold onto what was mine.

"We'll have a separate agreement with that person so they can't turn around and claim the songs as their own. But Quinn, I can't stress this enough; it needs to be someone you trust with your life. Jake maybe? Would he be willing to sign something to that effect to protect your music? No one would doubt it, seeing that he's a songwriter too."

I knew Tucker meant well, but if he thought I was going to let Jake take credit for my music, he was seriously delusional. Besides, Jake and I weren't the only songwriters in the family. There was another, and she was incredibly talented in her own right.

"No. Not Jake. My sister Grace."

∽

"He lives," Grace teased the moment our Facetime call was connected. Knowing that Tucker expected an answer by tonight, I'd used the break in the audition process to contact my sister. "I was beginning to think you'd forgotten all about me."

"There's this funny thing about phones, Gracie. They actually work both directions."

"You don't think I haven't tried calling you? I can only assume you haven't answered because you've been busy with the show. I refuse to believe you've purposely been shading your own sister."

"We weren't allowed phones during *Next in Line* rehearsals."

"So, you're saying you were rehearsing twenty-four hours a day?" she asked, trying to box me into a corner.

I came up swinging. "Pretty much. What about you, Grace? I heard from a reliable source that you've been holding out on me."

The guilty expression on Grace's face was all the confirmation I needed. She'd been actively keeping a secret from me. "Quinn, don't make a big deal out of it."

"What? You have a boyfriend. I'd like to know something about him. Is that not allowed?"

"It's allowed. What do you want to know?"

"Why don't we start with the basics first?"

"Okay. His name is Elliott. He's a student here at UCL."

"British?"

"Yes."

"What's he studying?"

"To be an economist."

"So, then, no tattoos. That's good."

She grinned. "How do you know that?"

"He studies economics and his name is Elliott. Lucky guess."

"And he wonders why I keep him away from my man," Grace thought aloud.

My smile faded. "Is he good to you?"

I could almost hear that wide smile of hers. "The best."

"All right then. I forgive you."

"Forgive me? For what?"

"For telling Emma your secret before me."

"Well, if I didn't think you'd be a judgmental ogre, you'd have been the first to know."

"Me? Emma spent ten minutes criticizing my shoelaces the other day. They were white, Grace. Apparently she found them too bright, and they were giving her a headache. That's who you chose to confide in over me."

"Okay." She laughed. "I'm sorry. So, what's up, Quinn? You said you needed to talk to me about something important."

"I need you to take credit for my songs."

"Say what? Did you hit your head?"

I explained the entire saga for my sister and how I needed her signature as a shield. "Anyway, he said to choose someone I trusted, and I couldn't think of anyone more trustworthy than my baby sister."

"Ah, that's so sweet. Of course I'd be happy to help you. I guess the only thing left to discuss is how much my silence is worth to you."

I nearly fell from my chair. "Wait. You want compensation?"

"You need a service, Quinn," she said, appearing totally sane. "One that I'll be signing my name to. I don't think fiftyK is too much to ask."

What the hell? Had her economist boyfriend rubbed off on her, figuratively speaking?

"You understand you're not actually writing the songs, right? We're just pretending. You know, like when people pretend to understand bitcoin?"

"Oohhh." She laughed. "Pretending. Got it. I'm joking, dork. You should've seen your face. And yes, Quinn, of course I'll help you. But..."

"But?"

"I do have one request. I have a song I wrote. It means a lot to me because it's about us when we were little. Jake thinks I could sell it, but I don't want anyone else to have it because it was written for us. I just thought maybe you could…"

"Yes."

"You don't even know what I was going to ask you."

"I know exactly what you were going to ask. And yes, Grace. I want that song."

# 15

## QUINN: BAND OF BROTHERS

I t should have been an easy decision. A slam dunk. Eighteen guys in total auditioned, seven of them standouts, so it really was just a matter of whittling down from that elite group. While all eighteen waited out in the hallway for word, me, Tucker, and the group he'd assembled to help us pick the contenders, were sorting through the final lineup when nature called.

I was in the process of relieving myself when one of the musicians from the audition walked in and chose to stand at the urinal directly beside mine, despite there being a handful of free ones to choose from. I tried to focus on the task at hand, but the dude kept casting glances in my direction, not being the least bit subtle in his desire to talk to me. Still, I was confident he wouldn't do it—couldn't—because all guys know not to break the universally agreed upon etiquette rule: no talking in a men's bathroom while dicks are out.

"What's up?" he said.

Willing my eyes not to roll, I tipped my head up in a word-less greeting. It was enough to acknowledge him but not enough to encourage conversation.

"I'm Mike. Bassist."

Good god. This guy didn't take verbal cues very well, did he? I could feel him staring as if he were actually requiring a spoken response, and I had a strong suspicion he wouldn't stop until I obliged him.

"How's it goin'?" I replied. No eye contact.

"Goin' fine." He paused for a moment, and I thought I might be free and clear, but no. "Well-aimed steady stream with a nice flow. A little out of control but not dangerously so. Life's good."

My eyes darted from the wall to him and back. His face was alive with amusement, forcing me to suppress a smile while I broke rule number two of men's bathroom etiquette: laughing while dicks were out. But his jovial reply got my attention, reminding me of Kyle with just a splash of Keith to make things interesting. I remembered Mike from the audition. He was the guy who'd plugged his bass guitar into the amp and pretended to be electrocuted. Hilarity ensued—not. I saw Tucker cross his name off the list before he even played the first chord. And while he did prove to be a good bass player, there were better.

"Crazy in there, huh?" he asked, keeping up the chitchat.

"Crazier in here," I replied, shaking off and buttoning my fly. Thankfully, I'd had a head start on the bassist, so it was still possible to wash my hands and be rid of him before that well-aimed, steady flow of his petered out.

No such luck. He sped up—maybe even stopped in mid-piss —all in an effort to catch me before I left. And I knew what he wanted—to talk about the audition, make his pitch. He was wasting his breath. The reality was that unless a bolt of lightning hit the building and *actually* electrocuted the rest of his competition, this dude wasn't getting the gig.

He met me at the sinks. "I don't know if you remember me, but I'm Mike, and I just auditioned."

"I know. We were introduced at the urinals."

"Oh, right. I wasn't sure how good your memory was."

It was at least good enough to remember the unusually tall, skinny guy with the long black '80's metal band hair that reached down to mid-back. He also sported a virtual landscape of ink, my personal favorite being the memorial tattoo of his dog covering the entire landscape of his right arm.

"Quinn," I offered in return.

He grinned. "I know."

"Okay, I wasn't sure how good your memory was, you know, after the electrocution."

"Ah." He laughed. "Too much?"

"Are you kidding? Who doesn't love a good electric shock skit?"

"Right? I'm always telling people that and they look at me like, 'Dude, you're fucking weird.'"

I waved off his personal insult. "Fucking inspired if you ask me."

He tossed his head back, laughing. Even though looks-wise, Mike wasn't the kind of guy you wanted to meet in a dark alleyway, just by talking to him I could tell he was a decent, good guy. Hard not to like him.

"Do you always follow random dudes into the bathroom, or was there something you wanted? I've gotta get back."

"Now that you mention it, yes, there was something I wanted," he said, pausing as the first outward sign of nerves hit him. "Look, I know what you're thinking. 'No earthly way is this dude getting the gig.'"

Good god. Not only was he a comedian, but Mike was also a mind reader.

"I'm well aware that I'm not as good as half the musicians in there. Hell, I'm sure Russ and Echo were frontrunners before they even auditioned, and I don't blame you. Those dudes are..." He shook his head, almost wistful in his worship. "I mean you heard them; you know. They could play in any band or behind any big-name artist. So, you gotta ask yourself, why are they here?"

That was a good question. Why were they here? Both Russ and Echo had been in the business since I was popping pimples in the eighth grade. Each had impressive resumes a mile long. So what did they need me for?

I caught Mike's eye in the mirror, silently questioning. And then I got what he was saying without a word being uttered. Those guys weren't band-hopping because they wanted to. They were band-hopping because they *had* to. Russ and Echo did not play well with others.

"I'm not going to talk bad about anyone." He shrugged. "You can do your own research. But listen, man, this is going to be the ride of your life. Who do you want to share it with? Do you want the best musicians standing up on stage with you? Because Russ and Echo, they're it. Or do you want to have guys up there who'll have your back no matter what? Because I'm telling you right now, bro, I'd be proud to stand behind you, and there are a few others in there that feel exactly the same way."

I took a moment to really process his words. What he said would make sense... if we were a *real* band. But what Tucker was suggesting wasn't a real band. It was me... and them. Was that really what I wanted?

"Like who?"

Mike startled, like he couldn't believe I was actually entertaining his theory. "Uh... Johnny, Joel, Kevin. All solid dudes."

I nodded.

"Anyway." He grabbed a paper towel, dried his hands, and dunked it into the trash like a pro. "Whatever you decide, I wish you luck, man. You're going to go far."

Once he left, I stood at the sink staring into the mirror. What was I doing? I couldn't sleepwalk through this process. There were a bunch of studio types back in that room ready to choose for me, but this wasn't their decision; it was mine. There was a reason none of my other bands had worked out. I'd always been the odd man out, the front man hired into an established group. The outsider.

What Tucker was proposing—that I'd be the star and my bandmates nothing more than musical accessories—would thrust me into the same bad situation I'd been in before. I'd be alone on the road. Together but separate. That wasn't what I wanted. Not this time. I was done with short-term fixes. I wanted more this time around, and the only way for this band to succeed was for us to be just that—a band.

I passed by the waiting musicians on my way back to the studio. Normally they would have been sent home after the audition, but this was a unique situation, and Tucker's plan depended on speed. Whoever got the gig would be starting right away, and not like tomorrow or the next day. No, *right away* meant like immediately following the announcement.

I made eye contact and wordlessly greeted the guys with a nod of the head. All of them acknowledged me, with a few notable exceptions—among them Russ and Echo, neither of whom even looked my way.

"Ah, perfect," Tucker said as I reentered the room. He handed me a piece of lined paper. "I think we got it."

I glanced down at the list in my hand. Eighteen names, fifteen of which were crossed out. I searched for Mike's and found it solidly executed under the slash of a red pen, as were Joel and Johnny and a few others I'd gotten positive vibes from during the auditions.

Tucker saw me analyzing his list. "We good?"

I handed it back to him. "No. Not yet."

He blinked, then glanced around at the other guys in the room. "Quinn. This is a good list. These three are the best musicians of the bunch."

"I agree."

"Then what's the issue?"

"I want to talk to them first."

"Oh. Sure, we can do that. Robbie, get these three guys in here, would you?"

"No," I said. "Not just them. All of them. I already know how they sound. Now I need to know who they are."

"Does that really matter?" Tucker asked. "You know we've got a bit of a time crunch."

"I know. But, Tuck, I don't want to be Bruce Springsteen and the E Street Band. If this is going to work—really work—I want to be the Rolling Stones."

His eyes fixed on me curiously. "That's what you want? I'm promising to make you a star and you want to be... what... a team player?"

Yeah, I supposed that was exactly what I was proposing. The revelation was as surprising to me as it was to Tucker. I'd been a lone wolf for a long time now. Never asking for help. Never letting them get too close. Somewhere along the way, it had become engrained in my head that I was solely responsible for my own survival, because no one would be there to catch my fall. And maybe that had been true for a very short window of time in my life, but it wasn't true now. People were there, waiting and willing to take up arms for me. If I needed help, all I had to do was ask.

"I don't want to be a team player. I don't want to be a star. I just want to play in a band of brothers."

Tucker pondered for a moment, really taking in my words before responding. "Okay."

"Okay?" I confirmed.

He shook his head, laughing. "Okay, Mick Jagger. Let's make this happen."

"Far out."

"Oh, and Quinn, if you ever call me Tuck again, you can find yourself a new spin master."

~

"Mike, Brandon, Matt," I called out the names. "Everyone else. Thanks for coming out. You guys didn't make this an easy decision."

I wasn't sure who was more surprised—Mike, Brandon, and Matt, or the guys who'd assumed they were shoo-ins for the job. Echo was out the door before the dust had even settled, and Russ swore under his breath, something about not needing this shit, before stomping out.

Mike caught my eye, acknowledging my choice with a stoked nod of his head. I nodded back, grateful for the clarity he'd provided. Had it not been for him and his steady flow, slightly out-of-control stream of piss, I would've walked headfirst into another disaster. And while it still remained to be seen whether we could make something of our ragtag band of musicians, there was one thing I knew for sure—if I had to circle the drain, these were the guys I wanted to do it with.

~

The celebration was short-lived. There was a lot of work to do and a dwindling amount of daylight to do it in. With only two hours left of studio time, the focus shifted to putting all of our individual pieces together into a functioning musical unit. The four of us were left alone to plan, and even though I knew I was the front man of the band, I was still surprised when the guys took a step back and allowed me to lead. It had never happened in my professional life that others had yielded to my vision. But my bandmates seemed to trust the musician in me, and with the ideas flowing freely between us, I'd never felt so respected or welcome.

It was then I got my first real inklings of excitement. This could work. This was already working. It made me wonder how much of my earlier struggles had to do with the feeling of being pushed aside. Being overlooked, neglected, ignored. But it was time to stop living in the past.

A new dawn was coming.

~

"Give me something inspired, boys," Tucker said, fixing to leave after setting us up with dinner at the brewery down the street. The tab was on him, but he wasn't doing it for free. We owed him not in money but in brainpower. We'd been tasked to do what was arguably the hardest part of forming a band—picking the name.

"Hey, Tucker. Hold up," I said, sliding out of the booth and jogging over to him.

He turned back toward me, questioning. "Everything okay? Are you not happy with these guys? Because..."

"It's not that. It's something...uh...personal."

I pulled him out of earshot.

"I need your help with something, and you look like you've hired a few hitmen in your day."

His brow lifted. "Uh...how kind of you. Who do you want dead?"

"Nothing so drastic. I'm trying to find someone—a girl. Her name is Jess."

I told him the story of our meeting and then of her hasty retreat.

"What do you know about her?" he asked, pulling up notes on his phone.

"I don't have her last name, but I do know her real name isn't Jessica. It's Jesse. She works for RYde. She's originally from Norwalk. And she drives a tan Hyundai Elantra."

"No problem. I've had people whacked with far less information," he joked—I think. "Phone number?"

"No. I have the wrong number for her. And I know her last initial, but I can't for the life of me remember what it is. Maybe L."

Tucker shook his head. "Jesus, Quinn. Maybe pay more attention next time."

"I wasn't expecting her to leave so fast. Otherwise, I would have asked all the pertinent questions."

"I'll see what I can find. Now go back and get me a damn band name."

I headed back to the table before calling over my shoulder. "Hey, Tucker. You're all right."

"What was that all about?" Mike asked, clear suspicion in his voice.

"Relax." I slid into place beside him. "Your name's already on the banner."

He wiped the fake sweat off his forehead and laughed. "Whew. I'm not used to winning, as you can tell."

"Well, maybe you should get used to it."

"All right. That's what my landlord likes to hear," Matt said.

Matt, aka Matty, was the most unassuming guitarist I'd ever met. Unlike Mike, who screamed dysfunction, Matty, with his short-cropped hair and striped polo shirt, looked like a stockbroker who played Guitar Hero on the weekends. But Matty was the real deal. A former member of a now-defunct Swedish death metal band, he had the quickest fingers I'd ever seen. And having only returned home to LA a few weeks earlier, no one had had a chance to snap him up. He was a true find—and the only one on Tucker's original list to make the band.

"I've got an idea for a band name," the drummer said, lifting his weary head off his arms to speak.

And then there was Brandon. Let's just say every group needed a Shia LaBeouf, and Brandon was ours. Not that he looked like the actor, with his platinum-blond roller-coaster hair, but he sure as hell gave off the same vibes. Narcissistic, defiantly handsome, with just a touch of the creep factor, he was the only fence sitter for me. But out of the three drummers who'd auditioned, one was dogshit, one was Echo, and one was Brandon. We had a winner.

"I think we should be called Shaft," he said, simultaneously grabbing his own for reference.

"Right, because what could possibly go wrong by naming ourselves after a phallic symbol?" I reasoned.

"What? It's edgy. Fun. But whatever, man," he said, shrugging as if it didn't matter, although clearly it did.

"Sorry, Brandon," Mike said. "But I'm using my veto power on this one."

"We have veto power?" Matty asked.

I shrugged. "News to me."

"I think we should all have one no-go name that we can nix. Shaft is mine," Mike said. "See, I was once in a band called Defecation, and my poor mom was so embarrassed, she lied and told everyone who asked that our name was Def Vacation. I can't do that to her again."

"You were in Defecation?" Matty gushed. "I saw you on the Sewer Tour. *Shit Happens* was inspired, man. Loved that album."

Mike sighed. "We broke up on that tour. Never got to drop our second album, *Number Two*, or go on to release our *Greatest Shits*."

I grabbed his shoulder. "I'm sorry for your loss."

"Eh, it was just a shitty band anyway. Nothing like this one.

We need a name that will stand out, not *up*," he said, eyeing Brandon.

"Okay, you pick a name, then," he challenged.

"Uh..." Mike scanned the restaurant before adding his suggestion to the mix. "How about *The Wrap?*"

"As in the spinach wrap on your plate?" I asked.

He flashed me a sheepish grin. "I'm not good under pressure, and you make me nervous."

"*I* make you nervous?" I asked, more than a little surprised.

"You make us all nervous," Matty agreed.

"He doesn't make me nervous," Brandon replied, all blustery Shia confidence.

"Right," Mike addressed him. "But you were raised by wolves. The rest of us were raised by humans... except for Matty, who was raised by Travelocity trolls."

"Trolls?" Matty questioned. "Why trolls?"

"I don't know, weren't you living in Norway or something?"

"*For two years.* Not enough time to get adopted by hobgoblins."

I was still stuck on Mike's comment. "Why do I make you nervous? Is it because of my brother?"

"Jake might have something to do with it, but it's more you, man. You've got the same star power as him, but you're still untested. Raw. And then, like a fool, I corner you in the bathroom and talk you into picking a bunch of unknowns to take along for the ride. There's a lot of pressure. We don't want you to feel like you've wasted your faith in us. So, yeah, we're all a little nervous."

Brandon lifted his head off his arm again.

"We know!" Mike stopped him. "You're not nervous. But Matty and I are."

"I was gonna say I'm a little nervous."

The four of us were silent for a second before we burst into laughter.

"Well, welcome to the band, Brandon," Mike said.

"All right, since we're all about confessions here, step back, fellas, 'cuz I'm about to share. First, don't assume I'm something that I'm not. I'm the messed-up kid brother of a superstar. I haven't proven myself. I've barely even scratched the surface. I picked you guys not because Mike swung his dick around in the bathroom urinals, but because we're all the same. We're all struggling to find our place in this business. Separately, we don't work. But together, maybe we've got something. We won't know until we try. And I'm motivated. I want out from behind my brother's damn shadow. I'm tired of walking a step behind. With you guys by my side, I'm coming for Jake's throne."

I looked around the table at all the stunned faces. Okay, that was probably too much information.

"Holy shit, you self-serving asshole. I think I'm in love," Brandon said, raising a glass. "To overthrowing the king!"

Matty added his glass to the center. "To Travelocity trolls."

Mike added his glass. "To my big, swinging dick!"

And I was the last to clink my glass against the others. "I never said big."

After getting the important bonding stuff out of the way, we returned to the task at hand: naming the band.

"What about something like Delirium?" Mike suggested.

"Can't; that's already a band."

"Illusion?" Matty tried.

"Where'd you pick that one?" Brandon asked. "From the unicorn name generator?"

More suggestions were thrown out, but none landed on the mark. We needed something distinctive. Something that stood out and was uniquely our own. As I ran names through my head, I found myself drifting off in thoughts of Jess. She was everything I wanted the band to stand for—unexpected, cool, challenging, blazing hot.

And then it came to me. The name of the band. It was the combination of the sum of all of Jess's parts. When I revealed the name to the guys, they mulled it over, tried it on for size, and finally unanimously voted it into circulation. And while I was genuinely relieved to have the band naming behind us, I didn't reveal to the guys that I also had an ulterior motive for the moniker.

If this didn't send Jess a message, I didn't know what would.

## 16

# JESS: DROPPING CLUES

"Okay, Noah, my tour passengers are coming on in a minute. What's the rule?"

"Um... run up and down the aisle and be as loud as I can."

Gloria, the bus driver, glanced back at him and chuckled.

"Ooh. Nooo, I'm sorry. Wrong answer but you were so very close." I palmed his face, forcing him to pay attention. "Shall we try again? And this time remember that I'm bribing you with not one but two scoops of Baskin Robbins ice cream."

Noah sat up straighter in his seat and, now with chocolate chip cookie dough ice cream on the line, there was no confusion. "Stay in my seat and no talking."

"There you go," I said, patting his head. "You're so smart. Isn't he smart, Gloria?"

"I've got chills."

"Now, Noah, Gloria here has agreed to be my eyes and ears."

"I have?"

"Yes, Gloria, you have because I'm also bribing you."

"Keep talking."

"I think an extra ten dollars from the tip jar should suffice."

"All right. Yes. Listen up, boy: I'm your mom's eyes and ears, and if you think you can fool me, you can't. I raised five teenagers. I'm bulletproof. You hear me?"

He couldn't. Noah had already popped the earphones into his ears, and the portable Nintendo in his hand ensured many hours of compliance. Sometimes you had to do what you had to do. Rolling with the punches, that was how it was done in single mama world. See, Noah had been scheduled to spend a week of his ten-day spring break at the sleepaway camp. But that was before he accidentally *on purpose* jumped off the shed. I even tried to get him back in for the final few days, but the camp told me in no uncertain terms that they'd rather sop up an extensive sewer leak than to allow my bat-winged child back on their grounds. So now I had a logistical problem. I had to work, but I had no one to watch the flying squirrel for the rest of the week. If I'd had the means of staying home with him while he recovered, I surely would have, but that luxury was reserved for those with options. That was not me.

And so, it became 'Take your child to work' day even though it absolutely wasn't. Officially, Andrea didn't know he was here. It would set a bad precedent if the practice were to catch on, but after her visit to my place two nights ago, she'd agreed to look the other way. It was a stunning turn of events. I wasn't sure what to make of her sudden interest in Noah, but if it resulted in more favorable routes or mommy-and-son workdays, then I wasn't about to question the madness.

The tour got underway per usual, and I dropped into character with ease. I could recite the route in my sleep, and it showed. I noticed Noah occasionally looking up from his game or listening to my stories along the way. He'd never really cared what I did for a living, only that I earned enough to keep him in the lap of lower-middle class luxury, but as he got older, I noticed more awareness on his part of the star-studded land around us.

It was about three hours into the tour when Gloria turned onto Goldfinch Road. This was the moment I'd been dreading—the moment my bus would come face-to-face with the McKallister Mansion for the first time since I'd come face-to-face with its youngest son. If I could have avoided this road altogether, I surely would have, but this was the tour entitled 'Meet the Stars,' and like it or not, Quinn McKallister's family home was one of the highlighted attractions.

I found myself holding my breath, my brain fraught with anxious conflicts as we rolled down his street. In all the years I'd guided this tour, I'd never once given a thought to the people who lived behind the gate… until now. How could I, in good conscience, exploit Quinn's family for my own personal gain? On the flip side, how could I not? This was my livelihood, after all, and his house was the focal point of the tour. There was no getting around it. If I wanted to give my customers the experience they'd paid for, I was going to have to stop in front of his gates and share with my passengers the story of the McKallister family. Or at least, the story as I knew it. After sharing that heart-to-heart with Quinn in the fairy-golf castle, I now understood that the story I knew was nowhere near the one he'd lived.

Thinking of that shared moment with him only made me long for him more. Since placing Quinn on my Do Not Disturb list and turning off my read receipt, things hadn't been much fun in Jesseland. I'd watched his texts, so vigorous and hopeful to begin with, start to fall away as the message from my side came in loud and clear—*The girl's not interested in you, bud. Give up.*

But I was interested. More than he could ever know. I wanted it all. Him. Me. Noah. But I'd learned to live with not getting everything I wanted in life. Sometimes you just had to make do. And I was making do. I had a beautiful son, a good job—for now —and, if the interaction with Quinn was any indication, I had the ability to reel in a top-quality guy. If I'd done it once, I could do it again... with a man not as pedigreed as Quinn. A man whose family home wasn't on my tour route. I'd made the right choice. Yes, I surely had.

Every night as I kissed my son good night, I felt confident in my decision, knowing I was doing right by him. But every night as I tucked myself in bed, cold and alone, I longed for Quinn's company, his kiss, his touch. Selfishly, I wanted Quinn to keep trying. I wanted him to climb to the highest tower or to send his men out canvassing the land for any trace of me. But where would that devotion get either of us? Probably nowhere but a broken heart for me.

No, the sooner he gave up, the better.

That would free me up to find another handsome, funny, talented, and sure, why not, hot musician a few years down the road from where Quinn was now, a man who was ready for the life I had to offer him. The simple truth was that Quinn had just shown up at the entirely wrong time in both our lives. Things might be different for us if he'd already staked his claim on the music world and had come back home to settle down. But he was only at the beginning of what promised to be a bright future. Quinn McKallister was on a collision course with fame, and there was no going back—no holding on.

"Jess," a woman in the front row said. "What's going on up there?"

I turned my head in the direction of her finger and was startled to discover Quinn's house the focal point of a frenzy, so much so that reporters and paparazzi had set up shop outside of his gate. I looked to Gloria to see if she might have an answer to the perplexing situation, but she appeared as surprised by the scene as I did.

"Uh..." I grunted, wondering along with my customer how this sleepy street had been turned into a media circus, but instinctively I assumed it had something to do with Quinn and the media press he was garnering. "I'm not sure."

"Who lives there? Is it a celebrity's house," she continued, pressing me for answers.

"Yes, it's the McKallister house."

A buzzing sound picked up from around the bus as excitement grew. Noah looked up from his game and questioned me with his eyes.

But before I could give him a suitable nonverbal response, a squeal emanated from the back of the bus. "Wait, is that... is it... *Jake McKallister?*"

And like a choreographed scene, the left side of the bus emptied as rows and rows of eager celebrity beavers pressed into their comrades on the other side of the aisle, all with cameras at the ready.

I whipped my head around so fast that it took a moment for my eyes to catch up, but when they did, I saw who my squawking passenger was referring to... and it wasn't Jake. My eyes widened at the sight of Quinn, standing there flanked by several men, but my vision tunneled and I saw only him. It was like Quinn's broad shoulders and impressive height rendered the others wholly inadequate. Those were the shoulders that had carried me over puddles. Those were the lips that ignited the fire.

I couldn't speak. I couldn't think. None of this made sense. In the years I'd run this route, I'd seen vehicles go in and out of the complex, and on a rare occasion, family members outside, but never had I actually seen one of the McKallisters standing on this side of the gate with a team of cameramen lined up like a firing squad.

"What do you want me to do?" Gloria asked with urgency, as if weaving us through a war zone. Mind you, Gloria wasn't asking me whether I wanted her to leave Goldfinch Road. That would just be stupid. No, she was asking where on the McKallisters' front lawn I wanted her to park.

See, an honest-to-god celebrity sighting like this was as close to a coup in the Hollywood sightseeing business as one could get. Every once in a while, my kind got lucky and we'd spot the Hollywood equivalent of a white tiger on an African safari tour —the coveted A-list celebrity. My passengers would record the moment for posterity, popping it up on their Instagram and Facebook feeds, and if we were lucky, word would get around that Angel Line Tours was *the* place for all your stalking needs.

Shock at seeing my studly man crush took a backseat to self-preservation. Instinct took over.

"Just pull up right there," I said to Gloria, before turning to address my passengers. "Okay, Angels, this is a rare treat. It looks like we'll be able to catch this press conference. As Miss Elizabeth here points out, it looks like that might be a McKallister sighting, though while she got the ancestral DNA right, that is not Jake. It's the youngest McKallister brother, Quinn. If you'll remember, he just had a star-making turn on *Next in Line*." *And had his hand between my thighs.*

Gloria hugged the curb so tightly the tire edged up onto the sidewalk, tilting the bus at an odd angle but actually allowing for a better view of the proceedings. My driver eyed me, a confuddled expression on her face as if saying, '*I do good?*' I flashed Gloria a thumbs-up. Desperate times called for desperate measures.

"Angels, we're just going to stop and watch. Remember to stay silent so they don't kick us out... or, you know, thanks to Gloria, tip us over. I'll be going off mic until it's over."

Staying silent was for my benefit only. No need to direct the attention of anyone outside the bus this way, specifically one hot stud's attention. In fact, I was just going to duck right down here onto the first step of the bus and hide like the coward I was. The last thing I wanted was for Quinn to look up from all his glory and see the white mini bus with pink angel wings and discover that the devilish woman inside was the same one who'd kissed his lips, then sent his texts straight to the trash bin.

Taking in the scene from my hiding spot, I noticed Noah, his head craning out the open window, taking in the excitement with stars in his eyes. Oh, lordy. This. This right here was why Quinn could not be trusted around my kid. He'd bewitch Noah in seconds.

My dream-come-true stepped up to the microphone and began to speak.

"Thank you for coming. I'm sure by now many of you have heard or seen my performance on *Next in Line* and know that I unexpectedly exited the stage following my performance. There has been some speculation as to my motives, so I wanted to speak today to clear up any rumors. But first, I want to extend my apologies to both *Next in Line* and to the fans I let down when I left. I am so incredibly grateful for the opportunity I was given to perform on the show, and I had every intention of singing my song and going through the process as contestants have done for years. However, I was under the impression that the producers would not showcase my early childhood trauma, so when the video montage came up on the screen, showing footage of me as a child at a press conference for my brother, I was shocked. And as you could probably see by my reaction on stage, it triggered memories that I was not prepared for in the moment. My focus was all off, and in a split-second decision, I chose to sing my own original song.

"Because I feel that the intent of the footage shown was not done in good faith and was, in fact, used to exploit my family's tragedy, I can no longer remain a contestant on the show. I will not be returning for this week's competition. I'm sorry for any frustration this has caused my fans, and I hope you'll continue to support me. For those of you who want to hear more of my music, I've got a brand-new song coming next week with my new band, Sketch Monsters. Look us up. Thank you."

*Sketch Monsters? Did he just say Sketch Monsters?* Thank god I was sitting down, or I probably would have passed out. Quinn McKallister, with that brilliantly devious mind of his, had just stolen my blitzed-out imaginary critters and passed them off as his own. Who did that? But I knew. A guy trying to get a girl's attention. Quinn was sending me a sign. He wanted to provoke me...draw me out into the open. And I had half a mind to take him up on the offer, flinging the bus doors open and jumping into his clever arms.

My daydream came to a startling end with a bopping sound on the side of my bus. An unwanted head popped through the same window Noah was standing in front of, sending him stumbling back in surprise.

"You again? I swear, Jesse, we have to stop meeting this way." Cody Weller.

My brows furrowed, and I could almost hear the wild west pistol duel music playing in the background. If ever there was rent-a-cop I'd like to prematurely fire upon in a quick draw, it was him.

"Relax," I said, flicking on my microphone and instructing my charges to return to their seats. "We're leaving."

"I specifically recall telling you not to loiter, but then you're not much for following the rules, are you, Jesse?"

"And I specifically recall you not being an actual cop, but then, look at you policing."

His tongue clicked as he took me in with his beady eyes. "Take it easy, sweetheart. That mouth of yours has gotten you into a lot of trouble in the past. Unless you'd like me to do a little story time with your passengers, I suggest you leave."

Ooh, match point. What a dickhead. God, how I wanted to spit in his face.

Perhaps sensing the animosity, Noah came to my rescue, stepping between Cody and me.

"Leave my mom alone," he said in his strongest superhero voice ever.

Cody's eyes shot up, a smile invading his smug face.

"He's yours... and Nick's? This is Noah?"

Warning signs flashed in my head. "Bud, it's okay. Go back to your seat."

"You look a lot like your dad," Cody said, taking a more active interest in his buddy's offspring.

Although I couldn't see Noah's face, as he was still in front of me offering what protection he could at four foot eight, I could only imagine his surprise. "You know my dad?"

Grabbing Noah's hand, I pulled him behind me.

"Back off," I warned.

Hell hath have no fury like a mommy protecting her young.

Cody actually took a step back, smart enough to recognize the danger. I turned my attention to Gloria, imploring. She didn't need to be told twice, or be kicked in the shin like Vern. Gloria popped the bus off the curb and we made our hasty escape.

## 17

## QUINN: ON THE RISE

The heat from the lights prompted Tucker to reach into his pocket for his handkerchief and offer it up to me. I shook my head. He then proceeded to mime dabbing the sweat off his own forehead, perhaps to demonstrate how the old-time invention worked. Yeah, I got it. And it didn't make me any more eager to rub his snot rag all over my face. Again, I shook my head. He flashed me a look that said 'Your loss' before tucking it away.

Mike snickered on the stool beside me.

"Hey," he whispered, "if you need something more sanitary to mop up the sweat, I have a used condom in my pocket."

"Please don't flatter yourself. We both know it's not used."

Mike focused some of his nervous energy into a laugh but quickly returned to the leg bouncing he'd been doing since we'd taken our seats.

"Hey, Thumper, relax."

I should talk. My leg was doing the same thing, only not as pronounced.

"That's easy for you to say. You're genetically pleasing. I got nothing."

"Hey, don't be so hard on yourself. Without the ugly in the

world, there would be nothing beautiful. Thank you for your sacrifice."

He laughed. "Fuck you."

"Besides, no one's going to be watching us anyway. We're an unsigned band."

"With big potential."

"I had big potential with *Next in Line*, and look how that turned out."

"Because that wasn't meant to be. Sketch Monsters, man. That's the future. Besides, we've only been a band for a few weeks and look where we are already."

Mike was right about that. We'd come far in the past three weeks. Nearly every night was a new city where we'd perform a mini concert with our four measly songs at bars and smaller venues. We were getting our feet wet, Tucker said, proving to the studios that we could pack a room. There were parties and radio shows and heavy interest from labels, but still no firm offers.

And then Tucker got us this—the *Today Show* interview. How he'd done it I wasn't sure. We weren't big enough to warrant an interview on our own merit, so I had to suspect it was one of two things they wanted to focus on: my meltdown on *Next in Line* or my proximity to rock's biggest star. But Tucker reminded me that we took all publicity no matter the reason it was given to us. It was a hard pill to swallow, knowing that for the foreseeable future my success would be tied to things other than the music the guys and I were creating, but Tucker hadn't steered me wrong yet, so I agreed to the televised interview, with conditions—no, discussion about my family or my past. They were the same conditions *Next in Line* hadn't honored and the same ones I was pretty damn sure this show wouldn't honor either.

"Dude," Mike continued. "We're on the frickin' *Today Show*. How many other unsigned bands can say that?"

I nodded, not wanting to burst his bubble by telling him the truth. We weren't here because of Sketch Monsters. We were here because of Jake. Because of his tragedy. Because of my stupidity. My family. My drama. But we weren't here for our music. We just weren't.

I hoped I was wrong... and maybe I was. I couldn't deny this time felt different. There was an energy in the air, but so far, we hadn't managed to harness it. Don't get me wrong; we'd come a long way since standing in front of my parents' house as I issued my non-apology to *Next in Line*. As Tucker predicted, the free world press had loved my honesty, splashing it on news feeds and drawing the support we needed. Who knew sympathy could be such a powerful aphrodisiac? My feeds were flooded with women promising to fix my tattered soul. It would've been funny if it hadn't been so mired in truth.

But that worship led to followers, and those followers led to buzz, and that buzz led to views and clicks and sales, so that by the time the music video for our first single, "A Fine Mess," dropped, we already had a growing fan base, which pushed the YouTube views into the millions. More surprising, the single we'd independently released began climbing up the rock charts. And that was all *before* the nepotism kicked in with endorsements from some of the biggest names in music. My camp, as well as Tucker's, had really come through.

Sketch Monsters was launched.

∼

Cameras began to roll. The introduction was followed by the obligatory back and forth banter. It was easy. Fun. I got in a few barbs at the guys and they on me. Everything was going fine until the beat dropped, the fun-loving faces of the hosts morphed, and I knew... I knew what was coming.

"Of course, the creation of Sketch Monsters came from you stepping away from *Next in Line,* Quinn. Do you ever regret the way your time on the show ended?"

"I think everything happened for a reason. The show wasn't right for me. This band feels like home to me. So no, I don't regret anything."

"Speaking of home... you have been uncharacteristically open about your struggles. In a family that's as famously tight-lipped as yours, has there been any backlash to your speaking out?"

Backlash? Who did they think we were, royalty? We had no rules that needed to be followed. My family was like any other. We kept to ourselves because it was no one else's business. But I could almost hear Tucker whispering in my ear: *Easy, boy.*

"No, no backlash. I've always been a wild card. My family knows I speak my mind and they've never faulted me for it."

"Why haven't we heard from you before, then?"

"Because I've never been in the position where people cared to listen."

"I disagree. I think a lot of people would like to hear from you."

"Sure, but they only want to hear about my family, my past, my brother. They don't want to hear about me."

It was a moment of weakness, revealing my insecurities on national television. I had a bad feeling I was about to pay the price for my honesty.

"Fair enough. Tell me then, Quinn. Who are you?"

I sat up, surprised. "Really?"

The interviewer's face softened. "Yes, really."

"Okay. I'm... sorry, no one has ever asked me that before. I'm not sure how to answer."

"He's a great listener," Matty said, rescuing me.

"Am I?" I raised my brows.

"Yeah, remember the other day when I was telling you I thought that ingrown hair on my neck was infected? And you didn't walk away."

"That was only because Brandon was holding me down."

"And he's funny." Mike jumped into the compliment game. "You wouldn't think so by looking at him, because I mean, come on, he looks like a douche. But jokes really are funnier when he tells them."

"Gee, thanks." I laughed.

"And he's a good guy," Brandon said, surprising me. He wasn't the sentimental type. "When I first auditioned, I was determined to hate him. I thought he was a poser who'd only gotten where he was through nepotism, but the night we met, he told us why he picked us to be in his band and his reasoning—it was deep, man. From that point on, I had nothing but respect for him."

And just like that, the guys saved me from the black hole the interview was spiraling into.

"I have one last question that I promised my friend's daughter I would ask. Quinn, are you single?"

"I am." I grinned, coolly sliding my fingers through my fringe. On Tucker's advice, and that of thousands of internet girls, I'd decided not to grow my hair back to shoulder length just yet. Besides, Jess liked it short. Not that it mattered since she hadn't been found. Tucker's guy had looked for her, but I hadn't been able to provide enough identifying information to pull her up in a search.

The more days that passed without her, the more I realized how much I wanted her. Jess had become my obsession. Every show I scanned the crowd. Every car with a RYde sticker on the back, I peered in the window. And every opportunity I had to jump into bed with another girl to forget Jess ever existed—I passed on. Yes, that's right, I'd become a born-again virgin at the exact point in my life when females were literally dropping in my lap.

"But I do have a crush on a girl named Jess."

It just slipped out. Totally unplanned, but the minute I said it, there was no taking it back.

"Oh really?" The host's perfectly arched brows lifted higher. "And does Jess also have a crush?"

"That's the big question. I'm not sure."

I explained her being called away in the middle of our date and getting the wrong phone number from her.

"Can't you just look her up?" Matty asked.

"I could if I had her last name, but I don't. The only thing I can do now is wait and hope she reaches out to me. So Jess, if you're out there..." I looked into the camera. "Call me."

"How is she going to do that if she doesn't have your number?" Brandon questioned.

"Oh." I winced. "Yeah. Okay. Let me try that again. Jess, contact me through social media. I don't care which one. I just have to see you again."

Matty leaned in, overly invested in the story. "Dude, not smart. You need a glass slipper. Something Jess can slip her foot into and prove she's the real Jess; otherwise you'll get a million women sending you DMs."

"Oh yes," the host said, "I like this. A modern Cinderella story. You can have her answer a question only she would know."

I knew just the one. Looking into the camera, I said, "Jess. Don't leave me hanging. Contact me and answer this one question, so I know it's you. Where did I want you to take me the day we met?"

# 18

## JESS: JESSERELLA

I learned of Quinn's mighty quest from the local barista. I wasn't exactly sure where I'd been for the past few days, but it certainly wasn't anywhere near social media or I would have seen my name trending right alongside a certain promising young rock star. My only excuse for being out of touch was that Noah had no outlet for his pent-up energy and I had become his power cord. I worked all day and played all night. But not the fun kind of play. No, this was eight-year-old boy fun, which meant it either included electronics or copious amounts of bodily fluids.

But I'd managed to drop him off at school early today, and now I had twenty minutes of 'me' time to sip coffee and stare off into the abyss.

"Jess," the barista called.

She watched me intently as I approached the counter, a smile stretching across her face. I looked behind me to see if there was anyone more worthy of her attention, but no, it appeared to be me she was rooting for.

"You're not *the* Jess, are you?" she asked, her eyes twinkling.

I had no idea what the woman was talking about, but I offered up a friendly smile. "Um... I'm *a* Jess. Does that count?"

"Oh, sorry." She giggled. "I just assumed you'd heard of the quest to find Jess."

My brows furrowed as I picked up my cup. I think I would have remembered an expedition in my honor.

"I have not." I grinned, taking a trial sip of my coffee. "What is this quest you speak of?"

"Quinn McKallister from Sketch Monsters?"

The coffee was halfway down my throat when I choked, the brew spraying out of my mouth like a hot liquid sprinkler.

"Oh, my god, are you okay?" The woman rushed to grab some napkins for me.

Wiping the coffee from my chin and off the counter, I nodded as I tried to explain my behavior. "Fine, just... that was some hot coffee. Go on. Quinn? Sketch Monsters?"

"Oh, right. It's all over the internet. Even Jimmy Kimmel picked up on the hype and did a bit on it last night on his show, calling the search Jesserella... you know like, Cinderella and the glass slipper. Only this is Jess and the question."

If a swarm of bugs invaded the coffee shop at that very moment, they would have drowned in my open mouth. Nothing seemed to be functioning properly as questions rattled through my brain.

"What, uh... what do you mean by Jess and the question?"

"In order for him to know it's her, she has to answer a question."

"And what is the question?"

Almost breathless in her delight, she replied, "Ah, it's so romantic. She has to know the place Quinn wanted to go the day they met. I heard his social media accounts have been flooded with women whose feet don't fit into the slipper, so to speak."

I fought the swoony smile threatening to give me away. What

was he doing? Did he really want to find me that badly? I stood in place, processing the information before realizing how suspicious that made me look. The barista's eyes widened like she'd just uncovered a coup.

"Do you know where Quinn wanted to go, Jess?"

*Oh no. Abort mission. You are a damn-near professional liar —so lie!*

Holding up my coffee cup, I smiled and thanked her. "Damn. I'm outta luck. I got nothing."

But as I turned to leave, my heart soared as I tossed the answer around in my head.

*Someplace fun... but not too fun.*

If I thought the legend of Jesserella was just going to pass over limply like a deflated balloon, I was wrong. I couldn't escape the question as it just kept popping up throughout the day. *Are you that Jess?* inquiring minds wanted to know. Even the littlest mind I knew, my own son, demanded an answer once he'd arrived home from after-school care.

"Did you know that the man talking to reporters that day when I went to work with you is looking for a girl named Jess?"

"So I've heard...over and over all day long," I said, slapping peanut butter onto some bread before handing it to him and probing for more. "How'd you find out about that?"

"My teacher. She asked if it was you."

His teacher? Was that appropriate? She really shouldn't be bringing up the subject of my love life to my eight-year-old son. There went her end-of-the-year gift card.

"That's a weird thing for Miss Usman to ask you," I said, deflecting.

"Not really. Your name is Jess."

"I know, but..." I shook my head. "What did you say back to her?"

"I said my mom wasn't cool enough."

It was one of those soft insults that crept into a tiny cut and burned like hell for the rest of the day.

"Thanks a lot," I said, nudging him playfully. "I'll let you know I was plenty cool when I was younger."

"Sure."

"I was!"

He ignored my protest. "My teacher said that you were pretty enough to date a rock star."

"She said that?" I asked, sliding my fingers through my hair. I'd always liked Miss Usman. Perhaps I needed to up the gift giving this year. An 'I heart teacher' mug maybe?

Noah continued with his sharing. "But then I started thinking. Why did you duck in the bus when we stopped?"

Shocked by his sleuthing, I rocked back on my wedges. Since when had my kid become Magnum P.I.? "I... uh... I wasn't ducking. I was taking a rest."

"No, you were definitely ducking."

He had me cornered. I couldn't come up with even one excuse for my behavior except maybe to blame it on Cody, but I didn't dare. Not after Noah had grilled me on our exchange with him that day. He'd wanted to know who Cody was and how he knew his father. I'd been honest with him then, so why couldn't I be honest with him now?

"Okay, yes. You caught me. I'm Jesserella," I said, bending down and giving him a series of neck kisses that made him squirm.

"I wish."

"You wish? Why?"

"Do you know how cool it would be to have a rock star for a dad?"

And there... right there... was why I couldn't bring Quinn into Noah's life. Rock stars didn't stay.

## 19

## QUINN: A FAMILIAR VOICE

L ife took a turn toward the crazy after the *Today Show* interview. Who would ever have guessed a simple search for a girl would become a cultural phenomenon? Poor Jess. I honestly never thought things would get this out of control or that people would actively be trying to smoke her out. Jess was probably viewing the whole thing like a publicity stunt instead of what it really was: a genuine search for an incredible girl. If Jess had been skittish before my stunt on live TV, she had to be like a doe traipsing through a wildlife reserve by now.

At least one good thing had come out of the Jesserella search. As a result of the interview, we'd seen a surge of activity on all platforms, raising our profile and securing us a record deal. So in a way, Jess had helped me realize a dream. And as the guys and I worked on completing the album, plans were being made for a fall tour. Things were finally moving forward. Tucker's talk of a metaphoric rise never materialized. Musically speaking, we were on a slow trajectory.

Personally speaking, there was only an upward curve as I was treated to my first real taste of fame and it wasn't an entirely comfortable place to be in. To be recognized. To be lionized. To be demonized. I'd never fully appreciated the courage it must have taken for Jake to walk headfirst into a lion's den so soon after surviving the unspeakable. None of this was easy for me, but for him, it had to have been excruciating. So why had he done it? Why put himself out there for scrutiny when he could have faded into the background?

I supposed the same questions applied to me. I could've remained anonymous—the youngest brother hidden away behind the gates—but I hadn't. Somewhere inside me, like inside Jake, was the desire to lead. To be heard. And if this craziness was what it took to get my voice out into the world, then I'd find the same nerve Jake had found... somehow.

Pulling through the gates of my parents' house, I smiled when I saw the car in the driveway. Grace! And to a lesser excitement—Elliott. Why did I already not like him? I mean, my god, he sounded so perfectly perfect I feared I might mistake him for a Boy Scout. Yet still, I wanted to pop him in the nose. And we all knew that would not go well given my past involvement in Grace's suitors. Just because she'd forgiven me once didn't mean she'd do so again. One more infraction and I risked being cut from her inner circle where Emma now, apparently, reigned supreme.

Grace burst through the front door as I was making my way up the front stairs. She jumped into my arms, hugging me tight. No one gave unapologetic hugs like my sister. Back when we were kids, I could scarcely get her off me; now it seemed I had to beg for attention. I thawed in her arms. Grace was so delicate and virtuous. So pure and kind. People like her were gobbled up in the real world, and that was exactly why I'd pledged to protect her from the start.

"It took you long enough to come see me," she said as I set her back on her feet.

"Two days is long? You're lucky I managed to squeeze you in at all."

"Oh yes. You're so important now."

"Where's the dude?"

"He's napping."

I raised a brow. "Napping? Does he also eat dinner at four?"

"Stop." She slapped my shoulder. "He has jet lag, jerk. We both do. Besides, he's had a rough couple of days. Our family isn't easy on the nerves. Just when he starts getting more comfortable, another famous person strolls through the front door. I think his heart might have stopped for a few seconds when Jake came over after dinner last night."

"At least he won't have to worry about me. After Jake, I'll be a letdown."

"Hardly. You're the one he's most nervous to meet."

"Me? Why?"

She rolled her eyes. "I think we both know."

"You told him about Rory?"

"I tell him about everything."

"Everything?" I challenged.

Her eyes fluttered up to meet mine.

"Okay, maybe not everything," she admitted.

"What did you tell him about me?"

"Not much. I've told Elliott bits and pieces of our past. He knows the role you played in my life. He also knows you're a wee bit possessive of your baby sister, so that sort of terrifies him."

"Good." I perked up. "Healthy fear never hurt anyone."

"No, Quinn, *not* good. You promised me restraint."

"What am I going to do, Grace? He's an economist who naps. The chances of me having to drop-kick him back to England are relatively low."

"Actually," Grace said, looking back at the house before grabbing my arm and steering me away, "there will be no risk at all.

This whole alpha male routine you've got going on is tired and outdated. I'm not in danger if a guy gets within twenty feet of me."

"Okay, fine. I'll move the perimeter back—five feet and then I pounce. Are you happy now?"

She sat on a retaining wall, pulling me down with her. I watched as Grace opened and closed her mouth, clearly trying to find the words. This could not be good. She was never nervous around me. Grace placed her hand over mine and finally spoke her piece. "I need you to hear me, Quinn. Really, really hear me. Can you do that?"

"I've been working around amplifiers lately, so I can't promise anything."

"Quinn!" There was no room for humor in her glare.

"Jesus, Grace. Yes, I'm listening."

"Good. Let me start by saying, I adore you. You know that. I always have."

"Why do I feel like I'm about to be broken up with?"

"Shush." She laughed. "This is the part where you listen and don't talk. I like Elliott. No, I love him. We have a ton in common. We laugh together; we study together; we like the same type of shows."

"Sounds sexy. Go on."

"Quinn." She placed her finger on my lips. "Mouth closed. When we were kids, you stepped into the role of my protector, and I loved knowing you'd always be there for me. I counted on you. You were my knight. But I'm not that little girl anymore. I'm fully grown with a life of my own, and I no longer need your particular brand of savioring. I forgave you for what you did to my last, what, *four* relationships, but I'm telling you right now, Elliott is off-limits. Do you understand? Off. Limits. If you so much as raise your voice, or god forbid, threaten him in any way, you will lose your hug privileges, and worse, my trust—forever."

I sat silently, processing her words. All these years I'd spent keeping my baby sister safe, and now she was picking some dude... who *napped*... over me?

"Everything I've done has been to protect you, Grace."

"Maybe when we were kids, yes. But somewhere along the way, it became less about protecting me from harm and more about keeping me from living. It stopped being about me altogether. I was just the collateral damage to whatever crap was going on in your head."

"That's not true."

"Yes, it is. You seem to think I'm breakable. But I'm not blown glass, Quinn. I won't shatter if you drop me. I'm a McKallister, just like you. Just like Emma and Kyle and Keith and Jake. If the rest of you don't break, why do you think I do? It's insulting, honestly."

I didn't have an answer for Grace because there wasn't one. The truth was, Grace was every bit as resilient as I was. She'd survived right alongside me and had probably done a better job of it than I had. So why had I set different standards for her? Why *did* I see her as fragile?

Looking her over now, I could clearly see Grace was not the waiflike girl I'd always cast her in the role of. She was lengthy in height, not Great Dane like Emma, but she wasn't a corgi either. Somehow, when I wasn't looking, Grace had grown into a strong, sporty young woman with bright eyes and a kind soul.

"I'm tough and capable and smart. I demand to be treated with respect because I see it in how Dad treats Mom and how my brothers treat their women. But most of all because of you. You put me first, Quinn, when no one else could. You kept me safe and loved and cared for. I never wanted for anything... because of you. And now I'm asking you to keep putting me first. Let me love and live my own life and in return..." Tears welled in Grace's eyes as she struggled to maintain composure. "In return, I will absolve you of your duty. You served me well, big brother. So, sit back and relax, knowing you did your job well. I'll take it from here."

I grabbed my heart and groaned. Grace had always been the one constant in my life. By keeping her safe and protected, I'd guaranteed myself at least one person who wouldn't leave when I needed them most. But I couldn't keep her locked in a tower forever. I had to let her go. "You're killing me, Grace."

"I know." She laid her head on my shoulder. "But you're not losing me. I'll always love you forever."

"I know. And I love you too."

Just then a tall, lanky, bespectacled Harry Potterish hipster-looking dude stepped out onto the front landing looked fresh and rested. And thankfully, harmless enough. No blue-haired mullet. No tattoos. And he napped. How could I ask for more?

"Oh, sorry," he said. "Did I interrupt?"

"No, Grace has finished the lashing," I said, standing up. If I was going to be the person Grace needed in her adult life, I might as well start now.

Elliott walked toward me, hand outstretched, and we exchanged greetings. Normal. Friendly. Boring. Whew. I'd dodged a bullet with this one. He made *not* being a prick so much easier. And that accent. When he talked, I felt like I was flying around Hogwarts on a broom. Hell, if I wasn't already spoken for by a girl who wanted nothing to do with me, I'd consider dating the dude.

The three of us chatted comfortably for several minutes before a distant voice captured my attention.

*Okay, Angels, if you'll look to your right, you'll see the McKallister Mansion.*

I cocked my head. That voice—faintly projected over an intercom—I'd heard it before... at the press conference. I remembered thinking it sounded like Jess at the time, and I still thought it sounded like her now.

*Neither Jake nor Quinn live here, but we do spot them visiting on occasion...*

Grace and Elliott began to chat amongst themselves.

"Shhh," I said, putting my hand up. "Do you hear that?"

We all remained silent as the faint voice continued to talk. *And they aren't the only two famous family members...*

"It's a sightseeing bus, Quinn. Just like the thousands of others who've passed by us for years and years. We should probably go in. Quinn's a big deal now," she said, grinning as she offered each of us a hand. Elliott took it. I did not.

I glanced toward the street and spotted a bus. I recognized that one. It was Angel Line Tours—the sightseeing company with the pink-winged buses. They'd been coming by once, sometimes twice a day for my whole childhood. Grace had always been indifferent to these tours, but I hated them with a passion. My list of grievances was long, given the particularly sullied history my family had with these intruders rolling by at all hours of the day and night, angling their long-lens cameras through the slats in our security gates and snapping shots of us in our private moments.

To be sure, the evasive tactics started way before we had tall fences to protect us. In fact, the exploitation dated all the way back to the day Jake had gone missing. Camera crews, reporters, and lots and lots of the curious bystanders came out in droves and set up shop on our front lawn. Some of the bolder trespassers would knock on our door or peek in our windows. It was like living inside a reverse snow globe where the storm raged outside our fragile glass bubble.

The crowds multiplied by the thousands after Jake's miraculous return, packing us all in tighter. I remembered that time of fear and uncertainty. The onslaught eased months later, as Jake's story eventually became old news in the eyes of the media and life slowly began to return to normal...or at least a new normal. But as it turned out, Jake was never meant to fade away, and as he rose to fame, he dragged the rest of us along with him.

The day Jake bought this place for my parents was the day order returned to my life. Not only did we move into a virtual mansion on one of the most desirable streets in LA County, but I also grew up in affluence, never wanting for anything. And while the giant, sweeping security gates did their job of keeping intruders off our lawn, there had been no cure for the buses that sat out front with their tour guides regurgitating the story of our tainted lives over and over for the enjoyment of their giddy, snap-happy tourists.

*The McKallisters, of course...*

That voice. And then I remembered what Jess had said to me in the car that day when I'd ask what she did for a living.

She'd said, *"My duties consist mainly of being the head angel."*

I jumped to my feet. Holy shit.

"Quinn?" Grace swished her head around, alarmed. "Are you okay?"

"No. Yeah. Maybe. I don't know. I think that... that tour guide..."

I didn't finish my sentence because I was already sprinting across the driveway.

I wasn't just chasing down my girl.

I was running toward the enemy.

## 20

## JESS: STOWAWAY

S o wrapped up was I in my commentary that I didn't see the figure of a man sprinting down the long, fancily paved driveway. I didn't see the side door to the security gate swing open. I didn't see him race toward the bus.

But my passengers sure did. Every single one of them. I looked up from my monologue only to find thirty-five stunned expressions staring out the open windows.

"Jess!" he yelled, causing my head to whip around at record speed.

Quinn?

And then he was there at the door to my bus—his palms flat against the glass panes, wearing the same shocked expression as me. We stood there staring, me rocking in place, him panting.

He knocked. "Open the door, Jess."

I couldn't move. I couldn't think. Keeping him away was manageable when he'd actually been away, but now, standing so near with that impossibly handsome face... it was unfair. Inhumane.

"You want me to open it?" Delene, my driver and friend, asked with that cynical expression on her face never breaking.

She'd just as soon run him down than facilitate the first inklings of love.

I wanted to say yes, but if Delene opened that door, she'd unseal the last barrier to the make-believe world I'd been living in since the two of us parted. A world where Quinn McKallister didn't rule my heart. If she let him in, I'd never be able to kick him back out. I scanned the interior of the bus, trying to determine if I could use my passengers for cover, but I could tell by their eager and excited faces that they would be of no help. They wanted Quinn on the bus as much as he wanted an invitation.

"Jess," Delene said. "He's staring at me. If you want me to open the door, show me a sign."

Quinn popped his head into the first open window. "Jess, just show her a sign."

"Yeah, show her a sign!" multiple passengers agreed, the mantra repeating itself over and over.

I looked to him, that irresistible smile laying siege upon my heart.

"Come on, Jess. I've been looking everywhere for you. Just give me five minutes of your time. Please."

That started a new chant. "Just five minutes."

I turned to Delene and exhaled. "Go ahead."

She opened the bus door, and Quinn took a step in. But I was there, pushing him back out.

"Not here."

"Then where?"

I placed my palm against his chest and walked him away from my bus, back toward the gigantic security gate he'd just exited from.

"Uh, Jess, what are you doing?" he asked, amused, as he allowed me to control the backward direction of our reunion.

"Getting you out of earshot of our audience, Quinn. Everyone is staring."

"That's because you made a scene."

"Me? I wasn't the one standing there with those big ol' Puss in Boots sad eyes."

He laughed. "God, you've got a way of stripping away my self-esteem, don't you?"

When we hit his fence, he grabbed for my face, drawing me in, his lips against mine. An instant heat swept through me, my body already responding to his kiss. His touch. No. I disengaged from his hold on me and backed away.

"You shouldn't be here," I said.

"*I* shouldn't be here?" He chuckled, pointing toward the McKallister home. "That's my house. If anyone shouldn't be here, it's *you who* shouldn't be here."

Oh. Yes. Well, that was factually correct. But still, he should've just remained tucked away inside his castle. "This is my job, Quinn."

"Let me see if I have this right," he said, the look on his face indicating that he was as genuinely amazed by this turn of events as I was. "Your job is stalking my family?"

I paused. How to answer that one? "Um...I stalk other people's families too."

"Oh, well, that makes it all better."

But Quinn wasn't mad. Far from it. He was loving this, and if I weren't so blindsided, I probably would be too.

"Is that why you wouldn't return my texts? I mean, by your reaction it's obvious I had the right number all along, and you just weren't returning my calls."

"No. And then yes."

"What?"

"No to your first question. My job has nothing to do with why I didn't text you back. But, yes, to the second question. I was purposely avoiding you."

He searched my face for an explanation. "Why? I thought we

had something."

This was where I should have stuck the sword in and twisted, vanquishing him from my life forever. It would've been so easy. But it also would've been a lie. I didn't want him gone. And he needed to know that.

My shoulders drooped. "We did."

He exhaled. "So I wasn't imagining it?"

"No."

"Then why? I don't care about any of this," he said, sweeping his arms to encompass me and my bus full of eyewitnesses.

Yet he said it like he did care. Like maybe it actually could be a reason for my disqualification. "Wait. What do you have against my job?"

"Nothing."

But he didn't meet my eye. "Quinn?"

"What?"

"You obviously have a problem."

"Okay, fine. If I were going to handpick the profession of my one true love, it probably would not be as a tour guide for a 'map of the stars' sightseeing excursion, that's all. Okay?"

"What in the living hell, Quinn? Of all hang-ups in the world, that is a very specific one. I mean some folks have aversions to snakes or germs or people who take more than ten items through the express lane at the grocery store, but you... you draw the line at sightseeing tours?"

Quinn looked like a man caught in crossfire.

I slapped a hand to my hip, strangely pissed at his very elitist phobia.

"Oh, man." He sighed. "Let's just say I have an issue with my life being on display for the entertainment of others. And sure, you can say we invited it by courting fame, but in our particular case, we didn't... I didn't. Notoriety was thrust on us by a serial killer who picked the wrong victim. You don't know what it's been like for me to grow up with a lens always trained on me—with people looking in through these bars and oohing and ahhing as I ran past like I was some zoo animal. Maybe it would have been easier had I not been raised to fear strangers."

"So, why choose the exact same path for yourself, Quinn? If you think you're going to escape the lens now, you're crazy. You're everywhere, and it's only going to get worse. You'll never live a normal life."

"And that's my choice. Look, I'm not disputing that most celebrities need this attention to stay relevant. Probably most even crave it. But when I was a kid, I didn't choose it. Nor did my siblings or my parents. Hell, Jake didn't either. So, yeah, I have some weird hang-ups about your profession. But I can work through them"—he paused to flash me a killer-watt smile—"for you."

The idea that I'd played a part in his misery growing up bothered me. The McKallisters really were victims of circumstance.

"Quinn, I'm sorry. I never considered any of that. It's a job. It pays the bills."

He reached over, sliding his finger gently across my lips. "I'm not mad at you, Jess. This job allows you to buy those pink swoosh Nikes. Besides, I might start loving these bus tours, now that they brought you back to me."

"I still don't know how you found me," I said.

"And I still don't know why you didn't want me to."

My cheeks flushed. "It's complicated."

"Not from my end, it's not. I like you, Jess. Hell, I've been beating women off with a stick since the whole Jesserella thing blew up. Who knew chicks loved grand gestures?"

"Who knew?" I grinned. God, he was so endearing.

"I mean, I always knew it was a possibility that you were avoiding me, but imagine my surprise when I'm in the driveway of my family's home and I hear your voice projected over a 1970's intercom system. I think, 'Huh, that sounds like Jess, but no way could it be the girl I've spent weeks searching for over the internet, because if it is, that would mean she's known where I've been all along and purposely did not want to be found."

He stopped, scanning my eyes with his own. "Have I missed anything?"

Even when he was irritated, he was giving me an out. He wanted this. He wanted us. And I wanted the same.

"You missed the *why*," I replied.

"There's a why?"

"Of course there is. No woman in her right mind would walk away from you."

He stepped in closer, gripping my arms. "Then why? Tell me."

I looked back at my bus. "I can't. Not here. I'm working, Quinn. This isn't professional. I'm not giving my passengers the experience they've paid for."

"Actually..." Quinn glanced over to the bus and waved. A chorus of swoons followed. "I think they've been fully compensated."

He had a point. And if it were just that, then there would be no issue, but what I had to say was not for public consumption.

"Listen, just let me get back to work, and as soon as I drop them off, I'll call you."

"Uh-huh. I've heard that before," he said, crossing his arms over his chest. "Excuse me if I don't believe you."

"I get it. But this time, Quinn, I promise."

"So last time you didn't promise? Because it sure seemed like you did."

The first inklings of anger crept in. And he had every right to be mad. I was one hundred percent in the wrong. If I'd given any consideration to his feelings, I would've afforded him an explanation, but instead, I'd been cowardly, all because I knew if I saw him or even just talked to him on the phone, I wouldn't have the willpower to stay away.

My fingers tiptoed over his forearm, his smooth skin as delectable as it had been that night on the couch. "I know I was wrong, Quinn. I should've texted you back. I'm so sorry. And I promise as soon as I'm done with this tour, I will call you. Just go back to your house."

"Actually, I don't think I will. In fact, I think I'm going to take your tour."

"Oh no, you're not."

He smiled. "Oh yes, I am."

"There's no room on the bus for you."

"Then I'll sit on the floor."

"That's against the law."

"Since when do you care about the law?"

He had a point. I hadn't given him any indication that I was a rule follower before, so why would he believe me now?

"Quinn. Stop being difficult. It's like the pink ball all over again."

He was not impressed by my argument. "You brought this on yourself. I don't trust you, so I'm going to stick right by your side until I get an explanation I can live with."

He jogged off in the direction of the bus as I followed close behind. "Seriously, Quinn. Not cool."

"I agree, Jesserella. Totally not cool."

He cleared the two steps into the bus like a gazelle and headed straight for Delene.

Reaching a hand out, he introduced himself to her. "Hi, I'm Quinn."

She took his hand, almost smiling. "Yes, you are."

"Delene, Jess says there's no room for me. Is that true?"

Her eyes rolled over him. "Baby, if you can't find a seat, you can squeeze right in here next to me."

My eyes widened to unsafe levels. Was she...was Delene flirting?

Quinn threw his head back, laughing. "See, Jess? Delene likes me."

"And I like you. But that's not what this is about."

"I look forward to the explanation. But until then, I'm just going to make myself comfortable."

Quinn didn't give me a chance for rebuttal. He'd already taken his charm on the road, casually making his way down the single aisle in the bus, shaking hands and taking selfies with anyone who asked.

Delene looked up at me. "That boy is all trouble."

"Don't I know."

"Um...dude?" A young woman appeared in the doorway, her eyes settling on Quinn. "What are you doing?"

"Being friendly," he replied. "Jess, this is my sister Grace. Grace, this is my tormentor Jess."

Our eyes settled on one another.

"You're Jess?" she asked, totally baffled by the unexpected turn of events. "As in Jesserella Jess?"

Oh god, if I never had to hear that name again, I'd be a happy woman. "Or, you know, just Jess."

"I'm so confused right now. Were you taking a sightseeing tour?"

"No, Grace," Quinn butted into our conversation. "She's the guide. She's been rolling by the house this whole month I've been looking for her. Haven't you, Jesserella?"

"Quinn, can we save this for our private conversation?"

"Wait," Grace replied, the wheels in her head obviously turning. "So, you've been..."

"Ghosting your brother. That's correct."

Grace burst out laughing. "This is... this just gets better and better. You and me, Jess, we need to get a drink."

"Hey, stop fraternizing with the enemy," Quinn called to his sister.

"I'm the enemy?" I protested.

"You are until proven otherwise."

"Then what are you doing on my bus?"

He paused a moment, perhaps considering why himself. "Proving otherwise."

Grace looked back at me. "You can't reason with that logic."

"No, you can't."

Just the way she looked at her brother told me she clearly adored him, and that made Quinn all the more attractive.

Quinn slid into a row next to a teenage girl who'd broken ranks with her family the minute she'd entered the bus for my afternoon tour.

"Hi. I'm Quinn."

The girl went temporarily mute, blinking up at him in awe. I knew the feeling well.

"Mind if I sit with you?" he asked, already getting comfortable as he stretched out like he had in my car. I smiled at his ease.

"Apparently you're staying," Grace said. "What do you want me to tell Mom? She's expecting you for dinner later."

"Tell her I've been abducted by a bus full of angels. That should calm her down."

"Right. Because any mention of abduction in our family is met with lighthearted giggles," Grace countered.

Their relaxed ribbing caught the attention of every person in the bus. It was so out of place with the image most people had of this famously reserved family.

"Okay, well. Sorry, Jess," Grace said as she moved off the bus. "I tried."

And just as Quinn's easy demeanor had captured my attention, so did Grace's. There was just no way not to like her.

"Nice meeting you," I called out to her as Delene closed the door.

I watched her wave as she walked up to a man and slid her fingers into his.

"This whole day..." Delene mumbled before putting her bus in gear.

"I hear ya," I said before turning the microphone back on and addressing my passengers. "Okay, Angels, I hope you don't mind, but we picked up a straggler. Give it up for Quinn McKallister."

There was a rousing round of applause.

"Answer the question," someone in the back called out.

"The question?"

"So, Quinn knows it's you."

"I think he knows already."

More chanting. "Answer the question!"

"Just answer the question, Jess," Quinn smirked.

I spoke low and deliberately into the mic. "Someplace fun—but not *too* fun."

My answer was met with roaring approval as Delene pulled back onto the road.

"Hey, Jess, I want to hear what you have to say about the people who live in that house," Quinn said, pointing out his own palace.

Oh, that smug look. He was playing with me. And not only that but he was looking frustratingly comfortable, with one leg crossed over the other and his arm resting on the back of his seat.

"I think I've said enough," I replied.

He held my stare, his lip curled up ever so slightly. "Humor me."

Fine. He wanted a tour? I'd give him a tour. Launching into a monologue about the McKallister family, I mentioned not only Jake but also Kyle's time on the reality survival show and the oldest sister's husband, Finn, himself a popular actor. And with my eyes never leaving his, I concluded with a piece about the family's youngest son.

"If you will remember, Quinn McKallister recently competed on the singing competition *Next in Line*. He was the awkward fella wearing a full-body sea lion costume, not because he was forced to but because he just really likes attention and doesn't care how he gets it."

Quinn laughed along with the other passengers. Snapping his fingers, he motioned me forward. "Give me that."

I handed him the microphone.

"Sit down now, missy. I'll take it from here." Quinn stood up and pointed out the window. "The house up there on the left belongs to actress Tara Agora. Every year, she throws a huge birthday bash—for herself."

Quinn went on to give deliciously detailed, inside trader accounts of all his neighbors. I found myself as engaged as everyone else, watching him shine by just being the guy I fell for that one rainy California day. And although I hadn't been with him since, I'd been following along in the media like everyone else. I'd watched in awe as Quinn had gone from an internet sensation to a vulnerable heartthrob to the frontman of a breakout band with a hit single that was taking over the airwaves.

Quinn's future was already outlined. Now all he had to do was fill in the blanks. I wanted to be a footnote on those pages... No, I wanted to fill every line. Maybe I hadn't given Quinn enough credit. I'd thought he'd just move on, but he hadn't. He'd held on... made a stand. Held himself faithful to me.

I owed Quinn the truth. I would tell him about Noah and

explain my reasoning. Maybe he would understand, maybe he wouldn't, but at least I would have said my piece so that both of us could move on.

Eventually, I wrestled the microphone from his hands and finished the tour. When Delene pulled into the parking spot nearly two hours later, there wasn't a person in the bus who wasn't smiling from ear to ear. Quinn had made today something special. Something unexpected. To have a celebrity wave and say hi on our route was one thing, but what Quinn had done was unlike anything I'd ever heard or seen. He'd put himself out there in a big way, and while it had paid off in the short term with a very pleased group of tourists, in the long run, I hoped he wouldn't live to regret it.

Just as the last passenger disembarked, I saw Andrea running toward the bus, waving us down. Delene opened the doors to let her in.

"Don't get off the bus," she said as she climbed up the stairs, panting.

"Quinn, this is my sister Andrea. Andrea, this is my stalker Quinn."

"Nice to meet you, Quinn. Were the two of you aware that the passengers on the bus have been livestreaming?"

Quinn's brows shot up. "Ah, shit. Tara will never speak to me again."

"You may need to move," I agreed. I was in as giddy a mood as my departed passengers. Quinn really had made my day. My month. My life.

"Actually, Andrea, I think we all know who to blame," Quinn said, clearing his throat. "Delene."

My driver shook her fist at him, but there wasn't an ounce of animosity. Dare I say the two had become friends along the route?

"I'm glad you all had such fun, but there's one person who isn't as happy—your manager, Quinn."

"Tucker?"

"Yes, Tucker. He called me. And has sent security to hold back the crowd."

"Wait," I said, looking out the window. "Why is there a crowd?"

Andrea gaped at me before tapping my chest. "Jess."

Her finger then tapped on his. "Quinn."

We both looked on, still not comprehending the connection.

"Wow, you two really are meant for each other, aren't you? Quinn McKallister just found his Jesserella. It's a real-life fairy tale, and people have been flooding onto the boulevard in hopes of catching a glimpse of the crowning."

"My god," Quinn replied. "I am Prince Gaston. My brothers are going to absolutely rip me to shreds for this one."

"At least you got a cool name. Jesserella sounds like someone's heaving up a hairball."

"Hey. Hello," my sister said, snapping her fingers at us. "You two really need to focus. Delene, drive them to the lot. Jess, you and your rock star can make your getaway from there. Oh, and Quinn? Thank you for the best publicity a tour company could ever have."

## 21

## QUINN: THE UNBROKEN

It wasn't until I was sitting in the passenger seat of Jess's car that I realized the significance of the moment. We'd come full circle. I was back where I belonged. Twisting my head in her direction, I smiled.

She glanced back. "Wipe that smile off your face, Quinn."

A low rumbling laughter burst forth.

"You don't get to enjoy this," she said, her own amusement coming out to play. "If you'd just stayed home where you belonged, none of this would've happened."

"Fair. But if you'd just answered my damn texts, it wouldn't have happened either. In fact, I'll go so far as to say you brought this on yourself. You could've knocked on my door at any time in the past five weeks. You're the problem here, not me."

Jess bit down on her lower lip, staring straight ahead. "No, you're right. This is all my fault. For what it's worth, I'm sorry. This isn't what I wanted either."

"Then why do it? You make no sense."

"I know. And I will tell you, it's just... I have to drop something off really quick, and then we'll go somewhere and talk, okay?"

Did I have a choice? No. Her silence confused me. Why was she hesitating? There was no denying our chemistry was right where'd we'd left it. And now, seeing her again, I was more determined than ever to make her mine. But Jess was in charge of this negotiation, not me, and whatever was holding her back seemed major enough that I might not get what I wanted in the end.

Jess pulled into a parking lot and turned off her car. I read the sign on the front of the building—The Maas Transitional Housing Center—and then quickly glanced over at Jess.

"Do you work here too?"

"No. Someone I love lives here."

The revelation stunned me. Someone Jess loved was homeless? She reached into the back seat to grab a bag before turning to address me.

"You can wait in the car," she said, opening the door and stepping out. "I'll be back quick."

I opened my own door and climbed out.

"Quinn—I'm not going to abandon you. I'm coming back. It's my car."

"I know. But if it's okay with you, I'd like to meet this person you love."

She stopped, her eyes wary. "It's not pretty."

"I grew up in 'not pretty.'"

Jess considered my words before reaching her hand out to me. "Okay."

My fingers slipped into hers and we entered together. Jess didn't stop for directions, moving through the facility with purpose, her head held high. If I hadn't been convinced of this woman's worth before now, this moment sealed the deal. Like me, Jess would walk through fire to protect the ones she loved.

We moved down a hallway that led into an expansive rec room in the back. She made a beeline for a man sitting in a wheelchair, his leg in a cast that reached up to his knee. He was staring at the wall. He must have heard us approach because he turned and reached his hand out to Jess. She dropped mine and took his, leaning down to kiss his cheek.

"Hi Dad. How are you feeling today?"

The desperation on his weathered face was clear. "Not good. I need a drink, Jesse. They won't give me one, and I can't go out and get one myself because of my leg. Just one. Please, help me."

"You know I can't do that."

He pulled her in closer, whispering, "They're trying to kill me."

"No, they're helping you, Dad. It should only be a few more days and then they'll get you in the rehab facility. I know it's hard, but you're doing great."

"No, I'm not! I'm not doing great at all. I need something now," he barked before spotting me and jabbing his finger in my direction. "You!"

I shot to attention.

"You look like you've got a secret stash somewhere. Weed. Coke. I'll accept any and all donations."

Jess caught my eye and rolled hers. Her dad's request seemed more serious than the roll of an eye, but if she said so.

"Sorry, man. I'm clean out of blow."

His eyes narrowed in on me. Pissed. Then he cast me off. "Go away then. Get!"

"Dad. He's not a stray dog. This is my friend Quinn. Be nice."

"Nice? You want me to be nice when you've imprisoned me in this hell?"

"Would you rather be on the streets?"

"Is that even a question?"

"Okay, then. Tell me how you'll manage in a wheelchair. How will you go to the bathroom? How will you sleep?"

"I'll do it all in my chair."

"Oh, sure."

"You don't believe me? I'm sitting in a load of crap right now."

Jess cocked her head back before a laugh shot from her mouth. Sometimes laughing was all you could do. I knew with my own family how powerful humor could be. It had gotten us through the worst of times, and it had clearly also seen Jess through.

Upon hearing her laughter, her father snapped his grumpy mouth shut. But I swear I saw the very slightest flicker of amusement pass through his eyes.

"You're ridiculous, Dad. Now, get your head back in the game. You wanted this, remember? You're just frustrated because it's taking longer to get you into a facility than we anticipated. Once you complete your rehab, you'll thank me."

"I'll do no such thing. You're dead to me, Jess. Dead."

"Uh-huh. Okay. I love you too," she said, handing him the bag she'd brought in for him. Damn, I loved the way this woman handled stress.

He grumbled something incoherent.

"I have the clothes you asked for, and there might be a bag of your favorite gummy worms in there."

"Are they infused with whiskey?"

"Nope. Plain old gummy worms."

"Well, fuck!"

"I'll be back tomorrow. Love you, Dad."

She grabbed my hand, raised that head of hers high again, and strolled out of there like she owned the place. I was awestruck. This woman was my queen.

We didn't speak again until we got back in the car.

"Sorry about that," she said, making no excuses. "He's always such a cuddly little fella."

"Adorable, really," I agreed. "My favorite part was when he thought I looked like someone who'd have cocaine on me."

She gripped my cheeks in her fingers. "You dime-bag tweaker, you."

I laughed even though so many questions were running wild through my head. Was this her secret, the reason she felt she could no longer see me? If so, she had to know I'd be here to support her, not knock her down.

"How long has he been homeless?"

"Off and on for years. I've tried to bring him in, get him help, but he never stays."

"That's a gnarly injury. What happened to his leg?"

"He was sleeping in some bushes when a car jumped the sidewalk and landed on his leg. He had surgery, and once he'd recovered enough to be moved, I brought him here. He's waiting for a spot to open up for him in a rehab facility. In the meantime, he's withdrawing hard."

"Shouldn't it already be through his system?"

"Technically, yes, but Victor Bello is nothing if not resourceful. He always finds a way to poison himself. If licking windowsills would get him blitzed, he'd do it. Some days I visit him and he's flying so high he doesn't know who I am."

"When will a spot open up?"

"It's hard to say. These are public rehab centers. They're free, so that's good, but there's always a wait and they're cookie cutter. Very generic. My dad's been in these before, and... I mean, they're better than nothing, but I wish I could get him into a private facility because they're customized to an individual's specific needs."

"But the private ones cost too much money?"

"Yes. I've tried to get Andrea to help me, maybe split the cost, but she and our father don't get along."

"That sucks. I'm sorry."

She trailed her fingers over the back of my hand so absently that I wasn't sure if she realized she was doing it. "I wish you could have seen him before. Back in the day when he still had a job and was taking care of himself, he was strong and robust, filling out a suit with such swagger. I can still remember the smell of his cologne and the way he slicked his hair back. I didn't think there was a dad alive as handsome as mine. I barely recognize the man in there. If we passed on the street, I might not even know it was him. But I know he's still in there, my handsome, loving dad, and that is why I fight."

I nodded, finding her passion so appealing and real. She made me wonder why I'd ever wanted an uncomplicated girl when I could have one like Jess, a woman who lived and felt and fought like hell.

"He's lucky to have you."

"Yes, he is." She smiled. "Who's lucky to have you, Quinn?"

"You."

Jess blinked, surprised. "Are you mine?"

"I could be."

She studied me, like an experiment she wasn't sure had gone right. "Why do you like me so much? You basically have your pick of amazing women, and yet you go on a worldwide hunt for one working class girl. Why?"

"Because my whole life I've struggled to connect with people. After the kidnapping, I was different. Changed. For the longest time I thought I was broken because I could never relate to anyone outside of my family. And then along came my getaway girl, and suddenly I realized maybe I just needed you to fix me. Jess, I think you unbroke me."

She appeared almost shaken by my words. I pressed my thumb against her lip and she turned her head into me, her eyes closing, giving in. I kissed the line of her jaw, then her ears, and finally started working down over her throat.

She didn't resist, but she didn't encourage, either. I could feel a heaviness coming off her that hadn't been there before. "Hey, what's wrong?"

"Listen, Quinn," she said, running her finger through the wayward strand of hair flipping around my ears. "Remember when you told me all I needed was one piece of your puzzle to know everything about you? Well, I also have a missing a piece of the puzzle—one that explains everything about me. It explains why I'm no longer that girl who broke into my mother's home. It explains why I didn't text you back. This piece is everything. And I didn't tell you the day we met because I didn't think you could handle it. I like you way more than I care to admit, and it killed me to ignore your texts. But this piece, Quinn..." She shook her head. "It could be a game changer for us."

As far as I was concerned, there was nothing she could say, short of telling me she was married that would detract me from my mission—which was winning the girl.

"Hey." I kissed her. It was brief and tender, but it was only meant for comfort. "I think you forgot that I grew up in a tornado. There isn't much I can't handle."

She watched me, analyzing. Deciding.

"Actually, change of plans. I was going to tell you, but I think maybe it's better if I show you instead."

I followed Jess inside a seventies-style brown and brick building —a community center, according to the sign out front. There were a handful of entrances, all appearing to lead to different offices. But Jess knew exactly where she was going, and with each step I took, so did I. The sounds of children playing was my first clue. The second was the large multipurpose room decorated in colorful splashes of paint with child-friendly activities all around. The third was the large play area out back with scores of kids running about. It was then that I knew. Jess had a kid.

Her eyes locked on mine. What did she want me to say? I wasn't opposed to kids; they'd just never been on my radar of must-haves. But now I understood why she'd kept me at bay. Jess was a mother, and I was pretty damn sure I knew who the father was.

A boy broke free from the group and ran up to us. He was a skinny kid with floppy brown skater hair blowing in the wind. He was sporting a cast on his arm, the second relative of hers wearing one today. They were an injury-prone group.

"Mom," he said, catapulting himself into her. She wrapped her arms around him, kissing him in his wayward hair.

I tried to stay neutral and project the required 'Relax, girl, I got this' swagger. But I didn't 'got this.' I was rattled. People didn't shock me often, but Jess managed to do just that.

She had a kid... a fact that was currently freaking me out. I'd thought I knew who she was, but I didn't know this woman at all.

The boy disengaged from his mother and squinted up at me. "You're Quinn McKallister, aren't you?"

I looked to Jess, wondering what she'd told him about me. "I am."

"I saw you at the press conference."

"He was with me that day in the bus." Jess immediately clarified his statement as if she were always a step behind sweeping up after him. "We saw you talking to the reporters."

His eyes widened, and he poked her in the stomach. "Wait —*are* you Jesserella?"

"I'm never going to live that name down. Yes, I'm Jesserella, but it's Mom to you. But look at me, Noah." She lifted his chin up. "Quinn and I are just friends. Don't be blabbing it all around that we're anything else, okay?"

"Sure, Mom," he said, full-on face-winking at her like he didn't believe a word she was saying but that he'd play along if she insisted.

I laughed. My god. He was like a carbon copy of his mother.

"Quinn, this is my son, Noah."

I could hear in her tone how difficult this was for her, and it occurred to me then that she didn't do this very often—introduce men to her son—and even though I was still working my way through the shock, I wanted to make it easier on her. Besides, kids didn't scare me. I was the fun uncle, and as far as these little booger-eaters went, this one seemed fairly easy.

"Hey, dude," I said as I bent over and offered a hand for a high five.

Noah readily accepted the greeting, even winding up to take his shot.

"Ouch." I jumped back, shaking out my hand out. I knew how little boys worked. The more perceived damage they did, the better. "Dang, you've got an arm on you."

"Baseball," he offered up as explanation.

"Ah, okay, I thought maybe you punched walls or something."

He laughed. Hysterically. Which, in turn, made me laugh. This kid was full of it. Whatever *it* was. I glanced up at Jess. She looked nervous, a row of perfectly lined teeth trapping her lip below. I mustered up a smile even though I was still losing it on the inside.

"Do you have any more of these guys?" I asked.

"Uh...no. Noah is my one and only. He's eight years old."

"I'll be nine soon. Can you come to my birthday party?"

"Oh, I..."

"It's a ways away, Noah. Quinn might not be in town then," Jess said, wiping something off his face. "How was school today?"

He looked down to the ground, toeing the dirt.

Uh-oh. *That* didn't look promising. I suppressed a smile. The kid was going down.

"I kinda got in trouble."

"What?" Jess jerked back. "Why?"

"I ate the science."

"Noah! Not again. We talked about this."

"I know, but we were learning how marshmallows get fluffy. I just ate a couple, and then Reese narced on me."

*Narced.* I laughed. Okay, he was growing on me.

"Did your teacher send you to the principal's office?"

"Not for that."

Jess shook her head. "What does that mean? Did you get sent to the principal's office for something else?"

I already knew the answer. Oh yes, he'd been there. But I kept mum as I was enjoying the show.

"Noah?"

"I called Reese a snitch." He sighed. "And then he got mad and told the blacktop lady."

"Ugh, Noah." She shook her head. "Why can't you just keep your mouth shut?"

"Because Reese was being a snitch! And then he proved he was a snitch by snitching again."

I chuckled. "He isn't wrong, Jess. A snitch is a snitch."

She backhanded me. "We don't encourage bad behavior, Quinn."

Too late. Noah was already looking up at me like I was his savior. He lifted his arm up. "You wanna sign my cast?"

It all made sense now. The emergency. Noah was why she'd

rushed off that night. Noah was why she hadn't texted me back. Noah was the piece of her puzzle.

"He was the emergency," I said to Jess.

She nodded.

I returned my attention on Noah. "Sure, I'll sign, but first you gotta find me some real estate."

"I don't know what that means," he said.

"Real estate? Like a place to sign."

"Ohhh," he said, and I could see his brain turning, committing the phrase to memory for future use on the blacktop. "Real estate."

I grinned. He was funny. A free spirit. So much like his mother, it was eerie.

Noah went to work examining his cast, searching for an empty spot, but there wasn't an inch of spare space. He was a popular kid. Good for him.

Finally, he came to a decision. "You can sign on top of Joey's name. He's my least favorite friend."

Ouch. Poor Joey.

"You got a pen?" I asked.

"No. I thought you guys carried them around."

"A pen? Why would I do that?"

"'Cuz you're famous."

"Barely. I'm like this much famous," I said, using Jess's finger measurement scale. "And besides, famous people don't carry pens."

"How would you know, if you're barely famous?"

Both Jess and I laughed. Damn, this kid was a firecracker. But then, why wouldn't he be? Jess's Bond DNA had obviously been passed down to him.

"Because my brother is Jake McKallister, and I guarantee you, he doesn't carry a pen."

Noah's eyes widened to unsafe altitudes. "Jake's your brother?"

"Yep."

"Noah, you already knew that," Jess said.

"I know, but it's cooler when he says it. Mom, can Quinn have dinner with us?"

Jess looked at me, questioning. "I... I don't know if he can, Noah. Quinn's a busy guy."

She was giving me a chance to tap out. She'd presented the evidence for review, and now it was up to me to accept it or not. I'd never dated a woman with a kid and had no idea what that would be like, but meeting Noah hadn't dampened my feelings for Jess. It may have slightly derailed them, but the more I talked to her little boy, the more the train seemed to be righting itself on the tracks.

Looking from Jess to Noah and back, I noted her uneasy stare and his expectant shine. I made a preliminary decision—the only decision that would accommodate the lust I had for this woman.

"Are you too busy?" Noah asked, disappointed.

"Not too busy for you and your mom."

Dinner turned out to be an ambitious endeavor. I knew from the minute I walked into the restaurant that something had changed. Things had been crazy before but adding Jess to the mix had tipped it over the edge. The stares. The cameras. The behind-the-hand whispers. My instinct was to look around for Jake because this was his deal, not mine. But the name being called was my own. The requests for pictures. The autograph seekers. The giggly girls. They wanted me. And for the first time in my life, I felt the weight of my own celebrity.

Jess seemed amazed. Excited. Shocked. And then protective, shielding Noah from the cameras even when he wanted to jump in every picture with me. As for Noah, he was having a great time, becoming my madam and pimping me out to the highest bidder.

"Did you want a picture?" he asked, so accommodating to the two college-aged girls lurking about. "It's okay."

"Noah." I puffed out a laugh.

"No more," Jess said through a spattering of giggles after the girls left. "Noah. Look at me. Let Quinn eat in peace."

But he didn't, inviting ever more strangers to our table for photo ops. Jess was finally forced to ask for a couple of to-go containers after the trip I took with Noah to the bathroom ended up being a meet and greet.

"I am so sorry." She laughed through her apology as we made our way out to the car. "I wish I could say this was out of character for him."

"Don't be," I said, sliding an arm around her waist. "As far as plus ones go, Noah's the man. It was the most fun I've had since I went on a date with this girl at a mini-golf course. It rained, and I carried her to the car."

She pinched me to prevent me from going further. "Sounds fun."

"Oh, it was."

Noah climbed into the back seat. "Can Quinn sit back here with me?"

"No, bud," Jess replied. "His legs are too long."

I loved the way Jess parented Noah. It was both matter-of-fact and fact-based. This wasn't a coddled kid. Jess didn't lie to him to protect his innocence, answering his precocious questions with not always age-appropriate results. Something about it was authentic and fun. Noah was free to be who he was... to an extent... but Jess also kept him from tipping into brat territory with firm rules—that he listened to. Or not.

"Can you tuck me into bed later, then?"

Whoa, he'd jumped way ahead. I laughed, wanting to respond with 'If I get that far,' but instinctively knew Jess wouldn't appreciate the innuendo.

"We'll see. Now strap in," Jess said, placating both Noah and me in one fell swoop. This woman was good.

Noah did as he was told, and after I slid into the passenger side, he placed his hand on my shoulder. "Are you going to be my mom's boyfriend?"

I looked back at him and then over to his mom. "How would you feel about that if I did?"

He was silent a minute, thinking. "It's okay."

"Yeah?"

"Uh-huh. You can teach me how to be a rock star."

"I can do that." I laughed, impressed with how well this kid coped with change.

"Hey," I said, looking back at him. "You're okay, Noah."

We didn't even make it out of the parking lot before the call came in from Tucker. Actually, many calls had come in from Tucker, but I'd had my phone off since the homeless shelter and had forgotten to return it to the normal settings.

"Hello?"

"Chili's, Quinn? You're at Chili's?"

How the hell did he know that? I looked out the window for any signs of a drone hovering about or even a swarm of Tracker Jackers. Upon finding none, I was left assuming the worst.

"Have you put a tracking device on my phone?"

"Yes, Quinn. It's called fans, and you put a tracking device on yourself. You're like a walking bullseye. All I have to do is type your name into Twitter and I can follow you all over town."

"Well...shit." The word just slipped out. I glanced back at Noah. "I meant poo."

A smile spread across his face. "But you said the other one."

"But you didn't hear it," I said, trying to use the force to direct his mind.

"Yes, I did."

"No, you didn't."

Jess stopped the childish duel with a swish of her hand.

"Are you still there?" Tucker asked.

"Yes, sorry. Jess and I picked her son up at his after-school program and went to dinner."

"I know."

"I find it creepy that you know that."

"Don't be. Pretty much anyone under thirty knows where you are. Listen, Quinn, I know having the spotlight on you and not Jake is a new thing, but you need to be more careful. For example: dinner. I could have called ahead. Got you in a back door, found a private corner."

"Chili's has a back door?"

"You know what I mean. I'm used to dealing with excitable fans—I managed a boy band, for god's sake—but I can't help you unless I know where you are and where you're going."

"Okay. Sorry."

"So where *are* you going?"

I paused. I knew where I wanted to go, but that didn't mean it was where we were going to go. "I don't know."

"Quinn!" He tsked.

"Seriously—it's up in the air."

Jess eyed me, mouthing 'Who is it'?

I mouthed back, 'My manager, Tucker.'

'What does he want?'

I ended our mime sesh. "He wants to know where we're going, and I don't really know."

258 | NEXT IN LINE

"Where do you want to go?" she asked, a raise of her brow letting me know she was open to suggestions.

I eyed her, letting her know I thought her place sounded dope.

"Would you like to come over and hang with us for a while?" she asked.

I glanced at Noah, then back at her. "Are you sure?"

"Sure, I'm sure. Noah, don't you have a fun game from your aunt Andrea you want to play with Quinn?"

"Yeah! It's going to be awesome!"

I flinched. By the *way too* excited expression on Jess's face, I knew it would be the opposite of fun. "I'm not going to like this game, am I?"

"No. You are not." Jess laughed, taking a glance in the rearview mirror before gently swiping my thigh with her finger, her subtle way of giving me hope that tonight might go my way after all.

"Quinn," Tucker said my name in the phone.

"Oh, sorry. Forgot you were still there. We're going to Jess's."

"All right. Just do me a favor. If it looks like people are following you, call me, and I'll send a security guy out there."

"I really doubt that will be necessary."

"You'd be surprised, Quinn. After the whole bus Romeo and Juliet thing, you've got a target on your back. Don't get me wrong —from a PR point of view, the entire stunt was pure genius. And it was all caught on film, every adorable cutesy word you two spoke to each other. Hell, I'm the least romantic guy in the world, and even I got a flush. But now that you and your lady friend have entertained a nation, you'll have to deal with the starry-eyed fallout of your actions."

"Oh boy, sounds fun," I reflected.

"Oh yes, it surely does," he agreed.

"I'll keep my phone on."

"Wonderful. That would be the smart thing to do. And, Quinn, as things progress through the evening, if you could just send me a quick text and let me know where you'll be spending the night, that would be swell."

Yep. There was no other way to interpret his request. My manager had just asked for a high-tech sock on the door.

"Will do."

I hung up and then turned to flash her a thumbs-up.

"I don't know if I like that smile," Jess said. "You look like an anime cartoon. What did he say?"

If it had just been the two of us, I would have had a frank discussion with her about the spectacle our reunion had caused, but as the uncle of many little human sponges, I'd learned to keep my explanations PG-friendly.

"So, fun news," I said, raising the excitement to pee-the-pants levels. "It seems that our bus reunion was conveniently recorded by your awesome passengers, Jess. And then, not to be outdone, Noah here, through his very energetic soliciting at the restaurant, has made us all—you, me, and the little man himself —internet stars."

I shook my fists in the air and cheered. "Yay!"

Noah, instantly picking up on the excitement but not the sarcasm in my words, yelled. "Whoa, cool!" His legs pumped up and down, kicking the back of my seat.

"Quinn?" Jess's fake smile was as big and animated as mine now. "What's going on?"

My voice was warped by the sheer wattage of my grin. "It seems we've become the number one target of your buddies."

"My buddies, you say?" she asked, flashing me that counter-feit smile.

"Yes, the super-duper fun paparazzi." I raised my arms in the air and did a little jiggy dance, bringing down the roof. "Isn't that the best news ever, Jess?"

"Wah-hooey-woo!" Noah pumped his fists right along with me.

"Wah-hooey-woo!" I mimicked. "Come on, Jess. Isn't this sooo fun?"

She laughed, shaking her head. "My god. What have I gotten myself into?"

"Strap in, you lucky lady, you," I hollered. "You're going for a ride."

_____

## 22

## JESS: PLAY FOR ME

What happened to my conflict? What happened to protecting Noah at all costs? What happened to my dignity? I'd let Quinn stroll back into my life, and now he basically ruled it. Maybe if he wasn't so hot. Or so fun. Or so hot. Oh, I already mentioned that one. But it was true. If I'd thought Quinn was female catnip before, he was a hardcore heroin overdose for me now. It was like, Noah who? All I could think when I looked at my child was 'Is it your bedtime yet?' Make no mistake, once that kid was tucked away for the night, Quinn would be on his back. Or me on mine. Oh, god! What was I saying?

I needed to beat myself with a Swiffer mop for even thinking about moving this thing with Quinn forward. *Noah comes first.* Yes, of course he did. Noah. Yep, he was just the best...love the kid... but, okay, just hear me out. What if Quinn stayed? What if we fell madly in love, got married, and popped out a few more McKallisters for his clan? He would then be a permanent fixture in Noah's life and not just his mom's ultimate fantasy. Well, then I'd be putting Noah first. What a fabulous mom I'd be. I mean, just look at those two. I smiled to myself as I eavesdropped on their conversation from the kitchen where I was cutting up Noah's nighttime snack.

"I saw you on *Next in Line.*"

"Ah, man." Quinn sighed. "Gotta tell ya, Noah, not my finest moment."

"Mom said it was the best song she's ever heard. She plays it a lot."

"Does she?" He looked my way, but I quickly averted my gaze because of... the eavesdropping and all.

Noah continued with his twenty questions. "Do you play in concerts?"

"Not like full-on concerts yet, but I might have a tour coming up in September. Still trying to figure it all out. But it won't be an arena tour or anything."

Quinn's explanation went straight over Noah's head, but that didn't stop his follow-up question. "Why not?"

"Why not? Because I'm still like a baby fish getting eaten by the big fish."

"When will you be a big fish?"

"That's a good question. I have to prove myself first."

"How do you do that?"

"I'll let you know when I figure it out."

"When you're a big fish, are you going to eat the little ones?"

Quinn laughed. "I haven't decided yet. Probably. Would you?"

"Yeah. Probably," Noah agreed.

"Why?"

"Because I like to eat fish."

Quinn dropped back in his chair laughing. "Little dude, I'm not sure if we're talking about the same thing."

I loved the way Quinn interacted with Noah. He didn't talk down to him; he showed him respect. I'm sorry, but it was ovary-busting.

"Do you ever get scared on stage?" Noah asked.

"No. I get scared off-stage, though."

"Really? Why?"

"Because I'm not as comfortable on my own when it's just me. But in front of the lights, with the audience cheering and the guitars blaring... yeah, that's my idea of heaven."

"I want to do that someday too."

Quinn knuckled Noah. "Right on, dude. I didn't know you liked music."

"I don't like it that much now. But I wanna be rich like you, so I'm going to learn it."

*Priorities*, I chuckled to myself. My son had a life plan. Good for him.

"If that's your goal, I hate to break it to you, but I'm barely making rent," Quinn said. "Like, what's your definition of rich?"

"Can you buy an Xbox?"

"I think I might be able to swing that."

"What about an elephant?"

"An elephant?" Quinn asked. "Why would I want to buy an elephant?"

"So you could ride it to work."

"Or I could leave my elephant at home and drive my car to work. That way I wouldn't have to stop and pick up dump-truck-sized turds when my elephant crapped all over the freeway."

Noah collapsed into a pile of giggles, helped in part by Quinn's laughter.

If I'd thought Quinn was irresistible before, this conversation with my son sealed the deal. I was in love.

"If you could buy anything in the whole world," Quinn asked him once they'd both settled down, "what would you buy? And don't say elephant."

"I would buy"—Noah put his finger to his mouth—"jewelry for my mom."

What? My heart swelled. Of anything he could have said, that was by far the sweetest. I stepped behind the wall so as not to let them see me swoon.

"Really? Not an Xbox for yourself? Why?"

"Because my mom likes pretty things, but she can't buy them because she has to spend all her money on me."

"Huh. Sounds like your mom really loves you."

"Yeah, she's the best mom ever."

Quinn high-fived my son. "You're a cool dude, Noah. I like you."

I dropped back against the wall, completely sidelined by the heartwarming interaction between the two. Noah's answer was proof enough that my policy of putting him first had been sound. He was a loving kid, and with any luck, he might grow up to be a great man. That conversation proved to all the naysayers out there that I could do it on my own... but how nice would it be not to have to? Was it so outrageous a thought that I could have it all? That Noah could have it all?

Grabbing his bowl of apples, I walked back out to the boys only to find Quinn and Noah each standing on their own individual chairs.

"Wow. Okay, guys," I said. "I can't think of any other reason for the two of you to be up on those chairs unless there's a mouse on the floor. So I'm going to go back into the kitchen and scream."

"We're playing hot lava, Jess," Quinn called out. "And it's coming your way."

My eyes widened at the news of a natural disaster materializing in my living room. I set the apples down and jumped onto the chair with Noah. We moved around the room on chairs and pillows and coffee tables until the three of us collapsed into a pile on the sofa, laughing and winded. It might not have seemed like much—a simple, silly game—but *this right here* was my dream come true. Without thinking, I cupped Quinn's face and kissed him. It was spur of the moment and stupid, but sometimes life just needed to be risked in that way.

"Blech," Noah articulated, complete with retching noises.

I grabbed my son and proceeded to drown him in a sea of kisses, making sure not to miss even one of the cute little freckles that inexplicably poked through his tanned complexion.

"Wait a minute," Quinn said, spying something across the room. "You have a guitar?"

"It's my dad's. When I was a kid, he used to play it for me. He was an amateur and only knew a couple of songs, but I've held onto it all these years, hoping someday he'd play it for me again."

"Do you think he'd mind?" Quinn asked, already headed over to grab it.

"You saw my dad. He's got bigger things on his mind."

Quinn returned to the spot beside me with the guitar in hand. He plucked one string and a puff of dust floated up. "Nice to see you wipe it down once in a while."

"I haven't cleaned it in all the years I've been holding on to it."

Quinn waved the now-airborne particles from his face. "Yeah, I can tell."

As Quinn twisted and turned the metal heads on my father's guitar, he patiently explained to Noah how everything worked, even trying to get him to use his ears to hear if something was out of tune. I smiled, watching them work together for a common goal. To think how many kids had this gift every day— fathers who cared enough to pass their wisdom on.

Quinn began to play, the song an extension of him as his fingers moved effortlessly over the strings. Such ease. Such beauty. The tendrils of his music wrapped themselves around me and I tingled, imagining his hands drawing skillfully across my own skin.

"I have an idea," I said, standing up and pulling a protesting Noah off the couch after Quinn's impromptu concert was complete. "Let's get you all ready for bed, and then maybe instead of a bedtime story, we can get Quinn to sing you that song from the *Next in Line* performance."

Quinn's eyes flickered with what I could only assume was the memory of what had happened the last time I'd heard that song. It had ended up with me on my back and him between my legs. And in all honesty, it would probably end that way again.

Noah took longer than usual to calm down, and that had everything to do with Quinn. He didn't want to miss any of the fun. I couldn't blame him because neither did I. It was only after Quinn promised to see him again that Noah finally lay down and fell asleep. But it wasn't enough for me to know that he was in the lullaby stages of sleep. No, my kid had to be full-on into the deep stages of REM sleep before I dared go back out to the musical stud in my apartment.

I quietly shut Noah's door and made my way into the living room, lovingly decorated in a combination of beach décor, Noah's various art projects, and framed photos. Quinn was standing near my front door, a photo swiped off my entry table in his hand.

"What are you looking at?" I asked, wrapping my arms around him from behind, already feeling uncommonly comfortable laying my head against his back.

"Jess and Noah," he said, replacing that photo and picking up another. "Jess and Noah." And another. "Jess and Noah. It's just the two of you. No other family. No other friends. No father for Noah."

"There's an explanation for that: it's just Jess and Noah."

"Is his dad NL from the heart in the mini-golf castle?"

"Yes. His name is Nick Ledger."

"And you were pregnant during the burglary, and the juvenile hall, and the high school shunning?"

"Unbeknownst to me, but yes."

"So, Nick's not in your life at all?"

"He's around, sort of, but only when he wants to be, which isn't often. I used to try to force it, but he just doesn't want to know his son. It's heartbreaking."

"Does he at least pay child support?"

"Not in a couple of years, no."

Quinn shook his head, upset for me. It was nice that someone was. It took two to tango, but I was the only one still dancing.

I took the photo out of his hand, set it down, and led him to the kitchen table. "Sit."

Once we'd both settled in, I finally explained. I told Quinn about Noah's accident and his insistence that my past boyfriend loved him and the way his father had forsaken him in his time of need. "I knew he'd bond with you. Who wouldn't? You're an amazing guy. But look at your life. It's big. It's crazy. You have this amazing future right in front of you. And then look at me. Compared to you, I'm small and insignificant. It doesn't take a big leap of the imagination to assume I'd be a passing phase for you. And if it had just been my heart on the line, I would've rolled the dice and risked it all, but it's my baby's heart too. I couldn't let you crush it. Do you understand? It was never about disrespecting you and always about protecting my child."

Quinn rose from his chair, laying his body across the table to reach my lips with his own. He dispensed a series of short, sweet pecks between the words he spoke. "You're not small. You're not insignificant. You're brave and funny and exciting. Any guy would be lucky to have you. And I understand why you made the decision you did not to text me back. I can't say I blame you. I'll be honest with you, Jess, when I saw Noah, my first instinct was to bolt."

I kept my expression neutral despite fighting off the feeling of impending doom. "It's a lot, Quinn. I get it. And it's obviously not what you signed up for."

"No," he agreed. "But am I what you signed up for? A McKallister? I know my backstory isn't a slam dunk either."

"Please—I'm sure you've never suffered with the ladies because of your lineage."

"No. But you're not just any lady. I can tell it freaks you out."

He wasn't wrong. But it wasn't because of his family's past; it was because of his family's present. They were like royalty, and I was... well... me.

"I just have doubts they would accept me. I mean, what would they think of you dating a woman with a child?"

"I don't know. I've never dated a woman with a child. Uncomplicated, remember?"

I smiled. "How could I forget?"

"Here's the thing, Jess. I've had a lot of time to think about my uncomplicated girl policy, and I've come to the realization that I need complicated. I need *you*. Everything else will work itself out. Noah. My family. You stealing my favorite t-shirt. The point is we owe it to ourselves to see where this goes. In twenty years, do you want us to look back and wonder *what if*?

"No," I admitted. "I don't want to live with regret. But it's such a balancing act of doing what's best for me and doing what's best for him."

"So, what's best for you?" he asked.

I paused. Should I say it? Should I open up my heart to

possible disaster? "You are, Quinn. Of course."

"And what's best for Noah? You have a lot of photo frames over there with just the two of you. Are you willing to expand your twosome?"

My heart fluttered at just the thought of what he was suggesting. The three of us, in a picture. A perfect little family.

"I'm willing... with hesitation. Listen, Quinn, I know you can't promise me a future. I get that, and I'm willing to take this chance on us if you at least promise me that you'll be gentle with Noah's soul. If you can promise me that one thing, you can do whatever you want to mine. I always survive."

He gripped my neck, his fingers tangling in my hair. "I will promise you that."

I stood up and took his hand. "Good. Now that we have that out of the way, come with me... and bring the guitar."

~

I stood with my back against the newly locked door, watching him with a predatory eye. I'd taken the liberty of changing into something more comfortable, which happened to be that damn Van Halen t-shirt he'd just accused me of stealing. The one I'd worn nearly every night since. He'd liked it so much the last time, I figured why mess with temptation?

"What do you have under there, Jess?" His voice was husky and tipped with lust.

"What I had last time." I pulled on the hem, revealing a black lace thong and a matching bra.

"You weren't wearing those last time," he said, near drooling. "I would've remembered."

Our eyes were locked in a battle of wits. Who would bend first? What did it matter? As long as we both got what we came here for, there would be no loser.

"I want you," he said feverishly.

I stayed at the door, slightly arched so my breasts were prominently displayed. "Play for me."

"Nah. I want to play *with* you."

"Then play for me."

He sighed. "Fine. But guitar only so I don't wake Noah."

I nodded, exposing some skin to show what awaited him once he upheld his end of the bargain. I didn't need to tell him twice.

"Wait." I stopped him seconds after he began strumming the guitar. "Lose the shirt."

He smiled, shaking his head as he laughed softly, and stopped his plucking for only the amount of time it took to strip the shirt from his body. Holy hell, his chest was a thing of wonder, and used as the backdrop for the guitar, I could barely keep from touching myself. "Is that all you want me to lose?"

I scanned my hungry eyes over him. "For now."

Quinn resumed strumming the guitar, playing a tune I'd never heard before.

"Did you write that?"

"I did," he said, looking up from the strings. "For you, actually."

"For me? How do I know you don't say that to all the girls?"

"Because I don't say it to all the girls. I wrote this song for you, whether you believe it or not. Now, why don't you come over here... and lose the shirt."

I smiled, twirling a strand of hair, teasing. My feet moved forward, each step slow and deliberate. I stopped before we touched and lifted my shirt up and over my head, standing there before him in my lacey bra and panties.

Quinn set the guitar down as I took the final step. He placed his hand on my stomach, peering up at me. "I don't even know where to start. You're so beautiful."

I tipped my head into his, my hair fanning out around us. His hand slid up my back, unhooking my bra and allowing my breasts to break free. His mouth circled one. Then the other. I reached around him, dragging my nails along his skin. Quinn tipped his head back and moaned.

"Everything," he said. "I want to look at you."

Hooking my fingers into the waistline of my panties, I eased them down past my hips until gravity took them the rest of the way. I was standing before him vulnerable and aroused. Quinn adjusted, his hardness straining. I throbbed, resisting the urge to touch him... to touch myself.

"God, Jess," he whispered, gripping my wrist and running his thumb along the underside of the delicate skin. "Where have you been all these weeks when I needed you?"

His words, the need. Quinn's lips skimmed my cheek, drawing a gasp as he placed tiny kisses along my skin until he arrived at my lips. He kissed me, his lips deliberate as they drew me in.

My tongue circled around his mouth as I sank into him. With my legs straddling his waist, his stiffness was perfectly angled onto my sensitive spot. Slowly, I rotated my hips, and Quinn bit down on his lips, forcing the groan to remain silent in his throat. He grabbed my ass, pressing me down. I ground into him.

He shifted, severing our connection as he picked me up and deposited us both onto the bed. Running his hands up my arms, Quinn gripped me tightly and pulled me under him. Propped up by his muscled arms, he hovered over me, the lust nearly dripping from his eyes.

I was no tamer, my predatory instincts taking over.

With little effort, Quinn was on top of me in an instant. My legs wrapped around him, aching for him to be inside. Neither one of us was in our right senses, nearly frantic with need. My fingers gripped his jeans, wishing I'd made the removal of them also a condition of his guitar playing. I dipped my fingers into his waistband and slid them down his slim waist. He'd come prepared for action, hard and wanting. Still hovering above me, he dipped his head, flicking his tongue over my lips.

Already wildly aroused, I circled my hand around his hardness, giving him a tug. The groan that set forth required muzzling. We stopped, waiting, listening for a tiny spy, but when no sound came from the other side of the locked door, I squeezed harder, forcing Quinn to arch his back and silently scream with pleasure.

"No," he spoke in a ragged tone, pulling out of my grip. Heat radiated off him, quickening my own pulse. "First I want to see you squirm."

Every nerve ending in me was on high alert as those fingers of his dipped into my wetness. Now it was my turn to be muzzled as I plunged my head into the hollows of his neck, moaning behind closed lips. The pressure increased, and I was thrashing about. Too much of everything.

"I can't," I squirmed, every nerve tingling; even my toes were curling. Panic. "Quinn. I can't stay quiet."

Challenge accepted. He licked his way down, between my breasts, over my stomach, and then he was there, twisting me in place. The only way to stop his tongue from sending me into a high-pitched crescendo was to offer him the place between my legs, the spot throbbing for his company. I spread wide, trembling with anticipation.

Quinn reached for the condom, his fingers replacing his tongue and never letting up until he was at my opening and forcing me open. Everything quaked. Anticipation. Longing. Pure animal attraction. His hands traced the curves of my hips as he slid into me, taking me slow and steady.

"Do you have any idea what I want to do to you?" his voice

dipped, his hands sliding to my breasts as he drew in then out.

"I want you to do everything," I hummed, rocking my hips upward in time with his, meeting each thrust with my own. The sultry slickness of his skin under my hands kept me busy while I devoured the feel of his heaving back as he breathed harder and heavier.

I desperately tried to hold back the force brewing inside me, but his foreplay had deposited me right at the edge, and I wasn't sure how much willpower I had left. Quinn drove deeper, the tempo of his thrusts growing faster and keeping in time with our breathing, until we both came in a shared climax, perfect in our harmony.

"Tell me who you are, Jess," Quinn said, breaking the silence with his simple question as we lay in bed afterward—me settled into the crook of his arm.

It was clear Quinn was expecting a profound reply. But I wasn't an enigma. I was just a girl—living.

"I mean, I know you're a cool chick. Adventurous. Quick-witted. Caring. But who are you really? What do you think about when you lay your head on the pillow every night?"

That he cared to even ask set him apart.

"Honestly," I said as I turned toward him, "lately... you."

He smiled. "Obviously."

I agreed. "Obviously."

I got a kiss for my answer, but from the expectant look on his face he wanted more. Sighing, I answered his question. "I'm a girl who holds tight to what is hers."

Quinn studied me, absently sliding a strand of my hair though his fingers. "See, I knew you wouldn't give me a generic answer. You're too deep for that."

"I'm really not that deep. I want what everyone wants—to not lose the things I have."

"Like?"

"Noah. My job. My family. My apartment."

"Me?" he asked presumptuously.

I circled my finger over his chest. "Yes, and you."

A still fell over us. What was he thinking?

"What about you, Quinn?" I asked, trying to coax him from his silence. "What do *you* think about when you lay your head on the pillow every night?"

"What don't I think about is a better question."

"You have a lot going on inside your head?"

"Normally, it's like a battlefield in there, but lately things have calmed down."

My heart pumped a little faster. Did I have something to do with this easing of the mind?

"What's changed?" I whispered.

Quinn averted his gaze, fixating instead on the ceiling. "I don't know. I feel different."

The teasing words spilled out before I could stop them. "Oh, my god. Please tell me you weren't a virgin."

He laughed hard at that. "What part of today made you think that?"

My body instantly reacted to his suggestion, especially with the finger that was now lazily trailing along my skin.

"I'm kidding. Tell me," I insisted. "How do you feel different?"

The pause was so pronounced that I wasn't sure he would answer... but I shouldn't have doubted him. "With you, I don't feel like I have to prove myself. It's like a weight has been lifted from me. I can't explain it, but that's why I pursued you the way I did. It's almost like I need *you*—in order to be *me*."

His answer hit me in the feels. He was a surprisingly introspective guy.

"When we first met, Quinn, you said you wanted to be seen. I thought it was an odd thing to say because you're such a big personality. Everyone is watching you, wanting to be like you. Yet you don't feel that way about yourself."

"It's just..." Quinn closed his eyes, drawing in a deep breath. Something I'd said hit a raw spot. "Never mind, I shouldn't complain."

"Why shouldn't you?"

"Because I have nothing to complain about. I grew up never wanting for anything. My parents have a loving marriage. I was never abused or treated with disrespect. I don't have the right to be wounded. Jake, he has the right. My parents, my brothers and sisters—they have the right. But me? Grace? No."

"You were there. That's enough."

"But nothing happened to me."

"That's not what the video showed. The kid looking into that camera was traumatized. That's not nothing, Quinn."

I glided a finger along his face. "Has no one in your family ever acknowledged your suffering?"

His body tensed, and it was then I knew it to be true—six-year-old Quinn had suffered in silence.

I squeezed tighter and whispered in his ear, "Talk to me."

Quinn took another deep breath and then spilled. "No one told me what was happening, Jess. I had no idea that Jake had been kidnapped or even what that meant. All I knew was that Jake wasn't there anymore, and the predictable life I was used to vanished in an instant. It was like someone flicked a switch. Good to bad. And no one bothered to explain to me why. I get it now. They didn't want to scare us because we were so young. But what my imagination didn't fill in, the kids at school graphically did. And figuring things out on my own was way more terrifying.

"It had another effect too. I grew up feeling like I was on the outside of this exclusive club that the rest of my family belonged to—those who suffered versus those who didn't. I still don't think my family knows the damage it did to me. I was there the whole time, at their feet, but no one looked down and saw me. So now I feel like I have to be extraordinary to get their attention —which with a brother like Jake is near impossible."

I waited for Quinn's frustration to settle before replying. "I'm looking."

He tipped my chin up and kissed me. "I know. That's why I turned the world upside down to find you."

"Thank god you did. I needed you to fight for me because..." My voice faltered. "No one ever has. My parents never put me first. I felt invisible. Pushed aside. But despite that, I still try and hold on to the ones I love, even when they might not deserve it. I mean, you've seen my father. He verbally assaults me every time I visit him, but there I am, bringing him his favorite candy."

"But not his favorite cocaine."

"No," I agreed. "Not his favorite cocaine. I know I should probably give up on him, but I can't. I just can't. And then there's Andrea. Now, there's a special kind of narcissist. She's hated me my whole life *because I was born*. I mean that's f-ed up, right? And the one time in my life when I really, really needed her, she turned her back on me. And yet I work for her now. All is forgiven, despite her never having apologized. And you know why? Because I'm afraid to lose one more person in my life."

Quinn considered my story for the longest time before his lip curled up on one side. "Jesus, Jess, you're a fucking mess."

I laughed, smacking him in the chest. "You should talk."

Quinn pressed in closer, his lips brushing against mine as he whispered, "What if I promise not to leave you?"

I thought about that for a moment, the novelty of what he was saying.

"Then you'd be the first."

## 23

# QUINN: JUST RIGHT

J ess was not a snoozer. I discovered that the hard way when her alarm went off at six thirty in the morning and she leapt out of the bed so fast I legit thought her apartment complex had caught on fire.

"Uh... Jess? Should I drop and roll?"

She tossed on her clothes from last night then tiptoed over to me, pulling her lush mane to the side.

"Just one more kiss," she said.

Jess made that one kiss count, her soft lips against mine as her tongue took its lazy time. As far as I could tell, it was the only lazy thing about her.

She stood back up, her expression pained. "Quinn, I really, really hate to do this to you, but you have to go."

I lay there nodding.

"No. I mean right now."

"Like *now* now?"

"Like two minutes ago now. Noah will be up soon. Listen, Andrea rescheduled my shift so I don't work today. Give me like an hour and a half to get him fed and off to school, and then we'll have the rest of the day to ourselves."

Following Jess's lead, I was already out of the bed and dressing when she stopped mid-rush and said, "Please come back."

God, she was so gorgeous makeup-free with that hair cascading over her shoulders. I drew her in for a quick goodbye kiss.

"I promise I will."

"Good. Because I already can't wait to see you again."

And just before she slipped out the bedroom door, Jess added, "Now, don't take this the wrong way, but you have two minutes to get your ass out of my apartment."

My ass was out of her place with a minute to spare. The last thing I wanted was make the situation awkward for any of us, so I ducked out of her front door and ubered the ten-mile distance home.

Once showered, I texted Tucker.

It was only seven a.m., early in my world, but chances were that my energizer bunny manager would be awake at this hour.

*Got a minute?* I asked.

*I've always got a minute for you.*

Damn. Everyone needed to get themselves a Tucker.

*Do you have recommendations for a good private rehab facility?*

Those dots danced on the screen for a long while only to receive a two-word reply.

*For you?*

What? Did he not know me at all?

*No, not for me. I barely fucking drink.*

*Then I assume we're talking about Brandon. I've already had a discussion with him about his drug use, and he's promised to curtail it.*

And note to self: never discuss anything incriminating with Tucker.

*Okay. I can see I have to spell everything out in one long, detailed text before asking you anything of a sensitive nature. I want to get Jess's father into a rehab facility.*

*You could've just said that,* he answered. *And yes, I can help. I know of a good private facility but it's not cheap.*

*I know but I'm getting the money in from the record deal and royalties for that first song should be coming in soon too.*

*Look, I'm not going to tell you how to spend money you don't yet have but are you sure you want to do this? You just got back together with her. It's a lot of money to spend if you don't really know where it's going.*

*No offense but this is my money not yours. I'm sure.*

Again, lots of little bubbles. I waited. And waited.

Finally, the reply came—a thumbs-up emoji.

I had to laugh. I knew how this probably looked to him. A young guy captivated by a girl. Of course he'd see this as a passing phase. A sowing of oats. But he didn't understand the scope of the connection we'd made. He didn't know that for maybe the first time in my life, I had complete clarity. It was hard to explain how I knew; I just did. Jess and Noah would be a part of my life forever.

I'd won the girl over with my charm, my voice, and my newfound commitment to her son. Now I needed to dig deep. Make her see that I was a keeper. That I would do anything for her.

I looked up at the sign and sighed.

"Okay, I'm here," I said into the phone.

"Good. Now go inside," Grace replied.

"Is there any other way?"

"Quinn, we talked about this. You're Goldilocks eating the baby bear's porridge. We're not going for too hot or too cold. We're going for just right. You can't buy her a car—too hot. You can't buy her a gumball—too cold. But you can buy her the perfect cup of Starbuck's joe, now, can't you?"

"I could, but... you know my rule, Grace. I've never stepped inside a Starbucks. It's a personal decision."

"I know. But just think how romantic it is to shun your stupid, anti-elitist posturing for the girl you love."

"Love is a strong word. I like...lots and lots."

"Whatever. Just go inside, Quinn. I don't have all day."

I reached for the door before an alternative popped into my head. "Why can't I just get her donuts?"

Grace groaned. "It's like I'm working with an amateur. Listen, Quinn. Donuts are for well-established relationships. They say, 'I love you so much I don't care about your ever-expanding waistline.' Elliott and I have been together for five months now, and I'd nail him in the nuts if he brought me home an apple fritter."

"Jesus Christ. Who makes these rules?" I grumbled.

"Inside now!" she insisted.

"Fine. I'm hanging up and going in."

"Is that"—she startled—"the best choice here, Quinn? Do you even know the difference between a grande and a venti, or that a tall is actually a small?"

My head spun with all the information, but one thing was for sure, having Grace in my ear would not help my rising heart rate levels.

"I don't know any of this, but I'm a grown man. I can figure out a Starbuck's menu. I'll call if I need you."

I could hear her begging for me to reconsider as I hit the red button on my phone. She was being ridiculous. I could do this on my own, and in return, I would wow Jess with my thought-fulness.

I opened the trendy doors and took my place in line. Grace was right; I had no idea how or what to order. All I knew was to avoid donuts at all costs.

The guy in front of me stepped up to the register. "Yeah, I'd like a venti soy quadruple shot latte with no foam."

I struggled to keep my eye roll to myself. This guy was why I avoided this place like the plague—these self-righteous hipsters. *We get it, dude. You're extremely important. Now why don't you go save the world on your own time?*

"I can take your order over here," a barista said, the cheery smile on her face fading fast as she saw me approach. It was clear she recognized me. "Oh, you're... wow... okay... what can I get for you?"

"I'm a virgin."

"I see." Her smile instantly returned. "You've come to the right register."

"I knew I could count on you, Debbie," I said, snagging her name from the tag on her apron. "I'm looking for the perfect drink to bring to my... let's just say, experienced... girlfriend."

She held up a hand. "Say no more. I know what you need. There's the vanilla latte with toasted white mocha *and* vanilla sweet cold foam. Total crowd pleaser, that one. Or if she's feeling a little frisky, she might prefer the non-fat, two-pump, peppermint frappuccino topped with double whip and cocoa powder."

I was momentarily stunned with the liquid monstrosities she was suggesting. "No, I think you misunderstood me, Debbie. My girlfriend is a real woman, not Mrs. Claus."

We had a good chuckle together over that. Were we bonding? I think we were.

"Oh, I know who this drink is for. Everyone does. And trust

me, you can't go wrong with either option. Besides, Jess doesn't seem like a picky woman."

My eyes widened. The way she said it made it seem like she was actually acquainted with Jess. Which wouldn't be all that much of a coincidence, given this was the closest Starbucks to her place. Now, normally I wasn't into strangers knowing my business, but in this specific situation, I wasn't above using Debbie's intel to my advantage. "You know her?"

"I don't *know her* know her, but she comes in here often enough that I know *of* her. Right after the whole Jesserella thing hit, I even asked her if she was *the* Jess. She spit her coffee all over the counter."

"That sounds like her." I laughed. "What did she say to that?"

"She made some excuse, but I couldn't shake the thought that it might be her, and then yesterday the two of you were all over the place and I was pretty damn proud of myself."

"I'm sure you were. Well, Debbie, you've been a wealth of information. Thanks to your patience, I think I'm ready to take that next step."

"Are you sure? I want you to feel comfortable with the process."

"I'm sure. Give me that toasted latte thingy. Now, about the pastries."

Jess opened the door and flung herself into my arms, almost making me drop the coffee and bakery items I'd brought.

"Whoa. If this is how food delivery guys get greeted, sign me up."

"Right—because those guys pull way more chicks than the rock star."

"I wouldn't know, because since becoming a rock star—in training—I've only had one."

"Your loss. I've banged the whole Door Dash fleet."

I pushed my way in. "You're lucky I'm not a jealous guy. Debbie says hi, by the way."

"Debbie?"

"The barista you spit all over last week."

"Oh, Debbie." Jess lengthened the name for comic effect.

I set the coffee on the table and handed her a bag. "I brought you a cake pop."

"A cake pop?" She giggled. "What am I, ten?"

"Debbie said it was the most popular bakery item."

"Yes. If you're ten."

"You want it or not? Because otherwise I'll eat it, and I've already consumed three."

"I want it. Geez. Back off, cake pop pusher!"

I laughed, sweeping her into my arms. "You're a firecracker today, aren't you?"

"You've spent a whole two days with me. How do you know I'm not a firecracker every day?"

My lips dipped into the hollows of her perfect neck. She smelled of sweet pineapple. I could easily devour her.

Reaching around and squeezing her ass, I said. "I'm counting on it."

~

Thirty minutes later we were getting dressed again—and the coffee was cold.

"I'm starting to see a pattern here," Jess said, hooking her bra.

I pulled on my jeans. "Yeah? What's that?"

"Our relationship's like eighty-two percent sex and eighteen percent cake pop."

"And that's a problem how?"

"I mean, do you think maybe we should attempt to do something else besides humping each other today?"

I sighed, long and heavy. "Are you *trying* to hurt me?"

She laughed. "I suppose we could stay here and talk about feelings."

"Oh lord, have mercy. Debbie warned me about this."

"Debbie seems to have made a huge impression on your life."

"If she was like twenty years younger... you'd have a problem."

We headed back into the kitchen where Jess was rewarming her fluffy fairy coffee drink when my phone buzzed. It was a text from Tucker.

*The Cliff Rehab in Malibu can take Jess's father as part of their community outreach program.*

*What does that mean?*

*It means you can hold on to that money you don't yet have.*

I stared at my phone, shocked. *How'd you manage that?*

*These private facilities are "encouraged" to take in county patients if they have an open bed. But they get paid county compensation too so most of these places officially have no beds open, even when they do.*

*Well hell, Tucker, you're a magician.*

*Nothing so exciting. Called in a favor.*

*You've got some powerful friends.*

*It's not about powerful friends. It's about powerful secrets.*

Damn. Tucker was impressive. Dangling threats seemed to be the name of the game in Hollywood, and Tucker was at the top of the game. Really, I didn't care how he got the job done, just that he did it. Now Jess would have one less thing to worry about and maybe, just maybe, we could nudge our 'sex to cake pop' ratio up a bit.

*I'm sending all the paperwork to you to pass on to Jess. He can move in tomorrow.*

*Thanks. I owe you one big-time.*

I set the phone down and smiled at Jess.

She was halfway through the cake pop.

"What are you smiling about?" she asked, catching on to my excitement and smiling herself.

"You're going to love me."

"Is that a dare?"

"No, Jess, it's a promise."

## 24

# JESS: ALL IN

I was used to fighting for everything I got. It was just the way things were done in my world, and I accepted it as fact. So, when Quinn told me what he'd done for my father—for me—I really wasn't sure how to react.

There were tears. There were thanks. There was laughter. And there were kisses. Lots of them. Thanks to this man, I had a real shot at getting my father back. If this was what it felt like for people to care and follow up, then I wanted more of it in my life. I wanted Noah to experience its wonders.

Quinn's phone rang. He checked the sender before sending it to voicemail. He'd been doing that a lot today. Quinn was a busy guy, and it wasn't lost on me that he'd forsaken everything to spend the day with me.

"More business?" I asked.

"Yes. Sorry. We're putting the finishing touches on our album. It's been hectic. Plus Tucker is trying to get us a tour this fall, but it's a monumental task with it already being July. Things are already booked up, so now it's looking like it might not happen until next year, which totally sucks."

All I heard was—*I'll be around many more months. Isn't that awesome?*

"Is that a problem?" I asked.

"It is in the sense that tours help promote albums, so if we aren't touring, then is it smart to release the album without one? But at the same time, Sketch Monsters has buzz now, so waiting is dangerous."

"Oh. I get it."

"Sometimes I wonder if people are just excited by the idea of us, you know. You've got the *Next in Line* stuff and my brother's awesomeness and Jesserella's fandom. We generate a lot of chatter. But will people want to buy our music if they view us as a gimmick?"

"You're no gimmick. The new single is everywhere. How can you fail?"

"You'd be surprised how fast things can fall apart in the music world. I feel like we're at this place where we're either going to take off or disappear. And the odds seem fifty-fifty. I just worry because what am I going to do without this? This is the biggest opportunity of my life. If it fails, I won't get another shot."

"But it's hardly been enough time. Sketch Monsters just formed."

"I know. Maybe it just feels slow. Not sure what I was expecting. Tucker made it seem like we would shoot into the sky strapped on the back of a rocket, but it feels more like we're tooling around town in a Prius. At this speed, I'll never catch up to Jake."

His admission surprised me. Was that what he was trying to do? Overtake his world-famous brother?

"I see your face, Jess. And yes, I know it's wishful thinking."

"Not wishful thinking, but Jake has a big head start. Do you think you're setting yourself up to fail by making him your barometer of success?"

"Of course I am, but it plays into my whole 'not being seen' theme, see. I can never be totally happy with my success unless I'm standing on stage next to Jake as equals."

Quinn's phone rang again. He flipped it over on the table as if he were planning to ignore the call when his eyes widened and he hastily answered it.

"Hello?"

I watched as the stress lines in his forehead disappeared, replaced with a genuine smile. "When? Where? Okay. I'll be there."

He hung up and looked at me. "Get up. We're going out."

"Where to?" I asked, already out of my seat and grabbing for my purse.

"My big brother, Keith, is about to become a daddy."

I put my purse on the table and slid back onto the chair. "That's really awesome, but, uh... no flippin' way."

"What do you mean no way?"

"I'm not going to the hospital, if that's what you're suggesting."

"That is what I'm suggesting. Why not?"

"Why not?" I repeated. So many reasons. Where to start? "Because I can't show up at a family function. They don't know me. And to the birth of a little McKallister? No. Just no."

"Uh-huh." He smiled, grabbing my arm and pulling me off my seat. "Let's go, Getaway Girl."

"Quinn, I swear to god."

"Jess, do you ever want to have sex with me again?"

I stopped, struggling to address his ludicrous threat. "Hold up, Romeo. Are you suggesting that you're going to withhold sex from me if I don't go with you?"

"Maybe."

My eyes narrowed. Oh, he wanted to play, did he? Let's go. "I have an eight-year-old kid, Quinn. I can assure you, other than the occasional Door Dash guy, men are not knocking down my door. I've been forced to make... shall we say... provisions."

He raised a brow. "Provisions, you say?"

"Provisions." I nodded. "Silent Bob, my battery-operated boyfriend. And you can be sure he doesn't withhold anything from me."

"Wow, Jess. Please be sure to share that happy tidbit with my mother when you meet her today," Quinn said, chuckling as he continued to manhandle me. "Come on. Where's that fighting spirit?"

"Dead. Totally dead."

"Jess." He eyed me. "I'm proud of you. I want to show you off to my family. They'll love you."

I scoffed. "I seriously doubt that."

"Because you believe what you've read about us."

"No, because I make a living exploiting your family. I hardly think that makes me a loveable character for them to root for."

"It makes you interesting. We like interesting."

"Oh yes, I can imagine I'd be very interesting. Should I bring Noah along? My dad, maybe? He'd add a little flavor."

Quinn lifted me from my seat, his arm circling around my waist. "Whatever floats your boat, babe."

"I can't." I pulled away from him. "This is a private family moment. I would be intruding on that."

He stared at me. "I accompanied you to a private family moment."

"Exactly. And my father was a disaster."

"No, he wasn't. Please, Jess. I want you with me. We've struggled so much as a family, and it's these little wonders that bring us together and make us whole. There is no better time to introduce my girlfriend than right now."

"That's what you think I am? Your girlfriend?"

"It's not what I think. It's what I know."

"After three days together?"

"It hasn't been three days for me."

The things he said, the way he said them. Quinn made me feel special in a way I never had before. Was this what it was like to be in a healthy relationship?

"It hasn't been three days for me, either," I admitted.

"Then it's settled. You're my girlfriend, and you're coming to meet my family."

"I don't remember settling anything," I protested. "You're very persistent, aren't you?"

"I know what I want."

"And Noah? Can you handle all that? Don't just be nice, Quinn. Really, truly think about it. I won't be mad, just a little maybe, if you decide dating a woman with a kid isn't for you."

"I *have* thought about it."

"For twenty-four whole hours," I interrupted.

He nodded. "Yes, this whole thing has been quick. I get that. But I'm not like most guys, Jess. I don't bond easily. So, when I find someone like you—or like Debbie—I don't take those connections lightly. You know, after the whole *Next in Line* fiasco, my dad accused me of not being a finisher. He said I walked away from things right when I got to the good part. I don't want to be that guy. I don't want to pull out of life anymore. Especially not now when I have a buzzy band. A record deal. The girl of my dreams. A barista to die for. And a cool little dude who eats science. Noah... he's not a burden, Jess. He's a bonus."

I reached for my purse.

I was all in.

## 25

# JESS: GRAPE SODA

A t my insistence, Quinn prepared his clan for my arrival. Nothing could be worse than bringing a newbie girl-friend unannounced to an intimate family gathering, except maybe bringing a newbie girlfriend unannounced to an intimate family gathering—with a child in tow. And not just any child, but the shed-jumping, celebrity-pimping Noah Ledger.

We stopped in front of the glass doors to the waiting room, and I bent down to address my son. "Listen up," I said, tilting Noah's head toward me to get his attention. Bringing him to the hospital with us wasn't really a choice, nor was leaving him at his after-school program after seven p.m. Knowing that babies were notoriously late to the party, we stopped at his school and pulled him out of his last hour of instruction before heading here.

"I don't think I have to tell you not to touch anything, not to talk too loud, not to curse, not to climb, not to steal, not to wipe boogers on the chairs..." I paused. Had I covered every scenario? I thought back to everything my son had done over the years to embarrass me. Nope. There were more. "Not to strip naked. Not to pee on a tree. Not to..."

"There aren't any trees in a hospital, Mom."

"The point is I don't want you peeing on anything or anyone."

"I only peed on Reid that one time and that was only because he got in my way."

"Noah! Zip it. I'm serious. Any funny business and you can't play with Quinn for a week."

"Nice, Jess," Quinn interjected. "Use me as a punishment."

"I'll stoop to any level I have to in order to keep his finger out of his nose in front of your family."

"You're worrying too much. Once he meets my dad, all these rules are meaningless anyway."

"What does that mean?"

"Oh, you'll see," Quinn said as he opened the waiting room door for the three of us to pass through. My legs wobbled, and I had a sudden urge to hide behind him. But of course, Quinn wouldn't allow it, thinking his family was just 'going to love' me. Yeah. Right. My step faltered. He grabbed my hand, dragging me along like a cartoon cat that didn't want to go.

His mother was the first to her feet as she crossed the waiting room to greet us. Her eyes, studying me, were the first thing I saw. So blue. So expressive. Those eyes had lived, and it was immediately clear, they did not trust easily. But like a trooper, she fixed a smile on her face and welcomed me. I took this woman in, nothing about her style vibing with the uppity image of her in the press. Michelle was not your average *The Real Housewives of Beverly Hills* woman. There was no Botox. No plumped lips. No trendy hairstyle. She was fit but not overly so, and dressed as she was now, in a baggy sweatshirt and leggings, Michelle could be any middle-aged mom in the world, even though she just so happened to have given birth to a superstar as well as the guy to my left, an icon in the making and my newly minted boyfriend.

"Jess. Hello. I'm Michelle. So happy to finally meet you," she said, shaking my hand before her eyes dropped down to the cute shaggy-haired creature beside me. "And you must be Noah. I'm Quinn's mom."

Noah glanced up at Quinn, then at me, pointing up with his thumb. "That's my mom."

"I know," she said, acknowledging me with a smile.

Whew! That wasn't so bad. Thank god for proactive thinking. Reporting the news of my motherhood to the clan before I arrived gave them time to prepare, as well as for me and Noah to avoid any awkward reactions.

Quinn hugged his mother. "Any baby news yet?"

"Nothing yet, but I don't think it will be too long because apparently Sam has been in labor all day. She woke up with contractions, and Keith was noting the time between them."

Quinn flinched.

Michelle instantly picked up on his reaction. "Exactly."

"How off were his numbers?"

"Off enough that the doctor, using Keith's calculations, told them Sam wasn't in labor and not to come to the hospital. So instead, they both went to work at the surf shop, where her water broke right in the middle of the bikini section. By the time they got to the hospital, Sam was fully dilated."

"There she is," said a man who could only be Quinn's father, Scott. "Good lord, you're a gorgeous woman."

I was totally taken aback by his compliment. With his salt-and-pepper hair, gregarious smile, and t-shirt that read, 'That's cute. Now bring Grandpa a beer,' Scott instantly put me at ease.

"Oh, well, thank you. And might I say you're an equally gorgeous man?"

"You might." He chuckled. "And I'm sure Michelle would wholeheartedly agree. Right, honey?"

"Yes. Wholeheartedly." Her monotone reply indicated it was a question she answered regularly.

"She's never been able to keep her hands off me," Scott continued, unfazed. "Hence all these damn kids."

Her eye roll didn't escape me. These two had a seasoned relationship worth dying for. I glanced up at Quinn. His look said, 'See, I told you there was nothing to worry about.' But I wasn't willing to hand him a victory just yet. There was still a long afternoon of childbirth to go.

A gaggle of kids ran up to their grandparents' sides. "And the welcoming committee has arrived. Noah, this is Max, Madison, Miles, Indiana. They've been excited to meet you."

Michelle continued rattling off the names of the youngest kids with a mixture of both joy and pride. She appeared so attentive and patient, which didn't square with Quinn's recollections of neglect so wrenchingly described last night. What horrors must have this devoted grand-mother gone through to leave her six-year-old son to fend for himself? And perhaps even more telling of the complex dynamics at work in this family was that despite the resent-ment Quinn held on to, he clearly had a loving relationship with both his parents.

Noah said his quick hello before disengaging from my hold. Typically, he had no interest in my coddling when there were other kids in the picture, and today was no exception.

"Can I go?" he asked.

"Sure, but stay with the others."

And then my security blanket was gone.

"Jess!" Grace skipped up to me with open arms, hugging me like we were the oldest of friends. "I'm so glad you came. It was sort of iffy on the bus if Quinn was going to win you over with that lackluster charm of his, but look at him—the persistent stud."

I laughed at her enthusiastic dig. "He brought me a cake pop. I was sold."

Her face melted in admiration of her big brother's romantic gesture before turning to the man beside her and tugging on his sleeve. "Why don't you ever bring me a cake pop, Elliott?"

"I didn't know that was a thing in the States."

"Oh yeah," Quinn said. "It's a surefire way to pull the chicks in America."

"You don't say?" He stared down at Grace, smiling. "Cake pop it is. I'm Elliott, by the way," he said, introducing himself to me.

"Oops. Forgot you didn't already know each other. Jess and I go way back."

"So far back," I agreed, realizing I was already forming an attachment to this bright and welcoming woman.

"Come," Michelle said. "We've sort of taken over the entire right side of the waiting room."

All eyes were on me as Michelle made the introductions. Because I stalked this family for a living, I knew who each member of Quinn's large brood was by name alone, but knowing their names and where they fit into the family did not tell me who these people were. Like Michelle and Scott, Quinn's siblings and their significant others were welcoming and friendly, but I sensed I was amongst a group of battle-weary survivors who kept their shields forever at the ready.

And that was even before I'd had a chance to meet the family's shining star. Once that happened—and I'd been told Jake was on his way—I assumed that was when the swords would come out as the McKallisters mobilized to protect their own. But as I waited for Jake and baby to arrive, all my preconceived notions about this embattled family went out the door.

These people were nice.

And surprisingly approachable. I'd only been there thirty minutes when Kyle and Kenzie had me enthusiastically agreeing to appear on their YouTube channel to discuss my experiences as Jesserella. And I had only been there forty-five minutes when I watched Scott teach my eight-year-old how to gamble during a rousing game of elementary school poker. And I was only there an hour when Jake's wife Casey suggested a playdate with her boys and Noah. A playdate. With Jake McKallister's kids. Pinch me, please. Only yesterday, it seemed, I was scrubbing toilets, and today I was at the glittery ball.

None of it seemed real. This was the family I'd always dreamed of having. I couldn't imagine what it would be like to love and be loved in return by people who'd always have my back. For all his suffering as a child, I wondered if Quinn even understood the gift he'd been given. His parents had made mistakes, no doubt, but clearly they'd atoned for them and had gone on to build this tight-knit empire. It was all I'd ever wanted my parents to do... but they'd failed miserably. Was it so inconceivable to think the McKallisters could be my saving grace, and that they might find it in their hearts to make room for two more... if it ever came to that?

"Mom." Noah pulled me out of my daydream by tugging on my shirt.

"What is it?"

"I'm hungry."

"Can you wait?"

"No. I'm hungry now."

Of course he was. "Okay. Let's go find the hospital cafeteria."

"I'm not that kind of hungry."

I blinked, confused. "What kind of hungry are you?"

"Max said there is a vending machine down the hall with candy and chips and soda. I'm that kind of hungry."

"Ah, I see. You're junk food hungry?"

"Exactly."

"I can take him to get something," Quinn offered.

"No, stay here, in case Keith comes in with word on the baby. I'll take him. We'll be right back."

I walked Noah out of the room... or, more accurately, *I* walked. He bounced. Clearly the kid was having the time of his life. Not only was he now best friends with the McKallister grandkids, but he and Scott had just had a lively discussion about throw-up that was as funny as it was stomach-turning.

I put a hand on his shoulder to slow him down. The last thing I needed was to add sugar to Tigger the Tiger.

"Mom."

"Yes."

"I wish Quinn's family was our family."

There. He'd said it. We were on the same page, both desiring the same thing. Those photographs on the side table in our living room, the ones of just Noah and me, weren't enough for him either.

"I wish they were ours too, bud."

"Maybe you can marry Quinn."

Ooh. That was definitely not where I wanted his mind to go. I could dream, but not Noah. Quinn and I were a long way off from a happily ever after.

"Maybe," I replied, knowing I shouldn't be giving him hope but not wanting to squash my own. After all, every so often, a girl got that dream. Why couldn't it be me?

We arrived at the vending machine, and Noah picked his soda first.

"Be careful with this, okay?" I said, popping the top and handing him the drink. Noah was the type of kid that, when it came to spilling, he was more likely to than not. "What snack do you want?"

"Cheetos."

Wonderful. His fingerprints would be all over the hospital.

I was crouched down waiting for Noah's chip order to fall

when I heard the collision. I cringed, hoping beyond hope my maximum-destruction son had simply walked into a wall.

No luck.

"Whoa, dude. Gotta watch where you're going."

"Sorry," I heard Noah say.

More cringing as I rotated in my crouched position only to see a pair of worn-out boots covered in grape soda. The owner shook the soda off his boots, then proceeded to rub the purple liquid around on the floor. If he thought he was being helpful, he wasn't. I don't know how I knew who owned those boots. I just did. My eyes slowly made their way up the long body of arguably the most popular rock star alive today before they finally came to rest on Jake McKallister's very famous face.

"I'm so sorry. My son is..." I shook my head. I had nothing. No way to defend his actions, given that I'd warned him to be careful no less than a minute before the collision. "Noah, go get some paper towels from the bathroom over there."

He took off, spilling more grape soda along the way.

"My god." My face overheated from embarrassment. "He's actually making it worse. How is that even possible? It's like a full-on crime scene now."

"He's leaving a trail of blood," Jake agreed. "You might want to consider hiring a lawyer now. The kid's going down."

I laughed. "Thank you for being so cool about it. It's like he's pocked with holes—pour something in and it squirts right back out."

"No problem. I have a little sprinkler myself named Slater. You're Jess, right?"

"How'd you know?"

"Casey said you were here with your son, Noah. I put two and two together. I'm clever that way," he said, offering me his hand.

I took it and he lifted me to a standing position.

Noah came back out with the towels and handed them to me. I handed them back and told him to do it himself. He appeared perplexed, and I didn't blame him. Cleanups had always been my job, and I desperately wanted to do it now, but Jake had just lifted me from the floor and I couldn't drop back down to it now.

Noah began.

Wordlessly, Jake and I watched as he missed large swaths of soda and smeared the purple mess around. My heart pumped a little faster as I tried micromanaging him from a standing position, but it was no use. I grabbed the paper towels from him and dropped back down to my hands and knees to complete the job.

While I was down there, I offered to clean Jake's shoes too, but he mercifully declined with an amused grin on his face before offering his hand to me... again.

From my subservient spot on the floor, I blew the hair from my face and said, "You must be very impressed right now."

"I'm entertained, that's for sure. You and Noah really need your own show."

Jake's personality, the way he phrased his words, the way he injected wit and humor into the conversation, it felt so familiar —like bantering with Quinn. He pulled me to my feet again just as a tousle-haired man in a hospital gown and board shorts called out his name as he hop-skipped down the hall.

"Jake!"

"Keith!" Jake mimicked.

"Jake," Keith repeated again, his face alight with joy. Keith looked to me, confused. "And random girl I don't know! And kid covered in purple. I just became a father!"

The brothers hugged. Noah got a fist bump. Then Keith turned to me—the random girl in the hall—and unexpectedly hugged me too. I laughed, genuinely overjoyed for him.

"Boy or girl?" Jake asked.

"Like I'm going to tell you first."

He took off down the hall to the room where his eager family was awaiting the news.

Jake and I exchanged an amused glance before we followed after him, arriving back just in time for the big reveal.

"It's a boy!"

## 26

---

# JESS: A NEW BOTTOM

Decorations—check. Goody bags—check. Store-bought cupcakes (no judging)—check. I wasn't sure who was more excited about this birthday party, me or Noah... or Quinn. Who would have thought Quinn would have lasted long enough to make it to Noah's ninth go-kart birthday party? But he did. And he showed no signs of stalling.

In the three months that we'd been together, Quinn had wound himself around us so tightly that I could scarcely remember life without him—nor did I want to. He hadn't officially moved in with me, still slipping out the front door in the morning before Noah woke up, but he was there every night—eating dinner, helping Noah with homework, teaching him guitar, and lulling him to sleep at night with a song. It was enough to nearly explode my heart.

But once Noah was tucked in for the night, that was when romantic, hot-as-sin Quinn came out to play. We really couldn't get enough of each other, which kept our sex-to-cake-pop ratio quite high. Because I'd never had *everything* wrapped up into a nice shiny bow, I wasn't sure exactly how to process it all. I had a boyfriend who loved my son. I had financial security. I had a father freshly released from rehab and getting stronger by the day. And I had a whole new family that was gradually becoming my own. And while most days I embraced the unknown with characteristic optimism, there were days my heart clenched in panic, waiting for the bottom to fall out from below me. When I'd related those fears to Quinn, he'd responded the way a true hero did—*If it happens, babe, I'll build you a new bottom.*

Our first real test was coming. Sketch Monsters was moving ever closer to the release date of their first album, scheduled to coincide within weeks of their upcoming tour. A tour that would take him and the band on the road for five months, maybe longer if the album performed as expected. And that seemed likely, given the buzz already surrounding them. I'd heard the songs. There was no way the album wouldn't smash all expectations.

As for myself, I'd actually cut back on my hours at work, bolstered by a second income that was much higher than my own. After years of struggling to make ends meet, Quinn's generosity was as surprising as it was welcome. In the beginning, unaccustomed to such pampering and privilege, I'd fought him, albeit somewhat feebly. But I had to say, the more he whipped that credit card out and paid for us, the easier it got to accept. The truth was, once Quinn's royalties really started kicking in, so went a lot of my financial worries.

The knock at the door drew me out of my thoughts. Had Quinn forgotten his key again? Or maybe his hands were just too full to dig it out of his pocket. Quinn had taken Noah to the store not only to pick up some last-minute items for the party but also to surprise Noah with his birthday gift before the afternoon party.

I swung the door open with a bright smile only to have it wiped clean away when I saw who greeted me on the other side —the man who'd stolen my foolish teenage heart.

"Nick?"

"Jess."

"What are you doing here?"

"Nice to see you too," he replied.

"You should've called. This isn't part of our custody agreement."

"The custody agreement you brokered."

"The custody agreement I brokered because you refused to support your son."

"That's the way it's always been with you, hasn't it, Jess? Gotta pay to play?"

"Well, I don't know, Nick, since you've never done either."

"Come on, Jess. That's not fair."

My eyes widened. I thought I was being generous. "You're off the hook financially. You should be happy."

"And what happens when your fancy boyfriend dumps your ass? Will you be coming after me again?"

There was just so much about what he'd just said that made me want to rip his nuts off, but I maintained my calm exterior, save for the slight quiver of my upper lip.

"What do you want, Nick?"

"To see my son on his birthday."

"He's not here." I opened the door wider for him to see the place was empty aside from me.

"Where is he?"

"Out."

"When will he be home?"

I didn't like this line of questioning. It implied that Nick would be back.

"Why now, Nick?"

"What?"

"Why this birthday? You've never been interested before. Is this because of Quinn?"

"I'll be honest. I don't like Noah around that family. You don't leave him alone with Jake, do you?"

"I hope to god you're not insinuating what I think you're insinuating here."

"The guy was kidnapped by a child killer, Jess. He murdered the guy. There's no telling what's going on in his mind. It's not a big stretch to assume he shouldn't be trusted around children— my child."

Now I was furious. What had happened with Jake and his abductor was self-defense. Not murder. Jake had never been anything but kind to Noah and me, and to have Nick hinting at nefarious intentions with our son made me sick.

"Get out or I'm calling the cops." I pushed on his chest. "Now!"

"I'm going," he bristled. "Oh, one more thing. I've hired a lawyer. Say goodbye to your protected custody."

A trembling unleashed inside me. No. He was just baiting me. No judge would give him custody.

"You haven't been in Noah's life for years. You don't even support him. They'd never give him to you."

"No? Courts don't like criminals, Jess. And only one of us is a convicted felon."

"I was a juvenile. My files are sealed."

"Bet your stepfather would be willing to testify on my behalf. I'm sure he doesn't think you're a suitable parent. He won't even let you meet your little sister. I wonder why?"

"That's none of your business," I seethed.

"All I'm saying is, don't think you're too good for me now, Jess. Just because you're hanging out with the McKallisters doesn't mean you belong. Don't forget, I know who you are. I bet Quinn doesn't."

"He knows exactly who I am."

"I highly doubt that."

Tears threatened to expose my weaknesses, but I fought them off. I hadn't hidden anything from Quinn, and he accepted me for who I was.

"I don't understand your angle. Did you come here to threaten me or my relationship? Because if that's the case, you're wasting your time. Quinn knows all about the burglary."

"Does his family?"

The question was wrapped in a threat. Nick had delivered the final punch, knocking the wind out of me. I leaned against the door for support. He wanted to destroy me. What had I ever done to him, other than to birth his beautiful son?

"What do you want from me?"

He leaned in, his voice low and vindictive. "For you to never be happy."

"Mom!" Noah rushed in, alive with excitement, throwing himself in my arms.

"Whoa!" I forced a laugh. Only ten minutes separated Noah's light from the darkness that had descended like a vampire to suck the happiness right out of me. "Obviously you had fun."

"Look what Quinn got me for my birthday! It's my very own guitar."

"Dude." Quinn shook his head, attempting to suppress a smile. "What happened to chill? You were going to walk in here like a stud. Go sit down and I'll hand it to you—gently."

"Okay," he said, eagerly assuming the position on the couch.

Quinn opened the guitar case, pulled the guitar out, and laid it carefully in Noah's arms.

His eyes lit up. "Isn't she beautiful, Mom?"

He spoke of 'her' with the same love and admiration that Quinn spoke of Lucia.

"She's gorgeous," I agreed. "Let me hear you play."

His composition was a disaster, of course, but it was also music to my ears. Noah was learning from a man who deserved to be emulated. There could be nothing more beautiful than that.

"You know, I was around your age when I got my first guitar. My brother gave it to me and he said to name it after the girl who meant the most to me in the whole world. Jake named his Shelle, after our mother."

Noah barely let Quinn finish his sentence before he said, "I want my guitar to be named Jesse."

"Perfect name for a perfect girl," Quinn agreed.

You could not have wiped the smile off my face if you tried. These two almost made me forget the threat at the front door. Almost.

Something occurred to me. "Wait—is Lucia your mom's middle name?"

"No," he replied, the flash of pain passing through his eyes a reminder of a past he'd yet to reconcile with. "Lucia is Grace's middle name."

His little sister. I didn't realize she meant that much to him.

"Noah," Quinn said, changing the subject. "I think we have something else to show your mom, don't we?"

"Oh yeah," he said, waiting for Quinn to take his guitar before leaping to his feet and grabbing a gift off the table.

Jumping in place, Noah handed over a shoebox-sized present all wrapped in gold and silver. I wasn't accustomed to getting gifts from my child, at least not ones that didn't involve construction paper, popsicle sticks, and glue.

"You didn't have to get me something, silly," I said. "It's your birthday, not mine."

"I know, but Quinn and me wanted to get you something special." More jumping. "Open it."

Quinn placed his hand on Noah's shoulder, the act of which calmed him right down. The gesture wasn't lost on me—the steady hand of a positive influence. What would that influence have looked like if Nick had been the one with his hand on Noah's shoulder all these years? If today was any indication, I'd dodged a bullet. I should thank Grandma Ledger for running interference. She'd saved me a lot of heartache.

Quinn settled his eyes on me, instantly understanding something was wrong and mouthing, 'You okay?'

I nodded, faking a smile as I removed the beautiful wrapping paper. Because of the size of the box, I had a strong suspicion that whatever was in there would wrap my feet in swagger. I glanced up at Quinn, my worried eyes instantly transforming when they settled on his proud face. He didn't have to buy me gifts to earn my favor. He'd won that on the first day.

There were no shoes in the box. In fact, the only thing inside was an even fancier wrapped smaller box.

"What's this?" I asked.

Noah, no longer able to jump with Quinn's hand on his shoulder, began to squirm instead. He couldn't be more excited for me. "Open it!"

My heart beat faster. It was jewelry, that much I knew for sure, but it couldn't be a ring, could it?

It wasn't.

Inside the box was the most beautiful diamond pendant necklace I'd ever laid eyes on.

"You guys," I said, my mouth agape.

"It's got a carrot in it," Noah said.

"Very nutritious," Quinn nodded before adding, "I'm not sure he fully understands it's not that kind of carrot."

"And there's a fiery heart inside too," Noah continued.

"It's a Hearts on Fire diamond," Quinn corrected.

"What's that?" I asked.

"I have no idea. The jeweler said it was the world's most perfectly cut diamond, but they all looked the same to us. Right, Noah?"

He nodded, aggressive in his agreement. "They were all so sparkly, Mom."

Never had I received a gift like this, and I wasn't sure even how to accept it. Or if I should. "Quinn, I can't..."

"It's not from me." He stopped me in my tracks.

"It's from *me*," Noah said, resuming his jumping.

Uh-huh. Like Noah had thousands of dollars lying around. But that look of sheer delight on his face laid siege to my heart.

"You deserve pretty things, Mom."

He'd said that before—to Quinn on the first night we were all together. That Quinn had remembered those words and allowed Noah to realize his wish said more about this man than anything he could ever say or do. It was the last barrier, the last question answered. Quinn would do anything for me and Noah.

I was unequivocally and desperately in love.

Tears flowed freely now as I gathered my son in my arms and squeezed. "I don't know what to even say, Noah. This is the most beautiful thing I've ever seen. You're the best son a mom could ever ask for."

I met Quinn's eyes and mouthed a 'Thank you.'

He smiled, nodding, perfectly content to allow Noah all the glory.

"Can you?" I asked, holding the box up to him.

He removed the delicate necklace and secured it around my neck before bending down and giving the skin it lay on one sweet and gentle kiss. "I can."

## 27

## QUINN: TESTOSTERONE

"You're going down," I said, revving my engine as I formed my fingers into a 'V,' pointing it first at my eyes and then back at his.

Jake, in the go-kart beside me, revved his own engine. "Whatever you say, cupcake."

"Like you two have a chance against me," Keith chuckled, his eyes glazed over from colicky baby insomnia. "I haven't slept in weeks. I've got nothing left to lose."

Noah's birthday bash created the perfect opportunity for a testosterone-filled day of fun not only for his little preadolescent friends but also for my big ones. The invitations to my brothers had gone out two weeks before, and I figured I might snag one or two VIP members of my clan, but I'd never considered the entire bunch would RSVP.

That my family embraced Jess and Noah, welcoming them in and respecting their place in my life with ease, made me reevaluate some of the lingering resentment I felt toward them. How many of the barriers I'd erected and the isolation I'd felt growing up had been of my own making? Somewhere along the way, I'd gotten it stuck in my head that I wasn't as loved and respected a member of my family as some of the others. But that had never been true. They'd always been there for me. Jess, she was the one who'd struggled for love. Not me.

"Please, you three don't have the balls to flip this shit over." Finn gripped his wheel, ready to rumble as his inner stuntman shone through. "But I sure as shit do."

"Sir, no flipping," the squeaky-voiced minimum-waged teenage girl warned. "It will get you banned from the go-kart track for life."

Finn's eyes widened. "For life? How do they keep track of that? Do they have go-kart mug shots?"

"Listen up," my father said from his vehicle all the way in the back. "Due to a possible fungal infection in my 'roast beef' toe, I'm going to take this race at my own pace. No one better touch my go-kart."

Jess's father, Victor, fresh out of rehab, had taken his spot in the go-kart beside my father. After a lifetime of living on the edge, he too was content to hang back and drive at his own speed. The man Jess remembered as a child had come back to her, albeit a more rugged and world-weary version, but Victor was actively trying to be an upstanding citizen, not only for himself but for the daughter and grandson who were counting on his sobriety.

The final drivers in the race were my nonbiological band brothers, Mike, Matty, and Brandon, who also hung in the back of the pack, but that was only because they were too intimidated by the company I kept to do anything else. Yet despite feeling out of place amongst my family, they'd come anyway. The four of us spent hours together every day preparing for our upcoming tour, and we'd grown close. There was nothing like having a shared dream to bind people together.

The flag rose. Our engines revved, and then Kyle yelled over it all, "I like how no one is even worried about me winning, you bunch of assholes."

The rest of us looked his direction, paused, then laughed. A second later, we were off.

Turned out we should've been worried about Kyle after all. He smoked us all, securing the winning time because he genuinely didn't care if he got banned for life from the go-kart place. And he nearly did, after repeatedly being reprimanded for ramming into any go-kart that dared to try to pass him. With Kyle wearing the crown and Jake pulling in right behind him, that put me solidly behind my brother once again.

But strangely enough, it didn't matter as much to me anymore. I didn't feel the same need to show Jake up as I once had, not with this hot, rockin' woman by my side giving me direction. Jess taught me humility and control. I could almost feel myself evolving into the man I could only have hoped to be.

Of course, my more relaxed view of sibling rivalry could also have had to do with the fact that I was killing it as frontman for Sketch Monsters. Our second single of the yet unreleased album was sitting high up on the music charts, playing footsie with Jake's newest tune. But I think the main reason I was suddenly okay with sliding into home plate behind my superstar brother was because I had a higher calling now, and his name was Noah.

Fatherhood had brought out the best in me. Yes, I knew Noah wasn't mine, but as he drifted off each night to the sound of my voice, I became ever more invested in his life. I wanted this boy to thrive, and to love and to be loved. I wanted to give him the security of knowing I was there for him and that he was important and safe.

Once upon a time, Jess had questioned my commitment to being a father figure for her son. No more. I'd proven I could be trusted, and even though I'd be taking off in a few weeks for the first Sketch Monsters tour, I knew there would always be a place for me to land. Because that was Jess. She held tight to the ones she loved.

~

The party wrapped up, the little guests were sent home with their goody bags, and all that remained was the cleanup. My brothers and Finn had stayed behind to help since we'd all decided to go grab a beer once we left.

We were nearly packed up when Jess dug her fingers into the waistband of my jeans and pulled me to her, pressing her lips to mine.

"Thank you," she whispered, her kiss lingering. "For making his dreams come true."

"Thank you for making mine."

She smiled at my saccharine response. "Now go. Have an awesome time with your brothers," she said. "You earned it."

"You sure it's okay? Noah won't be upset?"

"Are you kidding? He's on such a high after getting carried off the racetrack like a football star on the shoulders of like eight famous guys, I'm not sure he'll ever come down."

"He'll be a legend at school after that, for sure."

Jess's body went rigid in my arms. "Oh, god."

"What?"

"I'm sorry, Quinn. I should've told you," she replied, pulling away.

"Told me what?"

"Dad!" Noah screamed, breaking through my brothers and sprinting toward the taller of the two men. He flung himself into Nick's arms just as he'd done to me earlier. My chest splintered at the sight.

"He came when you and Noah were out," she hastily explained.

"He was at your apartment?"

I wasn't sure why that infuriated me, but it did. How dare he step foot into our space?

Jess put her hand on my chest. "Stay here. I'll take care of this."

She walked ahead. I followed. No way was I letting her go this alone. I understood now why she'd been acting strangely when Noah and I had come home with the necklace. She'd just had an encounter with *him*.

"This is a private party, Nick," Jess said.

"Tell that to the little man. You want your dad here, don't you, Noah?"

"Yes," Noah said, beside himself with joy.

"No. I'm sorry, Noah," she said. "But your dad is not allowed. There are rules..."

"That can surely be broken on his birthday. I brought you a present." Nick set Noah to the ground and handed him the gift.

"Jess, you remember Cody. I hear you've been breaking all the rules around him, haven't you?"

The way he said it, his eyes flashing suggestively, made it sound like something inappropriate was happening between the two. Jess ignited.

"Don't you dare!"

"Jesus. Chill. I was kidding," he said, aggressively rumpling Noah's hair as he spoke directly to him. "Your mom doesn't have any humor anymore, does she?"

It was the first time Noah seemed to understand more was at play. He looked to his mother.

I stepped beside her, grabbing her hand.

The other dude, Cody, perhaps trying to explain Nick's earlier remark, spoke up. "I work for the security company that patrols Goldfinch Road."

"Not anymore," I mumbled, my fist clenching.

My brothers made a tidy line behind Jess and me. Nick's eyes swept over them, appearing both irritated and impressed. "Well, shit. That's quite an entourage you've got there."

"Took years to assemble," I replied.

Nick scowled, reaching his hand out. "We haven't properly met. I'm Nick."

I had half a mind to slap his hand away but didn't want to make it awkward for Jess or Noah, so I shook it.

"And, hey. Thanks for helping out with my kid."

Helping out? I could feel my blood boiling. This douche hadn't paid child support in years. He didn't have the right to lump himself in with me.

Nick leaned in close, and the smell of alcohol permeated my senses. "And just so you know, I'm not here to scope out your girl. Trust me when I say she's safe with you."

Jess flashed me a warning with her eyes, leaving no question she wanted to handle this her way and for me to step aside.

"This isn't appropriate," Jess said, her voice strong and steely. "It's time to go."

Nick completely ignored her. "Go ahead, Noah. Open the gift."

"Can I, Mom?" Noah questioned, now painfully confused by the exchange happening between the adults in the room.

Nick issued the reply without ever looking Noah's way. His glare was on Jess. "You don't need to ask her. I'm your dad, and I say yes."

Jess was cornered, with only one way to answer if she didn't want to ruin Noah's day.

"Go ahead, bud," she relented. "And then your dad has to go."

"If *he* wants," Nick replied, so condescending.

"No," I stepped in, meeting his eye. "Not *if*. He leaves."

Poor Noah ripped open his gift in the middle of the show-down and hugged his dad for the Tech Deck set.

"I'm going to leave now, Noah. Your mom and her boyfriend aren't being real nice right now. But you were happy to see me, and that's all that matters, right?"

"Right," Noah replied, but he didn't sound sure of anything.

Father and son exchanged goodbyes, but before Nick left, he got one last word in. "I told you I wanted to see my son. No need for a formal invitation."

"Actually, there is. You only have supervised visitation rights."

"What more do you want?" he scoffed, his hand sweeping over the back row of my brothers. "It's supervised by half of fucking Hollywood."

"Nick, please don't swear," Jess replied calmly. "He's nine."

"Like he doesn't hear that shit coming out of your mouth. I know you, Jess. You're no angel. You might have him fooled, but you don't have me."

"I'd appreciate if you didn't speak to my girlfriend, and the mother of your child, that way."

Uneasy, Noah took a step toward Jess. She reached out and grabbed him, drawing him back to her and wrapping her arms around his chest protectively. My hand went over the both of them.

"Oh, you'd *appreciate* it, would you?" Nick stepped into me, his chest inches from mine. Another waft of the heavy scent of alcohol told me Nick wasn't in full control of his senses. "Well, I'd *appreciate* it if you took your hand off my kid."

The stress of the confrontation was too much for his mind to process, and Noah emitted a soft, whimpering sound. Jess hugged him tighter.

"Cody," she pleaded. "Please take him out of here before something happens that all of us will regret."

But there would be no regrets today, at least not on my end. My brothers stepped up, forming a line of defense. Any violence coming my way would also have to contend with my entourage.

Cody's eyes darted toward the door, making it clear he did not intend to throw himself on the sword for Nick like my brothers would do for me. He gripped Nick's arm and dragged him back. "Nick, come on."

I followed after them, making sure they found their way out. But Jess's ex wasn't ready to go. Ripping his arm out of Cody's grip, he stood his ground. "Noah, does Quinn scare you? Is that why you're crying? Come here, I'll protect you."

Clearly unsure what was expected of him, the boy looked to his mom and then to his father, dismay playing out over his face. It was a decision no child should ever have to make.

And, with tears trailing down his cheeks, Noah Ledger ran to me.

## 28

## JESS: THE DRILL

I climbed over the top of Quinn, his hard body sending a current through me. My hair fanned out like an upside-down umbrella as I arranged a series of kisses along his face.

"Is it morning already?" His voice was rough with sleep, but that didn't stop his barely awake fingers from sliding up my thigh. I wanted to be the first thing he touched every morning for the rest of his life. How lucky would that make me?

"It is," I said, sucking in my bottom lip as his hand moved up my sleep shirt and traced the swell of my breast.

"And you want me to leave," he said, knowing the drill well.

Every morning was the same thing. I set my alarm fifteen minutes earlier than Noah's, then tiptoed into the bathroom to do my business before brushing my teeth and fluffing my hair. I would then sneak back in and place kisses onto my sleeping prince.

And every morning, he slipped out the front door for his trip to the Starbucks on the corner, where he would chat up his coffee mistress for a while before returning to an empty apartment, or if it were a weekend, to a well-rested Noah who was none the wiser.

"I never *want* you to leave," I said, teasing him with the subtle swivel of my hips.

"How much time do we have?" he asked.

"Minutes."

"I can do it in sixty seconds," he bargained, grabbing his phone and setting the stopwatch.

I wrestled for his phone, snagging it out of his hand and holding it up.

"Look, woman." He swiped for the phone. "You're cutting into my performance time."

"As tempting as sixty-second sex sounds, you know the drill."

"I *know* the drill. I just don't *get* the drill. Noah knows what's going on. He's not dumb."

"He's nine, Quinn. He's a baby."

Quinn's brows rose.

"What?"

"Maybe I was an early adopter, but I was choking the chicken by the time I was his age."

"No you were not!" I gasped.

"Yes I was. Why do you think god made opposable thumbs, Jess?"

"To grip stuff, you perv!"

"Exactly." Quinn showed off his version of gripping 'stuff,' and it did not mesh with mine.

"All I'm saying is, I think Noah can handle me waking up here in the morning." Quinn sucked in a breath, hesitating. "Look, Jess, I didn't want to have to tell you this, but the other day when I was at Starbucks with Debbie... I had an espresso."

My eyes widened. "You didn't."

"I did. I'm not proud of it, but you forced my hand."

"How is this my fault?" I protested, struggling to fight back the giggle.

"Because you make me leave every morning. What do you

expect me to do, sip hot chocolate the rest of my life? I'm a man, Jess. I have needs."

I kissed his adorably sardonic lips before pushing him out of the bed. "Get."

"Fine." He rolled out of bed and headed for the bathroom. "But if Debbie forces a tall, non-fat latte with caramel drizzle and two percent foam on me, that's all on you!"

I knew he was kidding, but Quinn wasn't wrong in his desire to stay put in the morning. After what happened yesterday and the way he'd handled the situation with Nick, Quinn had proven his devotion to us. And Noah was clearly smitten or he wouldn't have chosen Quinn over his own father. So why keep up the charade? Maybe it was time to take the next step.

I pushed the bathroom door open and joined him at the sink, wrapping my arms around his waist and laying my head against his back. "I was thinking."

"I know what you were thinking," he said, wiping his face with the hand towel. "Two percent foam is just a jerk's order in sheep's clothing."

"No." I laughed. Good lord, I needed to save this boy from himself. "I was thinking... maybe you don't go."

He looked in the mirror. I peeked around the back of him to meet his eyes. He grasped my arm and brought me around to his side. "I'm listening."

"So, you know I implemented the exile rule at the beginning so Noah wouldn't get too attached in case you decided to leave, but..."

"After yesterday, that plan went all to hell," he finished for me.

I smiled. "Are you still gloating that he picked you?"

"I will always gloat about that."

I draped my arms over his shoulders. "Move in with me."

"Okay." No hesitation—it was like he was finalizing a pizza order.

"Okay?" I questioned. "It's a big step, Quinn. Don't you want to think about it for a minute?"

"I already live here except for the forty-five minutes a day in the wee hours of the morning where I have to sneak off for my coffee fix."

He had a point. "So, the answer is...?"

"Yes. Of course, Jess. You're my obsession. Why would I want to be anywhere else?"

"Exactly. Why would you?" I agreed, running my fingers up his back while pressing kisses to his chest.

He groaned. "I *wouldn't* want to, ever."

I tiptoed my fingers along his skin. "And I was thinking before you go off on tour, we should find another place to live. One with security. I don't want to be blindsided like I was yesterday when Nick showed up here unannounced. And your fans are also becoming a problem. They're starting to figure out where we live and knocking on the door."

"I'm all in with that, babe. I've been telling you for a while we needed to move. And if we get our own place, then your dad can have the freeway apartment all to himself without me ducking in every now and then for clothes."

I smiled, kissing his nose. "I like it. A solid plan, because god forbid we get rid of the freeway apartment. I'll start looking on the internet today."

"I'm still unsure about this morning. Do you want me to head over to Debbie?"

"Actually, I think it's about time the two of you broke up. Quinn, how would you like to have breakfast with Noah and me this morning?"

"I thought you'd never ask."

Quinn and I announced his live-in lover status that very morning, although in not quite as vulgar terms, by sneaking into a snoozing Noah's room, climbing onto his mattress, and jumping on his bed. If he was still traumatized by the events of yesterday, you wouldn't know it. Noah rose from a dead sleep to join us in a three-person bounce fest.

And when we made our way into the kitchen for breakfast, he never questioned Quinn's presence. Not once. Like, how many mornings had we wasted taking his feelings into consideration, when he couldn't care less? And to top it off, I'd made Quinn a raging caffeine addict for nothing.

When Noah got up to grab something out of the refrigerator, I reached over and cupped Quinn's cheek, feeling nothing but affection for this man.

"I love you."

His eyes held me steady. "I love you too."

Noah slid back into his chair, gripping the milk container, his head shifting from me to Quinn. And then, without a word, he poured the milk into his cereal.

Quinn was off to the studio early, as usual, and with Noah happily playing his video games, I took the opportunity to check apartment listings. I hadn't gotten far in the process when a text came in from Andrea.

*Have you checked social media, Jess?*

*No. Why?*

*You're trending.*

*You mean Quinn?*

*No. You.*

*Me. Why?*

*Nick. He posted all about your arrest. Says you're trying to trick Quinn into marriage. Says he's trying to warn the McKallister family before it's too late. I'm sorry to be the one to tell you but I thought you needed to know. Such a shitty thing for him to do.*

I dropped my phone and laid my head on the table, the fight beaten out of me.

Victory, once again, went to Nick.

## 29

# QUINN: ELEVENTH HOUR

"Brandon, how many days in a row have you worn that hat?" Matty asked.

During performances, Brandon went au natural, his bleached hair like porcupine quills. But during practice he was never without his black, green, and red Iron Maiden *Piece of Mind* cap.

"Don't be hating on my baseball cap. Nicko McBrain, baby," he said, pointing to the hat. "Only metal's greatest drummer. And if you disagree, I'll beat the bloody snot out of you."

Mike, knowing exactly what buttons to push, said. "What about Tommy..."

"No!" Brandon flicked a drumstick at him.

"Lee," Mike finished, getting the second drumstick catapulted at him.

"Let me tell you about Tommy Lee," Brandon said. "Think of it in terms of art. Tommy Lee is equivalent to the painter Thomas Kincaid. Nicko McBrain is Michel Frickin' Angelo."

"Who's that?" Mike asked.

"Michelangelo?" Brandon's forehead wrinkled. "The guy who painted the Sistine Chapel?"

Mike shrugged. "I've heard the name, but don't know who he is."

"Seriously? Quinn, please. Help me out here."

"Don't look at me, dude. I thought Michelangelo was a ninja turtle."

"Yes," Matty agree. "Me too."

"Guys." Tucker popped into the room. "Stop everything you're doing."

Since we weren't doing a damn thing, it was fairly easy to stop.

"What's up, Tucker?" I asked.

"Just got a call from the label," excitement lacing his words. "How would Sketch Monsters like to play The Basin?"

All four of our faces probably looked the same—stunned, excited, terrified.

"Hell yeah, we would," I blurted out, unsure how or why we'd been granted such privileges but not dumb enough to turn it down. The Basin was a large outdoor arena reserved for the biggest names. Sketch Monsters was not one of those names. "They're adding it to the tour?"

"No. Just one night. And you won't be headlining, you'll be opening—for Wylder."

"Opening?" I slid up in my seat. "Is that the right move?"

"Normally I'd say no, but this is a great opportunity. It's being filmed for a pay-per-view. They told me at least your last two songs will be on the recording, so we've got to save our best two for last."

"We're going to be on TV?" Matty asked.

"Well, *you* won't be," Brandon said. "The camera adds ten pounds of ugly. But the rest of us will be."

Tucker clapped once to focus our attention. "Hey! Listen up. There's just one catch, a rather large one. It's tonight. You go on at six p.m."

No way did I hear him correctly. "Tonight?"

"Yep. Not ideal, obviously. This is a last-minute changeup. The band that was supposed to perform woke up this morning spewing out both ends. Food poisoning, I'm told. Anyway, they're all too sick to play. The label knows you guys have been preparing for your own tour, so they're offering the gig to you first. It's a sold-out arena. It doesn't get much bigger than this. Are you in?"

There was no need to do a survey. Just by the hungry expressions on all our faces, I knew we'd be up on that stage tonight. "We're in."

"Quinn, can I talk to you for a second?" Tucker pulled me aside after all the details had been ironed out.

"What's up?"

"We've got a bit of an issue with Jess."

"With Jess?"

"Yes. Her ex is all over the internet accusing her of perpetrating a burglary. Says she was convicted of a felony. He's also alleging that Jess is scamming you... and your family."

I leaned back against the wall, speechless.

"Now look, I don't want to be insensitive in any way, but is it possible these allegations are true?"

"No. I mean, yes. She pled guilty to first-degree burglary in juvenile court like ten years ago. She was sentenced to detention, but her record was sealed when she turned eighteen. And, no, Tucker. Jess is absolutely not trying to scam my family."

"Okay. I know this is terrible timing, and I'm sorry this came out today. If you get a chance, let your family know what's happening before this gets out of hand."

"I will. I gotta go."

"Meet back here no later than two, Quinn. We'll do a run-through and then we'll head to the arena together. Don't be late."

"I won't."

He gripped my shoulder. "Hey, I'm sorry. Jess doesn't deserve this."

Just that Tucker took my side, took Jess's side, said so much about him.

"No. She doesn't."

~

Swinging the door open to the apartment, I called out to her. "Jess!"

I darted through the place and into the bedroom, where I found her lying facedown on the bed, Noah rubbing her back. I grabbed her and folded her into a hug. She was limp from crying.

"Hey, everything's fine."

"No, it's not. He ruined everything. Your family. They're going to hate me now. They think I'm a bad person."

"No, they don't."

Her face contorted in anger. "Please, Quinn. I'm not stupid. I know how this works."

Noah was watching and hearing everything, his head turning from side to side as if he were watching a tennis match.

"Hey, kid," I said, pointing him toward the door. "Why don't you go watch TV?"

His forehead was wrinkled with worry. "Mom didn't mean it, Quinn. She's really sorry. Please don't leave her. Please don't leave me."

I disengaged from Jess to deal with Noah. Grabbing him to

me and hugging him tight, I whispered into his ear, "I'm never leaving you or your mom. That's a promise."

Noah's tension unraveled before my eyes. He kissed my cheek. "I love you."

My heart melted at his words. "I love you too. Now go watch TV. I've got to turn your mom's frown upside down."

"Okay," he said heading for the door before turning back and kissing his mom's cheek. "It's okay, Mom. Quinn will make it better."

Once he was gone, she said, "I don't know how to fix this."

"I do. We don't."

"What do you mean, we don't?"

"We don't fix it. Do you really think this is the first time we've dealt with stuff like this? I called my parents on the way over here and told them what happened when you were a teenager. They're one hundred percent behind you. No one is blaming you. This kind of thing happens when you're famous. People make shit up all the time."

"But you don't think I'm trying to scam you or steal from you, do you?"

"Jess, don't even ask me that. Of course I don't."

"What did your mother say—really?"

"She asked about the burglary and about your situation growing up. My mother volunteers with foster kids, Jess. She sympathizes with the plight of at-risk teens."

"There's a difference between sympathizing with at-risk teens and being okay with her youngest son dating a former one."

"Grace dated a foster kid. She met him volunteering at the same place my mom works."

"And your mom was okay with that?" Jess asked, more than a little surprised.

"I mean, Grace was seventeen when she started dating Rory,

so my mom could have stopped it if she'd wanted to. They dated almost a year. My point is, Jess, you came to the right family."

Her forehead creased. "What does that mean?"

I tipped her chin up and kissed the worry lines in her forehead. "It means the McKallister family believes in redemption."

## 30

# JESS: I'M WITH THE BAND

I originally wanted to pass on the concert when Quinn sprang it on me, but I knew he wanted and needed me there. How could I deny him? Besides, this was a huge moment for Sketch Monsters. They'd been existing on the periphery, dropping singles while they waited to release their album, so this exposure would be huge for them—game changing. I wanted to be there to watch them take flight.

"Oh. My. God."

Grace perfectly articulated the narrative in my head as we drove past hordes of music fans lined up for entry into the stadium. Granted, most of these people were here for Wylder, but all of them would hear Sketch Monsters play, and I had no doubt they'd be wowed. "I hope Quinn is ready for this."

Again, my sentiments exactly. Grace and I were scarily on the same wavelength when it same to our shared favorite guy.

"Watch him choke. Get up there, open his mouth, and be like uh... uh... uh," Elliott replied, cracking himself up.

Okay. Apparently there was one person who wasn't on our wavelength: Elliott. Both Grace and I reacted with similar open-mouthed horror. He glanced between us, his smile quickly fading as he realized his mistake. Elliott should've known better. He'd been in the family longer than I had. Surely he knew the McKallisters were fiercely protective of their own, and that even sweet, easygoing Grace would morph into Buffy The Vampire Slayer if you threatened her coven.

Grace was slow to respond, like water receding in a tsunami seconds before the first wave hit.

"Why would you say that?"

"It was a joke, Grace."

"Is my family a joke to you?"

I flattened myself against the door, trying to make my physical presence as tiny and insignificant as possible in hopes I would not be dragged into the impending tidal wave.

"Of course not. I've got nothing but respect for your family."

Grace remained silent, peering out the window.

"Hey," Elliott said, stroking her arm. "It was a stupid thing to say. I'm sorry. Please forgive me."

And she did—but only in words. Her posture and subdued mood were indication enough that she hadn't forgiven him in her heart, and we girls all knew, that's where it really counted.

"Do you know where our seats are?" I asked.

"There's a friends and family section along the edge of the stage. Not that we'll need many of them."

Grace was referring to the lack of familiar faces that would be in attendance tonight. Per Quinn's request, she was the only McKallister invited. It wasn't a diss in any way, but rather a form of self-preservation. Quinn was worried his nerves would get the best of him, so he'd asked the others not to come. But Grace was different. I didn't really understand the dynamics of their relationship, only that whatever they'd gone through together as kids had solidified their bond into adulthood. He needed her here tonight as much as he needed me.

Plus, not gonna lie, the fact that the rest of the clan would not be in attendance was another reason why I decided to come. Regardless of what Quinn thought his family's reaction would be toward me, I remained cautiously on edge. Grace and I had yet to speak of the matter, and I hoped to get her take on things later tonight.

"I have explicit instructions from the man himself to bring you backstage," Grace said. "So you can give him a good luck kiss."

"Explicit instructions, huh?"

Grace shrugged. "That's what he said."

"Okay, well, am I even allowed?" I asked, unsure what the protocol was. I'd been to concerts before, but never backstage, and certainly never as the front man's girl.

"Jess, you can go anywhere." She tugged on my lanyard. "You're with the band."

Grace lived those words. She was always with the band. See, the difference between her and me was that she'd grown up going to Jake's concerts, so the almighty 'backstage' meant nothing to her. I wasn't even sure Grace realized how rare a life she led. I watched in wonder as she glided confidently through the narrowed halls, sidestepping equipment containers and chatting up tattooed roadies. Elliott and I, not having been fed a steady diet of cool growing up, followed behind, demurely watching her show.

She pushed open a door that looked as if it should've remained shut. But on the other side, standing in a circle with the other members of Sketch Monsters, was Quinn.

He looked up, smiled, and held a finger up to me.

"What's going on?" I whispered to Grace.

Grace tracked Elliott to the drink table, and once determining he was out of earshot, replied, "Probably praying they don't choke on stage—uh... uh... uh."

I couldn't help but laugh at her imitation of Elliott's diss.

"I think he suffers more from tone-deaf boy syndrome than the full-on asshole disease."

"I know," she said, slumping her shoulders. "I'm extra snappy with him. Poor Elliott. In England, at school living a simple life, he was the perfect guy. But back here, with my family... Things are weird. I don't know. I'm trying to figure it out."

"Are you thinking of br...?"

"There he is," Grace cut me off with a smile and a warning stare.

Ever the gentleman, Elliott handed us waters. "Here you go, ladies."

Quinn joined us, looking relaxed and ready. He gave his sister a hug and greeted Elliott before taking my hand and leading me away.

"I am lovin' those tight black pants," I said, allowing my fingers to discreetly roam over his backside. "You look so good it almost makes me want to start the stopwatch."

He cringed. "I can't believe I gave myself only sixty seconds."

"You couldn't have done it."

"If I was fifteen, I definitely could've done it."

My hand resting on his ass, I asked, "Did you get the hotel?"

"Oh, I got the hotel," he replied suggestively. "Did you drop the kid off?"

"Oh, I dropped the kid off," I mimicked. "On the car ride over, he was all whiny—*I want to go to the concert.* But then I pulled up to Casey and Jake's massive house, and Miles took him around back. One look at the three-story pirate ship play structure and it was all over. He wouldn't even look at me. Didn't get so much as a 'Bye, Mom.' So, yes, I think he'll be just fine."

"That's more than I can say. I'm performing in front of eighteen thousand people—most of who did *not* come to see me play. This has all the makings of disaster."

"So why do you look so calm?"

He shrugged. "Can't fail if you don't try."

"I think the word you're looking for is *succeed*."

"No." His smile spread wide. "I stand by my version."

"Okay, then." God, how I loved everything about this guy. I could easily see a future with him. If only I could keep my past from getting in the way.

Tucker arrived at the door. "Five minutes, guys, then we're heading to the stage. Anyone need anything?"

"Yeah," Brandon called out. "How's it coming with those anal beads you promised me?"

"Brandon, I've got my kid with me," he said, gesturing to the teenage boy beside him. "Can I get anyone anything that doesn't go in your assholes?"

"I didn't know you had another son," Quinn said. "You've been holding out on us, Tucker."

"Or... could it be that none of you give a shit that I have a life beyond the four of you?"

The Sketch Monster boys exchanged looks and replied in unison, "Nah."

Tucker rolled his eyes. "Everyone, this is Evan. Evan, these are the guys I told you to stay far away from."

Evan had no fear. With his messy black hair, bright-blue eyes, and a vintage rocker wardrobe to die for, he was the epitome of cool teenage confidence. "Actually, I believe your exact words were—'This is the best group of guys I've ever worked with.'"

"I said no such thing. Someone please shut him up."

Grace tugged on my arm. "We better get to our seats before the stadium goes dark and we have to stumble over people."

"Hold up," Quinn said. "She still needs to wish me luck."

He swished me into his arms and dipped me back. His lips pressed into mine, first soft, then insistent, and finally aggressively sucking on them as his tongue circled around mine. I sank into the kiss, reflexively moaning, completely oblivious to the helpless onlookers.

"Is anyone else as uncomfortable as me right now?" Mike asked, raising his hand. "Anyone?"

"I don't like it all that much," Matty admitted. "But only because it makes me look so bad."

"Okay." Tucker grabbed the back of Quinn's shirt and pulled him away. "Fun's over. Let's go."

Once he was gone, I followed Grace out the door, unconsciously trailing my finger along my swollen lips, smiling. If only I could wish him luck all day long.

From the darkness, a single spotlight rolled over the stage, and all that could be heard was the low, rolling beat of the drums, soft at first, then growing with intensity until I could feel it in my throat.

The spotlights stirred, the stage was lit, and Sketch Monsters came bursting to life. I wasn't sure anyone in the stands was prepared to be rocked the way those four boys shook the stage. Song after song, each one better than the last until it was all brought to a screeching halt. Sketch Monsters had arrived at their showcase song—Grace's breathtaking ballad, "Promises."

This would be the first time she'd hear it put to music and played live, and I could feel both her excitement and apprehension. She needn't worry. Grace's song was always going to be the shining star of the show, and somehow the crowd knew it. Phone flashlights rose to the skies as Quinn stood in a single spotlight with only the strum of his guitar and the hypnotic melancholy of his voice, prompting the listener to want to break from the pack and go save him.

Gradually the tempo increased as Quinn was joined first by Brandon on the drums and then Mike on the bass, and finally by Matty on the guitar, where he made those strings scream until they reached a soaring crescendo. And then suddenly nothing: empty air until Quinn's voice rose from the shadows and he sang the song's final, sorrowful notes.

So mesmerized was I by the performance, I hadn't felt Grace gripping my arm until the audience erupted in applause.

"Did he just..." Grace couldn't even form the words necessary to express what had happened on stage. It was a masterpiece, pure and simple, a song with the capacity to live on. This was why Quinn had wanted her here: to witness the moment their song took its first breath.

"I don't know what he just did, but it was amazing," I yelled over the melee.

From his place on the stage, Quinn sought me out. Sought Grace out. He placed a hand to his chest, then pointed her way. A tear rolled down Grace's cheek. Whatever meaning she'd placed on Quinn's gesture was enough for her to seek my shoulder to cry on... not Elliott's. The moment did not go unnoticed. Elliott looked on, troubled.

Quinn launched into their final song, a rock anthem that would bring the hearts he'd just broken back to life. I watched, amazed, as he expertly controlled the crowd. This wasn't something that could be learned. You had it or you didn't. And Quinn had it. The day we met, I'd suspected he'd be a star, but actually being here to watch it happen went beyond my wildest dreams.

As excitement mounted, the crowd surged. Screams filled the night sky. The popping sounds. The music. The confusion. The panic.

"Jess," Grace cried. "*Jess!*"

∼

Sketch Monsters would go down in history—just not as they had planned. See, while it was true that, after tonight, no one would ever forget their name, these four deserving guys would never get their moment of glory.

They would never get their triumphant bow.

What the band didn't know, what I didn't know, what most of the eighteen thousand people in the stadium didn't know, was that the first shots had already been fired.

## 31

## QUINN: RUN FOR COVER

I 'd dreamed of this. But that was all it had ever been—a dream. Tonight, on this stage, the guys and I had come together like an industrial-sized magnet, sucking everything into our core. Life was about to change for us. I could feel it.

The beat dropped at a spot in the song it wasn't supposed to drop. No, it didn't just drop; it stopped. I looked back to Brandon for answers just as an unknown force slammed into my shoulder. I stumbled, falling backward onto the stage.

It was only then I heard the pop of gunshots. And the screaming.

I lay there for a second, the breath knocked out of me, as I tried to clear my head. What was happening? Everything was moving in slow motion, like an illusion. I stared up at the ceiling. Wait, no ceiling. I was outside—on my back. On the stage. I looked down at my body, wondering why it refused to move. At my guitar, her elegant white wood splattered in blood. Wait, whose blood? And why did it suddenly feel like a brick was lying upon my chest?

I pulled Lucia over my head, discarding her unexpected weight. Turning my head, I looked back for my bandmates. No one was standing. Or lying down. I didn't see anyone at all. My head spun, trying to comprehend. Jess. Grace. My eyes shot open. Full clarity. *Jess! Grace!* I flipped to my stomach, staying low, crawling. My only thought was getting to them, protecting them. Arriving at the edge of the stage, I swung my legs over and landed in a heap onto a pile of overturned chairs, pain searing as I rolled to the ground from there. It occurred to me then that these had been Jess's and Grace's chairs. And Elliott's.

Where had they gone? The gunshots continued, but I no longer cared. I had to get to them. Willing my limbs to work, I hauled my heavy body off the floor and went in search of the woman I loved and the sister I'd promised my whole life to keep safe. If I failed now, what would it all have been for? I grew stronger. Steadier in my gait. My breath started coming back to me in waves.

Only a minute ago, this area had been packed with bodies, and now it was largely empty. Where had everyone gone? It was then I saw movement on the ground. The area wasn't empty at all. Upon closer investigation, there were hundreds, maybe thousands of people crouched under chairs, behind trash bins. And some—the unluckier ones—cowered in the open with nowhere else to go. Jess and Grace were somewhere in here. Strength in numbers, I hoped.

And then as quickly as it had started, the shooting stopped. All that could be heard throughout the arena now were screams. Had the gunman left? Was he reloading? Maybe he'd killed himself. Or maybe he was lurking somewhere, methodically searching for fresh victims or trails of blood to finish off the unlucky. Was I one of those?

Something familiar caught my eye—long, shiny black hair and the intimate curve of a back I knew all too well. Jess. She was turned away from me, motionless. On the floor. Under a chair. I sucked in a breath, wanting to scream her name. But I remained silent because I knew if I called her name and she responded, I'd put a target on her back. I dropped to one knee, fearing the worst.

"Jess?" I whispered, my hand shaky as I gently touched her.

She jerked, her head twisting, and upon seeing me, her body swiftly followed. She clutched me, touching my face, my ears, my neck.

"I thought you were dead." She gasped for breath through the tears. "I saw you go down."

Now it was my turn to grab her face, checking for injuries. "I'm here. You're not hurt, are you?"

"No."

"Where's my sister?" I asked.

"She's here," Elliott said, in a low, unsteady voice. "She's safe."

I looked under the chairs to see him shielding Grace's body with his own. I would never make fun of this napping hero again.

"Grace, no." Elliott tried holding onto her, keeping her safe, but Grace crawled out from under him, silent, and crept toward me. I could see the trauma in her eyes. I hadn't been able to protect her from this. Such a fail. I opened my arms to her and she sank into me, sobbing.

"You're okay," I said, smoothing her hair as I muffled her cries. "Shhh, Grace. We don't know where he is."

Elliott followed her out from under the chairs, again shielding her as he scanned the area for impending danger. And so he should. We were sitting ducks. Jesus, what were we doing huddling here in the wide open?

I passed Grace off to Elliott, trusting in him—not an easy thing for me to do.

"Quinn," he said, his eyes widening as he pointed to my shoulder.

It was then I saw that Grace was covered in my blood. Grabbing the back of a chair, I hoisted myself back up to my feet. Something was wrong. I knew it now. My black shirt disguised the blood somewhat, but it was there and spreading.

Jess bolted to her feet, her fingers grazing over the hole in the fabric of the shirt. "Oh, god. You *were* hit."

I flinched at her slightest touch, dots of black invading my vision. She jerked her hand back, her fingers tinted red.

Grace's head jerked up, newfound purpose erasing her fear. "We have to get you to a hospital."

"It's in my shoulder. I'll be fine."

But *was* it in my shoulder? It seemed lower than that, but what did I know? I'd never been shot before, nor had I ever paid much attention to human anatomy.

"It's not fine." She grabbed my right hand and pulled me. "Let's go."

"No," I said, turning her the other direction. The front, where the exits were and where Grace wanted to go, seemed the logical choice, but it was too far to travel. "Not that way. I know where a closer exit is."

As soon as I said that, chairs began to move as others crawled out from their hiding places and followed us. Handfuls of concertgoers, hearing my claim of an exit, my promise of safety, put their faith in me. I looked back to find scores of people trailing behind. I moved my crowd toward the back of the stadium, keeping them low and hugging the stage I'd been performing on only minutes earlier. Somewhere, toward the back of the long wooden platform, was a hatch door with no handle from the outside. It was used by the arena for emergency situations—a way to get security guards out into the crowd quickly. I was banking on the fact that they'd done just this and that the hatch door would now be open.

"Quinn." I looked up when I heard my name quietly called,

and saw him, his head poking out of the hatch door. Evan. He'd found the exit for me. "Over here."

Evan swung the door open wider as we neared.

"Where's Tucker?" I asked as my group began streaming through the exit.

"Looking for you. He ran out onto the stage, into the gunshots." The horror of the words he'd just spoken hit him hard. I was here; his father was not.

"Listen to me." I grasped his shirt and pulled him close. "I need you to lead this group out the exit doors in the back. Find someplace safe for them. Jess won't be happy. Tell her I'll be right back."

"What are you going to do?"

"Find your dad."

He nodded, in no position to resist.

I backed away from the door, pushing Jess through the opening and, as she was swallowed up by the others escaping, she grabbed for my hand. I didn't take it.

"No. No, Quinn."

"I'm coming after I get everyone in. Go."

Her objections could be heard even after Grace and Elliott and a flood of other bodies pushed her forward. I prayed Evan was doing his job and dragging her away. More people crammed through the door on the side of the stage, hopefully on their way out of the stadium and headed toward safety. But me? I walked away from that.

I didn't know what it was or why I had to go back, but I just did. Instinctively, I knew he'd been shot, that he needed help, that I wouldn't be able to live with myself if I let him die. The only positive to searching for Tucker was I knew exactly where he'd gone. To the stage, looking for me. And that was where I found him, bleeding out from a bullet wound to the leg. He'd managed to drag himself behind one of the amps and had carved out a nice little hiding spot for himself. Resourceful Tucker had already fashioned a tourniquet out of his belt by the time I arrived.

And I eyed another favorite accessory of his. "Good god, Tucker, tell me that's not your handkerchief?"

He'd tied it around the wound, stemming the flow of blood.

"As it turns out, I have everything I need to survive a gunshot wound except an extra leg to walk on." His eyes settled on my chest and his face twisted. "Oh, dammit, Quinn. What are you doing here? You've got to get to an ambulance. I'll be fine. Go."

"I'm going now. With you," I said, scanning the stage. "Do you know what happened to the guys?"

"Mike and Matty ducked out of the right side of the stage where I was standing. I didn't see Brandon, but I assume he went left. I saw you go down and was trying to get to you, but then this happened." Tucker grabbed my arm. "Did you see Evan?"

"Yes. Under the stage. He's fine."

Tucker exhaled, relieved. "That's where I told him to go."

"Yeah, well, he saved a lot of people opening that door under the stage. He has Jess and Grace."

"Smart kid, that one."

"He is. You did a good job with him, Tucker."

"Considering."

I wasn't sure what he meant by that but didn't have time to ponder. Even though the shooting had stopped several minutes ago, the situation still seemed unstable, like it could explode at any moment. With great effort, I wrapped my arm around Tucker and lifted him up onto his one good foot and together we hobbled backstage—where no one was left but us.

We made it out the back exits only to be met with chaos: eighteen thousand concertgoers trying to escape. Cops were already there, moving people away from the arena, but it was still too early in the disaster to have triage stations set up or safe areas to huddle. You just had to keep moving and hope you survived.

We were moving for a good ten minutes when we heard a familiar voice.

"Tucker!" Evan called out, breathless and red-faced. Clearly he'd been running around the backlot searching for us. His eyes zeroed in on his father's leg before he walked up to Tucker and threw an arm around him, hugging him tight.

"Jess? Grace?" I asked.

"Both fine, but dude, you've got some groveling to do. Jess is *not* happy with you... at all. Maybe chocolates might help. She thought you were following right behind. It took everything I had to keep her and Grace from going back."

I nodded, and the motion set my head swirling. I stumbled.

"Evan, help me get him to the curb."

"No. I want to get to Jess. I'm good. Let's go."

Tucker tried to get me to sit down, even suggesting Evan run ahead to get help, but my focus was on getting to Jess and Grace, and so I pushed through. The walk stole my breath, forcing me to stop several times along the way as each step became more strenuous. The adrenalin that had been pumping through me since finding the girls began to wane, and the heaviness returned. So did the pain.

When we finally arrived at the outcrop building, I had to lean against the doorframe, so light-headed now that I could almost feel myself fading away. Evan knocked and identified himself. The door swung open, and out came the girls. Hands were on me, guiding me in. The black dots swarming my eyes returned, and I had trouble focusing on what was happening around me. I was lowered onto a chair.

Jess's hands were on my face, her focus solely on me. "He's clammy. His skin's so pale. Someone hand me a water bottle."

I could hear her talking, but the change in altitude from standing to sitting caused my head to revolve like a Tilt-a-Whirl.

Grace crowded me from the other side, pulling down my collar in rescue mode. At least she'd found her strength again, I thought. She was going to need it for what was to come. "Is it the shoulder? I can't tell."

Elliott didn't wait to find out, instead ripping the material clean in half to reveal my bare, bloody skin.

"It's not in the shoulder," Grace said. I could almost taste her fear. "Where's the ambulance? Why aren't they here yet?"

I must have closed my eyes for a second because Jess was slapping me awake. "Quinn? Hey. Stay with me. Don't you dare go anywhere."

"I won't."

And then I was gone.

When I opened my eyes, I was flat on my back, with both Jess and Grace inches from my face. They were talking to me, asking me questions, but their voices sounded so far away. Both girls looked as if they'd been dipped in blood. It was on their hands, their faces, their hair, their clothes. I blinked, trying to remember who was injured.

Lifting a heavy hand, I touched a finger to Jess's cheek.

"It's not mine," she said, instantly understanding my concern. "You've been shot, Quinn. You've lost a lot of blood. Help is on the way."

I tried to sit up but was pushed back down by what seemed like a hundred hands. "Don't move. Everything's going to be fine."

That wasn't what it sounded like. Jess looked horrified. Grace looked worse. Even sedate Elliott looked panic-stricken. Was this really it? Was this really how I was going to die?

I grabbed Jess's hand. "Kiss me."

"Quinn, I don't think that's..." She met my eye. Whatever she saw stopped her protest. Sweeping her hair to one side, Jess pressed shallow kisses to my lips.

"My heart hurts."

Tears flooded her eyes. "I know, babe. Hang in there."

My eyes closed. She slapped my face. I opened my eyes.

"Hey. I love you," she said through more kissing sobs. "So much. You're going to fight for me, right?"

There was so much I wanted to say but didn't have the breath for. "Yes."

"For me and Noah. For us. You're going to fight for us."

"For us," I agreed, struggling to keep my eyes open as I slid my thumb over her blood-tainted lips. So beautiful. "Marry me."

A sad smile formed. "Quinn, you can't ask me that now."

Drawing whatever air I could into my lungs, I repeated, "Marry me, Jess."

I didn't get my answer because seconds after it was asked, the EMTs arrived, instructing everyone to back away as they assessed the damage and came up with a hasty plan to keep me alive. Jess stepped back but positioned herself in my line of sight. Our eyes held, and the love in hers soothed me.

She never looked away, even as I was lifted onto the stretcher and wheeled to the ambulance. And just as the doors were shutting, I implored her with my eyes. I needed an answer.

"Yes," she called to me. "I will marry you."

Now I had a reason to fight.

## 32

## JESS: THE TRUTH

Michelle's scream still reverberated through my ears. I could hear it through Grace's phone, out of the receiver, across the room. It was the call every mother dreaded. No preparation. Those moments of panic and fear. Your child injured. Maybe dying. There was no information—and nothing, nothing you could do. My own terror took a backseat to hers as I imagined what it had to be like to get that call *more than once.* Michelle had. And now began her agonizing wait.

By the time Grace, Elliott, Evan, and I were cleared to leave the area by police, the McKallisters had already begun arriving at the hospital. Grace had been in constant contact with Michelle, making her first call to her mother while we were in the outbuilding after running from the venue. Michelle knew every detail we did, but hearing what had happened over the phone was not the same as seeing the bloody evidence on our war-torn bodies when the four of us arrived in the waiting room. Michelle, and everyone else who loved Quinn, broke down.

It took three very long and very tense hours to get word on Quinn's fate. He'd survived the surgery, we'd been told, but just barely. This was no hero shot to the shoulder, as Quinn had suggested. Instead, he'd taken a direct hit to the chest. According to the surgeons who opened him up minutes after he arrived at the hospital, the bullet had narrowly missed his heart as it traveled through bone and muscle, lacerating a series of blood vessels before lodging in his lung.

Slowly he bled, compressing the lung from the outside, causing shortness of breath and the compounding of blood loss. The slow drip explained how he'd been able to move around for so long without collapsing and how he'd managed to get me and Grace and Elliott and possibly hundreds of others out of the arena before passing out on that chair in the outbuilding. It even somewhat explained how he'd had the strength to stay on his feet while saving Tucker, only to come back and hastily ask for my hand in marriage.

The proposal. Tears welled. Even him popping the question tonight was no cause for celebration. In fact, Quinn's proposal nearly broke my heart. It was honest; that much I knew, but it was desperate, too. It felt like he was grasping for a life jacket seconds before his head submerged under the waves. Quinn didn't really want to marry me. He just wanted to live.

Upon hearing my silent cries, Evan lifted his head off the bench where he'd been sleeping beside me. Ever since his father had followed Quinn to the hospital in his own ambulance, the teenager hadn't left my side. For all his confidence, Evan was still a kid... and a scared one at that. He swung his body up into a sitting position and rested his shoulder against mine.

"He's going to be okay, Jess."

I nodded, clinging to his optimism. Thank god for Evan, another outsider to lean on. Because for all the McKallisters' kindness and support, they didn't belong to me. They belonged to Quinn, and if he didn't pull through, this waiting room might be the last place I ever saw them. A wave of emotion overwhelmed me when I tried to imagine life without Quinn.

*Enough with the negative thoughts.*

"Distract me," I said.

Evan's eyes rose to the ceiling as he searched his brain for something worthy of my request. "Okay. Sometimes when I eat Doritos, I check to see what side has more flavor, and I lay that side facedown on my tongue."

Distraction complete. I chuckled. "What's wrong with you?"

"Hey, you asked." He grinned. "Your turn."

"I separate my M&M's and eat my least favorite color first. And then second to last. You get the idea."

He didn't even let me finish before replying, "Psycho."

See, I was already feeling more positive. Good for Evan.

"Okay, here's a good one," he said, lowering his voice. "Tucker's not really my father... not Bodhi's, either. And I don't know what I'm going to do if he doesn't make it."

I knew nothing about this boy, but I felt an overwhelming kinship to him after what we'd been through together. "Hey. Tucker would never let a bullet wound slow him down."

Evan nodded, clearly not convinced but still allowing my words to soothe.

"Is he your stepdad?" I asked.

There was no emotion in his curt laugh. "No, that would require a mother."

"So, who is Tucker to you, then?"

There was a long pause as Evan considered his response.

"The only person who ever cared."

Evan and I never got to finish the conversation because seconds after his confession, a doctor came for him, delivering the news of Tucker's successful surgery and whisking him away to his not-father's room.

But for the rest of us, there would be no whisking away— at least not yet. Quinn's condition was precarious enough that Michelle and Scott had been summoned to the Cardiothoracic ICU hours earlier, their infrequent texts our only connection to the man we all loved.

To their immense credit, the McKallister siblings, led by openhearted Grace, had not left me hanging. Despite what they'd all surely heard about me in the earlier hours of the day, none of them seemed to hold it against me. They welcomed me into their bubble, held my hand, comforted me when I cried. If I only took one thing out of this horrible experience, it would be an understanding of the humanity of this family, who despite their own vast sufferings, had found it in their hearts to tend to mine.

Michelle and Scott arrived back in the waiting room hours later, looking exhausted but relieved. They had the news we'd all been waiting for.

"Quinn has stabilized," Michelle announced. "The surgeons think he's going to make a full recovery."

The cheers that erupted could surely be heard from the street below.

"And get this." Scott's pride shone through. "He's awake and talking."

"Of course he's talking," Jake said, the relief evident on his tired face. "When does Quinn not get the last word?"

Hours passed. As we waited for updates on Quinn's continued recovery, answers began trickling in about the shooting. Names. Faces. The victims. The shooter. But the thing I clung to—what I took some bizarre solace in—was the fact that Quinn and Sketch Monsters had not been specifically targeted. They'd just had the extraordinary misfortune of being in the wrong place at the very worst time.

"I hear you're engaged," Michelle said, sliding into the chair beside me.

The half-hearted smile I offered up fooled no one. "Don't worry. I won't hold him to it."

"I hope you do."

I couldn't keep my jaw from dropping. She *approved* of Quinn's deathbed proposal?

"Is that so hard for you to believe?" she asked.

"A little," I admitted. "Especially after what my ex unleashed on the internet. It's hard to believe that you would be okay with your youngest son dating a single mom with a less-than-stellar past."

Michelle was slow with her response. "You know, I once fell for a single father with a less-than-stellar past. Star-crossed lovers, I guess you could say. I was from a very wealthy and connected family. Scott was not. I'd never known anyone like him. He was unrefined, vulgar, funny... everything I wasn't. Everything my family wasn't. Yet he was real and raw and exciting. I fell so hard. My parents—not so much. They fought our love every step of the way. Not only did they hate that he had a baby son, but also they didn't think Scott was smart enough, rich enough, or connected enough to provide for me. Without going into detail, it got very ugly, and I was forced to make a choice no one should ever have to make."

"Your heart or your family," I guessed.

She nodded, glancing around the room. "I chose my heart and then built myself a new family. I've never regretted it. In fact, I pity my parents. Think of all these wonderful kids they lost out on knowing. And for what? I swore I would never do that to my own children. Quinn loves you. He loves Noah. I've seen such a change in him. With you, he doesn't seem lost anymore. You make him happy, and that, in turn, makes me happy. So, when I say I hope you hold him to his proposal, Jess, those aren't empty words."

Stunned by her honesty, I whispered, "Thank you, Michelle. You don't know how much that means to me."

She smiled and then nudged me. "Quinn wants to see you."

My head shot up. "Really?"

"Really. And guess what the first word out of his mouth was?"

"If you say Debbie, I'm going to cry."

"Who?"

"No. Nothing. Just an inside joke between Quinn and me," I said, allowing excitement to creep in until realization hit. "Wait —isn't the ICU for immediate family only?"

"That's right. Scott and I let the staff know you're his fiancée. They're expecting you."

I jumped to my feet, feeling reinvigorated.

"Jess." Michelle grabbed my wrist, her eyes misting over. "Quinn doesn't know yet. So if he asks about the shooting, be cautious."

I paused, flickers of panic gripping me. "He doesn't know?" I whispered.

She shook her head.

"When will you tell him?"

"I don't know. We just don't want anything to stress him."

"What if he asks me? Michelle, I can't lie to him."

She considered my dilemma, no doubt comparing it to her own. "If you can sidestep the question, that's preferred, but I trust you to do what you feel is right. I suspect you know him better than any of us nowadays, so maybe the truth needs to come from you... when *you* think he's ready."

～

I considered Michelle's words as I stood outside the unit, waiting for the go-ahead to see Quinn.

*Maybe the truth needs to come from you.*

The truth?

My stomach churned.

The truth was that nine people perished in the shooting before security guards wrestled the man down. Fifteen more were wounded, and scores were injured trying to escape.

The truth was the gunman worked for the arena. He'd had a grudge and a death wish and a desire to take as many with him as he could.

The truth was Wylder had been the target of the night, not Sketch Monsters, and it wasn't anything Wylder had done wrong either. They'd been marked for death simply because they were the headliners on the very night the gunman had decided to die.

The truth was the perpetrator only opened fire upon Sketch Monsters because he'd been spotted with a suspicious bag and security was moving in.

And the truth—the big horrible, terrible truth that Michelle did not want Quinn to know, but that I'd now been tasked to tell —was that not every member of Sketch Monsters had survived.

Quinn slowly opened his eyes, focusing on me.

"Hey, babe," I said, stroking the back of his hand.

He didn't speak, just blinked.

I leaned in to place a light kiss to his cheek. "I love you so much. I was so scared."

"Who are you?"

I took a step back, shocked speechless. He didn't know who I was? How could that be? His mom said he'd wanted to see me, that the first word out of his mouth had been *Jess*.

"You don't remember?" I asked.

He blinked, no recollection in his gaze.

"I'm Jess. I'm your girlfriend."

"No, you're not."

"Yes, I am. We live together. I have a son. His name is Noah."

"You're not my girlfriend," he replied, his voice stronger and more determined now.

I stood my ground. "Yes, Quinn, I am."

"No, Jess, you're not. You're my fiancée." A grin broke across his lips.

I grabbed hold of the guardrail, my mouth agape.

Oh. My. God.

"You dick monster!" I said, the smile now racing across my own face as I smacked him—literally smacked the arm of a man who'd just been shot. "I cannot believe you just did that to me."

"I was just trying to lighten the mood."

"Well, you managed to do the impossible, because I'm smiling despite wanting to throttle you."

"Come here."

I bent down, kissing him for real this time, tears swirling in my eyes. "When you passed out... I thought..."

"I know what you thought, but you don't have to worry about me, Jess. Doctor said I was a stud."

"You are," I agreed, struggling to control my emotions.

"Hey. I'm going to be okay."

No, he wasn't. Not when he heard the truth.

"How's Noah?"

"He's okay. Really worried about you. He's being cared for by Casey's nanny. And Miles and Noah are best buds now, so that helps."

As I talked, I could see Quinn fading away in thought. "What happened, Jess? I know it's bad. My dad is a horrible liar."

My pulse quickened. I knew what he was asking, and I was in no position to deny him the truth. He needed to know.

"Is this my fault?" he asked.

"*Your* fault? Why would it be your fault?"

"Did they target me because I'm a McKallister?"

"No. It had nothing to do with you."

I related to him the story as I knew it: that the plan had been in motion well before Sketch Monsters had been asked to fill in for the other band.

"So, what are they keeping from me? Is it Tucker? Is he dead?"

"No, he's going to be okay. Quinn..."

"Then what? I can see it in your eyes. Just tell me, Jess."

Tears broke free, spilling down my cheeks. I wiped them away, but not fast enough to catch the ones that followed.

"Brandon." I sobbed out his name.

"What about Brandon?"

"He's gone."

## 33

## QUINN: BUILT-IN TRAGEDY

I had to watch Brandon's funeral on livestream—not by choice but because continued blood loss from the site of the bullet wound meant the surgeons had to go back in and ligate the leaking veins. All that meant to me was that I couldn't be there to see my buddy—my bandmate, my brother—be laid to rest. There had been no closure, and without it, I couldn't seem to move on.

I tried. I pretended. I convalesced with Jess and Noah by my side. Jess nursed my wound and kept my spirits up as best she could, despite struggling with her own frightening memories of the night as well as the continued fallout from the allegations Nick had made. Taken on their own, the rumors would have died off quickly enough, but the shooting thrust us all into the spotlight, where rumors and conspiracy theories thrived. And now my beautiful, resourceful girlfriend had a stain on her name that couldn't easily be erased.

I wanted to be her rock—I tried—but I couldn't because everything was off.

I didn't feel right inside. I seldom slept. I barely ate. And I was pissed. God, so pissed. Pissed at the shooter for being fucked up in the head. Pissed at Tucker for getting us that gig. Pissed at myself for surviving when so many others had died. Why me? Why had I, the easiest shot of all at the front of the stage, not been riddled with bullet holes? None of it made sense, but maybe it wasn't supposed to. Who lived. Who died. It was all just a random, heart-wrenching twist of fate.

A few weeks after the shooting, while everyone slept, I sat up watching the video footage of that night. I knew I shouldn't— and I'd never tell Jess—but the gory images called to me. Thanks to cell phone video, there was extensive film chronicling the minutes leading up to the shooting as well as those fateful seconds when everything went to shit. That meant I could watch myself get shot over and over until the end of eternity if I wanted to.

But it wasn't my fate I was tracking. It was Brandon's. I had some perverse obsession with the way he'd died and was not entirely surprised to discover that seconds before I was hit—that moment I realized the beat had dropped—was the moment Brandon lost his life. He'd fallen back off his stool, his body shielded from view by the drum set he'd loved so much.

Not that he would have been suffering. If the video footage proved anything, it was that Brandon had died instantly—a fact that both soothed and horrified me. It had been one swift deadly shot. He wouldn't have even known what hit him. One second he would have been in the prime of his life, and the next, gone. And that was what I couldn't square off with in my mind. The fragility of life. The only thing that had separated my fate from Brandon's was half an inch. Half a fucking inch!

The margins were too close. Too dangerous to live life with any security. At any minute, everything could fall apart. I began obsessively worrying about those I loved. Jess. Noah. My family. Had it been one of them, I wouldn't have wanted to survive. Nightmares flooded my sleep. Every night I was back on that stage, the guys and me joined up there by people I loved. People I would try my hardest to protect once the shots were fired and they all dropped around me. I'd be trying to save one while another was off to the side dying. I was growing more exhausted every night. The fear of losing them was so intense that I was losing myself in the process.

This wasn't me. It had never been me. I'd always been a fighter. A protector. I hated feeling this weak and vulnerable, and I knew I needed to pull myself together before it was too late and I lost it all. I needed help; I knew that. But asking for it, doing the work—that required a determined mindset I didn't have.

I sighed, flinging the sheets off me when it became apparent I would be getting no more sleep tonight. Walking toward the kitchen, I passed the hall closet and paused. I wanted to open the door, but did I dare? I stood there contemplating, even pressing my forehead to the wood. Should I? Fuck it! I opened the closet door, pulled the guitar case out, and set it down on the coffee table. And then I stared. And stared. I knew what lay inside: Lucia. Another casualty of the night. I'd only recently gotten her back from police evidence, and her smooth ivory body, accented in browns, had been entombed in its case in the closet ever since.

I wanted to cradle her in my arms again, but I knew from the videos what I'd find—my girl splattered in blood with a bullet hole lodged in her heart. She'd taken a direct hit for me. I'd taken two shots to the heart that night: one, half an inch above; the other, straight-on. Lucia had been there for me, absorbing the bullet into her long, smooth neck. She'd saved my life.

And I'd repaid her with neglect. Snapping open the guitar case, I removed my beloved Lucia, remembering the day Jake had given her to me. It was the first time in years he'd even really talked to me... seen me. I'd been in the music room when he'd arrived home from tour, and he'd just strolled in and thrust it at me.

*'Here,' he'd said.*

*I remembered gaping up at him, disbelieving. 'For me?'*

*'For you.'*

*'Why?'*

*'Because someday, you and me, we're going to sing on the world stage together, and no one will ever forget our names.'*

Remembering those words was like a punch to the gut. Jake had touched my soul that day, but he'd also set me up to fail. My whole life I'd been chasing that dream.

I ran my fingers along Lucia's stained surface. The blood was still there. It could never be erased. Well, that wasn't exactly true. She could be resurfaced and the neck rebuilt, but would I do it? Or would I allow Lucia to remain like this forever, as a living reminder of all the damage done?

Holding her in my arms awakened something in me. I longed to hear the music again. My music. But in order for her to sing again—for me to sing again—we both needed healing. And I knew the only person who could get me there was the one person I had no right to ask. I'd spent my life blaming him for a tragedy he'd had no part in making. I understood now. I understood the sheer magnitude of what Jake had survived, what hell he'd pulled himself out of to walk among the living. I understood because I was now living a similar nightmare.

I picked up my phone and pressed his contact number.

"Hello?"

"Jake, I know it's fucking late, but I need you."

I didn't have to wait long. Jake and I were practically neighbors now. After the shooting, Jess, Noah, and I had moved into the guesthouse in the backyard of my parents' house. We didn't have much of a choice in the matter after the bullseye Nick had placed on Jess's back and the notoriety I received from the shooting. It made staying in either Jess's apartment or mine impossible. We needed a safe place to convalesce, and the guesthouse provided that.

Having found a comfortable spot under the gazebo, away from prying ears, I watched Jake approach. He looked tired. But then it was one thirty in the morning.

"Hey," he said, taking the seat beside mine.

"Sorry about this."

"Don't be. Sleep is overrated."

"I'm not sure I agree. Haven't been getting much of it lately, and it sucks."

"I haven't gotten much of it in seventeen years. Trust me when I say you get used to it."

That surprised me. For whatever reason, I thought Jake had returned to a more manageable state of being, that the terrors of his past had subsided. I remembered the nights he roamed the halls. There had been something so off about him, so disconnected from reality. He used to scare the shit out of Grace and me. A living zombie. A ghost.

Much like I was now, I noted.

"I'm glad you called me," he said.

Okay. That was... surprising. Why did I always just assume I was a nuisance to him? "Are you?"

"I saw you spiraling, and I wanted to reach out, but I know how I react to 'help,' and you and I are, sadly, very much alike. So I figured you'd come to me when you were ready."

"What made you think I'd come to you? We're not exactly close."

"We're closer than you think."

I didn't understand what he meant by that, and Jake didn't explain.

"I mean, who better to talk you through this than trauma central himself, right?" Jake hiked a foot onto the table and leaned back. "Hit me, little brother."

"I'm just going to jump right in," I replied. "How do I move past this, Jake? How do I get back on stage? How can I give Jess what she needs emotionally when I'm a mess? Most importantly, how can I get to where you are without it taking seventeen years?"

"I'm not sure where you think I am. I hate to break this to you, Quinn, but I'm nowhere near healed. It took me seventeen years just to get here—at the fifty percent mark. If you think there's an easy fix, you're going to be very disappointed. The only way I've found to punch holes in the trauma is by talking about it, dispensing small bits at a time."

"Who do you talk to—Casey?"

"God, no."

"Why do you say it like that?" I asked, wondering how much of what I was going through I could share with Jess.

"The things I have to say... I don't feel..." Jake stopped himself and looked away. "Look, for me, the damage just runs too deep. If it takes me another seventeen years, I don't think I'll ever be able to talk about the worst of it. But I've learned to function... even thrive... on that fifty percent. And you will too."

"Well, that isn't very comforting."

Jake shrugged. "Sometimes there are no easy answers."

"But that's what I want."

He chuckled. "That's what you've always wanted, Quinn. An easy fix. There isn't one. You have to know that by now."

It was one of those Jake aphorisms that, in the past, I'd internalize as derogatory and allow to simmer. But I was hearing him with fresh ears tonight. And he was right. I always took the path of least resistance, only forging new ones when I was backed into a corner. Well, I was backed into a huge fucking corner now, and if I didn't do the work required, I was never getting out of it.

"I do know. I just don't like to hear it coming from you."

He smiled. I smiled back. An unspoken understanding passed between us. We really were so similar.

"I feel weak." I sighed. "Like I should just get over this and move on. I feel like I'm letting Jess down. Letting Noah down. How can they count on me when I can't even count on myself? And seriously, Jake, how am I supposed to support my little family if I can't get back on stage?"

"Why can't you get back on stage?"

"Uh, perhaps you haven't been watching the news."

"I know what's going on. You've got to stop being afraid of the stage. What's the worst thing that can happen up there?"

I gaped at him. "Um... getting fucking shot!"

"Exactly. And now you can cross that off the list. Next?"

"How about dying on stage? That sucks too."

"Not sure I agree with you on that. The dead don't suffer like us lifers do. Do you have any idea how much easier it would've been for me to have just died in that basement seventeen years ago? All the suffering I've done since. The suicide attempts. The nightmares. The ghosts that took up residence inside my head. It's mind-numbing. Do you think I did all that shit for me? No! I did it for Mom and Dad. I did it for Kyle. I did it for Casey. And then..." His voice broke. "And then I did it for my kids."

"What about you?" I asked. "Have you ever done it just for you?"

There was a long sigh.

"Not most days, no."

We sat for an extended period, both contemplating our own demons.

"You're not making me feel much better," I said.

"That's not why I'm here. I'm not trying to make you feel

better. I'm showing you that you can go on... if not for yourself, then for the people you love. You can do it and you can succeed because you're strong. And then, one day, you'll be outside watching your kid playing in the sandbox, and he'll look up at you with love in his eyes and he'll say, 'Daddy, I love you.' That, Quinn, that is when you'll know you did it for yourself."

I let out the breath I'd been holding. God damn, Jake was deep.

As I had my whole life, I didn't feel worthy... not even of this conversation. He was so much more than me. But maybe that was okay. Maybe I didn't have to be Jake. Right up until tragedy came knocking, I'd actually been loving being me. I loved Sketch Monsters. I loved our music. And despite everything that had happened the last time we'd been on that stage, no one could dispute that the guys and me—Matty, Mike, and Iron Maiden lovin' Brandon—we'd fuckin' shone.

"I wish I had a bottle of tequila so I could take a shot every time you said something profound, Jake."

"I have my moments." He grinned. "So, what do you want to do?"

"I don't know."

"Yes, you do. What do you want, Quinn? Really think about it. What is the most important thing to you? Focus on that first, and once you have that nailed down, go to the next most important thing and nail that down."

"Jess. She's most important to me. I don't want to lose her."

"Then you start with Jess. Here's what I've learned about women—get that shot glass ready—you can't just *say* it, Quinn. You've got to *show* it. Meaning you can't walk back into the guesthouse and tell Jess you love her and think that will make everything go away. First you show her. Then you tell her. Then you get your shit rocked. Easy."

I laughed. The first time I had in a while. In his straightforward, low-energy way, Jake gave me hope.

"Word of advice, though," he said. "Put a stop to the rumors. Don't let Jess shoulder this herself. She's only in this position because she had the misfortune of stumbling into the McKallister family. However you have to do it, fix it!"

A plan began to populate in my head. I could do that. This was good. At least now I had goals. A purpose. Maybe it wasn't too late to turn this sinking ship around.

"What do you think I should do about the band?" I asked. "Do we retire Sketch Monsters or rename it? Or do we keep it the same now that we've got the sympathy factor on our side?"

Jake's face soured. "Like I do, you mean?"

I froze. "That's not what I meant."

He shook his head. "You think I had it so easy, don't you?"

"No. I know you've never had it easy."

"I mean professionally. You think they took one look at my tragic backstory and swung those doors wide open for me. Jake McKallister. The kidnapped kid. Come one, come all. But what you don't know, Quinn, is that I was a joke. A novelty. I was supposed to be a one-hit wonder—a way for music execs to make a quick buck off my tragedy. And they were right. People did come. They came to gawk. To point. To laugh. To pity. But they didn't come for me. And they sure as shit didn't come for my music. I don't think you understand what it took for me to get up on that stage, knowing what I knew. Knowing that I was a joke. And then add to that, I was still a kid. A kid with a lot of psychological issues. I wanted to quit every day. I hated everything about the exploitation and the mocking and the disrespect. So, when you say my tragic backstory got me in the door, technically you're right. But it only got me in the door so they could slam it in my face. I could have given up and come home. I could have put my guitar down and never played again."

Jake paused a moment, maybe collecting his thoughts.

"So why didn't you?" I probed, needing the answer more than he knew.

"Because I refused to let them win. If they insisted on turning me into a circus animal, then I insisted on getting my just dues. I started defying their orders, and instead of playing the cover music they tried to force on me, I started singing my own songs—the ones I'd written from that place inside that makes *me* great. And people stopped laughing. They stopped talking and started paying attention, even singing along. And I got stronger and stronger until finally no one could stop my forward roll even if they tried.

"That's what you have to do, Quinn. Stop listening to the noise. You're not the poster boy for this tragedy. Get back on that stage and shut them up!"

I had no words. Nothing. We sat in silence for a long while until I finally found my voice.

"All these years," I said, shaking my head. "I've treated you like shit, blaming you for everything that went wrong in my life and my career. You must hate me."

"I don't hate you. I've never hated you. You are a pain in the ass, though."

"I know." I agreed. "I'm sorry if I ever implied you sailed along on your name alone. It was easier for my ego to credit your success to the kidnapping rather than admit it was your superior talent that got you where you are today. In my defense, I've never known much about your early life. Mom and Dad kept it from me, and once I got old enough to go searching for the information myself, I was too wrapped up in my own pettiness to care about you. The truth is, I've always felt like an outsider in this family. You guys all have this shared experience, and then there's Grace and me. We're like imposters in your world."

"You're not imposters. Maybe your experience wasn't the

same as mine or Emma's or Kyle's, but you had struggles none of us faced. My childhood, before Ray, is something I can look back on and smile about. Can you say the same?"

I thought about that, trying to remember the good times, the ones that genuinely filled me with joy. Where were they?

"No," I admitted, surprising myself with the reply.

"That proves you're not a hanger-on, Quinn. You're a McKallister—just like the rest of us."

## 34

# JESS: JUMP BACK IN

"Wake up."

I felt the fluttery kisses first, then his soft voice urging me awake. For a moment, I forgot it all. There was no shooting. No wounded boyfriend. No damning information about me circulating. It was just Quinn and me in my apartment, simple and free.

I opened my eyes. He was standing over me with a lopsided smile on his face. I looked him up and down. Had he...? Yes. My god. He'd showered and gotten dressed. Something about this scene wasn't right, and it wasn't just his newfound interest in grooming. Maybe I was dreaming. Because when we'd gone to bed last night, Quinn had been solidly stuck in his head.

I shot up in bed.

"What is it?" I asked. "Is everything okay? Do you need to go to the hospital?"

"Easy, chick."

Chick? Was he joking? I blinked, not understanding. "Am I dreaming?"

"That's a valid question for sure. I am pretty dreamy, but no. You're awake."

I looked around the room, then whispered, "Blink twice if you were abducted by aliens."

He blinked once.

"Who are you?" I asked.

All joking aside, he said, "I talked to Jake last night."

"On the phone?"

"No. He came over."

I had no recollection of that happening. "When?"

"About one thirty in the morning. I couldn't sleep, so I called him. Turns out he *never* sleeps, so it worked out perfectly. Who knew? Anyway, I think I now understand what needs to be done."

"You do?" I asked, hope blossoming. If Quinn could be all right, then so could I. I just needed him to walk through the fog first. "What needs to be done?"

"It's a complicated series of steps. Jake's going to get me a printout. But all you need to know is that you're number one on my list."

A smile swept over my face. "I am?"

He leaned down to kiss me. "You are, and I won't mess us up, Jess. I can't risk losing you."

I slipped out of the sheets, stood up, and threw my arms around him. "You could never lose me."

"You underestimate how resourcefully dumb the McKallister boys can be."

"I factored in for that."

He smiled. This all seemed too good to be true. For the past six weeks, Quinn had been spiraling into a dark place, and today he magically woke up a changed man? I wasn't sure I was buying it. "Don't get me wrong, I love this new and improved showered version of you, but how can you have one conversation with Jake and then suddenly everything is all better?"

"It's not all better... but it's been put into perspective. I don't want to wake up seventeen years from now and realize I forgot to live for myself. I want to live like Brandon, drumming until I take my last breath. You and me, Jess, I want us to leave something beautiful behind when we go. I want Noah, and our future babies, to know we went out on a high."

"Yes." I kissed him. "Yes to everything."

Quinn circled his arms around my waist. "Now. To Jake's list. The first order of business is Nick."

"Nick?"

"Yes, Nick. See, he's going to be issuing a retraction today. Isn't that nice of him?"

"How are you going to manage that?"

"I'm going to manage him just how you manage Noah. With bribery."

~

I'd never been to Nick's place, mainly because I didn't know where he lived. But thanks to Tucker's intel, we pulled up in front of his adorable cottage-style house.

"Seriously?" I protested. "Nick lives on a cul-de-sac? I'm going to kill him."

Quinn unhooked his seat belt. "Maybe you should let me handle this."

"Please." I waved off his concern. "I'm fine."

We got out of the car, and as we strolled up his decorative stone walkway, I couldn't believe my eyes. "He's got a succulent garden, Quinn! *And* mature olive trees. I bet his grass is even sod. The fucker."

"Jess... I will buy you a flat of succulents if you keep your mouth shut when he opens the door."

"Okay, but I'm just letting you know that if Nick has a hummingbird feeder—not the plastic red one but the bougie kind with the mason jar and the cute little yellow flowers—he will have to die."

"Honestly, Jess. If you just want to fill the cart on Amazon, I can keep you out of prison. Now stay quiet and watch me spin my magic."

"Yes, this is extremely exciting for me."

Quinn knocked, and I bit my lip to keep from commenting on the gorgeous stained wood.

A moment later the door swung open— no need to check the peephole in this neighborhood. I nearly toppled over Nick's dry-stacked stone retaining wall when a highly pregnant woman appeared, looking from Quinn to me, then back to Quinn.

"Um... Nick?" she called over her shoulder. "It's for you."

I couldn't stop staring at her belly, but then that was the point, obviously. The woman was wearing nothing but a sports bra, short shorts, and her belly. I imagined she was a yoga instructor. I mean, why not?

How was it this man had been living the dream while Noah and I were eating off-brand peanut butter?

Quinn seemed to be reading my irritated mind and tapped my outer thigh with his knuckle. *Be good.*

Nick appeared at the door and immediately did a double take before settling into the reality of his ex-girlfriend and her rock star boyfriend standing on the other side of his farmhouse front door.

"What, uh... my god. How... uh... how are you doing?" Nick stumbled over his words. "That shooting, man, that was..."

I caught Nick's eye, and mine rounded as I shook my head. Stupid. Stupid pampered Nick. Quinn was in the very earliest stages of drumming his way through life. He didn't need Nick ripping the sticks out of his hands.

"How's the band? Are you guys getting back together? I mean without Bran..."

My eyes couldn't get any wider nor could Nick get any stupider. Good lord, the guy was oh for two in tone-deaf remarks.

"I'm doing okay," Quinn said, not showing any emotion aside from a subtle tightening of his jaw. "And the band is up in the air at this point."

"Oh yeah. That's too bad. You guys were decent."

*Were? Decent?* What a douche.

"You got a second?" Quinn asked.

"Uh..." Nick looked back at his woman before stepping outside with us and shutting the door. We walked along the front porch to his—*breathe, Jess*—patio swing.

My lips pressed together in frustration. Now he was just showboating. I couldn't help but inquire. "Is Noah going to be a big brother?"

"Pending a paternity test, yes."

"You always were so romantic."

Nick shot daggers at me. "What do you want?"

"So, here's the deal, Nick," Quinn replied. "I need you to retract your comments and posts about Jess on social media. All of them. And then I need you to issue an apology."

Nick scoffed.

Quinn didn't flinch. "I'm not joking."

"And I'm not doing it. No way am I going to issue an apology. Fuck you both."

"You know what's so awesome about being famous, Nick? I have a manager who does all my bidding. And you want to know what my latest bidding was? You. And your family. And all the shady deals you've got going on to keep your baby mama and son from getting a dime of your money."

Quinn held up a folder. "It's all in here, Nick. I can bury you. I can bury your family's business. All you've got to do to prevent that is show some grace and do the right thing by your son's mother."

Nick wasn't fighting back. Obviously, whatever was in that folder was damning enough that Quinn's offer was at least somewhat appealing to him.

"And to further sweeten the deal, you're off the hook financially—forever. I've already set up a trust for Noah. He'll never want for anything. Imagine the relief of not having to hide your assets when it comes time for college."

My ex was not finding Quinn's wily digs amusing.

"So what? I make a deal with you and I never get to see my kid again? Is that what you're saying?"

"Is that what you want?" Quinn asked, almost hopeful in his tone.

"No, it's not what I want," Nick blasted back. "He's my son. Not yours."

"Then act like it. Be a father, Nick. Go to the hospital when Noah jumps off a shed. Go to the principal's office when he gets caught pranking his teacher by having his classmates move their desks back every time she turns her back. Go to his baseball games. Answer his phone calls. If you want to be his father, then *be* his father. Otherwise, get out of his life. Because I'm there, and I'd be more than happy to step into your empty shoes. I love Noah. I'll provide for him and do all the things you won't do. So, unless you want to lose him for good, I suggest you step up—right now."

Quinn's speech was like a mic drop. We all stood there, stunned. Quinn had laid it all out on the line, professing his allegiance to Noah while still giving Nick the ultimatum—the solution of which was entirely in his hands.

"I never wanted any of this, Jess. I was eighteen. A scholarship in my hands. And then you came to me, pregnant and threatening to derail everything I'd worked so hard for. I didn't want Noah back then. I admit it, okay? Doesn't mean I didn't want to be part of his life. But between you and my mother and now Quinn... it's like I can't make any decision that doesn't have everyone screaming. You think I liked seeing my kid run to you on his birthday, Quinn? Tore my fucking heart out."

Nick dropped into the swing, pissed. Defeated.

Quinn and I exchanged a glance. We'd hit a nerve neither one of us knew was there but now was not the time to cave to sympathy.

"So, what do you say, Nick? Are you going to retract the things you said about Jess so the contents of this file will go away?" Quinn asked, waving it around.

"What about the financial stuff?" Nick pressed. "Will I be totally off the hook?"

"Yes. You will have no further financial obligations to Noah or Jess."

A clear line had been drawn in the sand, and which side Nick chose would determine all our lives going forward.

"Okay," Nick said. "I'll retract all the statements and issue an apology. But in return I want to see Noah from time to time."

"Supervised visitation," I agreed.

"Whatever," Nick replied. "And Quinn? I'll want that financial agreement in writing."

"So what damning information was in that folder anyway?" I asked as Quinn and I strolled hand in hand along the beach walk. We took it slow because, despite his changed attitude, Quinn was still a man recovering.

"It was filled with empty pages."

I stopped, staring. "What?"

"I was bluffing, Jess. I haven't been playing poker with my dad since I was two for nothing."

"Oh, my god. You got so lucky." I laughed.

"No, *we* got so lucky."

"He's not going to be a dad to Noah, is he?"

"Probably not much of one. Do you care?"

"No. I'd prefer him out of my life, but Noah loves him so I think we did the right thing by throwing him a bone. I will say, however, it would be nice if he could take over some of the principal's visits."

"Uh-oh. Was there another one?"

"Unfortunately, yes. I didn't want to bother you with it because you were all smelly and sad."

"So kind of you. What happened?"

"Um, let's just say Noah aced his science experiment."

"That's good. Isn't it?"

I cringed. "Wellll... not exactly. He brought bags of powdered instant mashed potatoes to school and scattered them all over the grass just before the sprinklers came on. I don't think I have to tell you what happened next."

"Oh, shit." Quinn grinned. "It must have been like Thanksgiving on that lawn."

"Oh yes, it surely was. And guess who got marched into the principal's office, *again*."

"Hmm... I'm going to go out on a limb here and say you."

"Ding, ding, ding! Mother of the Year right here, baby!"

Quinn laughed, the raspiness warning me he was out of breath.

"Here," I said, pointing to a bench. "Let's take a break."

We sat and watched the waves roll in. What a difference a day made. This time yesterday, hope had been slowly fading, and now our lungs were filling with fresh ocean air.

"I called Andrea this morning," he said.

I looked over, again stunned. "My goodness. Where did you find the time?"

"She's accepted my offer to buy her soon-to-be ex-husband out of Angel Line Tours—in exchange for fifty percent of the company going to you."

Thank god I was sitting because I probably would have fallen over from hearing that news. "Me? Why?"

"Because this is your family business as much as it's hers. And this way, she can still partially own... and run... her grandfather's company. Oh, and as part of the deal, your dad can go back to the workplace he loves—under his daughters' supervision."

"Quinn..." I was still too stunned to process everything. "It's like everything stays the same, but it's all different. I don't know what to say. How can I ever thank you?"

"I accept sexual favors."

"And you shall receive them." I laughed, grabbing his jaw and kissing him.

"Just know it wasn't done for altruistic reasons, Jess. I wanted you to be able to go on tour with me, at least when Noah doesn't have school."

Every word he spoke fell on eager ears. I wanted everything he was offering. "Your face," I said. "It needs my kisses."

I proceeded to shower him with them. "You just lifted the weight totally off my shoulders. Look! I can shrug again."

"That a girl." He wrapped his arm around my waist. "I think I'm going to be okay, Jess."

I leaned into him. "I think so too."

"I'm just not sure what I want to do about the band. I hate the thought of going on without Brandon, but I also hate the thought of starting over. Despite everything, I love that band."

"You need to talk to Mike and Matty. They're as lost as you are. They've been trying to reach out to you, but..."

"I know. They're next on my list. I just needed to make things right for you first."

"You'd never been wrong."

His fingers folded into mine, and we kissed. It was soft and sweet, filled with the promise of a future that hadn't been there only hours earlier.

Quinn stood and pulled me to my feet. "Come on. I need a fix."

"A fix? What do you mean?"

"You'll see."

It didn't take me long to figure out what type of fix Quinn was referring to when I saw Keith's surf shop up ahead on the beach walk. The shells jingled as we entered and I was instantly struck by the relaxed feel of the place, matching perfectly with its owners.

"Quinn! Jess!" Keith bounded over to us, like a grown-up version of Noah. "You should've told me you were coming. I would have slipped into something a little more formal—like shoes."

I glanced down at Keith's bare feet. Clearly there wasn't a 'no shirts, no shoes, no service' rule here.

"I can't believe my eyes," Sam said, skipping out from the back room in a long, flowing dress with a beautiful baby accessory strapped to her chest. She too was barefoot. Sam enveloped us in welcoming hugs. "What are you two doing here?"

"Came to do some research," Quinn said, sliding his fingers over the soft, wispy hairs on his nephew's head. "I'm thinking I want one of these soon. What do you say, Jess? You wanna make a baby with me?"

"I just might," I teased back.

Keith glanced between the two of us. "There's a cot in the back. Be our guest."

## 35

## QUINN: FRAGILE DREAM

We'd been summoned. Matty, Mike, and I sat at the large oblong table occupied by the top tier at our label. These were the wallets. The deal makers. The ruthless dream killers. But today they were mere humans with their heads hung low.

"The decision is up to you," one said.

Situations like this didn't happen every day. There was no playbook, no right or wrong answer. We were just people trying to make the best of a horrible situation. At first glance, it would seem an easy decision. Retire Sketch Monsters. Brandon was dead. The rest of us were traumatized. But not so fast. Our first album, conveniently released a week after the shooting, went straight to the top of the charts and had not left. The album had even earned us two Grammy nods.

Was some of that success due to tragedy porn? Yes. Just like Jake before me, doors may have opened because of our back-story, but that didn't mean they'd stay open. Our future was a decision away. If we wanted it, we could have it all. The money, the arena tours, the fame.

If we wanted it.

"What happens if we decide to dissolve?" Matty asked.

"Then we'll amend the contract to a one-record deal instead of three. There will be no further albums and no legal ramifications. The only catch is, should you decide to ever use the Sketch Monsters name again, you'll be required to fulfill the remaining two albums from the contract."

"And what happens if we decide to continue"—Mike paused, glancing at both Matty and me—"as a band?"

The label head scooted right back up in his chair, hope playing out over his face. Of course they wanted us to stay. Sketch Monsters might possibly be the most recognizable band in the world right at this moment in time. The name alone stood to make us all a fortune. But the question remained—did we want it? Could the three of us stand on that stage and perform not only without Brandon but also without fear?

"Should you decide to stay, we'll set you up in the studio to get going on your next album and, when you're ready, a tour. I'm sure Tucker has told you about the offer to perform at the Grammys. It would be the perfect opportunity to show the world you're back but also to help ease you back into performing."

All eyes shifted to me, waiting on my response. I pushed a pencil around on the table with my finger, weighing my options, which were: everything or nothing or something in between.

"Can we have a minute?" I asked. "Just the three of us, please?"

I'd never seen men of such stature clear a room as quickly as these guys did. They'd stood by our side in solidarity hoping, maybe even praying to whatever god men like this prayed to, that the decision we made would be in their favor.

Once the door was shut behind them, I looked up at my bandmates for the first time since the shooting—really looked at them—and as our eyes met, I realized we were all suffering the same. We all felt the loss and the pain. What would be the benefit of breaking up and going our separate ways?

"Can you do it?" I asked Mike. "Can you perform?"

"I can," he said, holding my eye. "I'm ready."

I turned to Matty and asked the same question.

"I've got some things to work through, but if you guys are going on stage, I'll be standing up there with you."

"What would we do about a drummer?" I asked.

"I've been thinking about that," Mike said. "I think we should wait awhile before replacing Brandon. I say we get guest drummers. At least until we go on tour."

I liked the idea of keeping Brandon's spot open for the right guy. And by *right*, I didn't mean the best drummer. I meant a brother from another mother.

"What about you?" Matty looked my way. "What do you want?"

What did I want? I thought of Jake, that wronged kid who'd put everything on the line for a fragile dream—his safety, his sanity, his happiness. That's what had been necessary for him to be great. And what would be necessary for Sketch Monsters, too.

"I want to keep drumming."

"Are you sure about this?" Jess asked as I pulled the guitar strap over my shoulder.

"Oh, I'm sure." I nodded.

"I was afraid you were going to say that."

Tucker came ambling up, his cane barely slowing him. He saw my guitar and frowned.

"Quinn, this is the Grammys."

"Yes, Tucker. I'm aware."

Mike and Matty joined us.

Tucker's lips flattened as he shook his head. "This is not the stage to make a stand."

"We disagree. This is *the* stage to make a stand."

"So, is this your new thing?" he asked. "How you're going to tackle every concert?"

I laid a hand to his shoulder to calm him down. "One stage. One stand. One time—for Brandon."

Tucker met my eye, emotion passing through his as he nodded.

"Well, at least that's settled." Mike grinned.

Our guest drummer walked up.

"Echo," Tucker called out. "Great job in rehearsals. I knew you'd master the song in record time."

"Getting the song down wasn't the problem. It was stepping into Brandon's shoes." Echo turned to me. "Thanks for trusting me to fill them."

"Thanks for doing this, dude," I replied, bumping fists.

"Happy to help. Hey, they're calling me over. See you on stage, boys."

We watched Echo walk away.

"Excellent. You four seem to be getting along well," Tucker said with just the right amount of smugness. He was, after all, the one who'd suggested Echo fill in last minute.

"Hate the dude," I answered.

Mike nodded. "Fucking douche."

"He's like my older brother who used to stick his armpit in my face and wouldn't let me up until I licked it," Matty replied.

Tucker's eyes widened. "All right, well. It looks like Echo won't be staying."

"We told you, Tucker. None of them will. We aren't filling Brandon's spot permanently until we're ready."

A stagehand hurried over. "Okay, guys. It's the commercial break. You can take your places."

I turned to Jess. "Wish me luck, Getaway Girl."

"I can do better than that."

She stepped in and kissed me. This was not a quick peck that said, 'Good luck, honey,' but a kiss with full-on tongue and the promise of treasures to come.

She shooed me away with a swat on my ass. Just the sendoff I needed to make this performance count.

The stage was dark when we stepped out and took our places. My new guitar was sitting against the amp waiting for me. I grabbed it and moved it around the back. Tonight it was going to be about me and Lucia... her white wood still stained with blood and the hole blasted into her body visible. But I'd had a change of heart. I didn't want the guitar to remain locked away and neglected forever, so I had Lucia meticulously repaired to honor its history while still allowing me to work the strings.

Not to be outdone, Mike and Matty were wearing matching shirts with dates, one marking the day Brandon was born and the other, the day he died. Dangling from each of their guitars was one of Brandon's drumsticks. From my back pocket, I removed Brandon's signature Iron Maiden baseball cap, and combing my hair back with my fingers, I fixed it on my head.

We would not let these people forget, or worse, pretend it had never happened. We would go out there and wear our pain and anger and sadness... and we'd be great.

Only then would we move on.

## 36

# QUINN: BUCKET BOY

I looked down at the address on my phone. Then up at the apartment complex. Then back down. Wow, talk about false advertising. Someone had taken creative license when they'd slapped up a picture on their website. This place was a dump—and that was coming from a guy who used to have a freeway going through his backyard.

Broken windows. Rickety stairs. Trash strewn about. Of all the days not to bring security—or bug spray—this was it. I considered going back to my car and waiting for backup, but this was a delicate matter, and one best done alone. We needed this. We needed *him*.

I zipped up my sweatshirt and yanked the string tight, sculpting the hood to contort my head into a snug-fitting condom. A pair of sunglasses completed the ensemble. Couldn't be too careful nowadays. Sketch Monsters had hit the big-time after the Grammy performance, and with only weeks away from a sold-out arena tour, this secret mission of mine—and by secret, I meant that Tucker did not know—was all the more important. Although our plan had been to employ guest drummers indefinitely, that was easier said than done. We needed something more permanent for the tour, but no drummer we'd auditioned fit the bill. However, there was one... one drummer I couldn't get out of my head.

I climbed the outdoor stairs to the second floor and arrived at 217, the apartment I'd been assured he lived in. He'd gotten no warning of my arrival. If he had, no doubt he wouldn't have been home when I knocked. We hadn't exactly parted on the best of terms, and my guess was, he still held a grudge.

I could hear music inside blaring as I walked up. I rapped my knuckles against the splintering wood. The blinds next to the door shifted as a finger lowered one of the slats. I pulled my sunglasses off and loosened my hood.

"Surprise," I said.

He let go of the blinds. The door remained closed. Really? The fucker wasn't going to open it. "You've got thirty seconds to open this door before I start blasting an Oingo Boingo song and telling your neighbors you're the lead singer."

"Go away, Quinn."

"No can do, bud."

"I got nothing to say to you."

"Fair enough. Just open up and listen, then."

No movement. I checked my watch. "Fifteen seconds. Let's see, should I play 'Weird Science' or 'Just Another Day'?"

The door swung open, and I jumped back. Wow. Hello, Chewbacca. It was clear he'd fallen on hard times, but then, when had he ever not been in the throes of a hard time? His hair fell down to his mid back, which in and of itself wasn't bad, but his coif had begun matting, and not in the cool way. Deodorant: needed. Toenail clippers: industrial-size needed. But that beard. Holy fuck. We might need a weed whacker for that monstrosity. Clearly I'd underestimated the project he would be.

"What do you want?" he asked.

"There's this thing called a razor, dude."

"I like my beard."

"Ah, high self-esteem. Way to go. Just one question: isn't your beard annoying in the summer?"

"No, Quinn, manliness is not seasonal."

I laughed. "Can I come in?"

"I'd prefer you not."

It was then I saw his red-rimmed eyes and the blood-tinged tape wrapped around his wrists and fingers. What had he been doing in here before I knocked?

"This is actually really important, dude. You'll want to hear it."

His expression shifted. Worry. "Grace?"

I rocked back, stunned. Why would he ask that? Did he still have a thing for my sister? Ah, shit. Maybe I hadn't thought this through clearly.

"No. She's fine. Great, really."

Was that relief? Frustration? I wasn't sure what he was projecting under all that hair.

"I've got things to do, Quinn. I'm shutting the door now. Say goodbye."

"Come on, man. I drove all the way out here. Aren't you the least bit curious what I have to say?"

"I think last time we talked, you said everything I wanted to hear. Look, I'm really sorry about what you went through, and I wish you luck, but you and me, we don't do well in enclosed rooms."

"All right. Then talk to me here."

He looked behind me, clearly not wanting his neighbors to overhear our conversation, before sighing and allowing me entrance. I scanned the scantily furnished room. Tan everything. A sofa I just knew had been dragged in from the dumpster sat in the middle of the room. A TV. A tray table and half a dozen overturned buckets with a stool in the middle. That was what I was looking for. I smiled.

He followed my gaze. "I can't afford a set."

"But you still play."

He looked down. "I still play."

"Good. I need you."

"For what?"

"To take Brandon's place at the drums."

His mouth dropped open, and then he looked around as if trying to spot the hidden cameras. "Fuck you, Quinn. I don't know why you're here, but don't you think you've screwed me enough for one lifetime?"

"Look, I'm sorry for anything I've done to you. Obviously you hold a grudge, and that's something we'll have to work on, but I'm not kidding. I want you to join Sketch Monsters."

"Sketch Monsters?" he asked, still not believing my words. "You want some guy who plays buckets to join your Grammy-winning band?"

"Yes."

"Why?"

"Because despite our past, you're still the best drummer I've ever seen. Sketch Monsters needs you, Rory."

## 37

# JESS: RICOCHET

I lined up my shot, knowing quite well where the ball needed to go—right into the rectangular opening in the front of the mini-golf castle. From there it would fall into a box, where four separate tunnels could spit the ball out in different directions on the putting green below.

Quinn had taken two shots to get his ball into the opening. Noah... we won't talk about how many times it took him. But then his score didn't count anyway. It always remained a solid five whether it took him two or fifty tries to get his ball into the hole.

No. This was a two-man competition, and I was up by six.

"I bet it's really hard for you to lose all the time," I taunted my hot rival.

"Actually, I don't lose all the time. My album is sitting at the top of the charts, but sure, yes, big loser." He formed an *L* over his forehead with his fingers. "You know, Jess, you're a mean golfer."

I pointed my club at Quinn. "Watch and learn, son."

"Are you talking to me or your actual son?"

"You. Now shush. Mama's about to show you how it's done."

I tapped my ball with just the right amount of speed, direction, and intensity to hit the box straight-on. And when it disappeared into the castle, I lifted my iron and hooted, doing a little dance in place to rub it all in.

I wasn't prepared for what happened next.

My ball rolled back out.

"What the?" I protested.

"Noah, were you paying attention?" Quinn asked. "Apparently, that's how it's done."

"That was a perfect shot, Quinn, and you know it."

"No, Mama, I don't know it. If it had been perfect, it wouldn't have come back out. Now try again."

I huffed, picking up my ball and placing it right in front of the opening. "I already took a stroke, so I'm starting here."

Quinn raised his brows but didn't object to my cheating.

I lined my ball up again and, using a firm easy stroke, shot it into the hole.

A second later, it rolled back out. Holy shit. Someone was taking a page out of my playbook. I grabbed Quinn's shirt and pulled him to me so I could whisper in his ear. "Someone is in there, rolling my ball back."

"Yeah, sure, Jess."

"No, I'm telling you—someone is hiding in there and sending the ball back out, just like I used to do."

He exhaled, then rolled his eyes. "Can you never just admit defeat? You suck at miniature golf. There. I said it."

"Fine. I'll show you."

I lined my ball back up and shot it up into the castle for a third time. I waited. The ball didn't roll out.

Quinn smiled. "Will there be anything else?"

Now I was totally confused. Tipping my head over the elevated ridge, I waited for my ball to drop from inside the castle onto the green below, but it never did.

"What the heck?" I exclaimed. "Where's my ball?"

"Is that it?" Quinn asked.

A clear ball, larger than a golf ball, rolled out of the castle and down the ramp, passing me right on by.

Quinn watched it roll. "Aren't you going to get it?"

"I told you. Someone's in there," I said as I stomped over to the imposter ball and retrieved it. The plastic ball was heavy, and there was something inside. I shook it. "What is this?"

Noah came skipping over. "Open it."

"I'm not going to open it. What if it explodes?"

"What if it doesn't?" Quinn asked.

"Is that really a chance you want me to take?" I scoffed. "I'm just going to ask for a new ball."

"Give it to me." Quinn swiped it from my hand. "I'll open it."

Noah, standing off to the side, caught my attention. He was jumping in place, his smile a mile wide. What had gotten into him?

I turned my attention back to Quinn, my eyes tracking down. He was on one knee, the plastic ball open... and so was the black box inside. A diamond ring sparkled against the velvet backdrop.

"Let me try this again now that I'm not dying. Marry me, Getaway Girl."

## 38

## EPILOGUE ONE: JESS

"Listen up, Angels, we're now coming down Goldfinch Road, where more celebrities exist per capita than anywhere else in the world."

I waited for the oohs and ahhs. And they came. Oh yes, they came. Certain things never changed. The love of celebrities being one of them. Of course, I might have a different take on it now that I was married to one. But none of these people knew that. Whenever I climbed onto a bus, today or any day, I was just Jess. No one knew my last name was McKallister or that Quinn and I partly owned the tour company they were taking this ride on or that I'd once been the infamous Jesserella.

A lot had changed for me in the three and a half years since meeting Quinn, but some things remained the same: like these tours that I ran a couple of times a week. Granted, I no longer needed the money, and I donated my tips to whatever driver was assigned to my tour. But I continued to climb onto the busses and take passengers for a ride because it was fun. It was cathartic. And it gave me a chance to meet people who made lasting impacts on my life, like old hard-of-hearing Lloyd. Without his out-of-the-blue prophecy, I might never have spent that day with

Quinn and might never have experienced every fantastical thing that followed.

"Whose house is that up there?" a passenger asked.

I glanced out the window, seeing balloons and a big banner that read, 'Happy Birthday, Jess.'

My smile spread like wildfire. "That would be the McKallister house."

"Wait a minute," another called from the back. "Isn't that your name?"

"Such a coincidence," I replied.

"Didn't you say it was your birthday today?" the clever man in the bucket hat asked.

"It is." I nodded. "So weird, right?"

And just as the words left my mouth, Quinn stepped out of the gate, holding our two-year-old daughter, Sadie. With her dark hair pulled up into wispy pigtails high up on her head and those dueling dimples of hers, Sadie had earned the nickname Boo from her daddy's side of the family. As the current youngest grandchild, Sadie was arguably the most adored McKallister of the bunch. In fact, when she was visiting Grammie and Grampie at the 'castle,' as she called it, her feet rarely touched the ground.

Noah stepped out of the gate, flinging his arm over Quinn's shoulder and adding a tickle to Sadie's neck. At thirteen years old, Noah was in that awkward stage of adolescence, but his long, skinny body and shiny row of braces did nothing to dampen his game—because he used Quinn to round the bases. Noah—bless him—had become an expert at pimping poor Quinn out for his own benefit by offering his stepdad up for school functions or impromptu backyard concerts to impress his other dentally disadvantaged friends.

"That's Quinn McKallister," Tammy from row eight screamed.

And just like an earlier Quinn sighting had done years

before, the left side of the bus emptied onto the right side as sightseers craned to get a look at the man who warmed my bed at night. From my perch in the front, I could see him talking to Sadie, pointing out the bus, probably telling her I was on it as he urged her to wave. Those two. My god. They were heart-melting goodness.

And as my little family waved, Delene hung a hard right, surprising us all. I looked to her. She winked as she pulled into the driveway.

"What are you doing?"

"I'm just following orders. If you've got a problem, take it up with management."

"Uh, folks," I said into the microphone. "I have no idea what's happening here, but if I had to guess, I'd say we are all in for a really big treat, because see that hot rocker right there? That's my husband. And if there's one thing I've learned being married to him, it's to expect the unexpected."

Delene opened the door, and Quinn sent Sadie up the steps with a birthday balloon.

"Is that for me?" I asked, bending down to accept her gift before sweeping her into my arms and nuzzling her neck. "Thank you for my balloon, Boo."

Noah was next. Climbing the two stairs, he handed me a balloon and kissed my cheek. "Happy birthday, Mom."

"Thank you," I said, attempting to give him a peck on the cheek, but he cowered away. Noah had entered the 'Everything Mom does is horrifying' stage of teendom. Quinn, being a famous musician and all, was still acceptable—for now.

Once he'd completed his duty, Noah turned to Quinn. "Can I go now?"

"Yes. Sorry for taking time out of your busy schedule of staring at your phone."

"That's fine. Just try to be more considerate next time." He chuckled, sidestepping Quinn on the stairs. Once he was through the security gates, I heard him yell, "Love you, Mom."

From his spot on the bottom step, Quinn said to me, "And just so you know, that small amount of interaction took an hour of negotiations, and I think I might have promised him that we'd invite some famous dancing TikToker to our house for dinner."

"Oh, well, that's alarming."

He shrugged. "But you got your balloon, so that's all that matters."

"I did." I laughed.

Quinn took the final step, handing me another balloon and kissing me. "Happy birthday, babe."

There was a collective sigh. I'd nearly forgotten about my passengers.

"This is so sweet. Thank you. Now, take Sadie. I have to finish my tour."

"Not so fast," Quinn said, producing another balloon from behind his back. He bent down and kissed my pregnant belly. "And one more. From Liam."

## EPILOGUE TWO: QUINN

I sat on the darkened stage, guitar in hand, my boots propped up on the bottom rung of the stool. A fluttering in my chest was the only indication of the monumental moment that was about to occur.

*Someday, you and me, we're going to sing on the world stage together, and no one will ever forget our names.*

How many nights had I fallen asleep to Jake's long-ago premonition? All my life I'd dreamed of this. Jake and me, side by side. We'd played together in the past, but never like this. Never as equals on a world stage.

Jake lifted his eyes, settling on mine. I think he knew the significance of the moment as well as I did. In my mind, we'd been rivals from the start. But that might have been more wishful thinking than anything else. If I were Jake, looking down from his place of glory, would I have regarded me as anything more than a spastic bug avoiding a solid squishing by scurrying about in the cracks of the sidewalk? Probably not.

But times had changed, and Jake had had a front row seat to the proceedings. He'd watched me rise. Show after show. Concert after sold-out concert. Slowly but surely, our names appeared side by side on awards shows and on the music charts, our songs playing back-to-back on the radio. There was no denying the distance I'd erased between us. Yes, Jake still existed on that top rung where the biggest and brightest got to shine, but so now did I. And like Jake, I was here to stay.

My eyes still trained on my brother, I smiled. He tipped his head down, laughing absently to himself before looking back up at me through the strands of his shoulder-length hair. He nodded. It was a welcome of sorts, an acceptance that I'd earned my spot beside his throne.

The lights went up. And we began to play.

## The End

# BONUS SCENE

## QUINN (SIX YEARS OLD): THE PROMISE

I knew I wasn't supposed to go in her room. Emma said no. She said Mommy was sleeping. But I was hungry... and Mommy was always sleeping. Before Jake went away, she didn't sleep a lot. She was always awake before me so she could get me dressed and brush my hair and make me breakfast. I didn't have to do anything back then. I just got out of bed, and Mommy did the rest. I liked it that way.

Emma said Mommy wouldn't sleep so much once Jake came home. But I didn't know when that would be. I didn't even know where he was. One day he just went away and police came and then everyone screamed and cried. Jake was bad to leave us like that and I didn't like him anymore.

"Mommy," I whispered in her ear. "Mommy, I'm hungry."

She didn't say anything back. She didn't even tell me to go away like she usually did.

I touched her face. "Mommy, wake up."

She didn't move.

I lifted her eyelid to look inside. Her eyeball stared back but I don't think she really saw me. My stomach growled louder.

"I'm going to starve," I told her. "Do you want me and Grace to starve?"

She didn't answer.

Now I was mad. I kicked her bed. I pulled down her sheet. I flicked her bedside lamp on and off. But she still didn't open her eyes.

When was Jake coming home so Mommy would wake up?

I stomped down the hall to my big sister, Emma. She told me not to bother her when she was doing homework... unless it was an emergency. Well, this was an emergency. I was starving.

I poked her arm. "Emma?"

She looked up from her book, saw me, and then her face got all sad. Since Jake left, Emma and Mommy stared at me weird. Sometimes they cried. I didn't know why no one liked me anymore. This was all Jake's fault. He left us and now everything was so bad. And I was hungry.

"Emma?" I repeated.

"What is it?"

"I'm hungry."

"Go ask Mom or Dad for food. I'm doing my homework."

"I can't find Daddy, and Mommy is lying in bed. She won't answer."

"She won't answer?"

My sister stood up real fast and then ran down the hall. I followed after her. I was a fast runner. One of the fastest in my class. Emma was already shouting at Mommy when I got to the room but at least that made her wake up. Maybe I needed to start being mean like Emma. Maybe then Mommy wouldn't sleep when she was supposed to be awake.

I was only sorta listening to Emma and Mommy fight. They did it a lot now and I didn't like it. They were too loud. I put my hands to my ears but I could still hear them.

*"How many of these pills have you taken?"*

*"Not enough."*

*"Mom, please. You're not helping Jake like this. What if he comes home and finds you like this?"*

*"You don't get it, do you, Emma? He's dead. Jake's dead, and he's never coming back."*

The words got stuck in my ears. My legs went all wobbly and I fell against the wall.

"Jake's dead?" I screamed.

Emma grabbed my hand and took me out of the room. "No, Quinn. No."

My bones shook and shook. How could he be dead? All his stuff was still in his room. I collapsed onto the carpet, burying my head into the soft bristles.

"Jake's dead?" I cried over and over.

"Don't listen to her, Quinn. She doesn't know what she's saying. Jake is alive, and he's going to come home."

"Why would Mommy say that? Where's Jake?"

Emma picked me off the floor and hugged me. She was a good sister and I let her hold me. I didn't understand what was happening. Nobody said he was dead. They said he was gone. Not dead.

I heard a noise and opened my eyes. My brother Kyle was there, leaning against his door. Since Jake left, something happened to Kyle. He looked like a monster. His eyes were red and he had a knife in his hand. I buried my head in Emma's neck and cried. I didn't want to see anything else. I didn't like this family anymore. No one was like they used to be. And nobody cared.

Emma carried me back to the sofa and sat me down next to Grace. I saw her go back to Mommy's room. When was she going to make me some food?

My little sister got to her knees and wiped my tears away

with her blanket. She cared. I still liked Grace. And Emma. But none of the others.

"Why are you crying?" Grace asked.

"Because I hate them."

Grace's eyes got all big. "You hate Mommy? And Daddy too?"

I put my arm over her shoulder. "Nobody cares about us anymore, Grace. They want us to starve. But I won't let that happen. I'll take care of us. From now on, it's just you and me."

Grace got all sad. "But I don't want us to be all by ourselves. I want everyone to be smiling."

She didn't understand. I had to make her see.

"We can't smile anymore, Grace, because Jake died."

Her lip was shaking. "What does that mean?"

I leaned in and said, really quiet, "It means he's a ghost."

Grace covered her mouth. So scared. I hugged her tighter. "Don't worry. If he comes back, I won't let him hurt us."

And I meant it. If Jake came back, I would kick him and punch him until he went away again. I didn't need him. I didn't need any of my family anymore. I was going to take care of myself... and Grace. And the first thing I was going to do was make lunch.

Because I was hungry.

# MEET THE REAL SKETCH MONSTERS

Fun Fact! Sketch Monsters was a real 80s metal band.

Sketch Monsters was the brainchild of my brother Mike, who played in a number of metal bands growing up in Eureka, California, including Addiction, Sketch Monsters, and 'the shittiest band in town,' Defecation. It is true that my mother was so embarrassed by the band name Defecation that she told anyone who asked that the name of Mike's band was Def Vacation.

It is also true that the way Jess came about the name 'Sketch Monsters' is an accurate depiction of how Mike and his equally inebriated buddies first discovered the imaginary creatures amongst the redwood trees in Humboldt County.

A very big shout-out to the original Sketch Monsters: Mike Wheeler, Matt Faulkner, and Brandon Gambles (my sincerest apologies, Brandon).

A special mention goes out to family friend Joel Krueger, the guitarist for Defecation.

# ALSO BY J. BENGTSSON

Cake: A Love Story

The Theory Of Second Best

Fiercely Emma

Cake: The Newlyweds

Rogue Wave

Hunker Down

Like The Wind

Next In Line

Ripple Effect